W9-BRG-446

"If you like your romantic fantasies delivered with all the wit, fireworks, and tenderness of a Tracy/Hepburn movie, Elizabeth Bevarly can't be beat."—*New York Times* bestselling author Lisa Kleypas

To save his soul, she'll have to steal his heart.

"Elizabeth Bevarly knows how to show readers a good time." —*The Oakland Press*

"Elizabeth Bevarly writes for today's woman."—*New York Times* bestselling author Christina Dodd

**Praise for Elizabeth Bevarly
and her bestselling novels:**

"Elizabeth Bevarly writes with irresistible style and wit."
—*New York Times* bestselling author Teresa Medeiros

"[Bevarly's] writing is quirky and funny and her heroes are hot." —*The Oakland (MI) Press*

"Full of hijinks and belly laughs." —*Detroit Free Press*

"A super-steamy beach novel." —*Cosmopolitan*

"This is a book that's like a drink of fresh water to all of us who are tired of reading about perfect women. There's a bit of a mystery, a sexy hero, and a lot of terrific one-liners."
—*New York Times* bestselling author Eloisa James

"A delightful, humorous, and smoothly written book—a must read." —*Rocky Mountain News*

"This practically perfect romance has . . . writing that is pure joy." —*Library Journal*

"Wyatt and Julian are quirkily appealing romantic heroes, and Bevarly's voice is fresh and funny."
—*Publishers Weekly*

"Full of the author's trademark humor, this witty romance is a jaunty romp through the world of the rich and mischievous."
—*Romantic Times*

"Enjoyable and funny." —*Booklist*

**Turn to the back for a sneak preview
of Elizabeth Bevarly's next novel!**

READY

&

WILLING

• Elizabeth Bevarly •

BERKLEY SENSATION, NEW YORK

THE BERKLEY PUBLISHING GROUP
Published by the Penguin Group
Penguin Group (USA) Inc.
375 Hudson Street, New York, New York 10014, USA
Penguin Group (Canada), 90 Eglinton Avenue East, Suite 700, Toronto, Ontario M4P 2Y3, Canada
(a division of Pearson Penguin Canada Inc.)
Penguin Books Ltd., 80 Strand, London WC2R 0RL, England
Penguin Group Ireland, 25 St. Stephen's Green, Dublin 2, Ireland (a division of Penguin Books Ltd.)
Penguin Group (Australia), 250 Camberwell Road, Camberwell, Victoria 3124, Australia
(a division of Pearson Australia Group Pty. Ltd.)
Penguin Books India Pvt. Ltd., 11 Community Centre, Panchsheel Park, New Delhi—110 017, India
Penguin Group (NZ), 67 Apollo Drive, Rosedale, North Shore 0632, New Zealand
(a division of Pearson New Zealand Ltd.)
Penguin Books (South Africa) (Pty.) Ltd., 24 Sturdee Avenue, Rosebank, Johannesburg 2196,
South Africa

Penguin Books Ltd., Registered Offices: 80 Strand, London WC2R 0RL, England

This is a work of fiction. Names, characters, places, and incidents either are the product of the author's imagination or are used fictitiously, and any resemblance to actual persons, living or dead, business establishments, events, or locales is entirely coincidental. The publisher does not have any control over and does not assume any responsibility for author or third-party websites or their content.

READY & WILLING

A Berkley Sensation Book / published by arrangement with the author

PRINTING HISTORY
Berkley Sensation mass-market edition / November 2008

ISBN: 978-0-425-22477-9

BERKLEY® SENSATION
Berkley Sensation Books are published by The Berkley Publishing Group,
a division of Penguin Group (USA) Inc.,
375 Hudson Street, New York, New York 10014.
BERKLEY SENSATION and the "B" design are trademarks belonging to Penguin Group (USA) Inc.

PRINTED IN THE UNITED STATES OF AMERICA

10 9 8 7 6 5 4 3 2 1

For the faculty and staff
of St. Francis School in Goshen, Kentucky.
Thank you for giving my son
an educational garden in which to blossom.

· One ·

AUDREY MAGILL WENT INTO THE THIRD STREET ANTI-
que store looking for a chair and found a man instead.
His gaze caught hers within moments of her entering, no
easy feat since the place was crowded with Gilded Age
furnishings, Baroque mirrors, Victorian serveware, and Art
Deco lamps. He watched her no matter where she moved,
with dreamy brown eyes beneath a fall of dark hair that
tumbled insouciantly over his forehead. And he smiled at
her, too, in a way that was shrewd, sexy, and seductive.
Without saying a word, he enchanted her. Unable to help
herself, she picked her way through the shop's wares until
she stood in front of him and met his gaze full-on. Up
close, his eyes were even more eloquent and his smile even
more succulent, and she was helpless not to return it.

And when she discovered it would only cost a hundred
dollars to take him home with her, she was delighted.
Especially since that hundred dollars included the frame.

"Captain Silas Leyton Summerfield," the woman behind
the counter said when she saw Audrey looking at the

portrait. She was in her midfifties, with chin length salt-and-pepper hair and eyes made large by the thick lenses of her even larger glasses. "He was a riverboat captain," she added as she came out from behind the counter. "He lived from 1839 to 1932, and when he wasn't shipping silk and coffee between New Orleans and Philadelphia, he called Louisville home." She came to a halt beside Audrey to look up at the painting, and judging by the smile on her face, the woman had very much enjoyed having the good captain's company in her shop. "He owned a house on this very street, in fact. Up near Magnolia."

"That's where my house is," Audrey replied.

The salesclerk turned to look at her. "What a coincidence. Captain Summerfield lived at number three-eighteen. Might he have been your neighbor were he still alive?"

Audrey's eyes widened in surprise, and she couldn't quite prevent the little gasp that escaped her. "No, he would have been my roommate. Three-eighteen is my address." She looked at the portrait again, and although she knew it wasn't possible, his smile seemed to have changed just the tiniest bit, looking even more shrewd and seductive than it had before. Although she knew she had a greater need to spend a hundred dollars on other things, she asked, "Why is he so inexpensive?"

The shopkeeper gave her a funny look. "He's not. That painting is priced at a thousand dollars."

Damn, Audrey thought. She must have missed a zero on the sales tag dangling from the frame. She looked at it again, arrowed her black brows downward, then lifted it for the salesclerk to see. "It says a hundred dollars here."

The salesclerk opened her mouth to say something, but looked at the price tag first. She saw what Audrey did—there were clearly only two zeros after the one and before the decimal point. She closed her mouth and frowned. "I guess Mrs. Tenney marked him down for some reason. That's definitely her handwriting. A hundred dollars he is."

Audrey smiled again. "Then I guess I'm just going to have to take Captain Summerfield home with me."

"Sounds as if it were fated," the woman agreed. But there was still a note of bewilderment in her voice, and she was still looking at the price tag when she said, "I'll wrap him up for you."

"Thank you," Audrey replied. "But I actually need to look at a few other things, as well. I'm just moving into the neighborhood, but my house is zoned for my business, too, and I need a few things for both."

She explained to the clerk that she would be opening a hat shop—which she'd dubbed Finery, after her maiden name of Fine—in less than a week, to coincide with the start of the Kentucky Derby Festival. The two weeks preceding the Derby, she hoped, would be enormously lucrative, since every woman who was any woman had to have a hat to wear on race day.

Audrey Fine Magill intended for her name to be the one dripping from everyone's lips when it came time to buy their Derby headwear, and she hoped to make enough in the next few weeks to sustain her for much of the rest of the year. She'd done reasonably well for herself the last few Derbies, making hats and selling them through local boutiques and on the Internet. Now, she knew, the time was right to open her own place.

At least, she hoped the time was right. Just as a precaution, she'd sold her house in the suburbs and bought a rambling brick Victorian in Old Louisville instead, intending to use the first floor as her business and the upper floors as her home. She'd learned working as an accountant that new businesses were risky ventures under the best of circumstances. But she'd also learned as an accountant that one's annual income could depend on a short span of time every year. She was, after all—or, rather, had been—a tax accountant.

She swallowed the fear that rose every time she remembered she'd left an extremely rewarding career to pursue what many of her coworkers had thought was a pipe dream. *Hats, of all things,* they'd said. *Who bought hats in this day and age?*

In Louisville? In April? Audrey had countered. *Plenty of women.* And a lot of them didn't even balk at price tags in excess of three or four hundred dollars, especially if it guaranteed that their chapeaux would be one of a kind and fashioned to match their Derby ensembles perfectly. Her orders alone—which she'd been taking since October— had kept her busy for months.

Before leaving Tenney's Antiques, Audrey found not only a chair, but a pair of lamps and a mirror, too, in addition to the delectable Captain Summerfield. She had no idea where she'd hang the good captain, since the business part of her house had deliberately been decorated in an impossibly feminine décor that his overwhelming testosterone—even if was oil on canvas—would in no way complement. But she'd figure out something. The coincidence of his having once owned the place, coupled with his very affordable price, had just made him too good to leave behind.

If there was one thing Audrey Fine Magill had learned in life, it was that good men were few and far between. She'd been married to one of them, once upon a time—the best, in fact, Sean Magill—and had lost him. Captain Summerfield would be the perfect companion for her: handsome, gentle, and easy to talk to, just as Sean had been. The three years since Sean's death had been the loneliest Audrey had ever known. It would be nice to have a man around the house again. Even a painted one. That was preferable, in fact.

"Since you're right up the street, I can have everything delivered this afternoon, if that will be all right," the salesclerk told Audrey.

"That will be perfect," she replied. And with a little wave to Captain Summerfield, she paid her bill and went home.

SHE WASN'T QUITE AS BEAUTIFUL AS HE'D FIRST thought. Oh, certainly, she was a handsome woman, with ebony hair that spilled like a curtain of silk to the middle of her back, and blue eyes that proclaimed her every emotion. But her mouth was a bit too full, and her nose not quite delicate. Her eyes, too, as clear and intelligent as they were, were almost too large for the rest of her. But her figure was exquisite, full where a man liked to see fullness and trim where he preferred a woman be small. And her smile . . . Well. That made up for much, for it, too, was larger than most women claimed. Mrs. Magill had a very good smile indeed.

She would do, he decided. *Yes, she would do nicely.*

Captain Silas Leyton Summerfield watched his houseguest with much interest—or, rather, his hostess, he supposed, since it was she, not he, who owned the house now—noting with masculine appreciation her poetic motion and economy of movement. And he marveled that she could manage both. Most women, he had observed on many occasions, were either poetic or economical, but rarely—if ever—both. They existed either to look beautiful or to work hard, and neither the twain should meet. Audrey Fine Magill, however, seemed to exist for both.

Intriguing.

Styles had much changed since last he was home, he further noted. Though he recalled seeing dungarees similar to those she wore on stevedores and crewmen in his time, he'd never known women to don them, even for cleaning and moving things into an attic, as Mrs. Magill was doing now. And the white shirt she wore—at least it had been white when she started working, even if it was streaked with dirt now—was strangely free of any sort of closures like buttons or laces, and it clung to her body like a second skin.

Very intriguing indeed.

What was less intriguing—and more than irritating— was the wall she had chosen for his portrait. A man of his stature and character should not be relegated to the third-floor landing. His painting belonged in the main room downstairs, over the fireplace, where it had hung for more than four decades when Silas was alive. *Ah, well.* He could fix that soon enough. After she went to sleep tonight. In fact, he'd be fixing quite a few things once Audrey Magill was asleep tonight. The portrait was actually the least of his concerns.

He did, after all, have a soul to save.

AUDREY DREAMED OF CAPTAIN SUMMERFIELD THE night after she hung his portrait in her home. In her dream she awoke in one of the bedrooms on the second floor, but it wasn't furnished the way she currently had it furnished—in Contemporary Living Out of Boxes. Instead, the room looked like something from a nineteenth-century novel. Written by Melville. During a testosterone surge. From using steroids. Abusively.

The bed was the only thing in the room that could be remotely called modest. But even it was a black, wrought iron monstrosity piled high with pillows atop goose down, instead of the low-slung platform bed with memory foam that she owned and had set up in the attic room on the topmost floor that she'd decided would be her bedroom. The rest of the furnishings were massive, aggressively hewn mahogany, from the oversized armoire to a highboy, which was so tall that Audrey, at five-four, could barely see over its surface. Hanging above the windows, where she had at least managed to get up some iridescent sheers, were heavy drapes of dark blue velvet that were held back with thick gold braid. And instead of the antique floor lamp with the embroidered, beaded shade she'd placed in that room, an oil-burning lamp whose fuse was turned low burned at the side of the bed. She wrinkled her nose at the unpleasant odor, thinking it odd, because she'd never smelled things in her dreams before.

As she sat up on the side of the bed and looked down at herself, she half expected to find herself clothed in an old-fashioned, white cotton chemise. But she was wearing what she'd had on when she went to bed: striped pajama bottoms and a Louisville River Bats T-shirt.

Somehow, she knew she was supposed to go down to the living room for something, so she made her way out of the bedroom and down the stairs, which didn't creak nearly as much as they did in reality. The rest of the house was furnished much as the bedroom had been. Her own sparsely scattered furnishings and half-empty boxes were gone, and in their place were pieces similar to what she'd seen in the antique shop that day. Only they didn't look like antiques for some reason, at least not all of them. The house was much darker than she was used to, too. And not nighttime dark. Just . . . dark. The colors, the furniture, the rugs, all of it. Even so, strangely, although there were no lamps burning in any of the other rooms she passed on her way downstairs, she could see everything very well.

Just as her bare foot connected with the hardwood floor of her living room, she smelled something burning again, but this time it was the more pleasant aroma of pipe smoke. Audrey smiled when she smelled it, because the fragrance reminded her of her father, who had died when she was in college. As a girl, she'd loved watching him fill his pipes, and still remembered the metallic snick of his lighter opening before he lit one. They were comforting smells and sounds still, the same way the aroma of meatloaf and the click of eyeglasses folding reminded her of her late mother. Halfway thinking she would enter the living room to find her father sitting there—and perhaps her mother, too—Audrey kept walking.

There was a fire crackling in the fireplace, even though the evenings lately had been too warm to warrant one, and a row of wooden ships lined the mantelpiece where there should have been a display of her hats. Above them, where Audrey had hung the stylized logo for Finery, was the portrait of Captain Summerfield. His face was bathed in dancing amber light, courtesy of another oil lamp that burned atop a ruggedly fashioned antique end table near an overstuffed Queen Anne chair. A book was turned facedown in the chair's seat, and as she drew nearer, Audrey saw its title was *Mr. Midshipman Easy* by an author named Frederick Marryat.

Not one of her father's. He'd preferred cop stories over anything else and had never touched historical fiction.

She looked up and was about to walk forward again,

toward the dining room, when a shadow in the stairway landing above and to her left seemed to . . . move. She would have been alarmed had she not been dreaming. But then, had she not been dreaming, she would have been alarmed the moment she woke up and found her bedroom redecorated by HGTV's latest makeover show, *Melville My Room*. So instead of running away from the shadow, Audrey turned around and walked back to the stairs.

It was then that the shadow took form and turned into Captain Summerfield. He stood on the second-floor landing gazing down at her, looking almost exactly as he did in his portrait. Though in place of the black uniform jacket with brass buttons, he was dressed in a roomy white shirt, open at the throat, and black trousers. His only accessories were black boots and a cut-crystal snifter half-filled with brandy that he cradled in one hand. His dark hair a was tad longer than in the painting, but his smile was every bit as tempting, and his brown eyes were every bit as knowing. He looked to be in his early to mid forties and was taller than she would have guessed, easily topping six feet. He, she was certain, wouldn't feel at all minimized by the stalwart furniture with which he had filled the house when it was his.

And how do I know this is the furniture that filled his house? she immediately asked herself. She was dreaming. All this furniture came from her own imagination, just like the good Captain had.

"Madam," he said by way of a greeting. His voice was as dark as the rest of him, yet as rich and mellow as the spirits in his glass. "How nice of you to visit."

She smiled at him, wondering why she didn't feel intimidated by him. "I'm not visiting. I live here now."

He smiled back, and something about the gesture made Audrey feel very intimidated indeed. The reaction was only compounded when he began a slow descent down the stairs, his eyes never leaving hers.

"No, *I* live here now," he told her certainly. "You won't live here for more than a hundred years."

"This is just a dream," she replied, the words coming out

a little shakier than she wanted. Then again, *she* was a little shakier than she wanted.

So that explained that.

"Yes, it is a dream," he agreed. "But whose? Mine or yours?"

She opened her mouth to reply, then realized she wasn't sure how to answer. *It must be mine,* she wanted to say. Because she wouldn't be conscious of one of his. She would only be a figment of it.

He came to a halt on the last stair before stepping down into the living room, something that only enhanced his overpowering height—and presence. "Actually, the *now* is immaterial," he told her. "Right now, there is no *now*. There is only this dream. And it doesn't matter whose it is. Only that both of us be in it."

"And why is that?" Audrey asked.

"Because I need to speak to you, and I can't do that outside of a dream. Well, I can," he corrected himself. "But I much prefer this manner instead."

Weird dream, Audrey thought. She was going to have to cut back on the Chunky Monkey ice cream before bed.

"What did you want to speak to me about?" she asked.

"About my great-great . . ." He paused, seemed to think hard about something, ticked off a few numbers on his fingers, then waved a hand in front of his face. "About a descendant of mine."

She hadn't thought about him having descendants. But he might very well have family still living in Louisville. People from here tended not to move away very much, so it was likely.

"What about him? Or her?" she added.

"Him," Captain Summerfield told her. "Nathaniel Summerfield. My great-great . . . Well, he's a grandson of some kind."

"I didn't realize you were married."

Not that she'd really given it any thought. After all, she'd just met Silas Summerfield that afternoon.

He took a step to the side, something that crowded his

body against hers, even though their bodies weren't quite touching. Instinctively, she took a step backward. When she did, her foot tangled with the edge of the Oriental rug, making her stumble for a moment, but she grabbed the newel post and righted herself just as the good captain had started to reach out to steady her. She was back on solid footing before he would have grabbed her, and she was suddenly strangely sorry she *hadn't* fallen. She would have liked to see what happened when he touched her. Would his hand go right through her arm? Or would she feel the warmth of his fingers curling over her bare flesh?

And why did she even ask herself that? Not only was this just a dream, but so far, everything else in it felt substantial enough. Why wouldn't Captain Summerfield be substantial, too?

After a small hesitation, he put down his hand and strode into the living room. Audrey followed until he came to a halt by the fire. He placed a hand on the mantelpiece and gazed into the flickering flames, lifting the brandy to his mouth for a generous taste before speaking again.

"My marriage only lasted six months," he said when he finally did. "We were both very young. She was the daughter of one of my father's business partners, and we . . ." He sighed deeply and turned to look at Audrey. "Well, as I said, we were very young. And impulsive. And neither knew to take the proper measures against . . ."

"She got pregnant and the two of you had to get married," Audrey finished for him.

His expression changed at her assessment, but she wasn't sure if it was because he was distressed at the mention of his wife's doubtless unwanted condition or because he was perturbed by Audrey's frankness. Finally, he said, "Yes. She increased. Unfortunately, she didn't survive our son's birth." Before Audrey had a chance to remark on that, he hurried on, "As her mother was also deceased, my mother took the child and raised him. After Rebecca and I married, I had taken a position on one of the riverboats that traveled between New Orleans and New York, so I was often absent.

I barely knew my son, Mrs. Magill. For that matter, I barely knew my wife." He looked into the fire again. "Even after the boy grew to be a man, married, and had children of his own, I saw him only sporadically. I wasn't suited to family life. I grew too . . . restless."

Really *weird dream,* Audrey thought. Captain Summerfield's portrait had definitely made an impression, if she was dreaming about exchanging deep, dark secrets with the guy.

"In any event," he continued, "my son's sons married and had sons, and then their sons married and had sons, and so on and so forth, and each new generation made the Summerfield name more honorable and more respected than the one before it." He looked at Audrey again, and the unmistakable, unmitigated fury in his eyes pinned her to the spot. "Until now," he said. "My great-great . . . et cetera . . . grandson Nathaniel Summerfield has been suffering for some time now from a slowly deteriorating sense of duty and obligation. Over the years, he has blurred his personal line between right and wrong to the point where it is nearly indistinct. The boy is in terrible danger from himself, and I need for you to go speak with him."

"Me?" Audrey echoed. "Why me? I don't even know your great-great-et-cetera grandson."

"There will be an article about him in tomorrow's newspaper," Captain Summerfield told her. "Read it, and everything will be made clear. You must go speak to him directly after reading about him."

"And tell him what?" Audrey asked. "That his great-great-et-cetera grandfather visited me in a portentous dream and made me go talk to him about his representation in the media?"

Silas Summerfield sighed heavily. "No, Mrs. Magill. Tell him I visited you in a portentous dream and asked you to tell him that he's in danger of losing his soul."

"*What?*"

"And that once lost," the captain continued as if she hadn't spoken—or, rather, yelled—"his soul will be gone forever."

"Oh, well, in that case," Audrey said sarcastically, "he's sure to listen to every word I say. Then call the guys in the white jackets."

Silas Summerfield's expression turned confused. "What men in white jackets?"

"It's a figure of speech," Audrey told him.

"Translation?"

"They'd haul me off to the loony bin." Then, in case that particular phraseology hadn't been around in the captain's time, she clarified, "An insane asylum. Madhouse. Bedlam. The place where they put people who see and hear things that aren't really there."

He smiled at that. "Ah. Then you shall have to phrase your admonition to my grandson about the loss of his soul in a way that sounds logical and credible."

"Oh, is that all?" Audrey said. "No problem."

"Do whatever you have to do, Mrs. Magill," the captain told her. "Because tomorrow, Nathaniel will enter into a business liaison with a very dangerous man. A criminal. One who surrendered his own soul quite willingly long ago. And the product of this enterprise will completely sever the tenuous hold the boy has left on his soul. You must speak to him, Mrs. Magill, and you must do it tomorrow. Otherwise, the boy will be lost. Forever."

· Two ·

AUDREY AWOKE TO FIND SUNSHINE STREAMING THROUGH the French doors in her bedroom and feeling more exhausted than she'd been before going to bed. It was as if she'd spent the hours between one and six, when she should have been sleeping soundly, partying instead. She even felt a little hungover, even though she hadn't imbibed anything before bed except Chunky Monkey ice cream.

Weird.

And she'd had weird dreams, too, she recalled, especially the one with Captain Summerfield. It had been so vivid at the time, but now she could only remember snippets of it. She hated dreams like that, the ones that felt so real, it was tough to shake them off in the morning. But her house now appeared to be just the way she'd left it, not the masculine domain of a dead riverboat captain. She looked over at the French doors leading to the widow's walk and noted how the gold voile panels she'd hung there bloomed inward from the morning breeze. Funny but she thought for sure she'd closed those doors the night before. Even though the April nights had been balmy and pleasant, she wasn't the type to leave anything in her house opened or unlocked after dark.

The April mornings were surprisingly pleasant, too, she thought further as she rose from bed, so why did she have goose bumps severe enough to make her rub her arms to warm them? After closing and latching the doors, she snagged a hoodie from one of the still-unpacked boxes and thrust her arms into it as she headed downstairs. She tossed a breathless "Good morning, Captain," to Silas Summerfield as she passed his portrait in the landing, then—

Then spun around, because Silas Summerfield's portrait was no longer in the landing. In its place was the Art Deco print she'd taken down in order to hang it there.

Okay, now that really was weird. She distinctly remembered hanging the painting right there the day before, and she recalled saying good night to the captain as she made her way up to bed.

Right? Wasn't that what she'd done?

She closed her eyes and rubbed her forehead, trying to remember. Though, granted, that was a risky business before she'd had her coffee . . .

Maybe she'd hung the portrait in the second-floor landing, she told herself. She had been working awfully hard this week, and she'd been exhausted yesterday. Maybe she'd confused the second-floor landing with the third floor. Hey, it could happen. The house was in such a state of disarray that it was hard to tell one room from another. But when she rounded the stairs onto the second floor landing, there was no sign of Captain Summerfield there, either. Feeling more muddle-headed than ever, Audrey continued down the stairs to the living room. The morning sun streamed through the east-facing mullioned windows, casting mottled light on the hardwood floors and pastel Orientals, and creeping toward the ornately carved Victorian furnishings upholstered in colors as soft as the rugs. The ivory walls glowed almost gold in the creamy light, and—

And then Audrey just about jumped out of her skin, because there, suddenly, was Captain Summerfield, right in the middle of her shop. He was hanging over her fireplace where yesterday had hung an oversized and stylized logo for Finery. And that wasn't the only thing that had been disrupted. On the mantelpiece below the logo, she'd displayed a half-dozen hats that she considered some of her best creations. A good three thousand dollars' worth of millinery fashioned from delicate lace and feathers to beadwork that represented months of work. Now, however, they were scattered all over the floor, the obvious result of someone having angrily swept a hand across the entire row, sending all the hats flying pell-mell to the floor.

Good God! Someone had broken into her house last night! For all she knew, the intruder might still be inside!

Audrey didn't waste any time after that. She ran straight for the front door, not caring that she was still in her pajamas and hadn't even put on any shoes. She ran to the house next door, having been welcomed to the neighborhood by its owners her first day in her new house. Stephen and Finn owned a restaurant on Main Street that didn't open until lunchtime, and they rented an upstairs apartment to a young woman Audrey had met only a couple of times and whose name escaped her at the moment. Surely, at least one of them would be home this morning.

In fact, all three were, but none was any more prepared to face the day than she was.

"Audrey?" Finn asked sleepily when he opened the front door. He was still in his pajamas, too, though his were paisley silk and tailored to match perfectly the robe he was knotting over them. He was in his midfifties, his blond hair liberally threaded with silver, with one of those perpetually thin frames that even being surrounded by food all day did nothing to fatten. "What's wrong? The sun's barely up."

"I need to use your phone," she told him. "Someone broke into my house last night, and I'm afraid they might still be there."

"Oh, dear," he said with some alarm, opening the door wider to let her in. "There's a cordless in the kitchen. Go straight back."

Stephen was coming down the stairs as she passed them, the utter opposite of his partner in virtually every way. Although the two men were about the same age, Stephen was a good six inches shorter than Finn, with a broad midsection and arms like barrels. And his sleepwear consisted of sweatpants and a Gold's Gym T-shirt.

"What's going on?" he asked. Though he was speaking not to the hastily departing Audrey, but to his partner.

"Audrey's been burgled," Finn said. "And we could be next."

"That's ridiculous," she heard Stephen say as she reached for the phone. "We have a better security system here than we do at the restaurant." To Audrey, he called, "We'll give you the number of our security guy before you leave."

She nodded as she punched 911, then dipped her head in a perfunctory greeting to Finn and Stephen's tenant, who sat at the kitchen table in pajama pants decorated with cartoon cupcakes and a shapeless Sullivan University sweatshirt. Her boyishly short auburn hair was spiked enough to indicate that she, too, had risen from bed only recently, and faint purple crescents beneath enormous brown eyes indicated she hadn't gotten nearly enough sleep. Neither feature detracted from her beauty, however, which was almost startling in its flawlessness. She flinched visibly at Audrey's sudden appearance, then relaxed—a little, anyway—when she saw who it was. Still, she clutched her coffee cup tightly with both hands as she muttered a greeting, and she looked at Stephen with alarm when he entered the room behind Audrey.

Cecilia, she remembered. That was her name. She looked to be in her late twenties, but even with the superficial knowledge Audrey had of her, she'd developed the impression that Cecilia was one of those "old soul" types who seemed to claim an ample and sundry collection of life experiences. Which was strange, since she never seemed to leave her apartment.

Any further reflection on Cecilia fled, however, when the 911 dispatcher picked up at the other end of the line.

After Audrey explained what had happened and described her fear that the intruder might still be in her house, the dispatcher promised to send a car. No sooner had Stephen dug out a card from a kitchen drawer for a local security company than they saw a Louisville Metro Police car roll to a halt in the alley behind the house, its blue lights tumbling.

For a second time, Audrey related what had happened to the two uniformed officers who emerged, this time adding a few more details about the vandalized hats and the mysterious moving painting. The more she talked, however, the less concerned the two police officers seemed to be. For that matter, so did Finn and Stephen. Even Cecilia, who had become so twitchy at the prospect of a break-in next door that Audrey had begun to think she would be jolted by the appearance of a piece of lint, grew noticeably less twitchy. And, okay, Audrey supposed in the scheme of things, hat trashing and portrait shuffling probably weren't up there with hate crimes and felony assault. It could still give a person a major wiggins.

"We'll have a look around," said the first officer, a sturdy-looking brunette with a sleekly arranged chignon whose nametag identified her only as Milosevic. "But I'm pretty confident whoever's responsible is gone by now."

Her partner, a blond, all-American-boy type who looked fresh from the academy, name-tagged Andrews, nodded in agreement. "If they'd wanted to hurt you, they would've had ample opportunity while you were asleep."

Oh, that was a reassuring thought.

"I mean," he added, "if you didn't even hear the guy going up and down the stairs lugging a heavy painting, you wouldn't have woken up if he'd snuck into your bedroom."

Really reassuring thought.

The kid smiled. "Jeez, think about it. He could've killed you if he wanted to. And you never would've known what hit—"

"Andrews," Milosevic said sharply. "Let's go have a look."

Stephen leaned in close and pressed the business card into Audrey's hand. "You might want to call the security guy today," he said too quietly for the departing police officers to hear. "If nothing else, you can rest easy knowing Andrews can't get in."

Audrey nodded but said nothing. It was hard getting the words past the unmitigated terror that was lodged in her throat.

Turned out, though, the terror was for nothing. The two officers gave her house a thorough search, telling her everything, save the hats in the living room, seemed to be fine. But they wanted her to come back and do a walk-through with them, just to be sure nothing was missing. Try as Audrey might to find something, however, nothing, save Captain Summerfield and the hats in the living room, seemed to have been disturbed. Even her purse, which she'd left sitting on a chair near the fireplace in full view of anyone who might have gone in there to, oh . . . she didn't know . . . rearrange a portrait and then sweep an angry hand across the mantelpiece to knock down three grand worth of hats . . . would have seen it. Her driver's license, cash, and credit cards were all accounted for.

"I don't understand," she told the police officers as they wrote up the last few notes for their report. "Why would someone come in and mess up a bunch of hats and hang a portrait somewhere else in the house?"

The officers exchanged a look that told Audrey they didn't think anyone had.

Oh, *fine*. No matter what they thought, she knew she hadn't been working *that* hard. Still, it wasn't like she could come up with a better explanation.

She cleaned up after the police officers left, doing her best to repair the damage to the hats that had been swept to the floor. Most of it was only superficial, but one or two were going to need to be reshaped. What bothered Audrey even more than any of that, though, was the fact that she couldn't shake the feeling of being watched. She was sure it was just a byproduct of having her home broken into—skeptical police officers and neighbors notwithstanding—but there it was all the same.

When she finally sat down at her kitchen table with a cup of much needed and long overdue coffee, she was still in her pajamas. Looked like it was going to be one of those late-starting days, she couldn't help thinking as she reached for the newspaper already opened on her table.

The newspaper she couldn't even remember bringing in from the front walk, let alone opening on her kitchen table. But the date at the top, she noted, was today's. Even stranger, it was open to the business section, which she usually saved for last, because it was her favorite.

She was about to fold it up again when her gaze lit on the photograph of a man who looked very much like Silas Summerfield. He had the same rakish expression, right down to the entrancing smile. The man had dark hair, too, and although it was a small photograph, somehow Audrey knew his eyes would be dark, as well. On closer inspection, however, she thought maybe it wasn't his face that had caught her attention. Maybe it was the name under the photograph that just so happened to identify the man as Nathaniel Summerfield.

Waitaminnit. Wasn't that the name of the great-great . . . however many greats . . . grandson Captain Summerfield had told her about in her dream last night? She closed her eyes as she tried to remember. She'd been in her house, but it had been furnished with Captain Summerfield's things, and he'd said she was the guest, not he. Then he'd told her his great-great . . . however many greats . . . grandson was in danger for some reason. He'd been very distressed about it. What was it he'd said? That his great-great . . . however many greats . . . grandson was . . .

She opened her eyes again when she remembered. He'd said his grandson was in danger of losing his soul. Something about a shady business deal, she remembered. Something about partnering with a criminal. But she couldn't recall the particulars. She did recall, however, that Captain Summerfield had told her she would read an article about Nathaniel in today's paper.

Wow, had she thought her dream was weird? Prophetic was more like it. And *that* was *bizarre*.

She looked down at the paper again, at the photograph of Nathaniel Summerfield. There was a photo of another man beside him named Edward Dryden who was as nondescript and bland as Nathaniel Summerfield was charismatic and handsome. The headline above the article read: "Dryden Properties set to develop downtown lofts and retail space." Reaching for her coffee, Audrey began to read.

When she finished, she wasn't exactly filled with a sense of foreboding. There had been nothing out of the ordinary about the development Dryden Properties would be undertaking. And his deal with Summerfield and Associates seemed to be that he was simply a client, and that Nathaniel, an attorney, wasn't doing much more than overseeing the legalities. It was clearly Dryden's project. There was mention made that the city block on which the developer was planning to build had originally been on the city's radar as property they'd wanted to develop themselves, but she didn't see how that could lead to any soul-sucking activity. Why on earth would Silas Summerfield be worried about his great-great . . . his descendant . . . over what appeared to be a perfectly legitimate connection to a perfectly legitimate client?

Then again, why did she think Silas Summerfield was trying to tell her something? She'd had a weird—okay, a bizarre—dream, that was all. Induced, no doubt, by the fact that she'd bought a portrait of a handsome man who'd been dead for three quarters of a century. And, *okay*, maybe too much Chunky Monkey ice cream. But she'd had bizarre dreams before and had never thought someone was trying to tell her something.

Audrey Fine Magill wasn't the type of woman to buy wholly into supernatural hoo-ha. Then again, neither was she the type to completely discount it. She believed that everything in the universe was connected, even if in some small, tenuous way, and that anything that happened in some far corner of the world could potentially have an impact on everyone in it. And she believed, too, that there were some people in the world who were able to . . . access things . . . that other people couldn't. Not that she thought she was a likely conduit to the other side herself, but . . .

Well. There had been times after Sean's death three years ago when Audrey had felt and heard things she would have thought impossible. Times when she had felt as if her husband—or some afterglow of him—was in the same room with her, watching her go about her daily life. And there had been mornings when she'd awoken and felt as if she could turn over in bed and find him lying right there beside her. And once, she would have sworn she heard the soft murmur of her name from behind her, spoken in Sean's voice.

Naturally, each of those experiences could have been explained away as a product of her grief. Of her desire to have him back. Some seemingly real hallucination manufactured by her brain because she couldn't cope with his absence. But maybe, just maybe, those experiences had been the result of something else.

Nothing like that had happened for some time now, but there had been enough instances of Sean's "return" in the year after his death that Audrey had adopted the opinion that the door to the afterlife was sometimes left ajar.

Had Captain Summerfield slipped through it? she wondered. Had he taken advantage of her presence in his house—his home—to relay a message to his great-great . . . however many greats . . . grandson? And, hey, while she was at it, had he been responsible for the moved painting? Had it been his ghostly hand that swept her hats to the floor?

Or had Audrey gone well and truly off the deep end?

She sipped her coffee and looked at the photograph of Nathaniel Summerfield again. And from some very dim corner of her brain, she recalled Captain Summerfield's admonition from her dream: *The boy is in terrible danger from himself.*

Audrey understood what that was like, too. There had been a time in her own life—though, granted, she'd been considerably younger than Nathaniel Summerfield—when she'd been in a similar state. Fortunately, Sean Magill had come along and helped her find her way again. She wondered if Nathaniel had anyone to help him. Anyone besides a long-dead ancestor who showed up uninvited in people's dreams.

And she wondered, too, if maybe she should check up on him herself. Just in case.

· Three ·

NATHANIEL SUMMERFIELD WAS ALREADY HAVING A
rough day when his assistant Irene announced that he had a
visitor who hadn't made an appointment. Normally, he
would have told Irene to tell the person to come back when
they did, even if it *wasn't* a day when his phone was ringing
off the hook and he was fielding all kinds of obstacles to his
about-to-be-signed contract with Edward Dryden. Man,
everyone from the Fair Housing Commission to the Small
Business Owners Association was breathing down his neck
over this thing. Edward would be at Nathaniel's office in
less than three hours, and he still had to review part of the
contract before the man's arrival.

But it was just past noon when Irene informed him of
Audrey Magill's need to speak to him, and anyone Nathaniel
might need to call or do business with would probably be
breaking for lunch, anyway. Plus, Irene said Ms. Magill
promised she would only take a few minutes of his time.
What cinched it, though, was that he caught a glimpse of
Audrey Magill standing just beyond the door and decided he

could spare more than a few minutes for the woman, because she was, in a word, stunning.

So stunning, that he was momentarily taken aback when she strode into his office. The reaction surprised him, since she wasn't what he would have normally called beautiful— at least, not by his own definition of beautiful. She was too wholesome-looking by his standards, with her fresh-scrubbed face and hair pulled into a simple ponytail and attire that was better suited to a Sunday brunch than any kind of corporate affair, something that indicated she wasn't here on business. Which was just fine with Nathaniel, since a woman who looked like Audrey Magill didn't exactly inspire businesslike responses in a man.

Even though she wasn't conventionally beautiful, she was stunning. Had he mentioned that? The ponytail might have been simple, but it was nearly as thick as her wrist, holding razor straight, ink black hair that spilled to almost the middle of her back. It was the kind of hair that made a man itch to unfasten it, so he could thread his fingers through the silky tresses . . . and then splay them across the pillow on the other side of the bed. And her eyes. Good God. They were huge and abundantly lashed, as blue and clear as a Caribbean bay. She was slim but curvy, her generous hips and breasts only enhanced by the straight khaki skirt and pale blue T-shirt she was wearing. Her only jewelry was a gold chain that disappeared beneath the scooped neck of her shirt and gold hoops in her ears.

Not only was she not conventionally beautiful, but she wasn't the sort of woman to whom Nathaniel was normally attracted, either. He preferred women who went out of their way to play up their attributes, the kind who took hours to put on their makeup and fix their hair and choose their outfit for a date—provided they were ready when he got there and didn't make him wait. Women who wore lots of jewelry that swayed and glittered, and who chose outrageously feminine clothing meant to exaggerate their, ah, assets. Where a lot of men felt cheated by something like a Wonderbra, Nathaniel kind of liked them—though, naturally, he couldn't wait to get a woman out of one.

Wholesome-looking Audrey Magill, however, didn't seem like the sort of woman who would go for a Wonderbra. Which meant whatever she was packing, it was entirely hers.

Hell, yes, he could spare a few minutes for her. He even straightened his sapphire necktie and smoothed a few non-existent wrinkles out of his charcoal suit as he covered the few steps necessary to greet her.

"I might as well get right to my point, Mr. Summerfield," she said after shaking his hand. "I know you must be very busy."

Her handshake surprised him, too, as it was solid and masculine, the sort of handshake he didn't normally receive from a woman, even those who worked at the same corporate level he did. She took the seat he indicated on the other side of his desk, seeming in no way intimidated by his office environment, which he'd deliberately decorated in Early American Despot specifically to intimidate people. She just sat up straighter in the leather wing chair and met his gaze evenly over his expansive mahogany desk.

Then she had to go and ruin everything by asking him, "Do you believe in ghosts, Mr. Summerfield?"

Nathaniel hoped his feelings didn't show on his face. Because at that moment, what he mostly believed was that he should pick up the phone and call security, because stunning or not, he didn't have time for a nut job. Hopefully that didn't show in his voice, however, when he replied, "Ah . . . ghosts, Ms. Magill?"

She nodded. And said, "It's *Mrs.* Magill, actually."

His gaze dropped automatically to her hands, which she'd woven together and hooked over her crossed leg. Sure enough, there on the ring finger of her left hand winked a plain gold band.

Married and a potential nut job, he thought. *Two major strikes right there*. Good thing she had the stunning, no-Wonderbra-necessary-thing going, otherwise, she'd be out the door right now. "Mrs. Magill," he corrected himself obediently. "No. I don't believe in ghosts."

She expelled a soft sound that could have meant anything. "I don't either, actually."

Nathaniel expelled a mental sigh of relief. Then he reminded himself she was a *Mrs.*, so the state of her mental health—or anything else about her—made no difference. He liked women. *A lot.* He pursued women. *A lot.* But he drew the line at married. Not necessarily because of any moral leanings, but because the timing was a nightmare.

"I did have the strangest dream last night, though," she continued. "Your great-great . . . several greats grandfather was in it, and he told me you were—"

Nathaniel must have eyed her suspiciously, because she stopped talking, so suddenly that her mouth remained opened. Then she closed it and smiled in a way that made him think she realized how questionably sane—or sober— she sounded.

"Can I start over?" she asked. "I sound like a raging nut job."

Which may or may not be indicative of actual nut jobbiness. Willing to give her the benefit of the doubt, however, he said, "Of course."

She took a deep breath and tried again. "I recently bought a house in Old Louisville that, it turns out, belonged to one of your ancestors."

"Really," Nathaniel said, not sure how this was relevant to, oh . . . anything.

"Then yesterday afternoon, I went into an antique shop on Third Street and discovered a portrait of that ancestor— a riverboat captain named Silas Summerfield—for sale. I thought that was an interesting coincidence."

Nathaniel would have thought it interesting, too. Had he, you know, been interested.

"Naturally, I bought it," she said.

Naturally, Nathaniel looked at his watch.

"And then last night," she continued, "I had a very strange dream, and I woke up to an even stranger reality."

She launched into an account then that promised to take considerably more than the few minutes she'd already used up, something about his great-great-blah-blah-blah grandfather showing up in her dream and telling her that Nathaniel was in danger of losing his soul, followed by something about a break-in to her house that turned out to not be a break-in after all, but some kind of possibly-perhaps-sort-of ghostly mischief, and then . . .

Well, Nathaniel stopped listening at that point—not that he'd ever really started listening all that closely in the first place—so he really wasn't sure what she said after that. Or, *all right*, before that, either. All he knew was that she was about to use up his entire lunch hour—which, granted, he never used to actually eat lunch anyway—with some cockamamie story about an ominous warning from beyond the veil that if he entered into his partnership with Edward Dryden, he would lose his soul forever.

Stunning and no-Wonderbra-necessary notwithstanding, Nathaniel didn't have all day and did have a sound mind. So the next time she paused for a breath, he said, "Ms. Magill, I appreciate your concern, but you'll understand, I'm sure, when I tell you I don't share it."

"Mrs. Magill," she corrected him again. She studied him in clear confusion. "Why would I understand that? I mean, I know this sounds—"

"Ludicrous?" he finished for her. "Because it doesn't just sound that. It is that."

Now she studied him in clear offense. "Look, I realize what happened to me last night and this morning might seem a little out of the ordinary—"

"It doesn't seem a little out of the ordinary," Nathaniel interrupted her. "It *is* completely ridiculous."

"And believe me," she went on as if he hadn't spoken, "I weighed my decision carefully before coming here, for the very reason that I was afraid you'd think I'm nuts."

She paused, evidently awaiting a response to that. So he said, "And?"

Evidently that wasn't the response she had been ex-

pecting, because she narrowed her eyes at him. "And I
don't expect everyone to believe in the possibility of an
afterlife or any sort of conduit between that and the here
and now. I'm as skeptical as the next person about that kind
of thing. But I'm not completely closed-minded about it,
either. And I thought you might at least be like me in
finding the whole concept as . . . as . . ."

"As ridiculous?" he supplied helpfully. Well, okay,
maybe it was less helpfully than it was antagonistically. At
least he'd offered her something.

"As interesting," she finished tersely, "as I do."

"Ms. Magill—"

"*Mrs.*"

"*Mrs.* Magill," he amended again, wondering why he had
trouble remembering she was married, "You can't think I
would put stock in a dream you had, even if it did *allegedly*
feature one of my ancestors. Dreams are just images that
unroll in a person's brain while they're unconscious. All the
more reason to not put any stock in them. My advice to you
would be to lay off the Hostess Ho Hos before you go to bed
at night."

She narrowed her eyes at him even more. "It was Chunky
Monkey ice cream, and I know perfectly well this sounds
like nonsense. But don't you find it strange that I would have
a dream like that?"

What Nathaniel found strange, she didn't want to know.

"And then wake up this morning to see an article about
you in the paper?" she added. "One that your great-great-
et-cetera grandfather said I would see in the paper?"

"Ms. Magill—"

"*Mrs.*," she corrected him yet again, more vehemently
this time.

"*Mrs.* Magill," he amended yet again, less graciously
this time. "There have been articles in the paper about me
and Edward Dryden almost every day for two weeks. The
development he's undertaking—and which I'm investing
in heavily—is going to be one of the biggest ones this city
has seen for more than a decade. For all I know, that was

what caused you to have your dream, not some portrait of my great-great . . . whatever . . . grandfather. And certainly not any danger I might be in of losing my soul."

She opened her mouth to say something, apparently reconsidered what she was going to say, and closed it again. But she kept her gaze homed in on his as she stood and tugged her handbag over her shoulder. She started to turn toward the door, then looked back at Nathaniel. "I'm sorry if you think I've wasted your time, Mr. Summerfield. But as Shakespeare said—"

"Is this going to be the quote about 'More things in heaven and earth, Horatio'?" Nathaniel interjected before she could finish. "Because, quite frankly, *Mrs.* Magill, I can dream of a lot in my philosophy. And none of it has to do with ghosts or souls."

She nodded once, curtly. "Oh, believe me, Mr. Summerfield, I can see you don't spend much time worrying about your soul. What I'm trying to figure out is why Captain Summerfield was so worried about it. Since it's abundantly clear that any soul you might have ever had is already long gone."

And with that, she turned around and headed for the door. Nathaniel told himself he was grateful, even as he watched with something akin to wistfulness the way that long ponytail swayed even more seductively than her hips. The last thing he needed in his life these days was a raging nut job butting into it, even if she was stunning. Having Edward as a client was going to command more of his time than any other client he'd ever had, and it was going to ultimately net him more wealth. Hell, if that caused him to lose his soul, it was just one less thing Nathaniel would have to feel responsible for. He was sitting down to review his contract with Edward before the door behind Mrs. Magill was even closed.

"THIS IS THE START OF SOMETHING GREAT, NA-thaniel."

Three hours after Audrey Magill left his office, Nathaniel welcomed Edward Dryden into it. They'd gone over every clause in their contract together, had discussed the development in detail, had reviewed and approved all the arrangements left to make. All that was left was to sign on the dotted line—in triplicate—and the deal would be done. Edward signed his name where indicated with a narrow, crowded hand, then offered the pen to Nathaniel. He bent over the desk and placed the pen to paper and was about to scrawl the first of three signatures when his hand stilled. Because something Audrey Magill had said during her long spiel suddenly erupted in his brain.

If you sign this contract with Edward Dryden, you're going to lose your soul forever.

That was supposedly the gist of what his great-great-blah-blah-blah grandfather had told her, what the late, great Captain Silas Summerfield had come from the grave to say. That if Nathaniel went through with what would undoubtedly be the most financially rewarding deal of his career, he would be left soulless.

Nathaniel didn't even know if he had an ancestor named Silas Summerfield. He knew little about his family on either side, mostly because he didn't care. His mother had been estranged from her family, so he'd never met anyone from the maternal side of his family tree. His father had died when Nathaniel was too young to remember him, leaving his mother to struggle to provide for the two of them the whole time he was growing up. He wasn't big on heredity or genealogy, having never had much of a family to rely on. He knew there were other Summerfields out there— there must be, somewhere—but he'd never given any of them much thought. Present *or* past. And now suddenly, some strange woman—in more ways than one—had come barging into his life because of some dream she'd had about a long-dead relative.

He told himself she was crazy. She must be. One of those people who weren't content to go through life believing in things they had no business believing in to begin with, but who then had to foist off those bizarre beliefs onto others. They were people whose lives were so empty, and who needed attention so badly, that they had to harass other people to get it. True, Audrey Magill hadn't looked like that kind of person. She'd seemed normal enough. But sometimes it was the most normal-seeming ones who were the ones you had to watch most closely.

This deal with Edward was the start of great things. The sort of opportunity that only came along once in a man's career. So what if the land Dryden Properties was developing was originally targeted for quality, low-income housing that would have enabled struggling, single-parent families— families like, oh, say, Nathaniel's had been as a child—to live better lives? So what if, instead of safe homes for underprivileged kids, a new school to educate them, and a daycare to watch after them while their mothers worked, Edward was going to build overpriced lofts and boutiques for people who had more dollars than sense? That wasn't Nathaniel's problem. He wasn't the world's moral compass. He was just a guy trying to make a buck.

And this deal would make him a mountain of those.

"Having second thoughts, Nathaniel?"

He glanced up at the question to see Edward smiling at him, but there was something in the smile that wasn't quite genuine. As if the man honestly feared Nathaniel was about to change his mind. As if, should Nathaniel do that, there might be consequences. Consequences beyond the financial ones outlined in the contract.

Nathaniel shook the feeling off. Edward Dryden just wasn't much of a smiler, that was all.

"Of course not," he said as he dragged the pen across the line, leaving his signature in its wake. He repeated the action two more times, on two more copies of the contract. Then he tossed the pen onto his desk and turned to shake Edward's hand.

"No going back now," the other man said with a laugh.

"No way I'd want to," Nathaniel assured him. "It's a done deal."

As those last words left his mouth, Nathaniel felt a strange twinge in his chest, right in the area of his heart. Nothing scary, nothing that made him think he needed to head to the nearest ER, just . . . weird. Something weird. He felt as if something in his chest, something surrounding his heart, fluttered a little frantically and then just . . . evaporated. He couldn't think of any other way to describe it. As if a part of him suddenly panicked, then disappeared. And then, suddenly, he was overcome by cold. Cold so strong, it actually made him shiver.

Unconsciously, he lifted a hand to his chest and pushed against his breastbone, where he'd felt the emptying sensation, as if that might allay the uneasiness that was rushing into him almost as quickly as the cold.

"You okay, Nathaniel?" Edward asked. "You look a little pale."

Nathaniel nodded, even though he didn't feel okay at all. "I'm fine," he lied to the other man. "It's nothing. Probably just something I ate."

Yeah, that was it. He'd eaten something that disagreed with him, that was all. Because in spite of what Audrey Magill had tried to tell him, it couldn't be something he lost.

· Four ·

THE SECOND TIME AUDREY SAW CAPTAIN SUMMER-
field, it wasn't in her dreams in the middle of the night. No,
the second time she saw him, it was just past noon, when
she entered her kitchen pantry to retrieve a can of tuna to
make her lunch. She tugged on the string dangling from
the bare bulb overhead, spilled some frail white light into
the tiny confined space, and saw him standing right in front
of her, framed by a bag of Oreos and a can of artichoke
hearts on one side, a jar of Kalamata olives and a box of
Cheerios on the other.

She uttered a startled little cry at his sudden appearance,
leaping backward a step and nearly dropping the butter
knife she'd been holding absently . . . but now suddenly
clutched with great intent. Before she recognized the
intruder as the man in the painting upstairs, a million
thoughts dashed through her mind in a second's time. That
someone had broken into her house again, that this time
the intruder was going to try to do more than fling about
hats and portraits, that the only thing standing between her
and the great beyond might very well be her faded Levi's

and University of Louisville tank top and the blunt blade of her Oneida flatware.

Then, when she recognized the man in her pantry as Silas Summerfield, her thoughts went zinging off into a new direction. That she was seeing things that weren't there, doubtless because she was still carrying around some anxiety about the break-in to her house the day before. Or maybe the hallucination was due to a lack of sleep, since it wasn't easy to catch Zs when one was lying wide awake in one's bed, jumping at every creak and groan one's house made because one was still carrying around some anxiety about the break-in to her house that morning.

Even worse, when Audrey had finally managed to go to sleep, her dreams had been filled this time with images of Captain Summerfield's great-great-however-many-greats grandson, and that had been even more bizarre than the dreams about Silas. It had been bad enough confronting Nathaniel Summerfield in person. Though, truth be told, that wasn't entirely because he'd behaved like such an infuriating ass. It was because her reaction to him—even with the infuriating ass part—had been wholly unexpected and in no way welcome.

Simply put, the moment Audrey had laid eyes on the man, she'd responded to him in a way that she hadn't responded to a man for a very long time. Not since she'd laid eyes on Sean Magill, come to think of it. And even with Sean, there hadn't been that electric zing of immediate awareness. When she'd first met her husband, at a dinner party thrown by mutual friends, she'd thought him cute and funny and sweet, and she'd been charmed by him. But there had been no explosion of heat in the pit of her belly, the way there had been with Nathaniel. And when she'd shaken Sean's hand the first time, there had been no tingle of odd anticipation as there had been with Nathaniel. What on earth she could have possibly been anticipating, she couldn't have said. She only knew that, the moment her palm connected with his, she'd felt . . . hopeful somehow. As if something . . . major . . . was about to happen between the two of them.

She'd told herself that helping the man keep his soul was pretty major, but there had been something else there, too. Of course, once she'd realized what a jerk the guy was, that feeling of anticipation and hopefulness had fizzled. All she'd anticipated then was leaving, and all she'd hoped for was a swift departure. But the heat in her belly hadn't fizzled at all, and that had bothered her a lot. Heat was the last thing she wanted to be feeling for a man—any man. But most especially one like Nathaniel Summerfield, who was the complete antithesis of the man with whom Audrey had fallen in love.

Nathaniel, however, was the least of her worries at the moment. Because at the moment, there was a hallucination of his great-great-however-many-greats grandfather standing in her pantry, and that bothered her way more than bizarre dreams about either of them had. Bizarre dreams meant too much Chunky Monkey. Hallucinations meant . . .

Well. They just weren't good, that was all.

She squeezed her eyes shut tight for a moment—but didn't loosen her hold on the knife—then opened them again. Nope, Silas was still there. Dressed the same way he'd been in her dream, in black trousers and an open, collarless white shirt, its cuffs, wider than was fashionable these days, rolled back to his elbows. But where he'd been cordial and reserved in her dream, now he looked kind of angry and intense. He stood with his legs spread wide, his hands fisted on his hips, his dark eyebrows arrowed downward. His square jaw was set rigidly, and his black hair was in disarray, as if he'd swept both hands through it in frustration only moments ago.

"Madam," he said, addressing her as he had in her dream the night before, "you have failed me most egregiously."

Wow. He even sounded real. She truly had to get to bed earlier tonight. She closed her eyes again, this time accompanying the gesture with three long, steady breaths. Then she opened them again.

Silas was still there. Only now he looked even madder.

"I assure you I am no hallucination," he told her.

Oh, well, if her hallucination was telling her he was no hallucination, of course Audrey should listen to him.

She started to say something along those lines to Silas in retort, then decided that if she started talking back to her hallucination, she might as well start talking to the box of Cheerios behind him. And then to someone in the mental health field who might be able to help her separate fantasy from reality. So she only grabbed the can of tuna she'd come into the pantry for, tugged on the light string again to turn it off, completed two steps backward, and pushed the pantry door closed. Then she inhaled another deep breath and turned around.

Only to find Silas Summerfield standing in front of her again.

This time Audrey did drop the knife. And the can of tuna, too. And although she tried to close her eyes again, she found that she could not. Because the afternoon sun was streaming through the windows over the sink behind him . . . and through the good captain, too.

He'd seemed opaque enough in the pantry, but in the bright sunlight, he was vaguely translucent. She could just make out the line of her countertops behind him bisecting him at the waist, along with an occasional droplet of water from her perpetually drippy faucet that fell from just below his heart. When she studied his face closer, she could just discern the branches of the sugar maple outside the window, as craggy and jagged as his eyebrows.

In spite of her musings the day before about the door to the afterlife sometimes being left ajar, and in spite of what she'd said to Silas's great-great-however-many-greats grandson, Audrey told herself she couldn't possibly be seeing what she seemed to be seeing. Her house couldn't possibly be haunted by the ghost of Silas Summerfield. Not with a manifestation like this. Whenever she saw one of those ghost-hunter shows on TV, the evidence of hauntings was always as nebulous as the spirits themselves. Smudges of gray on camera film, wisps of faint light on video, scratches of sound on tape.

In spite of all that, too, Audrey heard herself say, in a rather shaky voice, "You're . . . you're not real."

He arched an eyebrow at that. "Am I not?"

She shook her head. "No. You're not."

"Then why are you speaking to me?"

She opened her mouth to reply, told herself that he was just trying to get a rise out of her, and closed it again. Just her luck that she'd have hallucinations that were sarcastic. Just how little sleep had she had last night?

When she said nothing, Captain Summerfield sighed with something akin to disappointment, and folded his ghostly arms over his ghostly torso.

Hallucinated arms over his *hallucinated* torso, Audrey quickly corrected herself.

"I am not a figment of your imagination, Mrs. Magill," he told her. "I am Silas Summerfield, and I am standing right before you. And yes, the sunlight does render me somewhat . . . thin," he finally concluded.

Oh, she didn't know about that. The guy seemed to be solid rock. Except, you know, for that translucent thing.

She said nothing in response, mostly because speaking to a man who wasn't there would make it seem as if maybe he were there. And if Silas Summerfield was standing in her kitchen, then the door to the afterlife was way more than ajar at the moment. Which meant that maybe, just maybe, Sean Magill could walk through it, too. And Audrey simply could not allow herself to have that hope.

At her reticence, Silas expelled a soft sigh and said, very quietly, "Please say something, Mrs. Magill."

But Audrey only shook her head in silence.

"What will it take to prove to you that I'm not a hallucination?" he asked. "That I am Silas Summerfield, former owner of this house, dead almost four score years and now returned because I must ensure that my descendant escapes a fate worse than death."

A fate worse than death? Audrey echoed to herself. Terrific. Her hallucination was sarcastic *and* melodramatic.

Silas nodded in response to her silence this time.

"Actually, I had anticipated this reaction," he told her. "I will prove to you that I am who and what I say I am. Come with me to Bellamy's room."

Audrey hesitated. And not just because she didn't know which room was Bellamy's room, either. Or who Bellamy was, for that matter. Was following a hallucination's orders the same thing as talking back to one? Would she be more crazy or less if she did what he told her to do? Then again, by virtue of this hallucination going on as long as it had, the level of her craziness was probably moot at this point. She just hoped her health insurance covered at least *some* of the cost of therapy.

She hesitated a moment, then thought, *What the hell.* Speaking to a hallucination couldn't be any crazier than having one in the first place. So she asked, "Who's Bellamy?"

He gazed at her blankly for a moment, as if she should know the answer to that. Then his expression cleared, as if he remembered why she didn't know the answer to that. "Bellamy is . . . *was,*" he quickly corrected himself, "my valet. He served me well for nearly forty years." His expression darkened some. "Of course, I had no idea the man was stealing from me at the time."

Audrey had no idea how to reply to that. So all she said was, "Gee, guess good help was hard to find in your day, too, huh?"

All Silas said in response to that was, "Come with me to his room." He made a face, then corrected himself again, "To his *former* room. I believe you're currently using it to store supplies."

Oh, *that* room, Audrey thought. The one that was little more than closet-sized and claimed only one tiny window and was wedged into a corner of the second floor at the opposite end of the house from the bathroom. Audrey had thought it too small and bleak to even use it for her office. No wonder Bellamy had stolen from his employer.

Silas suddenly frowned, as if she'd spoken that last

aloud. Then, as if to illustrate that very thing, he asked, "You think theft is an excusable offense, Mrs. Magill?"

Whoa. Now her hallucination could read her mind? Well, that was going to be inconvenient. Not to mention irritating. And embarrassing, too, on those occasions when she got Backstreet Boys songs stuck in her head.

She gave her forehead a good mental smack. *Well,* of course *her hallucination could read her mind,* she thought. That was, after all, where it had originated. Naturally it would have access to anything else that might be parading around in her head.

Not sure why she was continuing a dialogue with a figment of her imagination, she replied anyway, "No, I don't think theft is excusable. Well, unless you and your family are starving to death like Jean Valjean or something. I just meant, you know, if you'd given the guy a better room, he might have shown you better service."

"He might also have done that had he not been a damnable cur."

Yeah, okay. There was that. Point to the hallucination.

The hallucination in question smiled suddenly, doubtless because he had read her mind again, and something about the smile made her toes curl. It was amazing how much he looked like his great-great-however-many-greats grandson when he did that.

Not that *that* was what made Audrey's toes curl, no way. Heat in the pit of her stomach notwithstanding, Nathaniel Summerfield was the most odious man she'd ever met. He was everything she disliked in the opposite sex, epitomized all those things that gave the male gender a bad name. Overbearing, arrogant, short-tempered, self-important, more than a little sexist . . . The list could go on forever. The moment she'd stepped into his office and seen that it had been decorated by the design firm of Testosterone and Cash, Unlimited, she'd been reminded of all the reasons she'd left the corporate workforce behind. It was more than clear that what mattered most to Nathaniel Summerfield was money. And that power was a close second. For all she knew, those were the only things that mattered to him.

But he had smiled at her, she couldn't quite help recalling. Once. When she'd first come into the room, as he'd told her hello. And when she'd seen that smile . . .

Well. Suffice it to say something inside her had stirred to life that hadn't inhaled a single breath since Sean's death.

She shook the memory off almost literally, reminding herself she had a hallucination to dispel and some sanity to check. Captain Summerfield still stood before her, watching her with a curious expression.

"You found him handsome, my grandson?" he asked.

Audrey's mouth dropped open at that. "Of course not," she hotly denied. Okay, so there was more than Backstreet Boys songs that could embarrass her. Except that she *hadn't* been attracted to his grandson, she reminded herself. Which just went to prove that hallucinations didn't know everything. So there.

"If you must know, I found him loathsome, your grandson," Audrey added. "And I don't think you need to be worried about him losing his soul."

"Why not?"

"Because he lost that sucker a *looooong* time ago."

"Sucker?" Silas repeated, his expression turning puzzled. "What does candy have to do with anything?"

Audrey opened her mouth to explain, then decided not to bother. Her sarcastic, melodramatic hallucination was also, evidently, way uncool.

"Never mind," she said. Then she remembered he'd offered to prove his existence. Hah. So she repeated, "The storage room? You were going to show me something there?"

Silas nodded. "Meet me at the top of the stairs." And then he was gone, as if he'd never been there.

Well, that was one way to get rid of a pesky mental disorder, Audrey thought. Just agree to meet it somewhere else, and then don't bother to show up. No way was she going to go upstairs to meet someone who wasn't there.

"Mrs. Magill!" a deep voice boomed from overhead, so loudly, she could feel it reverberating inside her brain. "I'm waiting!"

She sighed. Fine. She recalled the old rhyme her mother used to say when Audrey was a little girl to make her laugh, the one about meeting a man on the stairs who wasn't there. Paraphrasing, she thought, *Today, I will go up the stairs and meet a man who isn't there. He won't be there again tomorrow, because . . .*

Because tomorrow, Audrey was going to get a complete medical workup. Starting with her head.

As she rounded the first-floor landing, she saw him standing at the top of the stairs, just as he'd promised, looking more opaque now, thanks to the lack of sunshine. But that lack of light made him appear darker in other ways, too, ways that reminded Audrey of Nathaniel Summerfield again, and, just like before, something hot and needy erupted in the pit of her belly. She closed her eyes and forced the sensation out, then opened them again and studied Silas, who still glowered down at her. For a hallucination, he certainly was stubborn.

"This way," he said. And, without awaiting a response at all this time, he moved to the left and down the hall.

With a soft sigh of exasperation, Audrey followed, trying not to think about being "visited" by a man who'd been dead for seventy-some years, even if he had once called the house home. Maybe she did believe in ghosts. Maybe, on some level, she didn't think she was talking to a hallucination. Maybe, on some level, she really did believe a spirit had manifested in her house as more than a smudge on film. Maybe that was why she was going along with this as easily as she seemed to be. But if ghosts were real, she thought further, then why hadn't Sean ever tried to cross the veil and come back to her? The way Silas had, manifested in all his glory, able to communicate as if he were flesh and blood?

She pushed that thought away, too, as she topped the last stair and followed in Silas's footsteps. But when she arrived in the storage-slash-Bellamy's-old-room, he wasn't there. So she ventured warily, "Silas? Where are you?"

"Behind you," came his voice from that direction.

She spun around, and there he was, standing in a spot she'd just passed herself, where he hadn't been before. She started to reach out a hand to see if she could touch him, then stopped herself. She still didn't know what was going on—whether she really was being haunted, or really was losing her mind—and she wasn't sure she wanted to know what would happen if she tried to push her hand through him. She remembered reading something somewhere about how there were supposed to be "cold spots" around ghosts. But even though Silas stood barely a foot away from her, the temperature in the room was in no way chilly. Was that more proof that this wasn't a haunting? Or did it just mean ghost-hunters were full of hooey?

The room in which the two of them stood was the one where Audrey had dumped everything she wasn't sure yet what to do with or hadn't had a chance to unpack. Boxes were stacked upon boxes, and a few odd pieces of furniture—chairs and tables mostly—were pushed against the walls. There was a plastic wardrobe full of her old suits shoved into one corner, and it was beside that that the good captain currently stood.

"Move this," he said of the rolling wardrobe.

Immediately, Audrey's back went up. It was the same sort of command, spoken in the same sort of voice, that had been commonplace at her former company, an old-boy accounting firm that had only changed its hiring practices at some point after World War II because the federal government had required them by law to do so. Their attitudes, however, had remained unchanged. Women, her old boss had firmly believed, should only work in offices to type, file, and make coffee. And to pick up dry cleaning and order lunch and make travel arrangements. And be leered at whenever the urge struck.

"Move it yourself," Audrey retorted, dropping her fists to her hips in much the way he had earlier.

His dark brows shot up at that. "I beg your pardon?"

She jutted up her chin at the wardrobe. "You want it moved, move it yourself," she repeated. "I don't follow orders."

He gazed at her distastefully. "Obviously not."

Point to the woman with the mental impairment.

Now Silas dispelled a sound of exasperation. "I can't move it," he told her. Then, to illustrate why, he placed his hand beside it and gave it a push, only to have his arm disappear into the wardrobe, up to his elbow. "I'm not corporeal," he said unnecessarily.

"Then how did you move the painting and toss my hats around?" she asked in a voice she hoped told him how much that had pissed her off. "That was three thousand dollars' worth of work you almost destroyed."

His mouth dropped open at that. "Three thousand dollars? For a bunch of hats?" he asked, aghast. "Madam, I paid less than that for my house."

"Yeah, inflation sucks," Audrey said blandly. Then, before he could ask for clarification, she told him. "Inflation is bad. So how come you were able to move the painting and hats? And open the newspaper on my kitchen table?"

He hesitated for a moment, as if he didn't know, actually. Then he said, "I don't know, actually. I wanted them moved, and they were moved. But afterward, I was exhausted to the point where I was unable to do anything for some time. I'm not certain of the mechanics involved. Only that I wanted something done, and it was done. But at great expense to my . . . presence." He made a pushing motion with his hand again, and, again, it went straight through the wardrobe. "I'm not certain how long it will be before I can do something like that again."

"But why did you want those particular things done in the first place?" Audrey asked.

He inhaled a deep breath and released it slowly. "Because . . . because I returned to my home and realized it was no longer my home. In a moment of terrible frustration, I tried to put things back the way they were when I was alive. Then I realized things could never go back to being that way." He made a face. "It was a childish thing to do. I apologize. I should have returned everything to its proper place."

Audrey could tell by the way he'd apologized that it was something he wasn't used to doing. So the fact that he had done it went a long way toward making her more amenable to him. And his edicts.

Nevertheless, she told him, "Well, the least you could do is say please."

He looked confused for a moment, then backtracked to the place in their conversation where he'd uttered his command. Then he gritted his teeth at her. In spite of that, he said, "Please move this . . . this . . . this thing."

"It's a wardrobe," she told him as she covered what little distance remained between them.

He looked at it with antipathy. "Craftsmanship has suffered greatly in the last century, I see."

"You have no idea," Audrey muttered as she pushed the wardrobe aside. She started to add that at least children weren't forced to work in sweatshops in this country anymore, as they had been in Silas's time, then she remembered that that was only because those sweatshop children's jobs had been outsourced to children in sweatshops in other countries. Craftsmanship may have suffered, she thought morosely, but corporate greed had advanced with enormous strides. Yay, progress.

There was nothing behind the wardrobe, so she turned to look at Silas questioningly.

"There," he told her.

She looked where he was pointing and saw an air vent cut into the hardwood floor, covered by a square, filigreed grate fashioned from black wrought-iron.

"Remove that," he told her. Then, when she snapped her head back to look at him with, she hoped, venom, he hastily added, "*Please* remove that, Mrs. Magill."

The grill was screwed onto the vent, so she went to a box upon which she'd scrawled the words MISCELLANEOUS

KITCHEN and picked through it, until she located a set of screwdrivers she normally kept in a drawer for easy access, but which she hadn't yet unpacked. She chose the one she knew would be the right size, then returned to the grate and effortlessly loosened each screw. She had to tug hard twice to free the thing, and after she did, a rather large spider came scurrying out to greet her. She immediately stepped on it, went back to the box to retrieve a roll of paper towels, then scooped up its squishy remains. When she turned to look at Silas again, to see why he'd wanted the grate removed from the air vent, he was eyeing her with something akin to admiration.

"What?" she asked.

"You dispatched that spider rather well," he told her. "And without squealing or some other feminine rubbish. You also used that tool with aplomb. As well as any man would."

"So?"

"So, Mrs. Magill," he said, "I don't think I've ever encountered a woman who could do both so comfortably."

"Yeah, well, I've come a long way, baby and all that."

His expression turned puzzled again, but Audrey didn't bother to explain. If this was a nervous breakdown, she wanted to get on with it and get it over with as quickly as possible. "What next?" she asked wearily.

"I'm afraid you're going to have to reach in there," he said.

"What for?"

"Because there's a pair of gold cuff links in there that Bellamy evidently stole from my room and stashed there, and you need to retrieve them for me."

This time Audrey was the one to be puzzled. "Cuff links?"

"Yes."

"You need cuff links in the afterlife?"

"No, Mrs. Magill. But they're rather unusual cuff links, and I shall describe them for you before you locate them, and then, when you do locate them, you'll have no choice but to accept the reality of my . . ."

"Haunting?" she said, even though she still wasn't convinced of that.

"Visitation," he corrected her.

"Why will that prove anything?" she asked.

He crossed his arms over his chest again. "Because right now, you can't possibly know what these cuff links will look like," he told her. "For that matter, you can't even know for sure there are cuff links down there. Once you discover them and see that they are exactly as I described them, you'll have to accept that the only way that could be is due to the fact that I, Captain Silas Leyton Summerfield, am standing here, speaking to you, and you are not enjoying a hallucination."

"Oh, I wouldn't exactly say I'm enjoying this," she told him. Whatever *this* was. Still, what he said did make sense. In a weird, beyond-the-veil, maybe-it-wasn't-the-Chunky-Monkey-after-all kind of way. "Okay, so what are they going to look like, these cuff links?"

"They are solid gold," he told her, "each with a lapis lazuli inset fashioned to look like a paddlewheel from the side. What appears to be a coil of rope surrounds the design."

Audrey nodded. "Okay. And how far down will I have to go to find these cuff links?"

"Just past the bend in the flue."

She dropped to her knees and stuck her hand down the vent, pushing her fingers through the dust and sediment until they bumped something that was small and blunt. Her heart hammered hard as she moved her hand further and encountered a second something that was small and blunt. Gingerly, she closed her fingers over what felt very much like two cuff links. When she withdrew her hand and opened it, she saw what also looked very much like two cuff links. Two dust-coated gold cuff links. She swiped her thumb over the flat part of one of them, and when she saw the asterisk-like design inset in blue stone and surrounded by a braid of rope, her mouth went dry.

It was only then that Audrey realized she had been convinced she was imagining the good captain. His appearance could have been triggered by her reaction to the
break-in, or might have even been the result of some leftover
grief for Sean at her sudden fear of being alone. She'd
always felt safer when her husband was alive, had never
worried about things like break-ins the way a single woman
would. A threat to her safety now might understandably
generate a desire to have Sean back, and with the recent
addition of Silas Summerfield's portrait to her house, her
brain could have manufactured him instead of Sean as a
suitable protector.

Up until the cuff links, everything Silas had said to her
could have been something she could have conceivably
invented in her own subconscious. Even the things he'd
told her about his great-great-however-many-greats-
grandson could have, as Nathaniel himself had pointed out,
come from her unconscious absorption of some news story
about the guy. But the cuff links . . .

There was no way she could have known they were there.
And there was no way she could have known what they
would look like. So her hallucination couldn't have plucked
that information from some dark recess in her mind. Having
found them here, this way, after Silas had told her what to
look for and where, could only mean one thing.

Her house was haunted. By the ghost of Captain Silas
Leyton Summerfield. And, judging by the look of him, he
wasn't going anywhere anytime soon.

NEVER IN HIS NINETY-THREE YEARS ON EARTH—NOR
his seventy-six years elsewhere—had Silas seen someone
go white the way Mrs. Magill did just then.

"Mrs. Magill?" he said. "Are you all right?"

She uttered a strangled sound in response, something
that reminded Silas of the creak and whine of the steam as
it primed the engine of *Desdemona*, his paddle wheeler.

The vessel had been as contrary as . . . as . . . Well, as Mrs. Magill. But he'd never lost his respect or admiration for the old girl.

"Mrs. Magill?" he said again. "Are you all right?"

This time she sputtered something that sounded vaguely like English, but Silas couldn't be sure. The language had, after all, changed rather a lot since his day.

"Perhaps you should sit down," he told her. Automatically, he started to reach out to her, then remembered he couldn't touch anything, so would be of no help. His temper flared at feeling so impotent—a condition he had *never* suffered in life—and his next words came out a little harsher than he had intended them. "Oh, for God's sake, woman. I'm just a ghost. I can do you less harm than the damned spider."

She worked her mouth a few more times, expelled a few more incoherent sounds, then, finally, managed, "That spider is something I can explain through rational means. You, on the other hand . . ."

He grinned at that, relieved she was regaining some of her spirit. "Are you calling me irrational, Mrs. Magill?"

She shook her head. "No. I'm calling myself irrational. This can't be happening. You can't be a ghost haunting my house."

"Why not? As you can see for yourself, I am here." He nodded toward the cuff links that lay open in her grimy palm. "I just proved it."

Instead of pursuing the topic of his existence or her own rationality, she asked, "How did you know they were there? I mean, if you knew they were there, why didn't you get them yourself while you were still alive?"

"Because I didn't know they were there when I was alive. I lost them not long after the set was given to me for my fiftieth birthday. I only found them myself this morning."

She shook her head slowly, then chuckled.

"What do you find funny, Mrs. Magill?"

She looked at him and smiled, albeit a bit shakily. "I just realized there's something that bothers me more than discovering I'm being haunted."

"What is that?"

She pressed a palm to her forehead and gazed at the iron grate lying haphazardly beside the square hole in the floor. "That if these air ducts are original to the house, I need to get them replaced, and that's going to set me back a lot more than I planned to spend just yet."

He smiled back at her, he hoped reassuringly. "Don't be concerned," he told her. "The house is quite sound."

She expelled a long, weary-sounding breath. "Too bad I can't say the same for myself."

"Have no fear, madam," he said. "You are one of the soundest people I have ever met." He was about to say more, but her legs suddenly buckled beneath her, and she landed on her rump with a resounding thump.

Again, he instinctively reached for her, and this time didn't check himself quickly enough before touching her. For the merest of moments, his fingertips grazed over her lower arm, and although he felt no physical sensation of touching her, something akin to an electrical shock leapt into his hand, sending a shudder of heat up his arm. Mrs. Magill must have felt something similar, because she jolted at the contact, scrambling away from him, pressing her own hand to her shoulder.

"What was that?" she asked breathlessly.

Silas, more than a little shaken by the sensation himself, replied, "I don't know. I gather we just discovered what happens when your world meets mine."

She looked as if she wanted to say—or perhaps ask—something else, then seemed to think better of it. She only nodded silently, pulled her dungaree-clad legs up to her chest and wrapped her arms around her knees. She still clutched the errant cuff links in one hand, and her bare arms were trembling.

"I truly won't hurt you, you know," he said softly.

"It's not that," she said quietly. "For some reason, I'm not afraid of you. It's just . . ."

"What?" he asked when she didn't finish the statement.

She blew out another breath, this one sounding a bit

shaky. "If people who die are able to come back, then why . . ."

He understood then. She was a *Mrs.* Magill, after all. And there clearly was no *Mr.* Magill living with her. "Your husband," he said simply.

She nodded.

"You want to know why I'm here and he isn't."

She nodded again, but dropped her gaze from his to study the floor instead. "It's nothing personal," she told him.

Silas took a few steps toward her. "I don't know why I'm here and he isn't," he said honestly. "I only returned here myself a few days ago. And only because of the fix my great-great-et-cetera grandson has managed to get himself into. When I realized what was about to happen, I had to come. I can't have him sullying the Summerfield name the way he is bound to sully it if he involves himself in a criminal enterprise. The only way to stop him was to come here. And the only way to come here was to join myself to something that belonged to me in life, something that represents the man I used to be."

"Your portrait," she said, sounding a little more steady.

"Yes, my portrait. When I saw you come into the shop, and when I heard you say you lived in my home, I knew it was fated that we meet. So I changed the price on my portrait to make it affordable to you. You are the perfect vessel to assist me," he concluded.

"Why?"

"Because," he said, "we Summerfield men are notoriously susceptible to beautiful women. Particularly those who have jet hair and eyes the color of a springtime sky."

Her mouth fell open at that. "You thought you could pimp me out to your great-great-whatever grandson?" she asked incredulously.

He looked at her blankly. "I'm sorry, Mrs. Magill, but once again, the language barrier impedes my understanding of the conversation." Although he was reasonably certain he understood the implications of what she was saying, and it wasn't a particularly flattering image. Nor was it, he was afraid, an altogether inaccurate one. So he hurried on before she could saying anything else, "If your husband has never returned to you, Mrs. Magill, it is doubtless because you have done nothing to sully his name or his memory."

When she looked up at him then, he saw that her eyes were filled with tears, and he cursed himself, both for being the cause of them and for feeling so irritated at their appearance. "I am sorry, Mrs. Magill," he said, doing his best to mask his annoyance. "But I'm still not certain how this works myself. There are some things I know with confidence—though I don't know how I know them—and other things that are a complete mystery."

She hesitated a moment, then asked, "What do you know with confidence?"

"I know that where my portrait goes, I go. I am bound to it."

She seemed to brighten some at that. "Then I can give it to someone else, and you'll haunt them?"

This time Silas was the one to hesitate, waiting to see if the answer would come to him. It did. "You cannot," he told her. "At least not yet. You were sent into the shop for the express purpose of buying it."

She shook her head. "No, I went into that shop looking for a chair."

"So you think."

"So I know."

"Mrs. Magill, there are forces at work here beyond both you and me. That, too, is something I know with confidence."

She eyed him warily. "Forces," she repeated. "Like . . . a supreme being?"

It was more her tone of voice than the question itself that caught him off-guard. "Do you not believe in a supreme being?" he asked, unaccustomed to such an idea.

"Not in the traditional sense, no."

"Then in what sense do you believe in one?"

She gave a little shrug. "I've always kind of considered myself an Emersonian Transcendentalist. That there's divinity in everyone, and we achieve it by living a good life and being good people."

"Emerson's essay 'Nature,'" Silas said, recognizing the philosophy and naming the title of the work in which Ralph Waldo Emerson first introduced it. "I find comfort in the knowledge that people still read Emerson. Though I myself found his suggestions in that particular work to be unsound."

"You read Emerson when you were alive?"

"Don't sound so surprised, Mrs. Magill. I read a great deal when I was alive, on a great many subjects. Yes, I read Emerson. However," he added, "I am reasonably confident that Mr. Emerson had nothing to do with my arrival in the shop up the street."

"And where were you before you arrived in the shop up the street?" she asked.

Silas tried to recall, but could not. "I don't quite remember. I only know that I entered the shop at roughly the same time you did."

He gave it some more thought, to see if any other ideas or images made an appearance in his head, then wasn't altogether surprised when a few vague ones did. "I have a somewhat indistinct remembrance of comfort and tranquility. And an absolute absence of fear." He waited for more impressions, but there were none. "Perhaps as time passes," he said, "I shall be able to remember more."

She studied him in silence for a moment longer, then nodded, once. With one quick swipe, she palmed her eyes, his cuff links still fisted in one hand. Then she pushed herself up to standing, inhaled a deep breath and released it slowly, and met his gaze again, this time dry-eyed.

"So if you showed up in the shop to meet me," she said, "and I can't give away your portrait, then I guess it goes to reason that you'll be hanging around until you do whatever you have to do. Save Nathaniel Summerfield's soul. Or whatever he has that passes for one," she concluded with clear disdain.

"In those assumptions, you are correct, Mrs. Magill,"

Silas said. "I won't be going anywhere until after that. And even then, I'm not entirely clear on the rules."

"But why me?" she asked. "Why don't you haunt Nathaniel yourself?"

The answer came to him immediately. "Because people without souls can't be haunted."

Her dark brows shot up at that. "Then that means his soul is already gone. We're too late. So you should be going." Hastily, she repeated, "Nothing personal."

"It's not gone yet," Silas told her, not questioning his knowledge of that. He only knew it was true, the way he knew other things were true. "Not permanently. It's somewhere between Nathaniel and the place souls go when they depart this world. Not here, but not there yet, either. It's in . . ." He wasn't sure what the word was for the condition.

"Limbo?" Mrs. Magill suggested. "Purgatory? The astral plane?"

"Not those, but something like them."

"So how do we get it back into your descendant?" she asked. "Because having met the man, I don't think he has room inside for a soul anymore. He's too full of loathsomeness."

"Yes, well, I can see how the lack of a soul might render one disagreeable."

"Oh, trust me, Captain, your great-great-however-many-greats grandson goes way beyond disagreeable. And I suspect he was that way a long time before he crossed paths with Edward Dryden."

Her tone of voice when she uttered the censure made Silas suspect there was something mingling with her disapproval that was not altogether disapproving. Mrs. Magill was turning out to be quite the intriguing houseguest.

He reminded himself that it was he, not she, who was the guest here. An uninvited one at that. The sooner he completed the task he had been sent here to perform, the sooner he could return to wherever he needed to return and leave her to move on with her life.

Strange, but even though he knew the place whence he

had come was one of complete peace, joy, and solace, a setting that wanted for nothing and offered every comfort, he found himself reluctant to go back.

He pushed the idea away. Nonsense. The world in which Audrey Magill lived was nothing like the one Silas had inhabited while alive. As many changes as the world had wrought in his own lifetime, they were nothing compared to the ones that had come since his death. He would never find solace or comfort in this world. From what little he had learned since his return—mostly by reading Mrs. Magill's newspaper—peace and joy seemed to be absent here. Certainly the time in which he had lived had had its share of woe and injustice, but this brave new world seemed neither brave nor new to Silas.

That thought, too, he relegated to the back of his brain. He had been charged with a task that must be completed. The sooner, the better. For everyone involved.

He was about to say that very thing to Mrs. Magill, but she spoke first. "Fine," she said. "I'll go see your loathsome grandson again. And I'll do whatever I have to do to get his soul back for him." She crossed her arms mutinously across her chest. "Even if I have to shove it down his throat."

· Five ·

AS AUDREY STOOD IN NATHANIEL SUMMERFIELD'S office the following day, she took perverse pleasure in the fact that she once again hadn't made an appointment to see him. Oh, she'd thought about making one the day before, after talking to Silas, but she'd decided the guy was probably booked up weeks in advance, and she wanted her house—and her life—returned to her as soon as possible. Besides, Nathaniel Summerfield seemed like the kind of guy who had to have his life all nice and orderly—something Audrey liked, too—and showing up unannounced would doubtless rankle him, a concept she liked. A lot.

Having some knowledge of her adversary this time, however, she'd decided to dress in the same uniform he did, so she had dug out the most masculine of her own power suits, a tailored black outfit pinstriped in a dark berry, to do battle with his. She'd also donned her pointiest-toed high heels to increase both her height and her sense of command. Her only concession to femininity was the Art Deco pin affixed to her lapel, black slants complemented by geometric shapes the same dark red color as her shirt.

His receptionist recognized her immediately and frowned, then reached for the telephone on her desk. Audrey half expected her to call security and have her thrown out, but, surprisingly, she announced her arrival to her employer. Except that she didn't announce Audrey by name. She simply referred to her as "that woman who didn't have an appointment yesterday, either," in a voice that, once again, let Audrey know that, to Nathaniel Summerfield, the only thing worse than not having an appointment was . . . Well, that there was nothing worse than not having an appointment.

Even more surprising than not being immediately accosted by burly security guards was the fact that Nathaniel Summerfield evidently told his secretary to send Audrey right in. So off she went, back into the lair of Silas Summerfield's loathsome grandson. Who, okay, didn't look all that loathsome. There was just no denying the resemblance Nathaniel bore to his dead ancestor. He even sounded like Silas when he thanked his secretary for showing Audrey in.

The resemblance ended, however, at his attire. As he stood up from his chair behind the big desk, she saw that he was dressed much as he had been the day before, in an overwhelming power suit that had doubtless set him back four figures. But where yesterday's had been charcoal, today's was dark brown. Coupled with the ocher shirt and a necktie splashed with a bit of swirling whimsical color that should have looked out of place on him, but somehow didn't look out of place at all, the ensemble made the brown eyes she'd found so tempting the day before look positively decadent now.

That almost forgotten heat erupted in Audrey's midsection once more, and try as she did to tamp it down again, it wouldn't quite go away. As had happened yesterday, the moment she laid eyes on the man, something inside her that had been smoldering slowly to death suddenly sparked to life again, reminding her of things—of feelings—she'd very nearly forgotten. Things—feelings—she'd been denied for far too long.

She told herself it was only because he was so handsome, a walking, talking piece of Greek god sculpture wrought by the hands of a master. But were she honest with herself— and Audrey always tried to be that—she would have to concede that it was something more than his good looks.

She'd encountered dozens of handsome men since Sean's death, more than a few of whom had made clear their desire to get to know her better. But none of them had even given her pause. There had never been any question since Sean's death that she would remain single for the rest of her life, because she knew she would never stop loving Sean or be able to open her heart to someone else. Even falling in love with Sean had come as a surprise. She had been convinced, even in adolescence, that she would never marry. Not just because she'd known she wanted to focus on a career, but because she'd always been a solitary person who simply didn't invite the interest of others. The shy, introspective only child she had been matured into a private, introspective adolescent. And after her parents' deaths, she had only retreated further into herself. Audrey had always liked her lone-wolf lifestyle, even if it had meant loneliness was a regular companion. She hadn't minded the loneliness. Not really. Not for the most part.

Until Sean Magill had big-shouldered his way into her life and swept her off her feet and shown her just how wonderful it could be with someone living it with her.

No one would ever be able to take his place. She was as certain of that as she was her own name. Especially not someone like Nathaniel Summerfield, who couldn't hold a candle to him. She didn't care how good the guy looked or how many fires he started in her belly. It was her body responding to the man who came from around the desk now, and with nothing more than the sort of physical response that even the most primitive creatures felt. Not her mind. Not her spirit. Not her emotions. The human sex drive, she'd read, was second only to the human will to survive. Having been without sex for three years, it was understandable she would react this way to a sexy man. All it meant was that she was someplace in her monthly cycle where her body needed something that the rest of her absolutely did not. In a few days, she'd doubtless find Nathaniel Summerfield as attractive as a pile of laundry that needed to be put away.

"Mrs. Magill," he said by way of a greeting, his voice lacking anything akin to warmth.

Which was ironic, because just hearing that velvety baritone again made the fire in Audrey's midsection leap higher.

She noted he remembered to refer to her as *Mrs.* this time, something he'd seemed incapable of doing the last time she was here, in spite of her insistence that he use the designation. And why had she been so insistent? she asked herself. Normally, she didn't correct anyone who wanted to call her Ms., mostly because it didn't bother her, especially when it came from someone with whom she would have only temporary contact. And she'd intended for her contact with Nathaniel to be very temporary indeed. For some reason, though, she'd wanted to make sure he understood from the get-go—and for good—that she was married. Even if she wasn't, technically, married anymore.

"Mr. Summerfield," she replied, striving for a coolness she was nowhere close to feeling. In fact, just saying his name added fuel to the flames in her stomach, notching them higher still.

"I see you once again arrive without an appointment," he said somewhat caustically.

"And yet you didn't hesitate to see me again anyway," she shot back.

Instead of tossing out another retort, he extended his hand toward the chair on the other side of his desk. After only a small hesitation—enough to let him know she was no happier about this meeting than he was—Audrey sat down, leaning back, and crossing her legs to at least offer the appearance of not feeling cowed by the man. She hoped.

Once he was seated, too—sitting in a way that made clear he was in no way cowed by her, the big jerk—she sorted through what she needed to tell him, not sure where to begin. She still didn't know how she was supposed to convince him that his soul was currently residing in some nether realm, and that if he wanted to get it back, he was going to have to accept help from both her and a long dead relative. But he took the choice out of her hands by starting the conversation himself.

"Would you care to enlighten me as to why you've darkened my door? Again? Without an appointment? Again?"

Audrey allowed herself a moment of smugness at having riled him, then answered his question with one of her own. "Care to tell me why you agreed to see me? Again? Without an appointment? Again?"

He frowned at that, then leaned forward to steeple his hands on the desk and look at her in a way that made her feel like, even if he wasn't cowed by her, she did kind of scare him. So that was cool.

"Because after you left the other day, Mrs. Magill, I experienced something kind of . . ."

Ghostly? she wanted to ask. Then she remembered Silas couldn't haunt his grandson now that Nathaniel's soul was no longer a part of him, so there was little chance she would convince him she was being haunted by anything other than prophetic dreams. Not that prophetic dreams were such an easy sell, either. But that was a better place to begin. So she only said, "Something kind of bizarre? Or otherworldly? Or surreal?"

"That last," he said, sounding grateful she had supplied the word, since he hadn't really known what to call it himself. "That means weird and dreamlike, doesn't it?"

"Pretty much. So what happened after I left the other day?"

He seemed reluctant to go into detail, but began, "I had an

appointment"—he stressed that word a little more than was actually necessary; somehow Audrey refrained from rolling her eyes—"with a client of mine. A man I'm representing on a real estate deal he's developing downtown."

Audrey nodded. "Edward Dryden."

He said nothing to confirm or deny her assumption. Probably that client confidentiality thing, though she couldn't see how his acknowledging the fact that Dryden was a client would violate any kind of confidentiality. He sidestepped an admission again when he asked, "How familiar are you with the development he's completing on Main Street over the next three years?"

"I only know what I've read in the paper about it."

What Audrey didn't add was that she'd gone online last night and pilfered the archives of the *Courier-Journal* to read everything she could about both men and the deal they were pursuing together. Main Street was an up-and-coming area with significant renewal, renovation, and revitalization going on in some areas, and entirely new buildings going up in others. What Dryden Properties had planned would contribute to the latter. They wanted to open a shiny new complex that would encompass nearly a full city block, with retail and entertainment on the first two floors and expensive condos on the four upper floors. The design was in keeping with the historic feel of the area, but it would still draw young professionals and single urbanites who wanted to live and play near where they worked downtown.

Nathaniel Summerfield, who specialized in commercial law, was acting as Dryden's attorney, since Dryden had recently parted ways with his previous counsel under circumstances that still weren't clear to Audrey—or anyone else, judging by the tone of some of the articles she'd read. But Nathaniel had also invested heavily in the project himself. Though that wasn't unusual, because he evidently had interests in a lot of downtown real estate and upcoming projects.

"So what was so surreal about the meeting?" Audrey asked now.

"It wasn't the meeting itself," he told her. "It was what happened afterward."

She waited for him to go on, but he seemed to need prodding. So she prodded, "What happened afterward?"

He opened his mouth to speak, then closed it as if he wanted to give what he was going to say more thought. Audrey sat patiently and waited. She understood surreal. Surreal was her life at the moment. It did give one pause.

Finally, Nathaniel said, "Right after I finished signing the contracts with Edward, I felt this . . . sensation."

"What kind of sensation?"

He lifted his hand to his chest, over his heart. *Or rather, what would have been his heart*, Audrey thought, *if he'd had one.*

"Right here," he said, his voice softer now.

"Like chest pains?"

"No. Like nothing I've ever felt before. I don't really even know how to describe it."

"Try."

"Like something inside me just . . . disappeared," he said, sounding genuinely mystified. "Nothing physical," he hastened to add. "But something that was a part of me nonetheless. One minute it was there, and the next it just . . . dissolved. And then I was overcome by cold. And I've been cold ever since. I thought maybe the air conditioner here in the office was on the fritz, but the cold followed me to my car. Even when I turned on the heated seat—high—I couldn't stop feeling cold. I've used an electric blanket the last two nights, but that didn't help either. I've been drinking hot coffee constantly, but I still feel so damned cold."

Wow. He actually sounded distressed. Maybe the guy wasn't quite as loathsome as Audrey had first thought. Maybe he *did* have a soul. Or, at least, *had* had one. Before he'd gone and thrown it away by being a soulless, heartless jerk.

Okay, soulless jerk, she amended. Obviously he had a heart. Otherwise he wouldn't be alive. He just hadn't ever used his heart for the stuff it was supposed to be used for, that was all.

"But even worse than the cold feeling," he said, "is the feeling that something is gone."

"Like maybe a soul?" she asked.

He frowned at that and immediately dropped his hand back to the desk. Where his eyes had begun to show what looked very much like fear, they suddenly went flinty again. Anything that had made Nathaniel seem as if he might, maybe, possibly, perhaps believe what she'd told him and was open to change fled in that moment. And any hope Audrey had that there might, maybe, possibly, perhaps be hope for him went with it.

"I don't believe in souls," he said crisply, his voice as adamant now as it had been the day before. "Or heaven or hell or any other spiritual hoo-ha. When a person dies, he dies, and that's the end of it."

"Then stop talking to me and go schedule an EKG and echocardiogram," she told him. When he said nothing in response and only continued to scowl at her mulishly, she continued, "The fact that you agreed to see me today after dismissing me as a lunatic two days ago means you must think on some level that what happened to you after I left has something to do with what I told you would happen a few hours earlier."

He leaned back in his chair again, but there was something in his demeanor that suggested he didn't feel nearly as relaxed as he was trying to look. "Is my PPO going to cover the charges for this psychiatric evaluation?" he asked. "Or is mental illness not covered by my healthcare provider?"

Amazingly, Audrey *didn't* pick up the heavy onyx-and-rosewood desk set that was easily within her reach and hurl it at him. "Look, I don't believe in eternal reward or damnation, either," she ground out, "but I certainly believe something happens to us after we die, and I absolutely believe in souls. How can you not? What do you think makes people alive, if not a soul?"

He seemed taken aback by the question. "I don't know. Some type of energy or something."

She nodded. "Right. A soul."

He made a face at that, but didn't pursue it.

"Look, whatever you want to call it," she said, "there's something in people that makes them do more than live and breathe. Something that makes them human. It's what gives them the capacity to feel joy and sorrow and anger and a host of other emotions. It's what makes people grieve when they lose someone, what makes them fall in lo—" She stopped herself before concluding *fall in love in the first place* not entirely sure why she did. The ability to love was the most ultimate gift a soul enabled a person to enjoy. It felt almost sacrilegious to speak of it in anything other than hushed, reverent tones. Or speak of it at all in the presence of someone unworthy of the gift who probably didn't believe in love, either.

"Souls are what make people human," she said simply.

He muttered something indistinct under his breath that mostly sounded like he was snarling. Jeez, only two days without his soul, and he was already turning into an animal. No, worse than an animal. Because animals had souls.

She shook her head, losing patience now. "Either you believe me about this, Mr. Summerfield, or you don't," she said.

"I don't," he immediately assured her.

Audrey felt like snarling herself. She didn't believe *him* when he said that. There must be some part of him that was open to further discussion about this, otherwise he would have had her tossed out on her keister. There had been three other people out in the reception area when she entered, and they'd all doubtless attained the nirvana of having an appointment.

But what was she supposed to do if he refused to acknowledge the possibility of something that was seemingly impossible? It would be pointless to stay here trying to convince him when he was clearly unwilling to be convinced. All it would do was make them both angrier at the other than they already were.

So, with a final sigh, she stood to leave, even going so far as to turn and take a few steps toward the door. But she couldn't go without one last attempt to sway him. Spinning around, she tried to meet his gaze . . . but found he wasn't looking at her face. Although he had stood when she had, his own gaze was still trained on a level with the chair, even as it had followed Audrey's moving person. Meaning he had been looking at her ass as she made her way out. She should have been incensed. So why was that unwelcome heat splashing through her midsection again?

Because you *need to find out if* your *healthcare provider covers mental illness,* she told herself. Honestly, this being haunted stuff wreaked havoc with a person's sanity.

"Mr. Summerfield," she said, feeling strangely disappointed when he lifted his gaze to look at her face. "I don't know the details of this relationship you have with Edward Dryden, so I don't know why this is true. But I do know that if you continue to represent him through whatever this project is, and if you profit from it, then you will lose your soul forever. As it is, right now, your soul is in a place that's inaccessible to you. You can't get it back by yourself. You need someone to help you."

He said nothing for a moment, only studied her in a way that made it feel as if someone had doused the heat in her belly with gasoline. Then he asked, "Why should I even care about that? I mean, what difference does a soul make anyway? If it's gone, the only thing I've suffered is being cold all the time. What I'll gain from this arrangement with Edward is potentially worth tens of millions of dollars."

Audrey's shoulders slumped in defeat. Even if there was something reasonable about being haunted by this man's angry, worried ancestor, there was no reasoning with a greedy SOB like Nathaniel Summerfield.

"Besides," he continued, "I've already profited from this deal, Mrs. Magill. Edward paid me a hefty retainer up front, and I've billed him for nearly a hundred of hours of work I and my associates have performed on his behalf."

"You can still rectify the situation," she told him. "According to your great-great-however-many-greats grandfather . . ."

"This would be the grandfather who's been rotting in his grave for decades?" Nathaniel asked, not even trying to hide the contempt in his voice.

Audrey bit back a sigh, feeling less angry and irritated now than she did weary and hopeless. "Yeah, that's the one. Except he's not the Summerfield who's been rotting for years. Trust me."

Nathaniel frowned at that. But all he said was, "And what pearls of wisdom fell from my grandfather's cold, dead lips?"

"He's not the Summerfield who's cold, either," she couldn't help reminding him. Before he could snap back with another retort meant to discredit a man . . . ghost . . . whatever . . . whom Audrey held in eminently higher esteem, she continued, "He told me that until the development is completed, and those buildings go up, your soul is still salvageable. As long as there's still time to undo what you've done, extricate yourself from Dryden, and make sure the project is scuttled, there's still time to have your soul returned to you."

To his credit, he hesitated before replying, almost as if he were honestly giving thought to what she said. Then, "Why would I undo what I've done?" he asked. "It's going to make me very rich."

Audrey straightened to her full height, which even in her highest pair of heels left her a good six inches shorter than he was. "Then you'd better invest in a lot of warm clothes. And you might want to brush up on your Dante. I hear the *Inferno* gets colder the deeper into the circles you go. And you, sir, are the kind of person who's going to be going very deep indeed."

Instead of being offended, Nathaniel smiled. A smile that was as lacking in warmth as he was himself. But all he said, as he extended a hand toward her the way men do when they want to shake hands and end an encounter, was, "Mrs. Magill, I'd like to say it's been a pleasure."

Yeah, he'd like to, Audrey thought, *but he wouldn't.*

And he didn't. He only added, "Please don't come back . . ." He hesitated a telling moment before concluding, ". . . without an appointment."

"Oh, believe me, Mr. Summerfield, I have no intention of ever coming here again."

Not sure why she bothered, Audrey accepted his proffered hand, intending to give it a single, vigorous shake to illustrate her annoyance and then release it. But she was so startled by the way his expression changed when she closed her fingers over his—and even more startled by how cold his hand was—that she couldn't bring herself to let go.

His skin was like ice. And probably not just his skin. That kind of coldness must go clear down to the bone. It was the sort of chill that made her start to feel cold, too. Then she realized no, that wasn't true, that her own body heat began to warm his fingers as she held onto his hand. Not a lot, but there was definitely some improvement. Nathaniel seemed to notice it, too, which was probably what had caused him to suddenly seem so . . .

What? she wondered as she studied him back. Just what was that expression supposed to mean? What, exactly, was it that entered his eyes just then?

Nathaniel was no help, because he said nothing. Only parted his lips slightly and closed his fingers more snugly over hers.

Since the conversation seemed to be over—it had probably been over before she even walked into his office a second time—she pulled her hand from his and turned to leave. Or, rather, she tried to pull her hand from his and turn to leave. But instead of releasing her, Nathaniel gripped her fingers tighter and began to tug her closer.

"Mr. Summerfield," Audrey said, tugging back, ignoring the way the heat in her belly suddenly blasted outward, filling her chest and her womb and parts of her best not thought about.

His mouth dropped open again, but still no words emerged. He did loosen his grip on her hand enough for Audrey to yank it free, however, which she immediately did. And then, because she was too agitated by now to linger, she muttered a hasty good-bye and fled.

Truly. Fled. There was no other way to describe what she did but flee. From a man she'd been so determined she would make understand the gravity of his problem.

Gravity, she echoed to herself as she punched the elevator button in the hallway outside his office. She bit back a chuckle she feared would become hysterical. The man's ancestor had returned from the grave to reclaim his grandson's soul, a soul Nathaniel didn't even think existed, let alone was missing. Yeah, that was a problem, all right.

But it wasn't Audrey's. Not anymore.

She didn't care what Silas Summerfield said. She was finished with his great-great-however-many-greats grandson. She'd take the portrait back to the antique shop, donate it to the Speed Museum, list it on eBay if she had to. Whatever it took to rid herself of the Summerfield men. Because Audrey was done. With *both* of them.

NATHANIEL LOOKED AT THE DOOR THAT HAD JUST closed behind Audrey Magill and waited for all the short circuits in his brain to stop *snap-crackle-and-popping* and reconnect. For the moment, the only recognizable concept he could grasp was heat. Because that was what he had felt when Mrs. Magill closed her hand over his. And not regular heat, either. Not the kind of warmth that spreads slowly when you come in from the cold and hold your hands in front of a fire. But an unnatural—even supernatural?—all-consuming kind of heat that had overcome his entire body within nanoseconds of contact with hers.

For the first time in two days, Nathaniel had felt not just warm, but . . . normal. Better than normal. Better than warm, for that matter. The coldness that had plagued him for the past forty-eight hours had thawed instantly after Audrey Magill touched him. And even beyond that, he'd been overcome by a feeling of well-being unlike anything he had ever experienced before. As if there were nothing in the world that would ever go wrong again. As if everything in his life was perfectly balanced. As if . . .

As if his soul had not only returned, but suddenly "fit" him in a way it never had before.

Ridiculous, he immediately censured himself. He'd thought the woman was a nut job yesterday, and she'd only cemented that conviction in their conversation today. Even if he did buy into her whole ludicrous fantasy, which he absolutely, unequivocally did *not*; even if he had lost his soul two days ago only to have it return today, however temporarily, which it absolutely, unequivocally had *not*, the new soul had felt different from the old one.

But there was no such thing as a soul, Nathaniel emphatically reiterated to himself. So there was no way he could have lost his.

Then why, he asked himself further, did he suddenly feel cold again, now that Audrey Magill was gone? And why did he feel empty again? And why had he started feeling that way the minute she removed her hand from his? Why was that feeling of well-being and balance gone?

He opened the door she had closed behind herself and, after only a moment's hesitation, stepped through it. His outer office was populated by his assistant Irene and three other people who, presumably, had appointments to see either him or one of his associates. At the moment, Nathaniel couldn't have recalled his day's agenda, even if he'd wanted to. Instead, he went straight to Irene's desk and stuck out his hand.

In her burnt-orange suit and red cat's-eye glasses, the fifty-something redhead reminded him of a plump pumpkin. A plump pumpkin who was obviously startled by his gesture and peered at him curiously over the rim of her glasses. "What?" she said.

"Shake my hand," he told her.

Her curiosity turned to suspicion. "Why?"

"Just do it," he told her, his voice edged with his impatience.

Gingerly, she lifted her hand and clasped it against his, then gave it a wary shake.

Nothing, Nathaniel thought. Not even a hint of warmth. Irene's hands weren't cold, but neither did they do anything to dispel the chill of his own.

"My God, your hands are like ice," she gasped.

Nathaniel ignored the comment, dropping her hand with much frustration. "Who's my next appointment?" he asked.

"Mr. Reinholt," Irene told him.

She gazed around Nathaniel at a man who looked to be in his early thirties, with hair as dark as his suit. Without having to be told twice, Reinholt rose, buttoning his jacket with one hand as he extended the other toward Nathaniel.

"Mr. Summerfield," he said with an ingratiating smile. "It's so nice to finally meet you."

Nathaniel said nothing as he grabbed the man's hand and gave it an unceremonious shake, holding onto his fingers longer than was necessary—or businesslike. But there was no warmth to be had from Reinholt, either. Damn him.

Turning from Reinholt, he looked at the woman seated nearby, who wore a suit not unlike the one Mrs. Magill had been wearing, except that she didn't fill it out nearly as well, and the dark color only washed out her pale hair and eyes, where it had made Mrs. Magill even more striking.

"And you are?" he asked the woman, dismissing Reinholt completely.

"Daphne McManon," Irene announced, her tone of voice indicating she was more than a little worried about Nathaniel at the moment. "She's here to see Eric."

"Ms. McManon," Nathaniel said, even though she wasn't waiting to see him, extending his hand to her before she even had a chance to stand up.

When she only looked at him with clear puzzlement and began to raise her hand slowly, he snatched it in both of his and held fast. Again, her skin was warm enough, but none of that warmth spread to Nathaniel. Even when he tightened his hold—and even after she stood and tried to tug her hand free, hard enough that there should have been some kind of static electricity or *something* generated that would heat his flesh—nothing changed within him the way it had the very second his hand had made contact with Audrey Magill's.

Hastily, he dropped the hand of . . . whatever her name was . . . and without even waiting for an introduction, he moved on to the fourth occupant of the outer office and grabbed *both* of the man's hands in his.

"Hey!" the guy objected, jumping to his feet. He, too, gave his hands a good, hard tug, yanking them free from Nathaniel's. But not quickly enough that Nathaniel knew with certainty there was no warmth to be had from him, either.

He was still cold. And he was getting colder by the moment. By now, Audrey Magill was, at the closest, walking down Main Street toward her car. At worst, she was already in that car, driving away from the narrow iron-front building that housed Summerfield Associates. It was almost as if the farther away she traveled from his office—and from Nathaniel—the deeper the cold sank into his body. He was practically shivering with it now. How bad would it be by the time he got home tonight? Especially if his house was in the opposite direction of hers?

And what the hell was he going to have to do to get warm again?

· Six ·

CECILIA HAVENS STOOD ON THE BUCKLED SIDEWALK
in front of her next door neighbor's big brick Victorian and
gazed at the third-floor windows of the turret on the left
hand side. The windows were straight across from her own
bedroom windows on the top floor of Finn and Stephen's
house, and looked into a room in Audrey Magill's that was,
at present, empty. Except for one thing.

The shadow Cecilia could have sworn she'd seen
moving around behind those windows a few minutes ago.

But she could see no shadow behind those windows now,
if indeed there had ever been one there at all. It wouldn't be
the first time her imagination had gotten the better of her.
And she'd overreacted to more than her fair share of shadows
in the past few years, many of which had looked like great
looming hulks poised to attack her one minute, and like the
coatrack or ironing board or shower curtain they actually
were the next. But that was only because, for some of those
years, the great looming hulk had been none too shadowy
and all too real.

This time, though, the shadow hadn't seemed particularly

looming or hulky or bent on attack. It had just sort of . . .
been. She had strode into her bedroom after showering, her
robe belted snugly around her waist, half bent over as she
scrubbed a towel over her hair to help dry it. When she
straightened and pushed the towel away from her face, her
gaze had automatically fallen on the window. She was about
to turn away when, through her own lace curtains and the
sheers on the house across the way, she'd seen something
move. Something significantly larger than Audrey Magill.

Before Cecilia had even realized it, she was walking
cautiously toward the window, narrowing her eyes to bring
whatever it was into better focus. But when she'd pulled her
curtain to the side to afford herself a better view, the shape
had . . . disappeared. Not moved away from the window.
Not bent down out of view. Just . . . disappeared. As if it had
never been there at all.

Not sure why she did it—probably because Audrey's
frantic visit of a few mornings ago was still fresh in her
mind—Cecilia had quickly dressed in faded blue jeans and
an even more faded black T-shirt, had tugged on her black
Converse low-riders, and had come over to make sure her
neighbor was okay. She knew nothing about the woman
who lived here, save what Finn and Stephen had told her.
That Audrey Magill, a woman in her late thirties, was a
widow, and that she made Derby hats, and that she was
trying to get a home business as a milliner off the ground,
even though Cecilia had thought the word "milliner" was
one that only showed up in historical romance novels
these days. She'd met Audrey herself only a handful of
times. They'd made the occasional small talk when they'd
encountered each other outside, but Finn and Stephen had
also had her over for a wine-and-cheese party a few weeks
ago. And then, of course, there was the other day, when
Audrey came running over because her house had been
broken into.

Correction. Because she *thought* her house had been
broken into. What she had described sounded more like a
run-of-the-mill poltergeist to Cecilia. Not that Cecilia was

an expert on the paranormal. She just watched way too much Discovery Channel, that was all. And way too much Learning Channel. And way too much Lifetime TV. And also HGTV, DIY, VH1, HSN, CNN, ESPN, and all those other channels that IDed themselves by letters. She *liked* TV. So sue her. It beat the hell out of having to deal with people on a regular basis. And what else was she supposed to do until she found a job? Or, at least, a job that didn't involve being around men, since the four jobs she'd managed to find during the six months she'd spent in Louisville had all ended badly the moment she'd had to interact with a heterosexual Y-chromosome.

Inhaling a deep breath, Cecilia smoothed one hand over the close-cropped and still-damp auburn hair she'd forgotten to comb, then made her way through the wrought iron gate at the foot of the front walk. It was never too late to drop in and welcome someone to the neighborhood, right? Even if that someone had lived next door for more than a month. And even if she'd already met her a few times and had neglected to say, "Hey, welcome to the neighborhood." And even if there might be a great, looming hulk poised ready to attack lurking in the shadows of said neighbor's home.

And even if, until now, Cecilia had gone out of her way to *not* run into Audrey. It was nothing personal. She went out of her way to *not* run into everyone.

But between the mystery shadow this morning and Audrey's panic the other day, something had crept into a place inside Cecilia that she'd been battling to keep locked up for months. Worse, whatever it was had started poking around and stirring up things she still struggled to keep battened down tight. She understood panic like Audrey had been overwhelmed by the other day. She understood fear. She understood not feeling—not being—safe. And if there was any chance her neighbor might be in danger, Cecilia felt duty-bound to help her.

But all those things she'd tried to keep locked up started *tap-tap-tapping* at the back of her brain as she studied her neighbor's third-floor turret windows, and they all urged her to run away. Fast. So she did what her therapist had instructed her to do whenever she felt the fears creeping in. She closed her eyes and reminded herself she *was* safe now. Vincent Strayer was thousands of miles away and would never be able to find her, even if he was looking. She hadn't just changed her address when she left him and moved clear across the country. She'd changed her name, her appearance, her friends, her job—well, she would change that, as soon as she found something besides pastry chef to which she was suited that didn't require her to be around men—straight men, anyway. Not that changing her friends had been very difficult, since Vincent had started systematically separating Cecilia from what few friends she'd had in San Francisco virtually from the moment she'd met him.

Besides, he probably wasn't looking for her anyway. As soon as she'd found her backbone and stood up to him, he'd lost interest in her. Though, granted, not without giving her a send-off she wasn't likely to forget.

I'm safe, I'm safe, I'm safe, she chanted to herself. *I'm strong. I'm independent. I'm self-sufficient. And as God is my witness, I will never date assholes again.*

Cecilia knew that, because she would never date *anyone* again. And after what she'd been through with Vincent, a haunted house—hell, even a burglar—was nothing.

She made her way up Audrey Magill's front walk and lifted the big brass knocker on the door, letting it fall three times before stepping back again. The house had been empty when Cecilia accepted Finn and Stephen's offer to rent the apartment upstairs six months ago, and it hadn't been in the best shape. But even after the short time she'd lived there, Audrey had already made some marked improvements to the place. She'd had the whole exterior pressure-washed, had fixed the cracks in the walk and porch stairs, had painted the wrought iron and shutters a cheery white. The front door, too, had been freshly painted, a rich violet color that always made Cecilia smile when she saw it, and which matched the semicircle of variegated stained glass overhead. Newly blossomed bleeding heart spilled from planters beneath the overhang in a tangle of red, pink, and purple, and bright, mosaic pots lined the porch and front walkway, awaiting more spring planting.

She was about to lift her hand to knock again when she heard shuffling on the other side, then the rasp of a deadbolt and the creak of a hinge. So she pasted on her best carefree smile—gee, she hoped she remembered how to do that— and, when Audrey appeared on the other side of the door, said brightly, "Hi."

Judging by her neighbor's appearance, it was obvious she'd been in the act of creation when Cecilia knocked. A stream of radiant ribbons in a dozen colors cascaded over one shoulder, and a handful of flamboyant feathers sprouted from the pocket of her white, man-style shirt. Straight pins were stuck haphazardly through the fabric of the shirt on its other side, and her blue jeans were littered with bits of thread and straw. Wisps of black hair had freed themselves from a not-especially-tidy braid that was slung over the unpinned shoulder, and her face was smudged here and there with bits of what looked like glitter.

Audrey pasted on a smile that looked almost as carefree as Cecilia hoped hers did, but it was clearly no more genuine than her own. "Hi," she replied. "Cecilia, right?"

Cecilia nodded.

"I'm sorry, I don't remember your last name."

"Havens," Cecilia told her. Not that that was the name she'd been born with any more than Cecilia was. She'd chosen both because of her love of sixties rock 'n' roll, even though she hadn't arrived in the world until more than a decade after Simon and Garfunkel and Richie Havens were first played on the radio.

"You work at the restaurant with Stephen and Finn, right?" Audrey asked. Then, before Cecilia had a chance to answer, she continued, with a smile that looked a little more genuine than the first, "The day they played Welcome Wagon, they brought me a basket full of food from the restaurant, including a caramel swirl cheesecake you made. It was incredible." She patted her flat tummy. "Not that my waistline thanks you, but my taste buds sure do."

"Cheesecakes are my specialty," Cecilia said. "But my tortes are coming along nicely. And I actually don't work *at* the restaurant with Stephen and Finn. Well, not anymore. I do prepare some desserts for them at their house for them to take to the restaurant, but I'm actually looking for another job." Without hesitation—or waiting for Audrey to reply— she added pointedly, "Listen, can I come in?"

If the intrusion surprised or bothered Audrey, she didn't show it. She just stepped aside and swept her hand toward the interior in invitation. "Sure. If you promise to forgive the mess."

The mess turned out to be considerably tidier than Cecilia's tidiest tidy. Certainly it was clear that the woman was still in the process of moving in, thanks to a couple of open boxes and a sparsity of furnishings. What furniture there was—a royal blue settee, two richly embroidered chairs to complement it, and an intricately carved secretary whose glass doors were thrown open to showcase a number of exuberant hats inside—was all as Victorian as the house and arranged with comfort in mind. Even the hats strewn seemingly carelessly about in display had the look of actually being carefully arranged. And the boxes were each labeled with its contents—HATS, they both read . . . gee, there was a shocker—in a neat and precise hand. *The boxes* clearly had been packed with great care.

When Cecilia had left San Francisco a year ago, she'd haphazardly dumped everything she owned into a couple of duffel bags and four nearly collapsed boxes she'd pulled from the Dumpster behind Vincent's apartment building. She hadn't cared at the time what went where or how much trouble they'd be to unpack later.

Of course, she'd had a very narrow window of time to escape from San Francisco and had wanted to be as far from Vincent's penthouse as she could before he discovered she was gone. That had rather hindered any sort of plan-making, never mind organization. Not that that had helped her get away from Vincent's penthouse before he discovered she was gone, anyway, since Dolan had caught her packing and locked her in the bedroom before calling Vincent and ratting her out. And then Vincent—

She shook the thought off almost literally before it could fully form. She'd done very well not thinking about Vincent Strayer for the past twelve months. So why was he suddenly crowding back into her brain today?

Oh, right. Great, looming, hulky shadows. The reason she'd come over to Audrey's in the first place.

Before her neighbor had a chance to say anything, Cecilia got right to the point. "The reason I came over is because I was up in my apartment a few minutes ago, and I just happened to look out my bedroom window, which faces the third floor of your turret, and something caught my eye, and it looked like—"

She halted abruptly, not meaning to, but couldn't quite get the words out. She wasn't sure if it was because she feared Audrey would start to think she was nuts or because she feared *she* would start to think she was nuts. She tried again. "What I mean is, I was worried there might be someone in the house who shouldn't be, and I wanted to check to be sure you're okay. So . . . are you okay?"

Audrey's eyes went wider the longer Cecilia spoke, and two bright spots of color that appeared on her cheeks grew redder. It was only then that Cecilia realized that what she'd worried might be someone in Audrey's house was, in fact, someone in Audrey's house. Like a man, maybe. Only he wasn't there to do her harm. He was there at her invitation. That possibility had never occurred to Cecilia, since she'd forgotten what it was like to actually *want* a man around.

"Oh, jeez, I am so sorry," she said. "I mean, I didn't realize you were involved with someone. I mean, I *should* have realized you were involved with someone. I was just afraid that maybe that really was a break-in the other day after all, and maybe someone had broken in again, and I just wanted to be sure you were okay, and . . . and . . . and . . ."

By now, she was beginning to babble, and Audrey's expression was changing from vaguely alarmed to fairly perturbed. Not that Cecilia blamed her. At the moment, she felt like the very definition of nosy neighbor.

"I'm really sorry," she said again.

"You think I'm hiding a man upstairs?" Audrey asked in a tone of voice that indicated she found the idea insulting.

"Well, no," Cecilia said. "I mean, I wouldn't say he was actually hiding. He just wasn't wholly visible, that was all."

"I do *not* have a man in my house," Audrey hotly denied. "I have a ghost." Her irritation immediately became embarrassment, and she muttered, "I can't believe I just said that out loud."

Cecilia hesitated, then asked, "Why not?"

Audrey eyed her with wariness. "Because it makes me sound like a lunatic."

"No, it doesn't."

Now Audrey eyed her with something akin to relief. "It doesn't?"

Cecilia shook her head. "Old Louisville is one of the most haunted neighborhoods in America. Didn't you know that?"

Audrey shook her head.

"There are whole books about it. Your house is only one of dozens around here that have ghosts."

Audrey's relief now turned into suspicion. Though it might have been amusement. Cecilia had trouble telling those two things apart. Which was what had landed her with a jerk like Vincent to begin with, and why she had stayed with him as long as she had.

"It's true."

"You believe in ghosts?" Audrey asked.

Cecilia didn't even have to think about that. "Sure. I used to live in a haunted house myself."

"Really?"

"Yeah. After my grandmother died when I was a kid, my

parents moved the three of us into her house. She stayed around for a long time after her death. Around dinnertime every Sunday, we'd smell fried chicken cooking. My grandmother always made fried chicken for Sunday dinner, but my parents never did. And sometimes, I'd wake up in the morning because I could hear her calling out—" She stopped abruptly, before saying the name with which she'd been born—Georgia—and which she could still hear her grandmother calling. "I could hear her calling out my name to wake me up," she concluded. "There were other things, too," she added. "But yeah. I believe in ghosts."

"But you've never seen one?" Audrey asked.

"Not really," Cecilia confessed. "I mean, there were times, especially when I was a teenager, when I caught a glimpse of something from the corner of my eye that I knew was Grandma Dorothy, but . . . No. I've never seen a ghost full-on."

"And you've never spoken to one?"

"Oh, sure I've spoken to one," Cecilia said. "I talked to Grandma Dorothy all the time. I still do."

Audrey brightened at that. "What kind of things does she say to you?"

Now it was Cecilia's turn to eye her neighbor with suspicion. "Well, she's never actually answered back."

Audrey deflated again. "Oh."

"Well, not in so many words," Cecilia amended. "But every now and then, I wake up to the smell of homemade doughnuts, which was what she used to make me for breakfast whenever I spent the night with her as a kid. Whenever I wake up smelling homemade doughnuts, I know it's Grandma Dorothy telling me everything's going to be okay."

What Cecilia didn't tell Audrey was that, the last time she woke up to the aroma of doughnuts was the morning after she moved into the apartment above Finn and Stephen. That was how she knew she was finally safe, that Vincent wouldn't bother her anymore. She'd spent six months on the lam by then, zigzagging across the country in an effort to elude him, because she'd feared he would try to find her and bring her back.

She'd become friends with Stephen years ago, when he'd been an instructor at the culinary school she attended in San Francisco after graduating with a business degree from Berkeley. When she heard from mutual friends that he had a restaurant in Louisville, she'd looked him up on the Internet and invited herself to visit. She'd only intended to stay for a little while, make the stop here only one of dozens to add to her convoluted trail. But when she'd awoken that first morning to the aroma of Grandma Dorothy's doughnuts, she'd known this was the place where she should stay. When Stephen and Finn offered her a job at their newly opened restaurant that very afternoon, she'd been convinced that fate—or maybe even Grandma Dorothy—had orchestrated the whole thing.

Of course, she'd had to give up the job within days of taking it since the kitchen staff was overwhelmingly male, but that was beside the point. The day after she'd told Finn and Stephen the facts about her flight from San Francisco and why she couldn't continue working for them, she'd awoken to the smell of Grandma Dorothy's doughnuts again. So she knew Louisville was where she should stay. She just wished she could find a way to stay here. Finn and Stephen had been great about her inability to pay rent some months, but Cecilia wasn't the type to take advantage of her friends. One way or another, she was going to have to find a job here she could keep.

So, yes, she believed in ghosts. In fact, before she could stop herself, she told Audrey, "Besides, I'd be way more worried if you had a man in the house than I would be if you had a ghost."

Now Audrey's expression turned puzzled. "Why is that?"

Oh, damn, Cecilia thought. No way was she going to open the door to a discussion on her feelings about the opposite sex. So she fumbled, "Just . . . um . . . ghosts don't eat as much." And then, to be sure they stayed off the subject of men, she added, "So do you know who it is haunting your house?"

"Oh, yeah," Audrey said. "It's a former owner and occupant. A Captain Silas Leyton Summerfield."

"How did he die?"

Audrey looked thoughtful for a moment. "Old age, I imagine. I think he was in his nineties when he finally went."

"So I guess he's the one who made the mess the other day, huh?"

Audrey nodded. "He was mad because the house was so different from when he lived here."

Cealia nodded sympathetically. "One of those petulant ghosts, huh?"

"*Petulant?*" a loud masculine voice boomed out of nowhere. "How dare you call me petulant, young woman? Have you no respect for your elders?"

At which point Cecilia was too busy jumping out of her skin to even know how to react. Other than to, you know, jump out of her skin. She wasn't just scared because the voice was disembodied, but also because it was extremely close. Even scarier, it was male. She spun around quickly, but saw no one. Even so, she knew what she'd heard. A man's voice. Which meant there must be a man around. Which meant it was way past time for her to be leaving.

She was about to announce that very thing—over her shoulder, as she sped toward the front door—when she heard Audrey say, "Damn. I keep forgetting he can be around even when you can't see him."

"Who?" Cecilia asked. Even though it was past time for her to be fleeing. Leaving. Whatever.

Audrey inhaled a deep breath and released it as a sigh that was clearly fatigued. She closed her eyes and pinched the bridge of her nose. "That was my ghost," she said softly. "Captain Summerfield."

Cecilia's mouth dropped open at that. Wow. Grandma Dorothy never sounded that good.

She didn't realize she'd spoken her thoughts aloud until

Audrey replied, "I wouldn't exactly call it 'good.' He can get pretty irascible."

"*Irascible?*" Silas boomed this time. "I'll have you know, Mrs. Magill, that I was considered to be a very gregarious and genial man in my time."

Audrey dropped her hand, met Cecilia's gaze levelly, and then looked at something over Cecilia's left shoulder. "Silas," she said, "this is my neighbor, Cecilia Havens. Cecilia, Silas. You two should have a lot to talk about. Because, Cecilia, you're looking at me as if I'm crazy, and, Silas, you're about to drive me around the bend."

SILAS GAZED AT THE NEWCOMER IN SILENCE FOR A moment, not certain what to make of her. When she'd first approached the front door, he had thought she was much younger. He had also thought she was a man. Her hair was cropped shorter than most men of his generation—or any other generation, for that matter—and her attire . . . Well. Her attire was anything but feminine. For that matter, so was the rest of her. With her hair so choppily shorn the way it was, she looked like an inmate, though whether one confined to a prison or an asylum, he honestly couldn't have said. There was an air of both mischief and madness about her, and not a little desperation. And although, upon closer inspection, he could see that she was considerably older than he initially thought, she was still a good score years younger than he.

Well, a good score years younger than he was in his current manifestation. Were he to take into consideration their specific dates of birth, he was a good century—and then some—older than she.

He tried to see into her, tried to read what she was thinking or feeling, the way he had been able to do with Mrs. Magill from time to time. But it was like trying to see through the murk of a river bottom. He'd come to understand that the only times he was able to breach Mrs. Magill's thoughts and feelings were when her emotions were running especially high. If he could read nothing of this Cecilia Havens, even when she was in a situation that caused her alarm—which this one certainly must—it was because she kept a very tight rein on her own thoughts and feelings.

She spun around and looked at where Audrey had indicated he was standing, but her gaze remained unfocused, and he could tell that she didn't see him. As if to confirm that, she said, "I don't see anything. Are you sure he's there?"

"Oh, he's there," Mrs. Magill assured her. "You can't see him?"

Miss Havens shook her head. "No."

"But you can hear me?" Silas asked, deliberately speaking even louder this time.

She flinched at the increase in volume, her hand flying to her chest in a gesture of self-preservation. "Dammit, could you stop yelling?" she demanded. "You're scaring the hell out of me."

Silas winced at her easy use of profanity. What had happened to women since his day that they bandied about such language with nary a thought to propriety? He'd heard Mrs. Magill, too, swear with both enthusiasm and creativity when she'd broken something or hurt herself while performing some task.

But it wasn't really the sad state of feminine vocabulary that made a ribbon of melancholy unwind inside Silas. It was the fact that Miss Havens couldn't see him when Mrs. Magill clearly could. Though why something like that should evoke melancholy was a conundrum. He wasn't here to enlist the aid of Miss Havens—or enlist anything else from Miss Havens—so why would she be able to see him? Nevertheless, she had obviously heard him speak. Why was she aware of him in one way, but not the other?

Before he had a chance to ponder that, he heard Mrs. Magill say, "Yeah, that's my ghost." Then, after a pregnant pause, she added, "I can't believe I'm able to say that with such matter-of-factness. 'Oh, don't worry, Cecilia. It's just my ghost,'" she mimicked herself in a Pollyanna voice. "'What? Don't you have one at your house, too? Doesn't everyone?'" She shook her head. "No wonder Nathaniel Summerfield thinks I'm a nut job."

Miss Havens ignored that last part of the statement—if indeed she even heard it—and continued look at the stairwell, where Silas stood in the landing. But it was clear she still didn't see him.

"He's standing right where you're looking," Mrs. Magill said.

"All I see is the stairs," Miss Havens told her.

"Silas, say something else," Mrs. Magill instructed.

He descended the two steps into the living room, his boots silent on the hardwood floor. But when he said, "Miss Havens," the woman flinched again, as if someone had just dragged a hot ember down her spine. Unable to help himself, he asked, "What possessed you to do that to your hair, woman?"

He saw Mrs. Magill lift a hand to cover her mouth, though whether she was shocked by the question or covering a smile, Silas couldn't have said. Miss Havens's reaction, however, was unmistakable. Her mouth dropped open and the color drained from her face, and her entire body began to tremble. *She's terrified*, Silas marveled. *Truly, terrified.* Even though she'd already claimed to have been haunted before.

He would have understood her fear otherwise, since the appearance in the here and now of someone who should have been dead for three quarters of a century defied both explanation and excuse. When he was alive, he'd been appalled by anyone who bought into the rubbish of psychics and the claptrap of spiritualists, because he'd thought them—no, he'd known them—to be utter nonsense. Those who thought otherwise were stupid and gullible. Ghosts? Preposterous. There was no such thing. When one died, there was only the harmony of heaven or the horror of hell in which to find oneself, and there was no escaping either one or the other.

Of course, now that Silas had arrived on the other side, he knew differently. Now, he knew . . .

Well, actually, he still couldn't remember much of the place he had left behind to come here, other than that he had been happy there. Something told him, though, that his afterlife had been nothing like he had anticipated. Nothing like he'd imagined. Nothing like what he'd been promised. It had in fact been even better than all of those things.

But he understood why someone still tethered to life and all things earthbound would be frightened of the unknown. Particularly when that unknown involved something that was inevitable to everyone—namely, death. However, this wasn't unknown to Miss Havens. She had admitted that her grandmother had crossed the veil many times to visit her, and she'd seemed to consider those visits comforting. So why was she so terrified of him?

"I apologize, Miss Havens," Silas said now, gentling his tone. "That was discourteous of me. I should have said something like, 'Hello, Miss Havens. It's lovely to make your acquaintance. What an interesting outfit you've chosen for the day. How interestingly you've chosen to arrange your hair.'"

"I bet you never said anything like that after meeting someone for the first time when you were alive, Mr. Gregarious-and-Genial," Mrs. Magill said. "Why would you do it now?"

"Excellent point, madam," Silas conceded. "So I shall start over by simply saying, 'Hello, Miss Havens.'"

He completed a few more slow steps in her direction and inspected her more closely. He'd been so preoccupied marveling at the specter of her hair and attire that he hadn't noticed what a beautiful woman she was. Genuinely beautiful. In a way that wasn't contrived or striven to achieve. Even the atrocious thing she'd done to her hair couldn't diminish it. Her eyes were enormous, the color of strong coffee, and her mouth was full and lush. Her cheekbones were well wrought and aristocratic, and she had one of those slender, elegant necks that drew a man's fingertips in idle exploration. Her skin was creamy and flawless, and he knew a poignant disappointment at not being able to touch her. Or smell her. Or simply walk with her along the river at sunset.

She suddenly turned and was looking right at him, and had he had any breath, it would have hitched in his chest, because he thought in that moment that she could see him. But her gaze remained unfocused, and she lifted a hand blindly, as if she were trying to detect his presence. Before Silas realized how close she was, her hand was passing through the middle of his chest, and something hot and frantic was shuddering down his spine and into his belly, where it exploded into every extremity.

And that was when it happened. That was when he felt himself slip inside Cecilia Havens, the way he had been able to do with Mrs. Magill. Only instead of being a simple matter of knowing what she was thinking, or gaining intimacy with what she was feeling, it was as if a great, cragged chasm cracked open in her psyche and sucked him in with enough force to crush him. And once Silas was inside Cecilia Havens . . .

Good God. There was more fear and pain in her than most men twice her size would be able to bear. That she was carrying it inside her slight, lissome frame, and holding it so tightly that it was undetectable to outsiders, was staggering. But the fear and pain wasn't a result of her alarm at coming into contact with his ghostly nature. She was afraid of him because he was a man.

Before he had time to discern the reason why that should be, Silas was being shoved back out again, and the chasm was closing, and Cecilia was dumping enough emotional rocks upon it that no one would ever be able to open it again.

She snatched her hand back toward herself, cradling it against her chest in her other as if she'd broken it. "My God, what was that?" she asked breathlessly, her eyes huge now. "What did you just do to me?"

"Cecilia?" Mrs. Magill asked with concern. "Are you okay?"

She covered the few steps between the two women and draped an arm over Cecilia's shoulders in a way that was meant to console. But the moment Mrs. Magill touched her, Cecilia lurched away, uttering a small cry that sounded as if she'd been hurt somehow. She stumbled backward, feeling her way blindly behind herself, presumably looking for the front door so that she could escape. But her aim was off, and she ended up backing herself into a corner of the room near the front window instead. When she realized what she'd done, she reached for the flowered chintz curtain hanging near her and pulled it across herself, as if trying to protect herself from something with a meager scrap of cloth. Then she shot her gaze around the room again, as if trying to identify her most imminent danger, so that she would know which way to run.

Silas had never seen anything like it. The woman was reacting to what should have been a simple, comforting touch like an animal who'd been beaten with a strap.

"Don't do that again," she gasped, still visibly shaking. But it wasn't clear if she was speaking to Mrs. Magill or to Silas.

Mrs. Magill seemed no more able to comprehend the other woman's reaction than Silas, because after a brief, anxious glance in his direction, she began to cross the room to Cecilia.

"Stop," Cecilia said when she saw her approaching, her voice little more than a whisper. "Don't come any closer."

There were tears in her eyes, Silas noted with no small distress, but she swiped them away fiercely before holding up her hand, palm out, to further illustrate her demand that her neighbor halt. Or perhaps she was telling Silas to do that. He still wasn't sure who Cecilia was talking to, even if she couldn't see him. But he wasn't sure she knew, either. And although he was no more certain of what had just transpired between himself and Cecilia than she seemed to be, his first instinct had *not* been to escape it. On the contrary, he'd found himself wanting to explore the incident further.

And just when, he wondered, had he begun to think of her as Cecilia, instead of as Miss Havens?

"Just . . . don't," she repeated. But her voice was a little hardier this time, and her panic seemed to be ebbing.

She looked down to see what she had done with the drapery, made a face that indicated she was quite disgusted with herself, and thrust the fabric away. Then she ventured forward a few steps, not looking especially sturdy, but no longer looking wounded and terrified, either.

"Are you all right?" Mrs. Magill asked the young woman again, concern still etched on her features.

"I'm fine," Cecilia replied in a voice that belied the condition. Nevertheless, she kept walking forward. She skirted Mrs. Magill noticeably, but instead of heading for the front door, as Silas would have thought she would, she came to a halt in the middle of the room.

"Captain Summerfield," she said to the room at large.

"Yes, Miss Havens?" he replied from where he still stood, a good eight feet away from her.

She turned in that direction. "What did you just do to me?"

Silas began to walk toward her, then, remembering how she reacted the last time he was nearby, made himself stop. "I did nothing," he told her. "When you reached out, your hand . . ." He hesitated. Her hand hadn't touched him, since there was nothing of him to touch. "Your hand . . . made contact with me," he finally said.

"It passed through him," Mrs. Magill clarified for her guest. "Your hand went through his chest. Right by his heart."

Cecilia's eyes widened at that, then she nodded. "That makes sense, I guess."

"Why?" Mrs. Magill asked. "What happened?" When Cecilia didn't reply right away, she continued, "The other day, my fingers just sort of brushed where he was, and I kind of felt this electric shock jolt through me. And that was just from the tiniest little contact."

Cecilia hesitated another telling moment, then said, very softly, "It was like a shock at first. But then . . ." She shook her head. "Then, suddenly, I felt like I was . . . like he was . . . like we were . . ." She shuddered visibly. "He was just way too close, that was all."

"And you don't like people getting too close," Silas couldn't help stating, since asking it as a question would be pointless after witnessing her reaction to Mrs. Magill's attempt to comfort her.

"No," Cecilia said. "I don't like people in my space."

"And why is that?" Silas asked.

"That's none of your damned business," she told him.

Silas knew her reluctance for people to be too close was related to the fear and pain inside her. He hadn't been privy to all of her thoughts and feelings in that brief collision, but it made sense to conclude that she'd experienced something very painful. Perhaps even very recently.

She suddenly lifted both hands to drive them through her spiky hair and expelled an incredulous sound. "I can't believe I'm standing here talking to a ghost."

Silas objected, "But you said your grandmother often spoke to you after she died."

"No, I said I woke up when I heard her calling my name, and that I still talk to her sometimes. I've never had a conversation like this with her. Talking to a ghost like this is just . . ."

"Bizarre," Mrs. Magill finished, with not a little derision.

"Yeah," Cecilia concurred with enthusiasm.

"Ladies, I am still present in the conversation," Silas reminded them, "regardless of whether or not you can see me."

Ignoring him, Cecilia turned to Mrs. Magill. "How long has this been going on? Was he here when you moved in?"

"He came with the portrait I bought," Mrs. Magill told her.

"What portrait?"

"It's upstairs." Mrs. Magill dipped her head toward the stairway. "Come on. You should be able to see who you're talking to."

With clear reluctance, Cecilia followed her neighbor up the stairs to the second-floor landing, where Mrs. Magill had hung Silas's portrait as a sort of compromise between the third-floor landing, where she had originally hung it, and the main floor, where he had wished it to hang. He watched as Cecilia stood before it, and was surprised when she lifted her hand to touch it, since she had been so reluctant to touch anything—anyone—before. He was further surprised that, when she began to stroke her finger over the more-than-a-century-old oil that represented his hand, he felt the caress as clearly as if she had drawn her hand across his flesh-and-blood fingers.

"He's very handsome," she said to Mrs. Magill. And then, remembering her manners, she added, "Captain Summerfield, you're . . . You *were* . . . You are?" Her face reflected confusion when she halted.

Mrs. Magill seemed to understand, because she said, "He still is. He looks just like he did when that painting was completed."

Cecilia nodded, but her expression didn't clear much. "You're very handsome, Captain Summerfield."

He wanted to tell her to please, call him Silas, but that would have been overstepping the bounds of propriety. His propriety, at any rate, since there seemed to be no propriety in current times.

So all he said was, "Thank you, Miss Havens."

He was surprised again when she replied, "You can call me Cecilia."

So what could he say but, "And you may call me Silas."

"Can I call you that, too?" Mrs. Magill asked.

"You already do," he reminded her, hoping his displeasure in that familiarity was evident. Oddly, however, he realized he wasn't as bothered by the prospect of her using his Christian name now as he'd been the first few times she'd done it.

"Then why do you keep calling me 'Mrs. Magill?' " she asked. "Or worse, 'madam'? Why don't you call me Audrey?"

"Because, *madam,*" he said, deliberately to provoke her, "you've never extended the invitation for me to address you so informally."

She rolled her eyes. "You are so Victorian."

"Yes, madam, I am."

"Yeah, okay. Point to the Victorian," she said with some exasperation. "Look, call me Audrey, all right? Since you're going to keep annoying me until I set your great-great-however-many-greats grandson straight. That's your reason for being, after all."

And it was the *only* reason, Silas reminded himself. He was here only to help Audrey help Nathaniel help himself. And once all of them had succeeded in doing what they were supposed to do . . .

Cecilia stroked her finger over the painting again, above Silas's hand this time, on his torso, and once again, he felt the warmth and tenderness of her caress as if she had touched him in person. Another twinge of heat splashed through his belly, and he marveled at feeling it. Save that brief shock he'd received from Audrey, he'd not felt anything physically—nor even metaphysically—since returning to this world until Cecilia Havens. And what he'd felt with her—what he felt now, as she touched his portrait—was considerably more vivid, more potent, more . . . more real . . . than what he had felt with Audrey Magill.

What would happen, he wondered, if their contact were prolonged?

Before he could think about that, Cecilia dropped her hand back to her side, and Silas was shaken by the depth of the emptiness that followed the separation. It had been so long since he had felt the touch of a woman. Of any human being. That was one thing he did recall about the place he had left behind to come here. There was no physical contact with others. No one seemed to think there needed to be, because the linking of spirits, of souls, was supposed to be so much better. And in a way, it was. But there was something about physical closeness that couldn't be achieved with a melding of mind or spirit. There were times when utter peace could be found in the simple touch of a loved one.

Then that thought, too, was scattered, because Cecilia was talking to Audrey, and Silas realized he'd already missed whatever question she had asked. When he heard Audrey reply, however, he realized Cecilia had asked about his great-great-et-cetera grandson, and why Silas was here annoying Audrey about him.

"Before I explain about Silas's great-great-whatever, I should put on a pot of tea. Because trust me, Cecilia, this is going to take a while."

BY THE TIME THE TEAPOT WAS DRAINED, CECILIA learned everything Audrey Magill knew about her ghost and his soulless—literally, at least for now—descendant. But, like Audrey, she had no good ideas on how to make Nathaniel Summerfield accept the truth of the situation. She wasn't even sure what to make of the situation herself. Cecilia definitely believed in an afterlife, but thanks to her experiences with Grandma Dorothy, she didn't embrace a conventional view of it. Nor had she ever really given any thought to the idea that a person's soul could actually be removed from him or her at some point while they were still walking around with a beating heart. But knowing that now, she realized it explained *a lot* about the state of the world.

"So what are you going to do?" she asked Audrey as she settled the porcelain teacup decorated with tiny pink roses back in its saucer.

Her neighbor's china was as impossibly feminine as the living room in which they sat. Which was odd, because Audrey herself didn't seem like much of a girly girl. Then again, she supposed her neighbor was going for the look of Ye Olde Hat Shoppe—or, even Ye Olde Hatte Shoppe—

and she'd achieved that in spades. If Cecilia didn't know better, she would have thought she'd just dropped into one of the historical romance novels she so loved to read.

"I don't know," Audrey replied, punctuating the statement with a soft sigh. She leaned back against the poufy sofa and rested her head on the intricately carved woodwork of its back. "The fact that I have to convince some guy of the seemingly impossible is bad enough. That it's a guy like Nathaniel Summerfield, who's pretty impossible himself, makes it even worse. And since it's coming at an impossibly bad time, that makes it even more hopeless."

"Why is this time worse than any other?"

Audrey threw out a hand at their surroundings. "Does this shop look ready to open in two days? Because I'm supposed to be opening in two days, and I'm not near ready. But I can't put it off any longer. I've already done something risky by waiting until two weeks before Derby to go live. A lot of the local boutiques and department stores have had hats on sale since February. I mean, I've been taking orders all along, but still. I have got to get this place up and running by Thunder over Louisville, because downtown will be crawling with people. Granted, most of them will be down by the river, but a lot of them will wander around town before the fireworks start, and they might just wander into Finery. But I haven't even found anyone to fill the salesclerk position I advertised for a month ago. *A month ago.* Everyone I've interviewed has been on the wrong side of suitable."

As they always did when she heard about some job prospect, Cecilia's ears perked up at that. "You need a salesclerk?" she asked. To herself, she added, *For your impossibly feminine hatte shoppe that no one with a Y-chromosome would dare enter upon pain of death? That any man with a mere drop of testosterone would run screaming like a girl from if he got within a hundred feet of it? You need a salesclerk for* that *shop?*

Audrey, too, seemed to perk up at Cecilia's question. "Yeah, I do. You sound like you might be interested."

"I am interested," Cecilia said. "I need a job."

"I thought you were making desserts for Finn and Stephen."

"That doesn't pay all that well," she said. "That's mostly to cover my rent until I find something full-time."

"I need somebody full-time," Audrey told her. "I'll be full-time in the showroom, too, for the first two weeks, of course, but after that, I'll need to spend my time making hats, not selling them. There won't be a lot of business after Derby, but I'll still need someone to woman the shop and take care of orders from the Internet. I'll only have weekend hours seasonally once Derby is over, so I'd need you Monday through Friday from eight to five, with an hour for lunch. Do you have any background in business?"

Cecilia smiled. "I have a business degree from Berkeley."

Audrey's smile fell at that. "Then you're way over-qualified. I can only afford to pay minimum wage right now. And the medical coverage is laughable. Which, I suppose, is why all my applicants have been on the wrong side of suitable."

Cecilia lifted a hand before she even finished talking. "Not a problem," she said. "I have simple needs, and my health is excellent."

"You'd take the job even with the ghost of Silas Summerfield lurking around?"

"Madam, I do *not* lurk," Silas complained. But he didn't show himself. "I live here the same way you do. If I happen to overhear your conversations, it is only because you speak overly loud. It's very unbecoming of a woman, actually."

Although the ghost's outbursts still gave Cecilia a start, she knew she could get used to them. His Y chromosome and testosterone had to have turned to dust decades ago. And the fact that he wasn't visible would make him even easier to handle.

"Even with the ghost of Silas Summerfield . . . um . . . living here," she said.

"Thank you, Cecilia," he said, his voice softening.

"You're welcome," she replied, smiling. And, strangely,

for the first time in more than a year, the smile didn't feel false at all.

"Are you serious?" Audrey asked. "You'd actually consider taking the position, even with the lousy pay, the lack of benefits, and Silas?"

"Madam . . ." Silas cautioned.

Cecilia nodded. "There's nothing to consider. I want the job."

Audrey's smile went supernova at that. And hers didn't look false, either. "Then it's yours," she said. "When can you start?"

Cecilia looked around the room, noting the boxes that still needed emptying, the displays that needed straightening, and the stacks of paperwork that needed sorting. "How about now?" she asked.

Audrey nodded. "Now it is."

· Seven ·

AT JUST PAST MIDNIGHT THURSDAY, NATHANIEL stood on the balcony of his sprawling condo at 1400 Willow, looking down at what few lights still lingered in the lesser-priced park-side apartments below. And he wondered what the poor people were doing tonight. Not that anyone who could afford to invest in Cherokee Triangle real estate was poor by any means, but they weren't as wealthy as he was. And a handful of those apartments—and maybe even a few of the smaller houses—were shared by penniless students who split the rent two or three or even four ways to make them affordable. Nathaniel knew that, because sometimes, when he stood by this window looking down into the park, he saw—and heard, even on the twenty-second floor, even when he wasn't standing out on his balcony—their battered, muffler-deprived cars rattle to a halt at the four-way stop below before churning to the left to go to some party in one of the less expensive apartments up on Everett.

He also knew that because there had been a time in his own life when he had been one of those penniless students driving one of those battered cars to one of those less expensive apartments on Everett. He'd shared a place on that street with three other guys from the University of Louisville when he was an undergraduate. So many nights, he'd looked out his bedroom window at the majestic brick monstrosity that was 1400 Willow, an icon of wealth and refinement, even amid wealth and refinement. And he'd sworn to himself that someday, some way, he would look out one of the windows in that high-rise and he would thumb his nose at his humble adode and the lifestyle it represented.

But as many times as he'd stood here looking back at that brick building on Everett, Nathaniel had never quite been able to thumb his nose at it. In fact, after enjoying a sip of the expensive single malt he'd poured into the Baccarat highball glass a half hour ago, he lifted his glass to the building instead.

Man, he needed to have his head examined, if he was saluting his old way of life. The last place he wanted to admire was that dump—both the apartment, and the lifestyle he'd had to suffer while living there. Being poor sucked, even if you could do it close to wealth, like you could in the Highlands.

But then, that wasn't the only reason he needed to have his head examined. Even though more than twenty-four hours had passed since Audrey Magill had made her second visit to his office, Nathaniel couldn't stop thinking about her. About the things she'd said. About the way she'd looked at him. About the way she'd made him feel.

Warm. That solitary, momentary physical contact he'd had with her had provided the only relief he'd enjoyed in three days from this damnable cold. He'd tried everything to allay the chill that plagued him, from generous pourings of the single malt he held in his hand—even the false warmth of alcohol would be welcome at this point—to wrapping himself in an electric blanket set on high. But nothing had made him feel even the tiniest bit warmer. He'd even spent time on the Internet, trying to find an explanation for what would cause a person to be cold all the time. He'd narrowed the possibilities for himself down to poor circulation, anemia, or a problem with his thyroid.

Never mind that he spent sixty minutes on the treadmill every damned day, something that gave him excellent circulation; or that he ate red meat—rare—the way a real man should twice a week, which meant his iron levels ought to be just fine; or that he'd had his thyroid, and everything else, for that matter, checked a month ago for the annual physical his insurer required, and had been given a thoroughly clean bill of health. Clearly, he'd come down with *something* this week that made him feel cold all the time. Because what other explanation could there be?

Audrey Magill had mentioned Dante's *Inferno* in their conversation, he recalled. How hell grew colder the farther down one ventured. He'd had to read the *Inferno* in college, so he already knew that. He knew how, by the time one reached the last circle, where Lucifer himself dwelled, hell was nothing more than a vast lake of ice in which the souls of the most heinous were frozen. So if he'd lost his soul, and now he felt cold all the time, did that mean that, when he died, he was destined for—

It meant *nothing*, he told himself. There was no pit of ice in hell, because there was no hell. When he died, whatever made him alive would go wherever it went when people ceased to be alive. There was no punishment or reward in the afterlife. Nor was there any in this life. Life was what you made of it, and this life was all you had. As he turned his attention to the unremarkable apartment house on Everett again, he reminded himself that he'd made a very remarkable life for himself. An enviable life. A life that included everything he could possibly ever want.

For some reason, that made him think of Mrs. Magill again. He told himself he felt sorry for *Mr.* Magill. Any woman that shrewish and indomitable couldn't be easy to live with. She'd been difficult enough just to converse with. Of course, he couldn't help reminding himself, she did have other things to recommend her. Enormous blue eyes.

Generous curves. A mouth that sent a man's thoughts spiraling into mayhem.

He pushed the memory of Audrey Magill's assets—and Audrey Magill's everything else—to the back of his brain. Not only because she was a married woman, but because he would never see her again. Whatever was causing him to be cold, there was bound to be some physiological explanation for it. He need only make an appointment with his doctor to verify that. And he would. For the very next day.

Soul schmole, he thought as he tipped the glass to his mouth and consumed what was left of its contents in one swallow. He had far more important things to think about right now. Which was why he would starting thinking about them right now. And he would stop thinking about Audrey Magill's—*Mrs.* Magill's, he reminded himself— enormous blue eyes and generous curves, and mouth that sent a man's thoughts spiraling into mayhem . . .

AUDREY COULD SAFELY SAY THAT THE ABSOLUTE last person she would have expected to darken her door— very nearly literally, since he practically filled it—was Nathaniel Summerfield. Though, judging by his expression when she opened her front door late Friday morning to find him there, she wasn't the only one who felt that way. In addition to looking like he had no idea what he was doing here, however, he looked like he hadn't slept for days. His espresso-colored eyes were smudged by faint purple crescents, dark stubble shadowed the lower half of his face like a Mack truck, and his black hair was rowdy and untamed, as if he'd driven restless fingers through it again and again and again. Instead of one of his faultless power suits and wing tips, he wore a pair of battered khaki trousers and a wrinkled white Oxford shirt, coupled with scruffy Top-Siders. And although the morning was on the warm side, he'd slung on a heavy brown cable-knit cardigan and was clutching it close to his body, as if he were cold.

Clearly he was not working today, which was, perhaps, the strangest realization of all. Mr. Darling of the Business Section These Days must have dozens of people lining up to see him, and Audrey would bet every last one of them had appointments.

"Mrs. Magill," he said, foregoing, as he always did, any form of greeting. The big jerk. "Normally, I wouldn't bother you at home this way, but since you operate your business out of your home—"

Ignoring, for now, the fact that he had gone to the trouble to find that out, Audrey interjected, "But my business isn't open yet. The grand opening for Finery is exactly two weeks before Derby, which means tomorrow, which means you are indeed bothering me at home." And since Cecilia was on her lunch hour, leaving Audrey here alone, that would make it look even more like he was bothering her at home. Even if she *was*, technically, at work.

But he didn't seem to notice her interruption, as he'd dropped his gaze from her face while he was talking to her. Not that Audrey wasn't used to that kind of thing from men, but Nathaniel hadn't focused his attention on the two things men usually focused on when they spoke to her. Instead, he darted his gaze between her two hands, one of which—the one she had fisted on her hip—was gripping a fairly large, and very pink, ostrich feather. Which, okay, considering the placement on her hip might make it look as if she'd just sprouted tail feathers herself, so she supposed she could see why he might be staring. Except that it was definitely her hand—and not the feather—he was staring at. And although her other hand held nothing and was hanging listless at her side, he looked at it as if it held the Holy Grail.

As an experiment, she fisted that hand, too, on her jean-clad hip. Sure enough, his gaze followed. She lifted it higher, adjusting the collar of her chambray work shirt, which in no way needed adjusting. Again, his gaze followed her hand. So she moved it over the crown of her head and back to her ponytail, and when his gaze started to follow

her hand again, she dipped her head to the side to meet his
eyes and wiggled her fingers in greeting to get his
attention.

That finally snapped him out of the strange stupor he'd
fallen into, because he made a face and met her gaze levelly
once again. But all he said was, "I'm sorry. Hello." Then, as
if he wanted to emphasize that he did indeed know who she
was, he added, "Mrs. Magill."

"Mr. Summerfield," she said, deliberately not returning
his hello, since, hey, he'd started it.

"Can I come in?" he asked.

"Gee, I don't know. I don't recall you having an
appointment."

She regretted the sarcastic remark as soon as she made it.
Because there was something in his eyes, and something in
his tone, that actually looked and sounded . . . solicitous? Oh,
surely not. A man like him wasn't capable of the condition.
But there was something there that hadn't been there before,
and it tempered the arrogance and crabbiness to the point
where she felt almost amenable to him. And since, she
reminded herself, she would be haunted by his great-great-
however-many-greats grandfather until she helped him get
his soul back, she relented. She said nothing, however, as she
stepped backward and opened the front door farther, silently
inviting him in.

He eagerly pushed past her to enter but halted almost
immediately once he was inside, his gaze ricocheting
around the room as if he were looking for something. Or
maybe he was just put off by the uber-feminine décor and
the scores of frilly hats scattered about. There were even
more now than there had been a few days ago, since
Audrey's grand opening was tomorrow, and she'd invested
in a huge weekend media blitz to promote Finery, so she
was counting on—*oh, please, please, please*—scores of
customers to show up over the next few days.

There were hats in every color imaginable, from small
boaters decorated with nothing more than bright bits of
ribbon and small silk flowers, to massive chapeaux piled

high with roses, feathers, and lace. She could never tell what would be popular in any given year, and women's choices in head apparel were as individual as the women themselves. So Audrey always made sure she had a wide variety of styles and colors available. She also had a room filled with . . . stuff . . . she could attach to hats for women who liked to design their own. Not just dozens of different types of ribbons, lace, feathers, and flowers, but novelty items, too, like birds, horses, jockey silks, mint julep cups, and any number of other bits of whimsy. There were a surprising number of women who thought that the more outrageous and fanciful a hat was, the better. And Audrey wasn't going to be the one to try and dissuade them. Hat-watching was half the fun of Derby, as far as she was concerned. But she was reasonably certain that Nathaniel Summerfield hadn't come here to pick out a hat.

That was made clear when he said, "I need to talk to you about . . ." He hesitated, as if he wasn't sure how to refer to their previous encounters. Finally, he continued, "About the discussion we had the other day."

Gee, had that been a discussion? Audrey wondered. She'd always been under the impression that a discussion was a thing where two people took turns talking and listening, and where each considered what the other had to say, even if they didn't necessarily agree with each other. She would have sworn that what she and Nathaniel had had the other day—and the two days before that, for that matter—was more like a . . . Hmm. What was the word she was looking for? That word that meant one person thought the other was a complete whack job and didn't even try to hide his opinion that she should be locked in a closet with a sock stuffed in her mouth and no one to talk to but a couple of bunny slippers. Surely there *was* a word for that, if she could just think what it was . . .

Détente. That was it. It was French for "bunny slippers" or "sock mouth" or something. She couldn't remember enough high school French—or political science—to recall exactly.

Anyway, she wouldn't have called what she and Nathaniel had the other day a discussion.

"What about it?" she asked. "I think you made yourself pretty clear. Sorry I'm not in the position to do a PowerPoint presentation for you, but here's the gist of it. You think that A: there's no such thing as ghosts or souls. B: even if there was such a thing as souls, keeping yours is less important to you than, say, choosing the right soap-on-a-rope. C: you'd rather make reeking piles of filthy lucre than do something that would make the world a better place. And D: I'm a whack job."

"Nut job," he said.

Audrey gaped at him. "Excuse me?"

He took a few more steps into her home-soon-to-be-business, looking less uneasy now, but still not exactly comfortable. "I thought you were a nut job," he told her.

She snapped her mouth shut and glared at him, even though what he said only confirmed what she'd already known. "Oh. Well. That's so different. I don't feel slighted at all."

He spun around to look at her, and she was once again taken aback by how dark his eyes were. Almost black, really. Just like Silas's. "The operative words here, Mrs. Magill," he said, "are *thought* and *were*. You might notice they're both in the past tense."

He had stopped clutching his sweater to himself once he was inside, and now shoved his hands into his pockets. But where the gesture might have looked casual coming from another man, with Nathaniel Summerfield, it just looked . . . She sighed to herself. Despite the fact that he clearly was not himself—or, at least, not the *himself* she'd seen before—he still looked supremely confident, supremely unruffled, supremely . . . well, supreme.

As much as she disliked Nathaniel Summerfield, she couldn't deny that she'd never met a man like him. He was like granite. Cold, rigid, and impenetrable, but also sleek, powerful, and beautiful. She couldn't help but admire him, simply because he commanded admiration. As much as she would have liked to disdain him, she couldn't. He was simply too daunting a figure for that.

"So you went to all the trouble to find me because you wanted to tell me you don't think I'm a nut job anymore?" she asked. "Wow, thanks for letting me know. That was really keeping me up nights. I ought to sleep a lot better now."

He ignored her sarcasm. Again. "I came because of what happened after you left the other day. Again. Then I saw an article about *you* in the business section this morning—"

Ah. Well, then. That explained that. He *hadn't* gone to any trouble to find out anything more about her. On the up side, it looked like her media blitz was working, if someone who didn't even care about hats knew about Finery.

"—and I thought," he continued, "I thought . . ."

When he let his voice trail off without finishing, she couldn't quite help finishing for him. "You thought it was your great-great-blah-blah-blah grandfather calling out to you from the grave? Or my attic? Whichever was closer?"

He frowned at her. "I thought maybe it would be a good idea to come and talk to you here." He looked around the room again. "Where you say my great-great-whatever grandfather has been haunting you."

If ever there was a cue for Silas to show up, Audrey thought, that was it. She waited a moment to see if he would, then bought herself a few more moments by moving slowly away from the front door and into the living room-cum-showroom, closer to where Nathaniel stood himself. But there was no sign of Silas.

Still holding the pink feather, she crossed her arms over her midsection and shrugged. "Well, he isn't haunting me at the moment. Which frankly amazes me, because he's asked a lot of questions about you, and I'd think he'd want to get a look at you. I told him how much the two of you resemble each other."

She would have expected Nathaniel to make some comment—or at the very least make some face—but he only nodded almost imperceptibly.

Not sure why she offered, she asked, "Would you like to see his portrait?"

He looked surprised by the offer, but nodded again, this time more vigorously. "Yes," he said. "Yes, I would."

Audrey was just as surprised by his response as he'd seemed by her question. Less than forty-eight hours ago, he couldn't have cared less about any of this. Now, suddenly, he almost seemed like he was open to at least the idea, perhaps even the possibility.

"It's at the top of the stairs," she said, absently jutting the pink feather over her shoulder in that direction.

When she realized she was still holding it, she set it on a nearby chair and turned toward the stairway. After only a small hesitation, Nathaniel followed her. He kept his distance as he did so, however. Her foot was hitting the top step when she heard his initial footfall behind and below her. When she stood in the second-floor landing, she turned to watch his ascent and was surprised to find that his head was bowed—he was watching his feet instead of looking up at the portrait or at her, even though he didn't strike her as the eyes-down type. Even when he crested the top step and came to a halt beside her, he didn't look up at the portrait he'd claimed he wanted to see. Instead, he looked past Audrey, into the room behind her that still bore the remnants of her recent move. Namely, sparse furnishings, bare walls and floor, and a jumble of boxes.

"You haven't lived here long," he concluded.

"Just over a month," she said. "I moved here specifically to open my business. I like the location."

He looked at her face again, and only then did Audrey realize how close he was standing. Mostly because she had to crane her neck back to meet his gaze.

He opened his mouth and hitched a breath, as if he were going to say something, then seemed to change his mind and closed his mouth again. But his gaze never left hers, and the longer the two of them looked at each other, the faster Audrey's heart began to beat, until her pulse was fairly pounding in her ears, and she grew hot all over. Good heavens, the man was potent.

"I," he finally said, very softly.

She narrowed her eyes curiously. "You what?"

"You said, 'I,'" he told her. "'*I* moved here,'" he echoed. "'To open *my* business.'"

"Yes."

He dropped his gaze to her left hand, then looked at her face again. "Is there no Mr. Magill then?"

As she did whenever she thought of Sean, Audrey automatically tugged on the gold chain around her neck and pulled free its sole decoration—a man-sized high school ring that had belonged to Sean. He'd been buried wearing the wedding ring identical to Audrey's, and she'd wanted something of him to keep on her person at all times. The way she kept her wedding ring on her at all times. Whenever loneliness, sorrow, or grief overcame her, she pulled out Sean's ring and cradled it in her palm, and she felt a little better, as if he were here with her. Even if he wasn't here with her. Even if he would never be here with her again.

Nathaniel watched her completion of the gesture with great interest, and when he saw the object she fingered with such care, his dark brows arrowed downward.

"There used to be a Mr. Magill," Audrey told him. Then, because she'd learned a long time ago that it was better to be blunt about it, she added, "He died. In the line of duty. He was a cop. He was only thirty-six. It was completely unexpected." The words came out in choppy, uneven sentences. Because choppy and uneven was still how Audrey felt whenever she thought about her late husband.

Nathaniel's expression changed not at all as she told him of her loss. When she was finished, he only asked, "How long ago?"

"Three years," she said.

He glanced down at her left hand again. "But you still wear your wedding ring."

She lifted one shoulder and let it drop. "That's because I'm still married."

Again, he seemed to want to say something, but decided not to. Instead, he only nodded slowly, as if he understood. But how could he? Audrey wondered. A man like him didn't seem capable of falling in love with someone. Certainly not with the depth of emotion that she and Sean had felt for each other.

She suddenly began to feel uncomfortable under his scrutiny—mostly because instead of diminishing upon her revelation that she still felt married, his scrutiny had only intensified—so she turned around to look at the portrait of his ancestor. "Captain Silas Leyton Summerfield," she announced, tucking Sean's ring back under her collar. And she told herself she only imagined the way her voice suddenly sounded all thready and rough. "Someday I'm going to have to sit down and figure out how many greats your grandfather he is," she added with a chuckle that was obviously forced.

Nathaniel moved forward a few steps, until his body was aligned with hers, and tipped his head back to look at the portrait, too. Audrey braved a glimpse in his direction, long enough to see the look of astonishment on his face.

"My God, he does look like me," he said.

"Especially around the eyes," she told him, lifting a hand to point to his ancestor's painted features. "I don't think I've ever seen eyes as brown as his or—"

She turned to look at Nathaniel, only to find that he was already looking at her, and in a way she hadn't seen a man looking at her in a very long time. The way Sean used to look at her when he was feeling especially hungry. Not sexually, but emotionally. On those occasions when he just needed to be close to her, needed to hold her, as if he needed to reassure himself that he wasn't alone in the world, that no matter what might go wrong in his life, he would always have her.

"Or . . . or yours," she finished in a much softer, much less certain, voice. Then, because she didn't like how she was beginning to feel a little hungry herself, she hurried on, "So, um . . . so what happened that made my status of nut job change from present tense to past tense?"

For a moment, he only continued to look at her in that strangely needy way. Then he slung his gaze back to the portrait.

"Do you remember how I told you I was feeling so cold?"

She nodded.

His voice grew even softer as he told her, "It's gotten worse. It's not like anything I've ever felt before. It goes beyond bone deep. It's like it's . . . it's . . ." He looked at her again. "Soul deep," he finally concluded. "Except that I'm actually beginning to think . . ."

He continued to gaze at Audrey's face but didn't finish that last statement. Not that it really needed finishing. He was starting to believe her. He was beginning to fear that he really had lost his soul. He lifted a hand, palm down, fingers rigid. "Feel this."

Audrey eyed him warily, but, reluctantly, lifted her hand to his. She didn't touch him right away, however. Certainly there was nothing untoward in his command, under the circumstances. All he'd asked her to do was take his hand. For some reason, though, she didn't want to. She just wasn't sure she wanted to think too hard about why.

So she stopped thinking and did what he'd told her to. She turned her hand palm up, her fingers pointing in the opposite direction of his own, and pressed it against his. As it had been in his office the last time she saw him, his skin was like ice. But he was right. It was even worse now.

Before she realized what he intended, Nathaniel slid his hand forward, off of hers and over the bare arm revealed by the rolled-back sleeve of her shirt. A shiver rippled through her entire body as his fingers crept over the sensitive flesh between her wrist and elbow, but it had nothing to do with the coldness of his hand, since it began to grow warm against her skin. She told herself to pull her hand away, that he *had* overstepped the bounds of propriety now, but for some reason, she couldn't make herself do it. She could only watch as the big, blunt hand peppered with dark hair moved with such gentleness over her smooth, slender arm, and she did her best to ignore the swell of heat inside her that seemed to be spilling over to him.

Because the longer he touched her, the warmer his hand grew, until it felt almost hot running over her flesh. This despite the fact that he wasn't touching her hard enough to create any kind of friction, nor was her own skin warm enough under his to generate such a response.

Well, her own skin wasn't warm enough *yet*. If he kept this up much longer, though . . .

Just as that thought unwound in her brain—and just as the implication of it began to unravel her—he slid his fingers back toward her hand and curled them gently around her wrist. Immediately, Audrey tried to pull her hand away, but he tightened his grip just enough to make that impossible without her having to violently snatch it back. What really kept her from doing that, though, was the soft, pleading way he said, "Don't. Don't let go of me. Please, Audrey."

Her mouth went dry at the husky timbre of his voice and the desolate way he spoke her name. When she snapped her attention back to his face, she saw that his eyes were desolate, too, and that the black of his pupils nearly eclipsed the brown irises surrounding them.

Somehow, she managed to ask, "Why not?" But her voice was barely a whisper, as if he'd sapped every ounce of strength she had.

His grip loosened a little, but he still clung to her with something akin to fear. "Because touching you is the only way I can feel warm."

She shook her head, the comment making no sense. "What are you talking about?"

He lifted his other hand and, after only a small hesitation, reached for her free one, moving slowly, as if he wanted to give her time to pull it behind her back. Audrey told herself that was exactly what she should do. Instead, she began to lift her free hand toward his, meeting him halfway. This time when he touched her, his skin wasn't cold, like it had been before. This time, it was warm and welcoming, and when he wove his fingers between hers, she did nothing to stop him.

He looked both surprised by and grateful for her concession. But all he said was, "That's why I came over here to talk to you. Just before you left my office yesterday, when you shook my hand, for one too-short moment, I felt warm. I'd been freezing ever since signing the contract with Edward, but the minute your hand connected with mine, that cold started to be replaced by warmth. Then, the moment you let go, the coldness came back. And I haven't been warm again since then." He looked down at her wrist and hand, both still enclosed in his own. "Until now. Please, just let me touch you for a few more minutes."

She shook her head slowly again, confusion muddling her thoughts.

"Please, Audrey," he said again. "I've been *so cold.*"

He sounded so desperate, she didn't know what to do. Nothing he'd said made any sense. How could he be suffering from relentless cold for days on end when the weather had been so mild? And why would touching her make him feel warm again?

"The boy is cold because his soul has gone missing."

Silas's voice came softly from behind Audrey, and she automatically spun around when she heard it, something that jerked her hand free of Nathaniel's. But he continued to hold onto her wrist. And she continued to let him.

Silas stood at the other end of the hallway, his legs spread defiantly, his arms crossed over his chest resolutely. His black boots were polished to a high sheen, his black trousers were crisp and pleated, his white shirt as starched and billowy as ever. Although he had spoken to Audrey, he was looking at Nathaniel. And he continued to look at him as he made his way down the hall.

"And he feels warm again when you touch him because you're currently the caretaker of his soul." When he came to a stop in front of his great-great-blah-blah-blah grandson, he added, without a trace of modesty, "He's a handsome lad. Takes after me in that regard."

Audrey ignored that comment and asked, "What do you mean, I'm currently the caretaker of his soul?"

"What?" Nathaniel asked, his voice puzzled. "What are you talking about?"

She looked at Nathaniel, then back at Silas. "He can't see you, can he?"

"Or hear me, either," Silas confirmed. "Once the soul is gone, that makes any contact with the other side impossible."

"Audrey, what are you—" Nathaniel began. But he halted when it became clear. "Are you telling me he's here now? My great-great-whatever grandfather? Is that who you're talking to?"

His voice had reverted back to its usual arrogant baritone, and he suddenly released Audrey's wrist. She felt strangely used, as if he'd only wanted one thing from her and, having gotten it, was now rejecting her.

"Still don't believe he exists?" she asked.

She thought he would assure her that no, of course he didn't believe that, that he found such a suggestion ridiculous. But what he actually said was, "I'm not sure what to believe anymore."

She saw Silas smile at that, with a smug satisfaction that was more than a little reminiscent of his grandson's smile. "Ask the boy if he remembers a girl from school named Monica Baranski."

"Why?" Audrey asked.

"Just do it," Silas told her.

She turned to Nathaniel. "Your grandfather wants to know if you remember a girl from school named Monica Baranski."

His entire body seemed to tense up at the question. "How do you know about Monica Baranski? She was in my third grade class."

"I don't," she told him. "Silas does."

Nathaniel looked at where Silas stood, but obviously

didn't see him. "How do I know you didn't do some digging into my past yourself?"

"Why would I bother?"

"Because—" he began. But once again, he didn't finish.

"Because I'm a nut job?" she finished for him. "I thought you said that was all in the past tense."

He turned to look at Audrey now. "Look, you have to concede this is all pretty hard to swallow."

"I will happily concede that," she said. "But *you* have to concede that it's at least possible."

He drew his head back a bit, then tipped it forward in consent. "All right. I'll concede that."

She looked at Silas. "What else should I tell him?"

Silas grinned. "Tell him that Monica Baranski knew it was Nathaniel who put the dead cricket in her milk, but she told the teacher it was Paul Delaney because he'd called her best friend Rhonda fat, and because Monica fancied Nathaniel. Up until the dead cricket incident, I mean. After that, her emotions were, shall we say, mixed."

Audrey smiled at that, related the story to Nathaniel, and took a twisted delight in seeing the color drain from his face.

"And tell him, too," Silas added, "that Monica Baranski now makes even more than he does as something called an anesthesiologist"—he stumbled a little over the word, but hurried on—"who has an excellent eye for investments."

Audrey told him that, too, and took even more pleasure in the way his mouth dropped open. "Guess the dead cricket wasn't such a good idea, huh?"

He snapped his mouth shut at that. "Oh, please. Monica Baranski was unbearable even in third grade."

"Look who's talking."

When Audrey realized that it was she—and not Silas—who made the comment, she slapped a hand over her mouth. Nathaniel seemed not to take offense, however, because he only muttered, "Touché," and went back to staring at Silas, whom he couldn't possibly see. When he lifted a hand toward his grandfather, Audrey started to warn him against it, but he pushed his arm through the ghost before she was able to do so. Just as had happened with Cecilia, his arm went right through Silas's chest. But where Cecilia had had a powerful reaction to the contact, Nathaniel showed none.

"Why can you see and hear him but not me?" he asked.

"Silas says it's because you don't have a soul. He can't haunt anyone who doesn't have one."

Nathaniel still didn't look convinced. "Has anyone else seen him?" he asked as he dropped his hand back to his side.

"Not seen him, no. But my next door neighbor, Cecilia, can hear him."

That surprised him, too. "What? Does she only have half a soul or something that she can hear but not see him?"

Audrey looked to Silas for clarification on that, but he only shook his head.

"I have no idea why Cecilia can't see me," he said. "Though I suspect it's because she isn't opening herself up to the possibility. Having seen inside her, I've deduced that she's somewhat . . . complicated."

Instead of relaying all that to Nathaniel, Audrey only said, "He doesn't know what's up with Cecilia."

"Can you get her over here?" Nathaniel asked.

Audrey looked at her watch. She'd asked Cecilia to run some errands for her after she finished with lunch, enough that she probably wouldn't get back for a few hours. "Not for a while," she said. Then, because she was beginning to lose patience—and because she wanted Nathaniel to leave before she started having to think about why she suddenly didn't want him to leave—she added, "So do you believe me about all this or not?"

He pulled his sweater around himself again, not seeming to realize he even did it. "I don't know yet," he said.

"When will you know?"

"After I go home and Google Monica Baranski."

Before Audrey could say another word, he was thanking her for her time, telling her he'd be in touch, saying,

"Good-bye, Audrey," and making his way downstairs. She heard the front door close behind him before she was even able to get out a good-bye of her own. Not that she'd especially wanted to tell Nathaniel good-bye, but having him just up and leave made her feel like the ill-used girlfriend again. Which was beyond weird, since she was in no way his girlfriend, and she hadn't been particularly ill-used. Blown off, sure. Ill-used? No.

Weirder still, she thought, just when—and why—had he started feeling so comfortable calling her Audrey instead of Mrs. Magill? More to the point, just when—and why—had she started thinking of him as Nathaniel?

·Eight·

SHE WAS A WIDOW.

A little more than two hours after leaving Audrey
Magill's house, Nathaniel sat in front of the computer in his
office at home, staring at the image on his monitor. It was a
photograph of Audrey Fine Magill on her wedding day. He
was supposed to be Googling Monica Baranski—and he
had, for all of fifteen minutes, which was long enough to
discover that she was indeed working as an anesthesiologist
for a hospital in Connecticut, and that she was living in a zip
code whose average annual income surpassed his own. She
also had an address in Naples, Florida, in a different zip
code whose average annual income surpassed his own. And
a house just outside of Paris, France, in a postal code whose
average income—oh, all *right*—also surpassed his own. So
having discovered that what Audrey had told him about his
third-grade crush was evidently entirely true, he'd started
Googling Audrey instead.

And he'd discovered quite a lot about her. He'd discovered
even more about her husband, Sean.

Late husband, he reminded himself. And then he tried to ignore, unsuccessfully, a pang of guilt for experiencing a twinge of . . . gratitude for the man's death? Oh, surely not. He might be a bastard who'd lost his soul, but he wasn't so far gone that he would be grateful for the most profound loss a person could suffer, even if it did mean that the loss made Audrey Fine Magill available.

No, not available, he reminded himself further. She'd said herself that she was still married. She continued to wear the ring her husband had given her ten years ago, even three years after his death. That didn't exactly make her available. Not that he should want that, anyway, regardless of how it had come about. The last kind of person he needed to get involved with was a woman like her. One who *wasn't* one-dimensional, undemanding, and decorative, the way he liked his women to be.

The wedding photo had shown up on one of those websites people used for uploading personal photos so they could be shared with friends and family. The person who'd uploaded them had done so after hosting a party for Audrey and Sean Magill's fifth anniversary. There were photos of both the party and the wedding and of the years in between. And in every one of the photos, Audrey looked happy. Genuinely, unabashedly happy, the way Nathaniel would have said it was impossible for anyone to feel. Her husband looked that way, too. There wasn't a single photograph of the couple where they weren't touching each other somehow. None where they weren't smiling or laughing. None where they looked anything other than besotted with each other. Nathaniel couldn't imagine what it must feel like to be that much in love with someone. And not just because he was currently without a soul.

Audrey Fine had been a beautiful bride, he thought as he took in the unadorned white dress that hugged her curves and the single white flower tucked behind one ear. She hadn't gone for the excessive look, and the simplicity of her attire only enhanced her beauty even more. Sean Magill was a handsome groom, blond, blue-eyed, and dressed in what Nathaniel supposed was the formal uniform of the Louisville Metro Police Department.

He skittered the mouse to the top left of the screen to scroll back to a previous one. An article in the *Courier-Journal* dated a little over three years ago described the death of a young police officer after he'd responded to a report of a domestic dispute. A man who had been threatening his wife and children with a handgun used the weapon on Sean instead, after Sean had tried to calmly talk the man out of doing what he'd been threatening to do. Audrey's husband had died at University Hospital five hours later, his partner and his wife of seven years at his side.

Nathaniel scrolled backward again, this time to the website for Audrey's Third Street hat shop, Finery, on the page that was headed, "Meet the Milliner." Audrey had been born and raised in Louisville. She was a graduate of Iroquois High School, class of '89, and Bellarmine University, class of '93. She'd worked for a prominent local accounting firm until a year ago, when she'd decided she simply couldn't ignore her passion for making hats anymore, a passion she'd indulged as a sideline until then. In Derbies past, her hats had topped the heads of some impressive local celebrities and socialites, and her clients this year included more than one Hollywood personality. Not bad for someone who had only recently started taking her business seriously.

He studied Audrey's photograph on the Finery website. She was smiling, but her smile in this picture wasn't anything like the ones he'd seen in the pictures on the photo-sharing website. Something fundamental had left her after her husband's death. Something had doused her buoyancy and dimmed her light. She was still grieving. Even though three years should provide a person enough time to start coping and at least begin to move forward. Audrey hadn't moved forward. She still loved her husband the way she had when he was alive. The " 'til death do us part" segment of the marriage vows obviously hadn't meant squat to her. Even death hadn't parted her from her husband.

Then again, he thought further, as he moved his gaze to

the word Finery, she referred to herself as Audrey Fine Magill on the website, and she'd called her business Finery, not Magill's. Maybe there was a part of her that was, subconsciously at least, ready to start identifying with the person she had been before marrying. Maybe.

But it wasn't up to him to try and figure out Audrey Fine Magill, he reminded himself. After all, they would only be in each other's lives for a short time. Just long enough for her to help him find his soul and put it back where it belonged.

Because as outrageous, ridiculous, ludicrous, and preposterous, and all those other "ouses" as it seemed, Nathaniel found himself believing what Audrey had told him. That she was being haunted by one of his ancestors. That Nathaniel had lost his soul. That it might be gone forever if he didn't figure out a way to get it back. As much as he tried to convince himself otherwise, he just couldn't do it. He'd felt that funny twinge around his heart immediately after signing the contract with Edward, which was what Audrey had told him had caused him to lose his soul in the first place. He was cold all . . . the . . . time, no matter what he did to try and warm himself. Everything she'd said the ghost had told her was true had turned out to be true. He just didn't believe anymore that Audrey Magill was an attention-seeker or nut job. He believed he had a metaphysical problem on his hand, and she was the physical solution.

Though maybe it would be better if he dwelled more on the *solution* part of that realization and less on the *physical* part of it.

His decision made—well, one decision, anyway—he reached for the phone and began to dial.

THE PHONE RANG JUST AS AUDREY WAS TRYING TO decide what to fix for her dinner. It was after six, and she hadn't eaten since noon, so her stomach was grumbling for something substantial. But she'd been so busy for the past

few weeks, she'd been living mostly on soup and sand-
wiches, and the thought of having to choose between turkey
or roast beef, wheat or rye, tomato basil or corn chowder
again was in no way appealing. Although she normally
loathed being called at the dinner hour, this time it was
almost a relief. Closing the refrigerator door, she crossed to
the telephone and looked at the number on the caller ID.
When the words *Private Caller* appeared without a number
to identify them, she did as she always did and let the
machine answer for her.

Hello, her recorded voice said, sounding cool and
professional and distant. *You've reached 502-555-5831.
Leave a message after the tone. Or, if you have business
with Finery, please hang up and dial 502-555-5832. Thank
you.*

"What a surprise, even your answering machine makes
you sound efficient."

Audrey's back went up at Nathaniel Summerfield's voice,
though she was surprised to discover that that wasn't
because it was his voice so much as it was that he'd called
her efficient, which wasn't exactly the adjective a woman
wanted to have ascribed to herself when the voice ascribing
it was dark and velvety and delicious. But then, she *was*
efficient, she reminded herself. She'd always considered it a
great compliment to be called efficient. And Nathaniel
wasn't delicious, she further reminded herself. Only his
voice was.

She snatched up the phone and snapped out a hello
without thinking, only to be met with silence at the other end.
But it was followed a moment later by a wary, "Audrey?" and
there was just something in the way he said her name that
made all the tension melt inside her. Because it was the same
something that had been in his voice earlier in the afternoon
when he'd told her not to let go of him, the same something
that had made her feel all warm and wistful inside.

"Nathaniel. Hi," she said, lightening her tone. Before
she realized what she was doing, she lifted a hand to her

hair to tuck an errant strand behind one ear. Then she cursed herself for doing it, because number one, he couldn't see how unkempt she was at the moment, and two, she didn't care if he *did* see her at her most unkempt, and number three, he already *had* seen her looking unkempt, and just because she'd felt frumpy and unattractive at the time didn't mean anything, and . . . and . . . and . . .

Where was she? Oh, right. Looking unkempt. No, not caring if Nathaniel saw her looking unkempt. Which she didn't. Right? Right.

"I'm sorry," she continued, pushing all other thoughts out of her brain before they made her dizzy. "I didn't mean to snap." And then, because she couldn't figure out why she had snapped in the first place, she brushed it off by concluding, "Long day."

He muttered a sympathetic sound. "Same here. It's not every day you find out your great-great-God-knows-how-many-greats grandfather, who just so happens to be dead, is telling a strange woman you've lost your soul."

Oh, fine, Audrey thought. Now he was calling her strange? Oh, wait. Maybe he meant the other kind of strange. Like *stranger* strange. Probably, she told herself, it was better not to ask for clarification. "Does that mean you believe me now?" she asked instead.

He didn't answer right away, as if he were afraid to speak aloud what he feared to be true. Then, when he finally did reply, it wasn't to answer the question she asked him, but to pose one of his own. "Have you had dinner yet?"

It was the kind of question that usually prefaced an invitation to go out on a date, and normally, it would have set off all sorts of alarms in Audrey's head. For some reason, though, the way Nathaniel asked it didn't put her on alert. In fact, the way he asked it, it didn't sound like he wanted to ask her out on a date. It just sounded like he wanted to know if she'd had dinner yet.

So, "No," she told him. "I was just trying to figure out what to fix."

"Let me," he began, then hesitated, and for a moment,

she actually thought he was offering to come over to her house and fix something for her. Thankfully, though, he continued. "Let me buy you dinner."

And suddenly, Audrey didn't feel thankful at all, because he had, in fact, just asked her out on a date, and she hadn't even seen it coming. Well, okay, she had sort of seen it coming, since he had prefaced the invitation with the sort of question men always used to preface an invitation like that, but even now, she wasn't feeling all nervous and uncomfortable, the way she usually did when a guy asked her out and she had to turn him down.

And then she realized the reason she didn't feel all nervous and uncomfortable was because she kind of . . . sort of . . . wanted to . . .

Say yes.

Oh, no, she immediately told herself. *No, no, no, no, no. You do* not *want to go out on a date with Nathaniel Summerfield.* What on earth was she thinking, for that to ever enter her mind? Yeah, okay, he was a handsome guy. And yeah, okay, she'd seen a side of him today that wasn't as brittle and unpleasant as what she'd seen of him before. The guy was soulless, she reminded herself. Even before he'd lost his soul, he'd been soulless. He was far more preoccupied by thoughts of business than of pleasure, of work than of play, of making money than of living life. He would be one of those guys who, on his death bed, *did* regret not working harder when he'd had the chance. He wasn't—

She swallowed hard. He wasn't Sean. But then, she thought further, no man ever would be. And that, if nothing else, was reason enough to decline.

"Um . . ." she started to say. But for some reason, she just couldn't get the rest of the words out that she needed to say.

He seemed to realize where she was headed, though, because he pushed on, "I'd really like to talk more about this . . . this . . . about what we talked about earlier."

Well, they did *need to talk about that,* Audrey thought.

And since neither of them had had dinner yet, it made sense to, oh . . . meet someplace for a bite. Nothing fancy. Nothing heavy. Nothing, you know . . . datey.

"Then you do believe me," she hedged.

But he hedged, too. "Please, Audrey," he said in much the way he had that afternoon, when she'd gone from feeling warm and whimsical to hot and bothered. And damned if it didn't do the same thing to her now, sparking that nearly forgotten heat that was becoming less and less forgotten . . . and more and more tempting.

All the more reason not to have dinner with him, she told herself. Besides, the darker hours had a bad habit of buffing all the edges and angles off of people. Darkness made people infinitely more mellow. Maybe she could meet Nathaniel during the day sometime, around noon perhaps, when the sunlight was at its most unforgiving and showed off every tiny blemish—though she doubted even unforgiving sunlight could make Nathaniel Summerfield look bad. And they could rendezvous—no, not rendezvous, because that was French and therefore sounded romantic. So they could . . . connect . . . yeah, that sounded nice and banal . . . someplace that was in no way evocative of a date. Like maybe the library. Or no, better, the Laundromat. Oh, wait, better still, the landfill. Yeah, that's the ticket.

She was about to say, "Hey, Nathaniel, I have a better idea. I'll meet you at the landfill at noon. Don't forget to bring a filter mask." But then she remembered that her days were going to be pretty full for a while, what with the opening of her shop tomorrow. If she was going to get together with Nathaniel, she would have to do something like—

"Meet me for dinner," he said, punctuating the sentence with a definite period instead of a question mark, something that ceased to make it an invitation and turned it into a command. Then, as if he hadn't already positioned himself nicely for Neanderthal of the Year award, he grunted an additional edict, "At Buck's."

As if, Audrey thought. For one thing, she wasn't going to

be told to show up someplace, nor would she be told where she wasn't going to show up. Those last two statements should have *really* put her back up. Instead, she found herself rising to the challenge.

There was no way she'd meet him at Buck's. It was far too affable and urbane, and way too cozily lit. It was a definite date destination. So she countered, "How about Third Avenue Café instead?"

Which was also *kind of* a date spot, but it was far too fun and too full of whimsy to give a man like Nathaniel—who would doubtless never eat in a place where the plastic tablecloths were deliberately gaudy—ideas of anything other than having dinner.

She could tell he wasn't happy about her having changed his plans, but he conceded, "Okay. But I'm buying."

Oh, no he wasn't. But they'd tackle that later. She would definitely pay own her way. Because this wasn't going to be a date. It was just going to be dinner. Dinner that wasn't soup and a sandwich. Dinner that they both needed to eat.

And also conversation, she added belatedly, wondering how she could have forgotten the reason they were doing this in the first place. Because it sounded as if Nathaniel did finally believe at least part of what she'd told him. Now all she had to do was convince him that the rest was true, too. Then they could figure out how they would win back his soul for him. And then, finally, she could go back to living her life. Alone. Just the way she liked it.

THIRD AVENUE CAFÉ WAS WITHIN WALKING DISTANCE of Audrey's house, but it was packed by the time she arrived. Belatedly, she remembered that it was Friday night, and Fridays generally meant brisk business for restaurants, especially popular ones like this. It had been so long since she'd done anything on a Friday night that she'd forgotten what a social event it was. That was reflected in her attire, as well, because she'd deliberately thrown on the first thing she pulled out of her closet, since she hadn't wanted to make a big deal out of this, because it absolutely, unequivocally, was just dinner and not a date. And, um, also conversation and not a date. As was reflected by the fact that she'd opted for a pair of blue jeans and a T-shirt.

Just because they were a pair of jeans she'd never worn before because they were embellished with a little beadwork around the waist, and just because she'd never worn the shirt, either, because it was decorated with a cool, glittery graphic of Paris and she'd been saving it for a special occasion didn't mean anything, either. It didn't. Jeans and a T-shirt was what she always wore for dinner at home.

Well, she *did*.

As she drew closer to the café she saw Nathaniel waiting for her just beyond the crowd of diners sitting at the dozen or so sidewalk tables, looking at his watch. He looked like he wasn't considering this a date the same way Audrey wasn't, because he'd cleaned up some, too. His previously rumpled khakis and shirt had been replaced by in no way rumpled charcoal Dockers and a different oxford shirt—still white, but this time pinstriped in the same color as his pants, its shirttail tucked in. In place of the sweater, he'd tossed on a tweedy jacket, even though, as far as Audrey was concerned, the night was a little on the warm side. Obviously, he continued to suffer from the cold, however temporary had been his relief when he'd held her hand that afternoon.

Something warm and wistful bloomed in her belly at the memory, something she hadn't felt since—

Her steps faltered at the realization. It was the same sort of sensation she used to feel in the pit of her stomach whenever Sean had touched her in a way that made her want to touch him back. Not a sexual feeling. An intimate one. A feeling of wanting to just be close to him physically. To run the pad of her thumb down the slope of his shoulder. To trace her fingertips over the camber of his biceps. To brush her lips along the curve of his jaw. Touches that told him yes, he turned her on, but, more even more important, she loved him.

She must not be remembering correctly, she thought. It had been so long since she'd felt anything like that, after all. Because she certainly didn't love Nathaniel Summerfield. She barely knew the guy. Nor did she want to touch him in any way that might be construed as intimate. He didn't even turn her on. Well, not in any way that led to intimacy. Just in a way that might lead to smokin' hot, steam-up-the sheets, deeper-baby-faster-baby-harder-baby-longer-baby sex, which wasn't nearly as important or significant as intimacy.

It *wasn't*.

At least, it might lead to that with someone other than Nathaniel Summerfield. Sex with whom wasn't even in the forecast. It *wasn't*. She was just feeling nervous right now, that was all. Anyone would feel nervous at the prospect of spending time with a man like him, one on one. A man who evoked feelings of smokin'-hot, steam-up-the sheets, deeper-baby-faster-baby-harder-baby-longer-baby sex—in other women, she meant—which wasn't nearly as important or significant as intimacy.

Ahem.

Just as she forced her feet to move forward again, Nathaniel glanced up from his watch and saw her. And, just like that, she stumbled over her own feet again. And heat exploded in her belly again, but this time it was unlike anything she'd felt before, not even with Sean— especially not with Sean—a confusing maelstrom of heat and combustion that was by turns fiercely frantic and sweetly seductive. He was just such a compelling mix of certainly and solicitude, of arrogance and apprehension. And suddenly, Audrey began to think that going to dinner tonight was a really bad idea, because she couldn't stop thinking about Sean, and about how much she wasn't thinking about Sean the way she should be thinking about him, because she was thinking about Nathaniel that way instead.

When he saw her approaching, he shifted his weight to one foot and hooked his hands on his hips, something that pushed his jacket open and pulled the shirt taut across his chest. His gaze captured hers, but not before she noted the dark hair coiling at his open collar, so different from the smooth flesh of Sean's chest. He was different from Sean in just about every way. Her husband had been blond, blue-eyed and fair, prone to broad smiles and laughter, his disposition easygoing and good-humored. He'd been nearly as tall as Nathaniel, and as solidly built, but he'd been as lean and slim as a diver, so hadn't seemed so . . . Well . . .

Potent was the word that came to her when she looked at Nathaniel. Potent and strapping and tough. The kind of man you didn't dare mess with. Which was odd, considering the fact that he was an attorney and her husband had been a cop, and Sean should have been the one who seemed more intimidating. But Sean couldn't have intimidated anyone if he tried. Which, she couldn't help thinking, was the very thing that had probably had gotten him killed. He'd tried to defuse a domestic dispute with his usual affable warmth, thinking he could sweet-talk an enraged—and armed—man into turning over his weapon. Instead, the man had fired the weapon. Three times. Into Sean.

Audrey pushed the thought away. She would *not* think about that tonight. She wouldn't think about it again. When she remembered Sean, she focused on his sunny smiles and loving embraces, not the way he had looked in the hospital. The good, not the bad. Because there was far more good to recall.

"Looks pretty busy," she said as she came to a stop in front of Nathaniel, trying not to notice how the heat in her belly had multiplied the closer she had drawn to him . . . and how thoughts of Sean had receded. "Guess we should have made a reservation."

"I *did* make a reservation," he told her, leveling a pointed look at her. "At Buck's."

Which meant he'd done it before he even called her to ask her—no, command her—to go out with him. Sean would never have done something like that. He'd been cocky, sure, but he'd never presumed that Audrey would do what he wanted to do. Or, if he had, he'd at least pretended her desires were as important as his own. No, he'd never pretended, she immediately corrected herself. Sean had always taken her feelings and likes and dislikes into consideration, and he'd never made even the most unimportant decisions without her input.

She had to stop comparing Nathaniel and Sean, she told herself. And really, why was she even doing it? Her relationship with Sean was nothing like the one she would have with Nathaniel. She wouldn't even be *having* a relationship with Nathaniel. She was here to help the guy get his soul back, however they ended up doing it. His place in her life and Sean's bore absolutely nothing in common.

"Oops. My bad," she said in response now to Nathaniel's remark. "Well, maybe the wait won't be too awful."

"It's more than an hour," he told her. "I asked."

Ah, yes, the beginning of the Derby Festival. Tomorrow was Thunder over Louisville, the official start of the Festival, but people started getting into a festive mood long before this weekend. The newspaper had been asking people to send in their Derby plans since January and had been showcasing Derby fashions for weeks. The mood and pace of the city truly did start picking up about now. Even people who didn't make it a habit of going out suddenly went out more than usual. As difficult as it was to get into restaurants and nightspots any other time of the year, this time of year, the difficulty—and wait times—multiplied as quickly as the tourists.

"There must be some Derby thing going on," she said. "But there are a million restaurants around. One of them is sure to have room for us."

"Buck's does. The reservation is for seven forty-five." He looked at his watch again. "That's ten minutes away."

"You didn't cancel it?" she asked.

The look he leveled on her then told her she should have known better than to even ask that question. "I was afraid something like this might happen."

Meaning he clearly *wasn't* a stranger to Friday night socializing, Audrey thought. For all she knew, he had standing reservations in restaurants all over town. He probably went out with a different woman every weekend. And they probably wore something nicer than blue jeans and T-shirts. Even if her own jeans and T-shirt happened to be pretty damned stylin'.

"We still have time to make it," he said.

She shook her head. "No, we won't. It'll take longer than that to walk there.

He covered the three steps necessary to put him beside a black Porsche Carerra, the passenger door of which he immediately opened. "Oh, look. I'm parked right here."

Unbelievable, Audrey thought. Anyone else would have been forced to park blocks away with this crowd. Even without a soul, he was the luckiest SOB on the planet.

"We're not dressed up enough," she pointed out.

"We're fine," he told her.

He was going to get his way, she thought. But then, why did that surprise her? Any man who got a parking spot like this for a restaurant with such a long wait was *of course* going to get his way. Surrendering to the inevitable, she crossed to where he stood and, after giving him just a little bit of a dirty look, folded herself into the sleek little car.

"Buckle up," he said just before closing the door behind her.

She did as he told her to, but only because it was the law.

She watched as he strode around the front of the car to the driver's side, his gaze never leaving hers as he stared at her through the windshield. He had some way of walking, she'd grant him that, full of swagger and confidence and masculine pride. The heat that was still reeling in her belly radiated outward, stealing into her breasts and pooling between her legs. Her heart hammered harder in her chest, making her hotter still. It did nothing to ease her distress when he opened the driver's side door and crowded himself into the little car beside her. And when the engine rumbled to life, vibrating the very air around her, she feared she might orgasm right there on the spot.

"So," she said suddenly, hoping to steer her thoughts into a new direction. She ran her hand over the warm black leather of the seat, but that only steered her thoughts right back to where they'd been before, because the smooth texture made her think about what it would feel like to run her fingers over Nathaniel instead. Curling her fingers into a fist, she stared straight ahead and said, "Nice car."

She could feel his gaze on her, and it felt curious indeed. Evidently, he wasn't experiencing the vibrating air/orgasm thing. "Thanks," he said, his voice, too, indicating that he wasn't quite sure what to make of her sudden demeanor.

Demeanor, hah, she thought. What she had going at the moment was more desire than demeanor.

"Are you interested in cars?" he asked, clearly in an effort to make conversation.

She nodded. "Yeah, I am, actually. I have an uncle in Florida who races them. When I was a kid, he lived in Louisville, and every time we went over to visit, he and my dad and I would go into the garage and look at whatever he was racing. Cars were the one thing my dad and I had in common."

"Is he still around?"

She shook her head. "My parents died within months of each other when I was in college."

He spared a glance from the road to her face, looking genuinely concerned. "I'm sorry," he said softly.

"Thanks," she said, just as quietly. Not sure why she was sharing the information with him, she added, "I was one of those late life surprises to my folks. They tried to have a baby for decades, but my mother just never got pregnant. Then, when she was forty-nine and my father was almost sixty, they found themselves parents for the first time."

"No brothers or sisters then?"

"No. You?"

"I'm an only child, too."

She'd suspected as much, since Silas had pretty much

indicated Nathaniel was on his own. "Cousins?" she asked. "Aunts? Uncles?"

"All of the above," he said. "But I'm not close to any of them. My mother and I kept to ourselves when I was a kid."

"Is your mom still around?"

"No, she's been gone fifteen years."

"Wow, you were young when you lost her."

He turned to look at her again. "So were you."

So they had that, if nothing else, in common, she thought.

He hesitated a moment, then asked, "What about your husband's family? Do you stay in touch with them?"

She wasn't sure why he would ask such a question. Nor was she sure why she was so reluctant to answer it. "Not really," she said anyway. "Sean wasn't that close to his family. He moved here from Ohio to go to college, and I only met his parents and sister a handful of times. Since his death . . ." She shrugged, but didn't continue. Then, because she couldn't quite stop herself from doing so, she added, "Why do you ask?"

This time, Nathaniel was the one to shrug. "I don't know. Just . . . You said you still feel married, and—"

"No, I said I *am* still married," she interrupted him, wondering why she suddenly felt so defensive. Wondering, too, why she felt the need to make that distinction to him so adamantly.

Instead of commenting on that, he only continued, his voice a little gentler than before, "—and it made me think you must still be involved with his family."

"No," she said. "I'm on my own."

He kept his eyes on the road and said nothing, then, after a moment, told her, "Yeah, me, too."

They entered Buck's with thirty seconds to spare and were immediately led to a cozy table for two by one of the front windows. Just as Audrey feared, the place was as cozy and intimate as she remembered, from its chocolate-colored walls to its white linen tablecloths and the cool jazz trio that was playing near the bar. The pale golden illumination of the restaurant brought out amber highlights in Nathaniel's hair that she hadn't noticed before, and softened the planes and angles of his face. He suddenly seemed more mellow, more relaxed, more accessible. And she couldn't help thinking that wasn't necessarily a good thing.

"I love this place," he said after the hostess left them to peruse their menus. "Not just for the food and service, but the wine list is phenomenal."

"Then you'll have to order for me," she said. "I don't know much about wine. I've been buying the same labels for years." She didn't add that they were labels Sean had introduced her to. Sean had already been far too present in her thoughts tonight. And she wasn't sure she wanted to think about why.

Their server came and described the evening's specials, took their wine orders, then departed. A few more moments of silence passed as they each decided on their choice for dinner, and just as those were made, their server returned. On the up side, Nathaniel didn't try to order dinner for her. On the down side, once those orders were given, the two of them were left staring at each other with neither seeming to know what to say next.

So Audrey asked him the question she had asked on the phone earlier, the one he hadn't really answered. "So do you believe me about the soul and the haunting and everything or not?"

She reached for one of the wineglasses the server had placed nearly side by side at the same time Nathaniel reached for the other, and as each made contact with their target, they inadvertently brushed their fingers against each other. Audrey jumped at the iciness of his skin, and he jerked his hand away, mumbling an apology. Only after she had curled her fingers around the stem of her glass and lifted it to her mouth for a taste did he reach for his again.

She remembered how he told her he had been cold since that first day she met him. She hated being cold herself. She hated those winter days when the wind whipped so harshly, rattling windows and rooftops, 'til the cold crept under her skin, right down to the bone. She hated layering sweaters over T-shirts over undershirts, thick slippers over socks, blue jeans over tights, and *still* feeling cold. Whenever she suffered from that kind of cold, she filled a bathtub with water as hot as she could stand it, grabbed a book and a cup of hot tea, and sank down until the water was at her chin. Then, and only then, would the chill begin to leave her body.

But Nathaniel's chill wouldn't leave. Not unless Audrey touched him. For days, he'd walked around feeling that kind of cold she hated most, his only relief those scant few moments when she'd held his hand in hers.

She watched as he filled his mouth with a generous taste from his glass and was mesmerized as his strong throat worked over it. When he set his glass back down on the table, she noted how strong his hand looked, how dark was the hair peppering its back, how blunt were his fingers. She looked at her own hand, so much smaller than his, at the slender fingers and smooth flesh . . . and at the plain gold band on the third finger, winking under the lamplight. Without thinking about what she was doing—because if she thought about it, that would make it more important than it was—she pushed her hand across the few inches separating it from Nathaniel's, and gently cupped her palm over the back of his fingers.

He'd been looking at his glass, his dark brows arrowed downward, his expression pensive, but the moment she touched him, he snapped his gaze up to meet hers.

And then, ever so slowly, he turned his hand so that his palm was resting against hers, and his fingers curled loosely into her own. His flesh grew warm beneath her touch, a warmth that purled through her, as well. When she braved a look at his face, he was smiling, a soft, gentle smile that very nearly took her breath away.

"Thank you," he said in a voice that was every bit as soft and gentle, every bit as breathtaking, as his smile.

"You're welcome," she replied, hoping she only imagined how breathless she sounded, too.

For a moment, they only sat silently holding hands, then a bus *whooshed* past beyond the window, rattling the panes and making them both jump. Audrey was the first to chuckle at their reaction, but Nathaniel followed quickly. And when he did, it was as if something that had been wound tight inside of both of them suddenly unknotted, freeing them both up to breathe a little more easily.

"Yes," he finally said. "I believe you. About everything. How can I not? You couldn't possibly have known about the Monica Baranski cricket incident, and this damnable cold that is only relieved by . . ." He glanced pointedly down at their hands. "By this . . . can't be the result of anything that's within my ability to explain it. It's not natural," he concluded with a shrug. "So it must be supernatural."

"So what are we going to do about it?" she asked.

She told herself she only imagined the way it felt like his fingers curled a little more intimately into hers. Imaginary, too, she assured herself, was the way his eyes darkened when he did it. And most imaginary of all was the little ribbon of pleasure that rippled through her. Okay, so maybe that wasn't so imaginary. It had nothing to do with Nathaniel Summerfield. It was just that it had been a long time since she'd held hands with a man. She'd forgotten how nice even that simple human contact could be.

"Well, that's the big question, isn't it?" he asked. "Even if I could get out of my contract with Edward, which is ironclad, I can't scuttle the development. There are scores of other people involved. He's contracted with a dozen different businesses who want to buy retail and entertainment space, and there are a number of other people who have already signed on for some of the condos. He's got architects and construction crews and equipment ready to go as soon as possible. The only way out of this thing is if Edward reneges on everyone. And he's not going to do that simply by my asking him to. Especially if I tell him the reason he needs to scuttle the project is because my soul is in danger."

"Then we have to make Edward renege on everyone," Audrey said.

Nathaniel expelled a single, humorless laugh at that. "Yeah, right. And what has my great-great-whatever grandfather proposed we do to achieve that?"

She tried not to squirm in her chair. "Actually, he's still working on it. He was sort of cast down here without much of a game plan."

Nathaniel sobered at that. "What do you mean, 'without a game plan'? I thought he'd have all the answers. I mean, what's the point of an afterlife if you don't get all the answers?"

"Well, his memory is a little hazy right now. He can't quite remember where he was before coming here, or what it was like, or how things worked there." When Nathaniel opened his mouth to object, she hurried on, "He does think that the key to your condition is Edward Dryden."

"What about Edward?"

"Silas says he's a criminal."

Nathaniel shook his head. "That would certainly make it a hell of a lot easier to halt the development if he was, but that's just nuts. Edward is as clean as they come."

"How do you know?" Audrey asked.

"Because I ran a thorough check on him before I took him on as a client. I don't want to get involved with a criminal element."

"But you're an attorney," she reminded him.

"I'm a commercial lawyer," he said. "Not a criminal lawyer. Not everyone with a law degree spends their time in a court room trying to prove someone's guilt or innocence. I mean, that would be like me assuming, just because you're a CPA and worked as an accountant before opening Finery, you figured people's taxes."

Audrey bit back a smile. "I did figure people's taxes, Nathaniel. I was a tax accountant."

He blinked at that. "Oh."

"And how did you know I was a CPA and worked as an accountant before opening Finery?" she asked.

She was certain the only reason he looked like he blushed in response to the question was because something must have happened to the lighting. "I read it on your website," he said. "On the Meet the Milliner page."

She nodded, but something in his voice told her he wasn't being entirely forthcoming.

That was made clear when he added, "Okay, I confess. Monica Baranski wasn't the only person I Googled today."

That surprised her. What surprised her even more was how he made Googling someone sound vaguely sexual. "You Goo . . . Ah, I mean . . . You did an Internet search on me?"

He nodded. "Just to make sure you were . . ." His voice trailed off without finishing.

"To make sure I don't have a history of mental illness?"

He colored again, and this time she couldn't quite convince herself it was a trick of the light. He was blushing, she marveled. And there was something in the realization that made her feel better about him. If a guy could blush, especially a guy who was clearly not prone to it, then his soul couldn't have gotten *too* far, could it?

"So . . . what else did you find out about me?"

He lifted his wine for another swallow, took his time completing the action, and avoided her gaze by dropping his to their hands again. Audrey's gaze followed, but the moment she saw the gold band on her left finger, she snapped her attention back to his face.

"I know you grew up here," he said softly. "I know where you went to school and when you graduated. I know you post with some regularity to message boards about hiking in Appalachia, Jane Austen books and Billie Holiday recordings." His gaze settled resolutely on hers as he added, "And I read the articles in the *Courier* about your husband."

Sean again, Audrey thought. Only this time it was Nathaniel bringing him into the evening. Was it some kind of message from the great beyond? she wondered. Was this Sean's way of reminding her that she was a married

woman? Or had it been—at least until now—Audrey's way
of keeping Nathaniel at a distance?

"I'm sorry, Audrey," he said. "I know you told me what
happened, but I didn't realize just how—"

"If you have all that information about me," she
deliberately interrupted him, "it's only fair that I have the
same information about you."

He hesitated for a moment, but whether it was because
of the sudden change of subject, or because he didn't want
Audrey to know as much about him as he did about her, she
couldn't have said. Finally, though, he told her, "I grew up
in J-town. I graduated from Manual, class of eighty-five,
then went to U of L for undergrad and law school. As for
message boards, the time I spend online is used for work,
not socializing."

That was doubtless because he did his socializing in
person, Audrey couldn't help thinking. He probably did
lots of that. Especially on Friday nights, with dinners that
were dates. And those dinners were probably with women
who considered them way more than dinner. He probably
considered them way more than dinner, too. After dinner,
they probably both, um, socialized. A lot.

Pushing the thought away, she asked, "Ever been
married?" Since he'd deftly avoided that part of his story.
And she told herself the only reason she asked was because
he had information about her own marital status.

"Never," he answered immediately.

"Ever come close?"

"Never."

Yeah, there was nothing like a little marriage to curb all
that Friday night, in-person socializing.

"You also know where I live," she pointed out, again
telling herself the only reason she wanted to know about
his home was because he had knowledge of hers.

He dipped his head forward in acknowledgement. "I live
in Cherokee Triangle."

That surprised her. For some reason, he seemed much

more the bright, shiny new development type. She would have put him in an east-end condo or one of the new downtown developments.

"Fourteen Hundred Willow," he clarified.

Ah. That explained it. Fourteen Hundred Willow might have been designed to blend in with the stately old houses surrounding it, but it was still comparatively bright, shiny, and new. It was also opulent, exorbitant, and magnificent, impossible to not notice or admire. Kind of like Nathaniel.

"Anything else you want to know?" he asked.

Nothing she couldn't Google later, she thought. She shook her head.

"Then we need to figure out what we're going to do about my . . ." He sighed with something akin to resolve. "My soul."

"So we do. I suppose we should start by comparing what I know about your great-great-whatever grandfather and what you know about Edward Dryden. See if there's anything about him that could make this whole project null and void."

"I still can't believe Edward has anything to do with this," Nathaniel said. "The man is controversial, certainly. But he's not dangerous."

"Controversial how?"

"Well, he's just one of those people you either love or hate. He doesn't inspire a tepid response. But those are the sort of people who make things happen." He met Audrey's gaze levelly again. "I'm telling you, he's *not* a criminal."

Says you, Audrey thought. Even if Nathaniel had done a thorough background check, there were some things that didn't show up in those. And there were other things that could be falsified. Even more that could be spun to look like things they weren't. Maybe it was because she'd been married to a cop, but Audrey had learned to trust her gut instincts. Silas had told her there was something shady about Edward Dryden, and Silas had been right about everything else. Audrey didn't trust the guy with whom

Nathaniel had gone into business. Now she just had to figure out how to get Nathaniel to open up to the possibility that his new BFF might be an AKA.

"Then let's compare," he said. "And we'll decide how to proceed from there."

· Nine ·

HIS HOUSE HAD BECOME A BROTHEL.

Silas Summerfield stood at the top of the stairs gazing down into his living room, marveling at the incessant chatter and laughter and bustle of the women below. There were more than a dozen down there, picking up hats and trying them on, vying for space in front of the half dozen mirrors. With their scanty dress—scanty by the standards of his own day, at least—there was nothing else to liken the scene to except one wherein ladies of easy virtue reigned.

Save one woman who had cleaned his house and one who had laundered for him, Silas had never allowed females into his home when he was alive. Not once. Certainly he had enjoyed the society of women from time to time, provided that society met the physical needs that every man experienced. He had kept women in a number of cities along his routes on the Mississippi and Ohio rivers, including a lovely one in Louisville named Daphne. But they were the sort of women who made their way in the world by being kept. He hadn't deluded himself that each of them hadn't had as many benefactors as he'd had beneficiaries of his own largesse. But that was what had made those relationships so ideal. There had been no troublesome feelings involved, no meaningless expectations, no silly exchanges involving anything other than commerce. Commerce was something Silas understood. Love, affection, devotion . . . those were as alien to him as the stars above.

His gaze lit on Cecilia then, who was aiding a rather indecisive woman on the selection of a hat. Silas shook his head. The woman was a homely creature who would be flattered only by headwear from which fell a heavy veil, but Cecilia smiled at and cooed over her as if she were the most handsome woman on the planet. Standing beside her, Cecilia was absolutely breathtaking. She'd tamed her short, unruly hair and tied around it a bit of lacy, pale yellow ribbon he'd seen her pluck from the assortment Audrey Magill provided for her clients. The dress she wore was of the same buttery color, a simple cut that only enhanced her natural beauty, something Silas would have thought it impossible to improve upon. Her smile today was dazzling, absent any of the sadness and shadow that had plagued it before.

She was genuinely happy in this society of women. What could the bastard have done to her that made her so fear men?

Because it was clear there was some bastard in her past who had mistreated her. It didn't require the supernatural ability to see inside a person's soul to deduce that. It required only to look into Cecilia's eyes to see the darkness that haunted her.

He smiled at his own choice of words. There was more than one way for a person to be haunted. Audrey was haunted by a ghost, the ghost of someone else's past, someone else's deeds, where as Cecilia . . .

Well. Now that he thought about it, he supposed Cecilia was haunted by the same sort of ghost. Now if only he could determine the identity of the cad, perhaps he could erase at least some of the shadows from her eyes.

She glanced up suddenly, looking directly at the place where he stood, as if she could see him. But he knew she could not. He hadn't even materialized to the point where Audrey could see him, lest one of the other women present have some kind of psychic inclinations. There was no chance Cecilia could actually see him standing there.

But she smiled at him, in a way that told him she knew he was there, and something unfurled inside him he hadn't even been aware was pulled tight until now. Perhaps she couldn't see him, but she could sense his presence, and pinpoint it to the very place where he stood. That had to be significant somehow, didn't it? And why did he want so desperately for it to be? The last thing he needed or wanted was the affection of a woman. Particularly a woman who was damaged. And most particularly a woman who was tied to this mortal world as surely as he had been pulled from it. Once Audrey had helped Nathaniel recapture his soul, Silas's work here would be finished. It made sense to conclude that, once it was, he would be pulled back to that netherworld he'd left behind and return to whatever it was he'd been doing there.

Strange that he couldn't remember much of his afterlife except that it had been pleasant. *That, too, must be significant*, he thought. But, again, he couldn't say just how.

He returned his attention to the activity in the room below—or, more accurately, he returned his attention to Cecilia in the room below—watching for another half hour, until the last of the women trickled out, and Audrey locked the door. She leaned back against it and spread her arms wide, as if barring it from a Viking attack. Then she looked at Cecilia, and the two women laughed the sort of laughter that comes with great relief. And then they did a curious thing, each lifting a hand into the air to smack their palms together. Audrey said something about having a surprise and headed into the kitchen, and Cecilia began to tidy up. Within moments, Audrey returned with a bottle of champagne and two slender glasses. Silas smiled at the crisp *pop* of the cork as she tugged it free of the bottle and began to pour.

"Silas, you should be here for this, too," she said as she filled Cecilia's glass to the brim.

"I, madam?" he asked as he descended the stairs. By the time he stepped into the living room, he had materialized the rest of the way so that Audrey could see him. He only wished he knew what to do to provide the same service for Cecilia. Because as much as he liked Audrey Magill, it was her companion who truly captivated him. "Why should I be a part of your celebration?" he continued. "Although you do certainly seem to have a successful shop on your hands, I was in no way instrumental in the accomplishment."

"Maybe not in the actual work," she said, "but you've put some good vibes into this house." She lifted her glass to toast him. "Plus, you're a nice guy. That, in itself, is cause to celebrate."

"I'll drink to that," Cecilia said, lifting the glass to her lips for a taste and closing her eyes to savor it as she did.

Ah. Just the entrée into conversation Silas had been looking for. "Do you not find most men nice, Cecilia?"

She had been swallowing when he asked the question and, by the time he finished asking it, was choking on her champagne. Audrey immediately went to her aid, patting her gently on the back until her coughing subsided.

"Was it something I said?" Silas asked innocently.

"Ah, no," Cecilia told him. "Not at all. I'm just not used to good champagne, that's all. I usually go for the cheap stuff."

"I see," Silas said. "I thought perhaps it was your way of indicating that no, you do not find most men nice."

"Audrey's the one who said that about nice men," Cecilia said. "She's the one who implied they're few and far between. Not me."

"Then you disagree with her," Silas said, deliberately clouding the issue. "You think the majority of men are quite nice."

She lifted her glass to her lips again, and for a moment, Silas didn't think she was going to reply. Then, just before taking another, much smaller, sip, she said softly, "Well, I wouldn't say that, either. Not if I were being honest."

Silas started to say something else, but Audrey cut him off. "Well, I must say, today exceeded my expectations. As much as I hoped we'd win more business with Thunder going on, I was worried, too, that we'd have to compete with it. But I think it was the opposite. While the husbands and sons were watching the Blue Angels and simulated dog fights, the mothers and daughters went shopping." Before Silas had a chance to ask for clarification, she told him, "Thunder over Louisville is the official start of the Derby Festival. The most humongous fireworks display you've ever seen. It's preceded by a day of revelry and mayhem, most of which is dictated by noise. They bring in all kinds of military aircraft, and—"

"Aircraft," Silas said. "Now that is something I should like to see."

"Weren't planes around when you were alive?" Cecilia asked.

"They were," he said. "But not in any great number. I've never seen an aircraft up close."

"It's too bad you're bound to the painting," Audrey said. "Otherwise, we could take you down to the Belvedere and show you around."

"It'll be packed, though," Cecilia said. "It usually brings in more than a half million people."

Silas's mouth dropped open at that. "Half a million people? In one place?"

Audrey and Cecilia exchanged smiles. "Sure," the latter said. "Thunder brings them in from miles around. It's pretty major."

"Good God. Louisville did attract a million people once, for the Southern Exposition in the eighteen-nineties, but they came over the course of four years, not in a single day." He shook his head in disbelief. "What's the population of the city these days?"

"Well, let's see," Audrey said. "The city and county merged a while back, and if you want to bring in southern

Indiana, and parts of Oldham and Bullitt Counties, since a lot of people commute from there, you're probably looking at about a million in the metropolitan area."

His mouth dropped open at that. "There couldn't have been more than two hundred thousand people who called the city home in my time. And that was plenty."

"Well, the city's spread out a lot since your time, too," Audrey said. "Old Louisville used to be considered a suburb, now it's considered part of downtown."

"I don't recognize this word 'suburb,' " Silas said.

"That's because you're not a baby boomer," Audrey told him.

He started to say he didn't recognize that phrase, either, then feared she would throw out something else he didn't understand, so refrained. It was amazing how much language could change in only a few generations. But then, having looked around Audrey's house and watched her use the things she used so matter-of-factly, particularly the computer, and having looked out the windows at the varying modes of transportation available and the speeds at which they traveled, he realized it wasn't just language that had changed so drastically.

He wondered again about his fate, once Audrey succeeded in helping his great-great-et-cetera grandson. Even if he could continue to haunt her house and be a part of this brave, new world in some way, did he really want to be? There was nothing in this time that harked back to his own. Even his old house bore no resemblance to the place he had called home. Her music was different, her fashions were different, the ways she entertained and expressed herself were different. The sounds, smells, and sights of his time had been replaced by new ones, as had the customs, practices, and laws. In the seventy-some years that had passed since his death, the entire world had become a place he never could have imagined. Did he truly wish to remain in such an alien environment?

He watched Cecilia sip her champagne once more,

noting the way she again closed her eyes as she did so, as if it might enhance her relishing of the experience. He watched the way she sighed with delight and smiled once she'd completed the action, as if such a simple pleasure brought her the utmost joy one could find. And he wondered how much pleasure, how much joy, she had been denied in her life.

Perhaps, he thought, there were some things that didn't progress. Some things that never changed, no matter how sophisticated and technologically advanced society grew. The enjoyment of champagne, for example. The pleasure of looking at a beautiful woman. The satisfaction that came with quiet conversation. The contentment of agreeable company. None of those had been altered by evolution, not really. Oh, the champagne may have been cold water in primitive times, and the conversation little more than grunting, but the pleasure received was the same, no matter the era or the age. Human beings, regardless of when and how they lived, had always claimed the same requirements. Nourishment and companionship. And if one was very, very lucky, that nourishment would include finer things like champagne, and that companionship would flourish into love.

"I need to tally the sales and make the bank deposit," Audrey said, her very down-to-earth statement pulling Silas's head out of the stars.

"Go ahead," Cecilia told her. "I'll clean up down here."

"And I shall keep her company while she does," Silas volunteered.

Both women opened their mouths to say something, then both closed them at the same time. Audrey only nodded mutely in a way that could have meant anything, and Cecilia smiled silently in a way that meant nothing.

Another vacant smile, Silas noted with something akin to anger. But it wasn't anger for her. It was for whoever the bastard was who had robbed her of so much. Maybe, he thought, he did still have work to do here. Work that didn't include his great-great-et-cetera grandson. Work that might, perhaps, take rather a long time to complete.

WHEN CECILIA HEARD SILAS'S ASSURANCE THAT HE would keep her company while she closed up, a ruffle of something fuzzy and flittery skittered up her spine that she'd thought she would never feel again. It was that feeling a thirteen-year-old experienced when she caught the cute boy in school looking at her, the feeling a sixteen-year-old experienced the first time she kissed the boy she'd been crushing on for months, the feeling a twenty-six year-old experienced when . . .

Well. When a handsome man said he would keep her company while she closed up shop. The fact that the handsome man in question just happened to be invisible was beside the point.

The point was that, for the first time in a long, long time, Cecilia was interacting with a man who didn't make her hyperventilate—in a bad way, she meant. In fact, she was interacting with him in a manner that made her breath catch in her chest in a way that felt kind of nice. She almost did feel like she was thirteen again and the cute boy in school was looking at her. The feeling was that innocent, that pure, that sweet. At thirteen, she'd been a happy, carefree kid who embraced all sorts of romantic notions about love. By twenty-six, every last one of those notions had been dashed and battered and trampled to bits. If it took a ghost to make her feel like a dreamy adolescent again, then . . .

She sighed and enjoyed another sip of her champagne. Okay, so maybe the fact that Silas was invisible *was* the point. That didn't matter. What mattered was that, for the first time in years, Cecilia wasn't frightened of a man. And if that was because the man was insubstantial and lived with someone else and would probably only be around long enough for him to rescue the soul of one of his descendants, at least it was something.

She turned her attention to the shop and smiled. The place was a wreck. But that was good, because it meant they'd been inundated with customers, and the majority of them had made purchases. Cecilia and Audrey had worked shoulder-to-shoulder from the moment the latter had unlocked the front door, often literally, helping customers choose hats. Many of the women who'd shopped today had even bought two hats, since many of them attended both the Derby and the Oaks, the race run by fillies the day before Derby. And it went without saying that a woman couldn't wear the same hat or dress to *both* races. That would be an unforgivable faux pas in Louisville.

Derby hats might be a seasonal business, Cecilia thought, but having guesstimated the sales figure for today alone, she knew Audrey would be *juuust fiiine* covering her annual expenses.

She shook her head at the amounts some of the women had paid. Four figures, many of them had added to their credit cards today. More than a thousand dollars for hats, of all things. Of course, they were *gorgeous* hats, into which she knew Audrey put *a lot* of work. But they were still hats. And when Cecilia thought about what a thousand dollars could also buy, things like food and clothing and a roof over one's head . . .

She sighed. Ah, well. Hers was not to judge others. People who worked hard deserved to be paid well, and if that wasn't always the case, it wasn't up to her to criticize. If she had a thousand dollars to blow on hats, she'd do it, too. Probably. And it wasn't like she hadn't lived *very* well when she lived with Vincent. He'd opened accounts for her in all the chic downtown boutiques, had bought expensive jewelry for her birthday and Christmas, let her drive one of his Mercs whenever she wanted. And his penthouse had claimed every luxury a person could want, from the Sub-Zero fridge to the cedar sauna.

Of course, there had been that small matter of him controlling every aspect of her life the whole time she was with him—even if she hadn't realized that at first. And his

domineering and his ugly mood swings. And then the back
of his hand. And her being absolutely terrified of him there
toward the end.

She wondered how many other women were trapped in
the same situation? Maybe even one of the women who
had been in the shop today—maybe more than one—
whom Cecilia had so envied for the ability to spend so
much so frivolously. To the outside world, Cecilia's life in
San Francisco would have looked pretty damned good.
She'd been envied by a lot of women, having come to work
for Vincent's restaurant right out of cooking school and
catching the rich boss's eye right off the bat. She'd had
nothing when she met him. She'd never known her father,
and her mother disappeared when she was sixteen. She'd
spent the two years before college in a foster home and had
gone to Berkeley on a handful of scholarships and by
working three jobs.

When she started working for Vincent, she'd been living
in a tiny apartment in a crappy neighborhood and had had
to rely on the BART to get around. Two months later, she
was living in his penthouse and driving his cars, wearing
the diamond earrings he'd bought for her and arraying
herself in Badgley Mischka. Hell, Cecilia would have
envied herself, too.

She pushed the thought away and tried to think about
something besides San Francisco and Vincent Strayer and
what her life had once been. Her life wasn't that anymore,
and it would never be that again. She was utterly content to
remain alone for the rest of her days. It was infinitely
preferable to being with the wrong man. And any man was
the wrong man, as far as she was concerned.

She drained the last of her champagne and went about
tidying up, always feeling Silas's presence, even if neither
of them said a word. After returning hats to their proper
places and straightening up the displays, she went to the
small room at the back of the shop where Audrey kept the
bits of ribbon, lace, and accessories that her clients used to
design their own hats. It hadn't gotten as messy today as she

would have expected, probably because Audrey had enough orders now for custom hats that she was no longer able to guarantee delivery of those by Derby day, two weeks hence. Someone had carried an already-completed hat in here, though, Cecilia saw, and set it on a shelf. So after setting the room to rights, she took the hat back out to the living room/showroom to try and figure out where it went.

Ah. Right there. On the empty display stand by the secretary. There was a big gilt mirror hanging near it, and as she passed it, she couldn't quite keep herself from trying on the hat, to see how it would look on her. There were some women who couldn't wear hats successfully, even if both the woman and hat in question were beautiful. Sometimes it was because something about their faces simply did not accommodate headwear. Other times, it was because they simply didn't have the right attitude. Not that most hats required a good deal of sass or sophistication, but a woman needed at least a little audacity.

Cecilia wouldn't have thought she would be suited to a hat like the one she held, a pale, frilly number piled with yellow silk roses that were topped with white ostrich feathers, and sporting a brim that was wide enough to put out someone's eye if she wasn't careful. After all, she hadn't been audacious since . . . ever. But she was delighted to discover that the moment she perched the hat on her head, she was transformed. In a good way. The yellow color gave her complexion a mellow tone and brought out flecks of gold in her brown eyes. She tilted her head one way, then the other, putting the feathers into softly moving motion, and that made her smile. A few more turns of the head and she might very well take flight.

"You look lovely, Cecilia."

Silas's voice, coming from directly behind her, made her jump. He'd been so quiet that she'd figured he must have drifted off. Literally, since that was what ghosts did. She turned slowly around and saw nothing—not that she was surprised by that—but smiled at the place where she suspected he stood. Closer than she would have thought she would be comfortable with, but making her in no way uncomfortable.

"Thank you," she said. Then she swiftly removed the hat from her head and repositioned the lacy ribbon she'd used to tie back her hair. Hair that was so short, it didn't need ribbon to hold it back. Hair she'd wanted to make look nice for her first day on the job. Because why else would she have bothered with a frivolous decoration like that?

"Don't take the hat off on my account," Silas told her. "You do look lovely in it. It reminds me of the sort of thing women wore in my time. Except that on them, I always thought such hats a ridiculous affectation. You, however, carry it off with aplomb."

She chuckled at that, a nervous sound, and fiddled with one of the roses, as if it were loose, even though it wasn't. Strangely, her nervousness wasn't because she was in the presence of someone male who, however invisible he might be, had the potential to hurt her. It was because she was in the presence of someone male who, however invisible he might be, didn't alarm her at all. Even stranger, she was beginning to think that wasn't because he was invisible.

"I don't think I'm much of a hat person," she told him, setting the hat carefully back on its stand.

"I disagree," he replied. "You have a beautiful face. And it's made more beautiful when it's properly attired."

She blushed at that. No one had ever called her beautiful before. Not even Vincent, when he was trying to coax her into having sex when she wasn't in the mood. He'd used other words to describe her and her body parts, words he'd thought were erotic and arousing but which had made her feel dirty and cheap. When she'd told him that, though, and asked him to stop, he'd only laughed and pushed her back onto the bed and crammed his tongue into her mouth. Maybe if he'd called her beautiful instead, he wouldn't have had to do that.

Again, she pushed thoughts of Vincent away. He didn't bear thinking about anymore.

"It's nice of you to say that, Silas," she told him. "Thank you."

"I wasn't being nice," he said. "I was being honest."

His voice was warm velvet when he spoke, something that fired sparks of heat through her entire body. Telling herself she was just trying to change the subject, and that she really didn't have any interest in his answer other than that, she asked, "What were the women of your time like?"

She heard him sigh. "They weren't like you and your employer, of that much I am certain." He hesitated, and when he spoke again, his voice was thoughtful. "Although perhaps I speak too quickly when I say that. Women of my time were, like women of your time, of varying types and conditions. Although the majority were not like you and Audrey, there were a marked number who were strong-natured and claimed many admirable traits."

She smiled at that. "And to you, an admirable trait would be . . . what?"

"Well, for example, the ability to converse about something other than the latest fashions or who did what at someone's latest soiree."

"Yeah, that would be admirable, all right," Cecilia agreed, biting back a smile. "What else?"

He must have needed to think about that, because he didn't reply right away. "Also, having skills beyond sewing and embroidery. The ability to ride vigorously, say, or enjoy a brandy without losing her faculties."

"Yep, those are pretty admirable qualities, too," Cecilia agreed. "But I can think of a few others."

"Such as?"

"What about refusing to submit to marriage and wearing bloomers and protesting for the right to vote?" she asked. "I'd think those things would all be traits of a strong, admirable woman."

This time, he didn't hesitate at all. "No, Cecilia, those are traits of a rabble-rouser."

She smiled again. "I would have been a rabble-rouser if I'd lived in your time."

"And yet," he said, "I would have welcomed your company anyway."

She chuckled at that.

He added, "Once I bailed you out of jail, I mean."

That made her actually laugh. Not a huge laugh, but a laugh nonetheless. And only after completing it did she realize how long it had been since she'd done that. Years, she marveled. It had been years since she last laughed.

"That, Cecilia, is the most delightful sound I believe I have ever heard," Silas said. "Yet something tells me it's one that isn't often heard."

He must have picked up on what she was thinking, she decided. Not that she was going to verify that for him. Instead, she only said, "Well, it's been that kind of day." For the last several years, she added to herself.

"No, that's not it," he disagreed with confidence. "I watched you today. You looked genuinely happy among Audrey's clientele. Not so happy that you laughed," he mused further, "but still happy."

He was right, she thought, realizing it only now. She had been happy today. Only it hadn't been Audrey's clientele that made her feel that way. It had been the fact that she was doing something. Something productive, something she was good at, something that made her feel worthwhile. Vincent had robbed her of all those feelings while she was with him. She hadn't felt like herself since . . .

Well. In a lot of ways, she'd never felt like herself. Because she'd never had a chance to figure out who *herself* was.

But today, some of herself had started to creep out. She had enjoyed working in Finery today. And she'd done a good job helping women figure out what they wanted and what styles suited them best. She'd enjoyed talking to Audrey, the first friend she'd made in a very long time. This had actually been a *good* day, she marveled. A very good day. And all because it was so wonderfully, astoundingly, deliciously . . .

Ordinary. The sort of day normal people lived. People who weren't cowed by fear and looking over their shoulder and trying to shrink from life so no one would notice them. Yeah, okay, so she was talking to a ghost at the moment, which maybe wasn't what most ordinary people did during their ordinary days. Somehow, Silas made it feel ordinary. Made it feel right. Made it feel normal.

Normal and ordinary, Cecilia thought with satisfaction as she surveyed the room she'd just tidied, knowing she would be back in the morning to do it all over again. She had a normal, ordinary life. With the occasional conversation with a dead guy. All in all, not a bad way to go.

No, not a bad way to go at all.

· Ten ·

WHEN NATHANIEL HAD AGREED TO LET AUDREY choose their dinner destination the next time they met, he hadn't realized she would pick the Chow Wagon, even if it was, as she had pointed out, a Derby tradition. For the few weeks prior to the race, a cornucopia of independent vendors—most of whom served their fare from garishly painted and luridly lit trailers more suited to a carnival midway—corralled themselves inside chain link fences in various places around town, serving the type of food that was guaranteed to harden arteries upon contact. Apple pie, barbecue, cole slaw—and that was just for the first three letters in the alphabet—along with ice cream, beer, pie, and deep-fried whatever-the-hell-you-want. And, it went without saying, that ancient, arcane gastronomic mainstay of Kentucky festivals, burgoo, a chililike concoction into which went everything except chilis. Inevitably, a stage was set up somewhere amidst the culinary mayhem for local bands to perform, making for often decent music, and always lousy acoustics. Acoustics made even lousier thanks to the accompaniment of the lawnmower-like din of scores of generators fueling all the garishly painted and luridly lit trailers.

In spite of that, the moment Nathaniel entered the Chow Wagon, he was transported back to his adolescence, when he and his friends would spend entire days here, wolfing down gyros and tiger ears and sno-cones, listening to Southern-fried rock and trying to buy beer with fake IDs that never fooled anyone. Even though nearly two decades had passed, the Chow Wagon hadn't changed one iota. Hell, he'd even bet some of the people beind the counters of those trailers were the same ones who had waited on him when he was a kid.

But he wasn't that kid anymore and hadn't been for a very long time. He told himself the kind of man he had become should look around this place and find it, at best, plebeian, and, at worst, grotesque. It was exactly the kind of environment he avoided now, expressly because he didn't want to be reminded of his humble beginnings. But he couldn't quite keep himself from closing his eyes, filling his lungs with the mingling aromas of fried onions and tepid beer, and filling his ears with a scratchy, feedback-laden rendition of that bluegrass staple, "Rocky Top." Somewhere in the distance, a woman laughed raucously, a man shouted coarsely to a friend, and a baby began to cry. And Nathaniel was surprised to discover that, contrary to being repelled by his surroundings, he actually wanted to smile. Because he realized that here, among the gaudy trailers and unhealthy food and blaring music, people were enjoying their lives. And they were enjoying them infinitely more than he had ever enjoyed his.

Well, except for a handful of nights as a teenager, when he and his friends came to the Chow Wagon.

He was grateful Audrey had selected the Chow Wagon downtown on the Belvedere so they had a gorgeous view of the Ohio River at sunset from the picnic table where they now sat. The *Belle of Louisville*, the city's resident paddle wheeler, had just set off for an evening cruise, but hadn't pulled so far away from the dock that she was out of view.

Her bright red paddle wheel churned the brown water behind her, her cheery white decks festooned with twinkling lights. If he listened closely, he could still hear the calliope belting out an exuberant rendition of "Alexander's Ragtime Band," punctuated now and then with the jovial *Bwaaamp! Bwaaamp! Bwaaamp!* of her whistle.

Traffic was still brisk on the Second Street Bridge above the steamboat, the cars' headlights bouncing along almost in time with the music as they headed to and from Indiana on the other side. The sun had dropped low on the horizon, tipping out a long, orangey spill of light over the shallow hills and historic buildings of New Albany, staining the rest of the skyline with pink and gold. The bluegrass band made way for one that played Southern rock, so at least they were giving the generators a run for their money. And although Nathaniel would have sworn he'd lost his taste for Lynyrd Skynyrd tribute bands when he was a teenager—mostly because he'd never had a taste for Lynyrd Skynyrd tribute bands to begin with—he had to admit the new guys weren't half bad. Even more surprising, he didn't mind drinking a tepid beer from a plastic cup when he could have been sipping a nice shiraz from Reidel crystal at any number of restaurants around town instead.

Tonight, for some reason, this wasn't such a bad way to have dinner. Even if he did suspect that Audrey's choice was probably her way of getting even with him for paying the bill for both of them three nights ago after underhandedly accosting their server for the bill when she slipped off to the ladies' room.

Well, the joke was on her, he thought further. Because he was having a damned nice time. Which was weird, because in addition to not normally being comfortable in such surroundings, he wouldn't have thought he would take pleasure in watching a woman sit at a picnic table covered with a plastic table cloth and eat burgoo out of a plastic foam bowl with disposable utensils. But damned if Audrey Magill didn't make the activity look downright erotic. Even though erotic was the last thing she should have looked when the two of them were dressed so similarly. But where his jeans and midnight blue sweater were fairly nondescript, her jeans hugged her body like a second skin, and her pale sweater was woven with flecks of gold that complemented the black hair plaited into a fat braid that fell over one shoulder.

Even better, the neck of that sweater dipped low enough for him to see the elegant contours of her collarbones and the faintest hint of the upper swells of her breasts. It also, unfortunately, allowed him to see the twin lines of the gold chain dipping into that neckline, reminding him of the heavy ring that pulled it to its lowest point. The ring that had belonged to her husband. The ring she evidently had on her person at all times, because every time he'd seen her, he'd noticed that gold chain disappearing into whatever she'd had on.

Inescapably, his gaze fell to the ring on her left hand, too, which was infinitely more meaningful—and, to him, more troubling—than the one she wore around her neck.

And why was it so troubling? he asked himself. From his very first meeting with Audrey Magill, he'd been struck again and again by how different she was from the women he normally dated. He'd reminded himself over and over how she was the last sort of woman with whom he should get involved. It didn't matter how beautiful she looked across a candlelit table. It didn't matter that he'd had more meaningful conversations with her than he'd ever had with anyone. It didn't matter how good it felt to have her weave her fingers with his. And it didn't matter that he could be sitting in the sort of environment he normally disdained and suddenly find it charming, just because she happened to be in it, too.

None of that mattered. Because Audrey Magill was the sort of woman who continued to wear her wedding ring years after her marriage had ended. She was the sort of woman who remained faithful to the memory of her husband, even after that husband's death. She was the sort of woman for whom feelings obviously ran very, very deep.

The sort of woman who, when she fell in love, stayed in love forever. And he . . .

Hell, he was a guy who was so detached from his emotions that he couldn't even hang on to his own soul.

Nathaniel shoved back a wave of discontent and returned his attention to her face, but all that did was make him realize again how beautiful she was, even absent any cosmetic enhancement. He also noticed how much she was savoring her burgoo, and that, finally, made him smile.

He'd never seen anyone enjoy eating as much as she did. Especially women. Usually, when he took a woman out to dinner, she ordered crap. Salads and broiled chicken and other such tasteless, texture-free fare. But two night's ago at Buck's, she'd eaten the bulk of their scallop appetizer, cleaned her plate of baked goat cheese salad, ate every bite of her strip steak—with blue cheese and mushrooms—and then had refused to share so much as a nibble of her mocha dacquoise with him, insisting he had to order his own. And tonight, the burgoo was just for starters. She'd also heaped high on her red plastic tray a bratwurst, an onion rosette, a corndog, and an elephant ear. Oh, and fudge, which she said she was taking home with her, but she was already eyeing it with as much interest as she was showing everything else, so his money was on mass consumption by night's end.

Still he had to admit it was good to see a woman with an appetite for a change. Inevitably, though, before he could stop the thought from coming, he found himself wondering if her appetites extended to something besides food.

Three years, he marveled. That was how long her husband had been dead. And since she'd told him she still considered herself to be married, it must mean it had been three years since she'd been with a man. He tried to remember what he'd been doing three years ago. Let's see . . . He hadn't opened his downtown office yet, and he'd been living in the east end. Wow. That was a long time ago. Then he tried to remember the last time he'd had sex.

Less than a month ago, he recalled, when an old college flame had come to town on business and looked him up for a weekend hookup. Even that felt like forever. He couldn't imagine going three years without sex.

But Audrey Magill had. The woman must be made of ice.

He watched as she picked up her corndog and nibbled the end, closing her eyes in near ecstasy and making one of those *mmm-mmm-mmm* sounds women made whenever they were close to orgasm or eating Godiva chocolate. Then she opened her mouth wider and covered the end of the corndog completely, her full lips closing around it in a way that made Nathaniel's cock twitch.

Oh, great. Just what he needed. A Beavis and Butthead reaction to carnival food. Being reduced to a hormonally driven thirteen-year-old in this, his forty-second year of life, after having bedded more women than a thirteen-year-old could even dream about.

Naturally, Audrey opened her eyes then and caught Nathaniel watching her. God only knew what she saw in his face, because her eyes went wide, and she gagged a little on the corndog before pulling it out of her mouth. But where that should have thrown a bucket of cold water on any errant erotic—and adolescent—ideas he might have been having, instead he found himself wanting to reach across the table to close his fingers around the corndog and guide it back to her mouth, then encourage her to try again, taking all of it this time.

It was immediately clear that she was uncomfortable under his scrutiny, which meant—damn—she'd probably known exactly what he was thinking about. Well, except for how he'd had her dressed in knee socks and a little plaid skirt, but they were both probably better off not having that part made clear. After mumbling something about saving the porndog—ah, he meant *corn*dog, of course—for later, she wrapped it in a napkin and went to work on her elephant ear instead, and Nathaniel resigned himself to getting no satisfaction tonight.

"So did you have a chance to talk to the ghost of Silas Summerfield again?" he asked.

When they'd parted ways three nights ago, they'd been no closer to laying out a plan of action than they'd been when they started dinner. Though, speaking for his own part, Nathaniel had at least enjoyed the evening. That wasn't why he'd asked Audrey out again, though. Or rather, why he hadn't suggested they meet for dinner again, since he wasn't asking her out, no way. She was a married woman after all. Dammit. They'd simply come to a mutual agreement to get together again after Audrey had spoken again to her ghost, and—

Her ghost, he repeated derisively to himself. He still couldn't believe he could think that with a straight face. He still couldn't believe he was buying into the whole haunted house thing in the first place. He, a man of utter pragmatism, was suddenly relying on a phantom from the great beyond to return balance—or, at the very least, warmth—to his life. And the plan upon parting ways with Audrey the other night was to see if that phantom could use his supernatural position to find out something more about why signs pointed to Edward Dryden, while Nathaniel rechecked his natural sources to see if they could do the same.

As for himself, he'd discovered nothing from his detective that he hadn't already been told about Edward. Just as he had known he would uncover nothing he hadn't already been told. When he did a background check on people, it was thorough. He had a team of unsavory PIs to whom he paid way too much money to make certain of that. So if he and Audrey were going to find out how to rescue his currently unavailable soul, it would have to come through supernatural means.

"I did speak to Silas, actually," she said after swallowing. "At first, he wasn't much help and kept insisting the link was Edward. When I told you you were sure that wasn't it, he called you a—" She halted abruptly, threw Nathaniel an uneasy smile, then hurried on, "He got a little perturbed and said he'd poke around some more."

"And did he?"

She nodded. "Last night, I had a dream that he and I were sharing a glass of port in his bedroom."

Nathaniel's eyebrows shot up at that. "You were in his room?"

And why did he care? What difference did it make? Not only was she only dreaming, the guy in the dream was a ghost. Not to mention a hundred-and-something years old.

"Well, it's not like it was the first time," she said. "I woke up in his bed that first night he was at the house with me."

Hmm, Nathaniel thought. Maybe it hadn't been three years since she'd had sex. Maybe it had only been a week. Did dream sex satisfy a person the way real sex did? Certainly, it was safer and there were considerably fewer strings attached, and it could go on for a lot longer, and—

And what the hell was he thinking? Jeez, one erotic corndog episode, and he'd turned into a jealous lover. Jealous of his great-great-whatever grandfather, no less. That was just . . . weird.

He made himself focus on the matter at hand. "So you woke up in my grandfather's bed," he said, telling himself he did *not* sound jealous.

"You sound jealous," she said with a smile.

"I do not sound jealous," he denied.

"Yeah, you do." Her smile grew broader. "What's the matter? Envious because guys in Silas's time may have gotten more action, since they knew better than modern men how to treat a lady?"

He nodded. "Right. By denying them the vote and the right to own property. That's the way to win a woman's heart all right." Before she could sidetrack him more—or make him feel more jealous—he continued, "Could we get back to the matter of what you dreamed last night?"

Unless, of course, she'd dreamed about having sex with his great-great-whatever grandfather, in which case, Nathaniel was going to need to find a place to be sick, because that was just too gross to think about.

"He gave me another name," she said. "He's not sure

how it's significant, or how it ties in, or who the guy is, if
he's even anyone. But he said the name Nicholas Pearson
kept circling in his head. And he said the last time a name
circled in his head like that, it was Edward Dryden's. But
he'd been able to find out who Edward Dryden was, and he
can't figure out who Nicholas Pearson is."

"Guess the afterlife doesn't have access to Google,
huh?"

"Evidently not. But I do."

"And?"

"It's too common a name. I got more than ten thousand
hits."

"Did any of them say, 'Nicholas Pearson is a notorious
murderer who just invested in a downtown Louisville
development that cost a man his soul'?"

She smiled at that. And Nathaniel tried not to notice how
it softened her features and lit up her eyes and made him
want to lean across the table and cover her mouth with his.

Obviously, Audrey Magill wasn't the only one who had
gone too long without sex. Because the last time he'd
reacted this strongly to a woman this soon after meeting
her had been . . .

Never, he realized. He'd never responded to a woman
the way he found himself responding to Audrey Magill.

"Alas, no," she said. "But there was a Nicholas Pearson
who pitched a no-hitter in the Peytona Little League last
year."

"I don't know," Nathaniel said, telling himself to get a grip
and stop thinking about Audrey the way he kept thinking
about her. "He sounds like he could be our guy."

Instead of laughing at that—or at least chuckling, as
he'd hoped she would—she sobered.

"There is something else I could do, Nathaniel."

She so seldom spoke his first name, that hearing it made
something in his chest that had been pulled too tight start
to loosen. And then . . . yes, there it was. Warmth. In his
stomach. Then his chest. And she wasn't even touching
him. He would have said it was only the sort of warmth

brought on by a chemical reaction to a sexual attraction, the kind that was only felt in the gut because something in the head had sparked it. But there was something else to this heat, something that went beyond both belly and brain, something that made it linger, if only for a moment. And then, just as he'd feared, it began to wither, because Audrey suddenly looked very sad, and there was nothing to bring warmth from that.

"You know my husband was a cop," she said, her voice softening to the point where he had to lean across the table to hear her.

He nodded, but said nothing. Mostly because he honestly had no idea what to say.

His silence seemed to encourage instead of deter her, though, because she continued, "His partner, Leo Rubens, was promoted to detective last year. I could ask him to look into both Edward Dryden and Nicholas Pearson. Maybe him being a cop, he could have access to information you wouldn't have."

Nathaniel doubted it. He'd put his money on unsavory PIs every time. Hadn't she ever read Raymond Chandler or Dashiell Hammett? Sam Spade and Nick Charles were always one step ahead of the flatfoots. The flatfeet. The guys on the police force.

"Do you see him often?" Nathaniel asked.

She shook her head. "Not really. Not anymore. But I know he's still at the same precinct."

Nathaniel wasn't sure what to make of Audrey's estrangement from her husband's partner. So he decided not to think about it. For now.

"The last time was . . ." She hesitated, mulling that. "Wow, I guess it was when Lucy had her bat mitzvah. That was . . ." She halted again, presumably to do some quick mental math. "Almost two years ago. I got an invitation to the party to celebrate Leo's promotion last year but I didn't go. I had something going on that night. I don't remember what."

Nathaniel couldn't help but think that was important.

Weren't partners on the police force supposed to be as close as brothers? Even closer sometimes? He didn't think that was just a TV affectation. Audrey and her husband had probably seen a lot of this Leo and his family when Sean Magill was alive. But she hadn't seen her husband's partner for almost two years and hadn't attended a party to commemorate what had to have been a major milestone for the man. Did that mean she was starting to put the past behind her? Or did it mean the past was still so painful for her to think about that she couldn't face any reminders?

And again, why did it matter?

It mattered, he immediately answered himself, because Audrey was a nice person. And there were precious few of those in the world today. It mattered because she shouldn't have had to suffer such a massive loss. It mattered because he shouldn't have to ask her to do something she clearly did not want to do. And it mattered, he made himself admit further, because he liked her.

He liked her a lot.

"What do you think?" she asked when he didn't reply.

Although it should have been an easy enough question to answer, Nathaniel wasn't sure how to answer it. Or maybe he just didn't want to. Because, of course, the answer should be yes. Yes, she should go talk to Detective Leo Rubens to see if he could shed any additional light on this mystery, the solving of which would mean the return of Nathaniel's soul. But asking her to do that would mean asking her to stir up memories and feelings she obviously didn't want to stir up, otherwise she wouldn't have lost touch with the Rubens family in the first place.

Did Nathaniel want to do that to her? No. He didn't. But the reason for that wasn't just because he didn't want Audrey to suffer. It was also because, if she was beginning to put the past behind her, he didn't want to bring it front and center again. Not just because it would make things difficult for Audrey. Because it would make things difficult for him, too. Because in spite of all his admonishments to the contrary, Nathaniel really did want to get involved with her. Involved with a married woman. Even if she wasn't really married anymore.

Man, he really was soulless, he thought, if he wanted to make Audrey forget about the man she married and whom she still loved.

No, not soulless, he immediately told himself. At least, not for that reason. He didn't want to make her forget Sean Magill or remove him from her life. He just wanted to help her create new memories with someone else. To find room for someone else in her life. Someone like maybe him.

If anything, Nathaniel's weird feelings tonight kind of reassured him that his soul must not have gotten too far. Because a man without a soul couldn't be falling for a woman the way he was falling for Audrey. Could he? And he wouldn't feel guilty about how doing so meant sharing her with another man.

"That would be great, if you could talk to Leo," he finally said, striving for a carelessness he was nowhere close to feeling. "If you don't mind. And if it wouldn't be any trouble."

After only a moment's hesitation, she shook her head. "No, it's no trouble," she assured him. But she said nothing about whether or not she minded.

Of course it wouldn't be any trouble, Nathaniel thought. It would only be painful. And difficult. And very possibly traumatic. And while she was going through all that in an effort to save his soul, he would pick up the phone and call a guy named Duke, ask him to run a couple of checks and then bill Nathaniel for his time.

"Hey, you feel like walking?" he asked impulsively, for no other reason than he was suddenly restless, and she didn't seem to have any more interest in her food . . . since she'd pushed the tray away the minute she'd started talking about her husband's old partner.

She looked startled by the question, but nodded. "Yeah, sure. I should probably walk off some of that elephant ear."

He rose and reached for her tray, moving the little white box of fudge to the table, before picking the tray up along with his own and carrying both to a nearby trash can to empty them. When he turned back around, he saw that Audrey, contrary to what she'd just told him, was still sitting at the table, running her thumb idly over the box of fudge, as if she'd intended to do something with it, then was waylaid by something else. Her thoughts, judging by the look of her. She was staring down at the box, her dark brows arrowed downward, her expression grim.

The Lynyrd Skynyrd wannaband had moved to a mellow song, one Nathaniel had never heard before, so it was easy to tune it out. Until, as he was ambling back over toward Audrey, some lyrics drifted into his ear, saying something about life having taken the singer everywhere, but that there was no place like home. It was a surprisingly pleasant lyric, even if it was followed by something about she-gators. But what really surprised Nathaniel was how much he found himself identifying with it. Even though he'd never really stayed in one dwelling long enough to think of it as a home. He and his mother had barely stayed one step ahead of eviction when he was a kid, and as an adult, he'd gradually moved into bigger and better places while awaiting that one big score of a condo at 1400 Willow. But even after living there for almost two years, the place didn't feel like home to him. He'd begun to think no place ever would. So why, suddenly, the big homecoming epiphany over a song he'd never even heard before?

Man, he was losing a lot more than his soul if he was enjoying plastic utensils and fried food and identifying with Lynyrd Skynyrd lyrics. Forget about supernatural forces. He should be a lot more worried about his state of mind.

As he drew nearer to the table—nearer to Audrey—she looked up at him, and, for a moment, she honestly looked like she wasn't sure where she was. She'd been that deep in thought. Then she managed a small smile and stood. He watched as she tucked the fudge into the oversized handbag she slung over one shoulder, then he stretched his arm out to the right, a silent indication that she should precede him. When she did, he placed his hand in the small of her back, a gesture he'd completed so often, with so many women, he didn't even think about it anymore.

He thought about it this time.

Because, this time, heat seeped into him at even that simple touch. Only instead of making him feel better this time, it only reminded him how very cold he was whenever Audrey wasn't around. And not just physically, either. Not lately.

She spun around at his touch, her eyes wide, her mouth open, obviously reacting to the cold from his hand that must have permeated her clothes.

"I'm sorry," he immediately apologized. "I wasn't thinking. I should have warned you I was going to touch you. I know the cold must be . . . uncomfortable for you."

Her expression cleared immediately, and she shook her head. "No, it's not that. It's . . ."

"What?" he asked when her voice drifted off without her finishing.

"Nothing," she replied, a little too quickly. A little too anxiously. "It's nothing. I just keep forgetting about your . . ." She hesitated, then finished softly, "Condition."

Nathaniel wished he could forget about it. Though, truth be told, he was starting to get kind of used to the cold, which was something he really didn't want to do. Because if he was getting used to the cold, it made him think maybe he was getting used to his "condition," as she'd called it. And maybe he was getting used to his condition because his soul was moving farther and farther away. Just how long did they have, he wondered, before it was gone for good? Audrey had said that as long as Edward's development didn't come to fruition, then he was in good shape. But how did she know that for sure?

Oh, right. Because a ghost told her. So, hey, why worry?

As if of one mind, they both turned toward the river and strode in that direction. As they walked, Audrey reached for his hand and twined her fingers with his, as if it they were a couple who did that all the time without even thinking about it. She'd done the same thing the other night as they'd left

Buck's. Even after chewing him out for paying the bill, as they'd made their way to the door, she'd slipped her hand into his as if she hadn't even given conscious thought to doing it. And then, when they'd been in his car, and he'd needed his hand back to shift gears, she'd still kept her fingers circled lightly around his wrist to keep him warm. She'd done it without him even having to ask, because she was a nice person who didn't want other people to suffer.

Eventually, though, he'd had to drop her off at her house, and she'd had to tell him good night and release his hand to dig her keys out of her bag. That was when the cold had washed over him again, from head to toe, from skin to marrow. She'd apologized for having to leave him, but she'd left him just the same. Not that he'd expected her to come home with him and climb into bed beside him and hold him all night to keep him warm.

Even if he'd found himself wishing she would do just that. Only his desire for that had had little to do with wanting to be warm and everything to do with—

Well. Wanting to be hot. And wanting to make her hot, too. What was remarkable was that he'd wanted that second thing even more than the first. Not that he never put a woman's pleasure before his own, but neither was it something he consciously strove to achieve. When Nathaniel made love to a woman, he did it in a way that was meant to generate and prolong the passion for both of them equally. There was something about Audrey, though, that made him want to go slowly and put the focus on her. Maybe because he knew it had been so long since she'd made love with anyone. Or maybe it was for another reason he hadn't let himself think about.

He thought about it now. Thought about being with her in his bed, tracing his fingers over her mouth and cheeks, her neck and shoulders, her breasts and belly. Then moving his hand lower, between her legs, stroking her with exquisite care and attention until she came apart at the seams. He thought about moving his mouth to that part of her, pushing her legs wide and—

"It's beautiful, isn't it?" she said softly, wrenching him out of what had promised to be a very pleasant fantasy . . . if not a particularly appropriate one for the moment and his current surroundings.

As evidenced by the fact that he'd completely forgotten those surroundings. So much so that he hadn't even been aware that the two of them had come to a stop at the railing that surrounded the Belvedere and now stood watching the river beyond. The sun had pretty much disappeared from the sky by now, and the cool breeze had picked up. He turned to look at Audrey just as it caught in her hair and tugged a wispy strand free from her braid, nudging it onto her cheek. Telling himself not to do it—and studiously ignoring himself—he lifted a hand to the flyaway tress and tucked it behind her ear. At the same time, she mimicked the gesture, and their fingers brushed against each other, and they both laughed lightly at the collision.

And then, although he honestly, genuinely, truly didn't plan it, he was dipping his head toward hers, and covering her mouth with his. He brushed his lips lightly across her own, once, twice, three times, four. Then, when she did nothing to discourage him, he cupped her face in both of his hands, tilted her head back, and kissed her again. Longer this time. More eloquently. Deeper. And then Audrey was circling her fingers around his wrists and kissing him back, and heat surged through Nathaniel like nothing he had felt before. It poured into his chest, doused his stomach and groin, then shot up like a volcanic explosion, filling and searing every last inch of him.

And then there was something else there, too, something as gentle and fine as the heat was jagged and fierce. Something unlike anything he'd ever felt before. It was something that tempered the passion with tenderness, and the need with hope. Something that comforted and consoled even as it agitated and aroused.

But before he could identify what it was, both the heat and the something evaporated, and he was enveloped in the bleak, soulless cold that had filled him before. Because

Audrey tore her mouth from his, dropped her hands from his wrists, took three giant steps backward and, after gazing at him in horror for a moment, turned away.

Not sure what to do—since, hell, he wasn't even sure what to feel—he covered the distance between them and, after only a small hesitation, settled his hand gently on her shoulder. She immediately shrugged it off and took another step away, so Nathaniel dropped both hands to his sides.

"I'm sorry," he said softly, even though he wasn't. Not sorry for kissing her, anyway. Not sorry she kissed him back.

When she said nothing in response to his apology, he strode around to her front, and wasn't much surprised when she dropped her head into her hands to avoid looking at him.

"Audrey, I'm sorry," he said again. "I shouldn't have done that. I just . . ." What? he asked himself. Couldn't resist her? Wanted to take a chance that maybe she was thinking the same thing he'd been thinking?

Then again, maybe he hadn't been thinking anything. Maybe he'd only been feeling something. Just what he'd been feeling, though . . .

"Audrey, please say something," he said. "Even if it's something like 'How dare you, you big jerk.'"

She dropped her hands at that and looked at him. "How dare *you?*" she echoed. Only she put the emphasis way different than he had and didn't include the jerk part, which should have made him feel better, but somehow only made him feel worse. "How about 'How dare *me?*'"

"What are you talking about?" he asked. "I'm the one who kissed you. After obviously mixing signals in the worst way."

She shook her head. "No, that's the problem, Nathaniel. You didn't mix the signals at all. I kissed you."

And that was a problem? he wondered.

Oh, yeah, he immediately answered himself. It doubtless was for a woman who wore a wedding ring that hadn't been given to her by the guy that kissed her.

"Audrey," he began.

"Nathaniel," she said at the same time.

Being a gentleman—yeah, right—he deferred to her. "Go ahead."

"That shouldn't have happened," she said plainly.

"Maybe," he replied softly. "Maybe not. No matter what, though, Audrey, you didn't do anything wrong."

"Says you."

"Says anyone who would have knowledge of the situation." She started to say something else, but this time, he plunged on, striving to keep his tone gentle. "You still wear a wedding ring, and it's admirable that you're still bound to the vows it represents. But one of those vows was 'til death do you part. And, Audrey, Sean is dead."

Tears sprang to her eyes at that, and Nathaniel cursed himself for not being gentle enough. But what was he supposed to do? What was he supposed to say? There was no good way to remind a woman that the man she used to love, the man she continued to love, was dead. But he didn't want her to feel guilty for something she shouldn't feel guilty about. She really hadn't done anything wrong. She hadn't even been unfaithful to her husband's memory. No one said she had to stop loving Sean, even if she started to care for someone else.

And Nathaniel, God help him, was hoping she had begun to care for him. Because he was beginning to care very much for her. No, he didn't know how far this thing between them would go. He didn't even know if it was borne of anything other than the fact that he knew she was the only one who could help him reclaim his soul. All he knew was that, since meeting Audrey, there was something there that he hadn't experienced with anyone else. He was feeling things for her he hadn't felt for anyone else. And maybe, just maybe, whatever it was would grow into something neither of them had expected, but that both of them welcomed. Because as much as it surprised him to realize it, he wouldn't object to having someone like Audrey Magill in his life.

No, not someone like Audrey Magill. Audrey Magill herself. Because if he was experiencing and feeling things he hadn't experienced or felt before, it was due to her. And something told him that even after they recovered his soul—and please, for the sake of all that was good and soulful, let them recover his soul—there would still be a bond between them.

"I know Sean is dead," she said. "Believe me, Nathaniel, no one knows that better than I do."

"Audrey, I didn't mean—"

But she cut him off before he could explain. "But this . . . this . . ." She waved her hand anxiously between the two of them to illustrate what she couldn't find a word for. "Whatever this is, it feels . . ." She expelled a restless sound, then her entire body slumped forward. "It feels . . ."

"Wrong?" he finished halfheartedly for her.

She shook her head, looking even more wounded than before. "No. That's just it. It doesn't feel wrong."

Heat filled his belly again, that same false-but-somehow-not-false heat that had overcome him before. "I don't get it then. If it doesn't feel wrong, what's the problem?"

A single tear slipped from her eye, but she swiped it away so quickly, Nathaniel was almost able to convince himself he never saw it. Almost.

"That *is* the problem," she said softly. "That it doesn't feel wrong." And then, before he had a chance to say anything more—not that he honestly had any idea what to say—she hurried on, "I'll go talk to Leo tomorrow. And I'll let you know what he says. In the meantime, see what your detective can find out about Nicholas Pearson." She finally looked him in the eye, but only long enough to look away again. "I'll call you tomorrow," she said.

And then, without another word, she fled.

· Eleven ·

AUDREY HADN'T VISITED SEAN'S PRECINCT FOR
nearly three years, not since collecting his effects from his
locker and formally thanking his fellow officers for the
scholarship fund they'd set up in his name. She'd stayed in
touch with some of them for a while after his death, but there
was only one she had spoken to with any regularity . . . even
if that regularity had become more and more irregular over
the years. Leo Rubens had been Sean's partner since before
Audrey met him, and the two had shared the same sort of
bond that was legendary among uniformed police officers.
They'd been friends both on and off the force, and, in many
ways, had been closer than they were to their respective
wives. Audrey had never really socialized with Leo's wife
Janet outside gatherings of their foursome, but she'd liked
her. And she still sent birthday cards to the Rubens kids,
Jacob and Lucy, even though she hadn't seen either of them
for more than a year.

As she stood on the steps of the precinct, shoring up her
nerve to enter, she tried to remember the last time she'd
physically spoken to Leo. It must have been on the phone,

but she honestly couldn't remember when it might have
been, or under what circumstances. Probably, she had
needed to know something about Sean's benefits. Or maybe
there had been some new development in the case against
the man who had killed him, a man who was serving a life
sentence in Eddyville, but whose conviction was under
continuous appeal. She hadn't seen Leo face-to-face for a
long, long time.

But she'd called before coming today to make sure Leo
still worked here, and she'd made it a point to come early
enough that he should still be at his desk. She'd stopped
short of calling him to ask when would be the best time to
see him, because . . .

Actually, she wasn't sure why she'd stopped short of
doing that. Just, every time she'd punched the Rubenses'
number into her telephone, she hadn't been able to hit that
last seven that would have connected her. She'd needed
more time to prepare herself, she'd told herself. Or she
hadn't wanted to call them so late in the day. Or so early in
the day. Or at lunchtime. Or at suppertime. Or at any other
time. It wasn't because she still felt guilty about the kiss
she'd shared with Nathaniel.

There. She'd made herself think about it again. Not that
that was such a difficult thing to do since, in the thirty-
seven hours, forty-eight minutes and—she checked her
watch—twenty-two seconds since that kiss had happened,
there had been times when she hadn't been able to think
about anything else. And not just during those times when
she was avoiding Nathaniel's phone calls, of which there
had been more than a few. And it wasn't just the memory
of the kiss she kept trying to bury. It was the feeling that
had come over her while she was kissing him. And the
feelings she'd had afterward. Because kissing Nathaniel,
before during *and* after, had made her feel . . .

She grew warm all over remembering. She wasn't sure
how it had happened or when, exactly, she'd realized he
intended to kiss her. But she *had* realized what he was
going to do, even before he'd lowered his head to hers. And

she'd done nothing to keep it from happening. Because she'd wanted to kiss Nathaniel. Holding hands with him the way she had when they were together, as polite as her intentions had been in making the gesture, had reminded her of how good it felt to simply be close to another human being. Another *male* human being. She'd forgotten how important even innocent touches were when it came to feeling human. And she'd forgotten just how a man could make a woman feel by simply touching her. Like . . . a woman. It had been a long, long time since Audrey had felt that way. Too long.

Much, much too long.

So she'd done her best not to think about those touches with Nathaniel. Because they'd begun to feel less innocent with each new encounter. And she hadn't thought about them. Until she and Nathaniel had been standing by the river, and the wind had nudged a strand of hair onto her cheek, and they'd both reached for it at the same time and gazed at each other at the same time, and then, suddenly, there was something arcing between them that hadn't been there before, and she'd found herself wanting to see if . . .

Well. She'd just found herself wanting, that was all. And when Nathaniel had dipped his head to hers and kissed her, that wanting had turned quickly into needing. And then need had become demand. A blind, all-consuming, damn-the-torpedoes-and-full-speed-ahead demand. And then all she'd been able to think about was how close her house was, how they could be there in minutes and fall into her bed, how it would feel to lie naked beneath him, her legs wrapped around his torso as he drove himself inside her, deeper and deeper with every thrust, until they were both insensate with—

She closed her eyes and inhaled a shaky breath, pushing the thoughts back to the dark recesses of her brain where she'd tried to keep them contained. She had to stop thinking about Nathaniel the way she kept thinking about him. Because every thought like that felt like a betrayal of Sean. Rationally, she knew that wasn't true. It was impossible to be unfaithful to Sean since she was no longer, technically, married to him. But Audrey's marriage had never been technical. It had been emotional. It had been spiritual. It had been physical. Even without the license and the white dress and the ceremony, she would have been married to him. Because the way she had felt about him had made her married to him. Just because he was gone, that feeling didn't change.

And even if she could find it in herself to have feelings for someone else, Nathaniel wasn't the kind of man to fall in love. Not the way Audrey did. Not with one woman, 'til death did they part. Especially since, in her case, anyway, even death couldn't put asunder what had been brought together.

She forced that thought, too, to the back of her brain, and focused on the task ahead. Smoothing one hand over her tailored blue shirt and khaki skirt, and the other over the tortoiseshell barrette she'd used to clip back her hair, she told herself to stop stalling and go inside.

When she did, she was immediately assailed by more forgotten memories. The incessant ringing of the phones, the unsteady thrum of voices, the sudden, unexpected burst of profanity. The glare of sunlight pouring through sooty windows, the unremarkable, government-issued furnishings, the acridly sweet aroma of industrial strength cleaner that could never quite mask the overripe smell of the detainees.

She held her breath as a maelstrom of impressions engulfed her, halfway expecting time and activity to come to a complete halt while she deflected them all, the way it might in the movies. But nothing stopped. Everything kept moving. The same way her life had since Sean's death, no matter how many times she'd tried to stop, if only for a few seconds, so she might have just a moment, one tiny, itty-bitty moment, of peace.

She darted her gaze around the room, looking for Leo. Finally, she found him, sitting behind a battered desk in the corner of the room. He was standing with one hand on his hip, a telephone pressed to his ear. He'd gained some weight since his promotion, she saw, and he was a bit grayer on top. He was the physical antithesis of Sean, with dark hair and eyes and a build like a sparkplug, but she'd always thought him good-looking, in a rugged, backwoodsman kind of way. Out of uniform, though, and dressed in a nondescript brown suit and patterned tie, he'd been robbed of some of his charm. Then he smiled at something whoever he was talking to said, and the gesture lit his features in a way that reminded Audrey of the way he used to be, and that made her feel better. She had been right to come, regardless of how strange it felt to be here. Leo, she was sure, could help.

She picked her way across the squad room to his desk, but stopped a few feet away and remained silent while he finished his conversation. He'd turned by now and sat on the top of his desk with his back to her, gazing out the window at the buildings on the other side of the street. He murmured a few more questions, received a few more answers, then hung up the phone and turned to sit down in his chair. That was when he saw Audrey, and halted before completing the action.

"Audrey," he said, his voice tinted with his surprise.

She lifted a hand in greeting. "Hey, Leo."

He smiled at that and came around from behind the desk, pulling her into a fierce hug she was certain resulted more from his feelings for Sean than his feelings for her. "It's good to see you," he said as he held her. "How the hell are ya?"

"I'm good, Leo," she said as she hugged him back, her response, too, stemming more from memories of how she'd felt when she saw him with Sean than how she saw him now. When they pulled apart, she added, "How's Janet? How are the kids?"

"Good," he told her. "They're all good."

What followed was a good ten minutes of getting caught up, not just with Leo's family, but with mutual acquaintances they used to share, some of whom Audrey genuinely couldn't remember, but pretended to, because it seemed important to Leo that she did. Finally, though, knowing she couldn't have come because she wanted to revisit the past, he asked the question she'd been waiting to hear.

"So what can I do for you, Audrey?"

She chose her words carefully, not wanting to reveal any more than she had to about the situation—particularly the part where she'd have to tell Leo she was getting her information from a ghost who was haunting her house—and because what she was going to ask him to do might be a no-no if there wasn't an official investigation into any wrongdoing. "I was hoping you could help me look into a matter that might, maybe, possibly have some criminal implications."

His dark eyebrows shot up at that. "You involved in something you shouldn't be, Mrs. Magill?"

He immediately looked contrite. *Mrs. Magill* was what both he and Sean had called her when they were kidding around, the way they'd called Janet *Mrs. Rubens* in the same spirit, and in the way Audrey and Janet had referred to their husbands as *Mr. Whatever.* "I mean . . ." he began. Then he halted abruptly, as if he wasn't sure what to say.

"It's okay, Leo," she said. "I'm still Mrs. Magill." Not sure why she did it, she added, "I'll always be Mrs. Magill."

He eyed her curiously. "Then you're not . . ."

"What?"

"Seeing anyone?"

The question surprised her. It also flustered her. Mostly because the answer should be cut and dried—not to mention obvious—and it was clearly none of those things. Not even to Leo. Nevertheless, "Of course not," she said. Sounding—oh, dammit—flustered.

"Oh," he replied. But there was a note of puzzlement in his voice, and she wasn't sure if it was because he'd picked up on the flustered part, or because he had thought she would answer differently.

Surely, it was the first, she told herself. How could Leo possibly think she might be seeing someone? Even if, in a way, she had kind of been seeing someone?

Telling herself to just drop it there, Audrey heard herself say anyway, "You sound surprised."

He lifted a shoulder and let it drop, then leaned back in his chair in a way that was probably supposed to look careless, but didn't really. "No, it's not that. Just . . ."

"What?"

He shrugged again. And looked even less careless this time. "I don't know. I just thought that by now . . . I mean, it's been almost three years . . . And you're so . . . And Sean wouldn't have wanted . . ."

For some reason, Audrey's back went up at that. "Sean wouldn't have wanted what?" she asked, a little more crisply than she intended.

But instead of being offended by her tone, Leo smiled a sad, gentle smile. "He wouldn't have wanted you to be alone, Audrey. Not for the rest of your life."

She wasn't sure how to respond to that, so she only said, "I like being alone."

He didn't look convinced. As if to illustrate that, he asked, "Do you now?"

She nodded. "Of course. I was alone when I met Sean, wasn't I?"

"You were," he agreed. "In fact, Janet and I used to wonder what a rowdy extrovert like Sean could see in a straitlaced introvert like you."

Now it was Audrey's turn to smile sadly. "You're not the only one. I could never really figure out what drew the two of us together, either."

"It ended up being a good thing, though," Leo told her. "You two rubbed off on each other in a good way. You brought Sean down to earth and smoothed his edge, and he brought you out of your shell."

Audrey had forgotten about that. About how Sean had been prone to wildness and frat boy behavior when she first met him, and how she'd been a little too cautious and uncompromising. They really had been very different from each other in so many ways. But they'd managed to end up on common ground and stay tethered there together.

"Anyway," Leo said, "I find it odd that some guy hasn't snatched you up by now."

"Some guy did," Audrey said. "Sean Magill."

Leo studied her intently for a moment. "So he did. And that guy wanted you to be happy," he said softly.

"He did make me happy."

Leo nodded. "Until the day he died."

Audrey could guess where this was going, so she softly petitioned, "Leo, this isn't . . ."

"He didn't just want you to be happy while he was married to you," Leo went on anyway, pointedly ignoring her. "He would've wanted you to be happy even after he died."

"Leo . . ."

But Leo obviously didn't intend to let up until he told her what he wanted—maybe even needed—to tell her. "He wouldn't have wanted you to always be Mrs. Magill, Audrey. He would have wanted you to move on with your life."

Still not sure what she should say, Audrey nevertheless objected halfheartedly, "Leo . . ."

"He would have wanted you to see other men."

Okay, she *did* know what to say in response to that. "You can't possibly know what you're talking about, Leo."

"Oh, can't I?"

She shook her head.

He leaned forward over his desk, resting his arms on its surface, settling one hand over the other. She couldn't help thinking he looked just like Ward Cleaver did whenever he was about to teach Wally and the Beave a lesson about life.

"Look, Audrey, when you're a beat cop, you and your partner talk a lot. It gets boring driving around in a car all day. And what you talk about more than anything—even sports statistics, which I know will come as a surprise to women everywhere—is your family. And when you're a cop, it's always, always at the back of your head that every morning, when you say good-bye to that family, it could be the last time you ever see them."

Audrey knew that. She knew that because, every single morning during her marriage, when Sean had kissed her good-bye, he'd done it with all the passion and Hollywood excess of a fabulous forties film. He could make that kiss on the beach in *From Here to Eternity* look like a quick peck on the cheek from great-aunt Edna.

"Sean and I both talked about what would happen to you and Janet if something happened to us," Leo continued. "And we both decided, unequivocally, that if we ever went to that great doughnut shop in the sky, you should both move on." He grinned. "After a proper period of mourning, of course. If either one of you ran off with some young buff rugby player named Serge the week after the funeral or something, we'd come back and haunt you but good."

Audrey's stomach knotted at that. If he had even an inkling . . .

"'Cause we knew that if anything happened to you or Janet, you'd want me and Sean to move on, too." He hurried on, "After a proper period of mourning, of course. It's not like we'd run off with some young, stacked cocktail waitress named Brandi the week after the funeral or something. We'd wait at least, oh . . . a month." He grinned again, to let Audrey know he was kidding . . . mostly.

She said nothing for a moment, and just tried to digest what he'd told her. She could believe the two men talked about such things. And she could believe they both said what they had. But had they meant them? Or had it all been talk?

"Do you think Sean meant what he said?" she asked.

"That you should move on? Sure."

"No, I mean the part about how he would move on."

Leo hesitated only a moment, then nodded. "Yeah, Audrey. He did mean it. The same way he meant you should go on, too. Especially if it happened at a time when you—and he, for that matter—were young and still had decades of life ahead of you. It's not right to expect someone to stay faithful to a ghost. Not when that person has such an incredible capacity to love. The way Sean did. The way you do."

She started to say something else, but, honestly, she was so knotted up inside by now that she wasn't sure what she was even feeling, let alone what she wanted to say. Leo seemed to understand, because after clearing his throat indelicately in a way that said, *Let's move on*, he changed the subject.

"So tell me about this maybe, possibly criminal activity you're involved in."

As grateful as she was for the switch to a new topic, she couldn't quite nudge the concept of Sean moving on to the back of her brain. Probably because she'd already pushed so much to the back of her brain today that there was no more room there for anything else. It did, however, step to the side enough that she knew it would wait while she finished with this matter before stepping forward to demand consideration again.

"What do you know about Edward Dryden of Dryden Properties?" she asked Leo. Might as well just get to the heart of the matter right off.

His expression changed not at all. In fact, he leaned back in his chair this time in a way that was genuinely relaxed and folded his arms to cup the back of his head in his hands. "I know he's a big shot developer who's got a lot of projects going up downtown, especially on those blocks of Main Street the city is most interested in revitalizing."

"That's all?" Audrey asked.

He did the shrug thing again, and again, this time it looked sincere. "What else am I supposed to know?"

"Oh, I don't know," she said. "Maybe that he's linked to some big crime syndicate on the eastern seaboard?"

Leo laughed at that. "You know, one of the nice things about working as a cop in this city is that we don't have a big organized crime element thriving here."

"There are gangs."

"Yeah, and that problem is one we're aware of and on top of. But we don't have any budding Tony Sopranos or Teflon Dons here, Audrey. And even if we did, Edward Dryden wouldn't even make the long list of suspects. He's an upright guy as far as I know. His business is legit enough that the city has hired him for jobs from time to time. He contributes to a lot of social programs, both private and public. A lot of his employees are regular volunteers. There's not even a whiff of scandal about the guy."

"So he's a regular bastion of the community," she said dryly.

"Well, I don't know that I'd call him a bastion, since he came here from Philadelphia, but—"

"Philadelphia," Audrey repeated as she sat up straighter in her chair. "They had a Teflon Don."

Leo laughed again. "They also have my cousin Patricia who teaches first-graders and does recordings for the blind."

"I know, but—"

"Why the interest in Edward Dryden?"

There was no way she could tell him a ghost had told her the guy was shady and needed looking into. So she only said, "A friend of mine has invested in one of Dryden's projects, and now he's worried about where his money is going. He's . . . heard things," she said evasively, "that make him think maybe there's something shady going on."

"*He's* worried?" Leo repeated, smiling. "*He's* heard things? So this friend of yours is a guy?"

"The *guy* is a *friend*," Audrey corrected.

"Oh. Okay. I see." But something in his voice told her he didn't see it that way at all, and that maybe their previous exchange had come about at just the perfect time.

"Anyway," Audrey forged ahead, "he has reason to think maybe Dryden isn't who or what he says he is. He has reason to think maybe the guy is or has been involved in things that might, maybe, possibly be illegal. And I was wondering if maybe you could . . . if it would be possible for you to . . ."

"You want me to look into the guy's background?" Leo asked.

"Can you?"

"Yeah, sure. I can run a rudimentary check on him. See if anything comes up that looks off."

"There's another name, too, that's come up," she told him. "Nicholas Pearson. Does that ring a bell?"

Leo shook his head. "Can't say that it does. But I'll add him to the list." As if to illustrate that, he picked up a pen and scribbled both names into a small notebook he pulled from his inside jacket pocket. "Gimme a call day after tomorrow," he added as he completed the gesture. "I should know something by then."

Audrey expelled a breath she hadn't been aware of holding and said, "Thanks, Leo."

"I'll do this under one condition," he interjected.

Uh-oh. "What's that?"

He grinned that knowing grin again. "That you bring this *friend* around to meet me and Janet sometime."

Audrey nodded unenthusiastically. "Sure, Leo. No problem." Provided, of course, Nathaniel was still around after all this. Because if they didn't figure out a way to get his soul back, there was no way of telling what would happen. And even if they did get his soul back, there was no way to know how long his interest in Audrey would remain. If it would even remain at all.

SEAN WOULD HAVE MOVED ON AFTER HER DEATH.

Audrey lay awake in her bed the night after talking to Leo—and after another day of avoiding Nathaniel's calls, of which there had been more than a few—thinking about everything her husband's former partner had told her. How Sean had said he would want her to move on in the event of his death. How he would have moved on himself in the event of hers. What did that say about his feelings for her? she wondered. What did it say about hers for him? Was she being unrealistic, thinking she would never fall in love again? Especially in light of the fact that she'd always been certain she would never fall in love in the first place, and then Sean had come along to make her see how wrong she was about that?

She wondered again where he was now. He'd been a good

guy in life, so he must have ended up in a good place after his death. But why had Silas been able to return from the afterlife to contact her when she was a total stranger to him, but her husband, who had loved her, had not. Just how did the hereafter work, anyway? Did souls interact with each other? Did people walk around in some alternate dimension looking the way they had in life, having conversations? Or was there simply some kind of disembodied state of consciousness where you were aware of things? Of other beings? Were there feelings in the afterlife? Was there laughter? Was there joy? Was there companionship? Was it possible that Sean had indeed moved on in the place where he was? Had he met someone there? Had he built a life for himself in the hereafter with someone else? Why hadn't he returned to her since it was clear that return was possible?

"Silas," she said softly into the darkness. "Are you around?" When he didn't reply or appear, she repeated, a little more loudly, "Silas? Are you there?"

She'd heard nothing of him for days, not since he'd given her the name Nicholas Pearson. Cecilia said he sometimes visited her when the shop was empty and Audrey was in the office seeing to paperwork or out running errands. But she said they only talked about the sort of getting-to-know-you things people talked about when they were getting to know each other. He'd told her nothing of Nathaniel's situation, clearly leaving that to Audrey. Cecilia said she'd learned more about the operation of paddle wheelers and the commercial routes between New Orleans and Philadelphia than she probably needed to know, but judging by the pink blooming on her cheeks when she told Audrey that, she clearly hadn't minded the lessons.

If Audrey didn't know better, she'd swear Cecilia was falling for Silas. But surely she knew better than to have feelings for a ghost. Yes, Silas was handsome and charming and strangely nice to have around. But there was that state of deadness to consider. That could really put a damper on any potential romantic relationship that might develop between the two. Who knew how long he was going to be earthbound? Not to mention, sometimes he could be so . . . so . . . Victorian. And how could you hug a ghost? Or hold hands with a ghost? Or have dinner with a ghost? Talk about your one-sided relationships. Surely those things had occurred to Cecilia. Surely the only feelings she had for Silas were platonic.

"Silas?" Audrey called out again into the darkness. "If you're home, pick up. I need to ask you something."

After another moment of quiet, she heard him say, "Pick up? What the devil does that mean?"

She cringed at his irritated tone. *Why so prickly?* she wondered. She hadn't bothered him for days. "Sorry," she said softly. "Did I wake you?"

"Of course not," he replied, still sounding annoyed. "Do you honestly think I sleep?"

"I never thought about it," she told him. "I mean, there is that old saying and stuff."

"What old saying?"

" 'I'll sleep when I'm dead,' " she said.

"People actually say that?"

"Sometimes."

He expelled a petulant sound. "Then they will be sorely disappointed when they arrive. There is no need for sleep here."

"But what if someone likes sleep?" she asked. "What if someone's an insomniac in life, and their idea of paradise is the ability to fall asleep whenever they want? What kind of eternal bliss is it if the thing they wanted desperately in life can't be found in the hereafter?"

He said nothing for a moment, then, "What do you want, Audrey?"

She turned to the left, toward the direction from which his voice had come. "You know, you don't have to be so snarky. Jeez, I don't hear from you for days, and then when I do, you're mad about something. And Cecilia says you talk to her all the time."

Gee, now who sounded irritated, annoyed, and snarky? Audrey asked herself.

Silas sounded less irritated when he replied, "Cecilia isn't in constant need of information or favors. Cecilia wants only to engage in interesting conversation. Cecilia is a lovely woman whose company I enjoy very much."

"Oh, and I'm not lovely?" she demanded. "You don't enjoy my company?"

"I didn't say that."

"But you implied it."

"No, I was simply stating that when I talk to Cecilia, it's because I wish to engage in lively conversation. When I talk to you, it's because I'm on a mission."

"So with her, it's an assignation and with me it's an assignment."

He said nothing for a moment, then, in a tone that revealed nothing, replied, "Perhaps."

Gee, maybe Cecilia wasn't the only one falling for someone she shouldn't be, Audrey thought. Because Silas sounded kind of besotted himself. She wondered if she should remind him that his world and Cecilia's had only come together because of the very mission he was on, and that there was no way to know what would happen once that mission was complete. Death may not be as final as she'd once thought it was, but it could still be a real conversation killer.

"I'm sorry if you think the only reason I ever want to talk to you is because of your mission or because I have a favor to ask," she said.

There was another brief hesitation, then he said, "I accept your apology. Now then. Why is it you wanted to talk to me?"

Sheepishly, she told him, "I need a favor."

He muttered something under his breath that sounded like "Damnable woman."

In her defense, she added, "Well, at least it's not about your mission in this case."

Sounding only slightly less irritable, he asked, "What is it?"

This time Audrey was the one to hesitate before speaking.

And when she finally did, it was to ask very slowly, "Can you . . . you know . . . find people? On the other side of the veil, I mean?"

He said nothing for a moment, then told her, "I don't know. I've never tried to find anyone on this side."

"Are you able to go back to your side from this side?" she asked. "Like can you move back and forth between this world and your world? Just where do you go when you're not—" She stopped before finishing with *Here bugging me,* and instead said, "Here visiting me."

"I don't go anywhere," he told her. "I'm still here, even when you can't see or hear me. I just . . . Well. I switch off, for lack of a better way to put it."

"How do you switch back on again?"

"When someone thinks about me, it brings me back."

Which explained why Audrey hadn't seen much of him lately, she thought. Her own thoughts had been so focused on Nathaniel that she hadn't thought of much else. But if Cecilia was seeing a lot of Silas, it must mean she was thinking about him a lot. In a word, *Hmm.*

"But could you go back and look for someone?" Audrey asked. "And then come back here and report to me? Is that possible?"

He said nothing for a moment, then, sounding very thoughtful, told her, "I don't know. I can't do it in the way you seem to think, though. I can't just open a door and walk through whenever I want."

"But you were able to find out about Nicholas Pearson after I asked you to see if you could learn more," she pointed out.

"That was merely a matter of the man's name popping into my head when I concentrated on the question you asked about him. I didn't go interviewing people on the other side, asking if they knew him."

"Well, could you do that then? Concentrate on a question I ask to see if you get an answer?"

"I don't know," he said. And something in his voice made her think he didn't want to even try. "Audrey, as I said, I'm not certain of how the rules work. I don't know if I can leave here and go back there. At least not until I've done what I came here to do. And even if I could go back before then, I'm not certain I would be able to return here again if I did."

This time it was Audrey's turn to be thoughtful. "You know," she said, "you kind of sound like you don't want to go back there. Even if you could."

He stepped out of the shadows then, and although he'd claimed to have no need of sleep, he looked more tired than she'd ever seen him. "That's because I'm not certain I do," he said softly.

Audrey pushed herself up on one elbow, cradling her chin in her hand. "Why not? I thought you said it was a nice place."

"It is a nice place, from what I recall," he agreed. "But then, so is this place."

"I thought you didn't like the way things have changed so much here in the time since you've been gone."

"Yes, well, I've changed my mind. Some of those changes have improved the world rather a lot."

"Like computers?"

He shook his head. "No. Like . . . something else."

*More like some*one *else*, Audrey thought. But she only said, "Then you do like it here?"

There was a pregnant pause, followed by a slow, meaningful, "Yes."

"So then what? You're just going to haunt me forever? Never leave me in peace?"

Instead of answering her question, he posed one of his own. "What was the favor you wanted?"

Audrey inhaled deeply and released the breath slowly. "I want you to find someone on the other side the way you found Nicholas Pearson."

"I didn't find Nicholas Pearson," he reminded her. "I merely received the man's name. So who is it you—" He halted abruptly, sighed wearily, and frowned. "You want me to look for your husband." It was a statement, not a question.

"Do you think you could find him?"

"I don't know, Audrey."

"Well, could you at least try?"

"Why do you want me to find him? What do you hope to achieve?"

"I just want to . . . talk to him," she said. "If I can. There's a question I need to ask him."

"Perhaps I could ask him for you. Assuming I find him. Assuming he wants to be found."

"He has to want to be found in order to actually be found?"

"I believe so, yes."

"How do you know?"

"I just do."

This time it was Audrey's turn to remain silent, since, really, what more was there to say?

"You're certain you want me to find him?"

"Yes," she replied without hesitation.

"Even if the answer you receive to your question may not be the one you want to hear?"

This time there was some hesitation. But she replied, honestly, "Yes."

"I'll see what I can do."

"Thank you, Silas."

He took a few steps backward, until he dissolved into the darkness. But she heard him say, as if from a great distance away, "Good night, Audrey."

"Good night, Silas."

And then, somehow, she knew he was gone. She was about to close her eyes and hope for sleep, but the phone rang suddenly, jarring her back. When she saw Nathaniel's cell number on the caller ID, she reluctantly reached for it. She couldn't avoid him forever. Eventually, they were going to have to talk. Not just about Edward Dryden and Nicholas Pearson, but about that kiss on the river two nights ago.

She pressed the phone to her ear and said quietly, "Hello, Nathaniel."

There was a pause much like the ones she'd just heard from his great-great-et-cetera grandfather, then, "You're home," he said, sounding slightly incredulous. *Translation*, she thought, *You're speaking to me.*

She sighed heavily but lay back down, the phone still held to her ear. "Yeah, listen, I'm sorry I've been incommunicado for the last couple of days."

"I'm sorry about that, too."

She told herself she only imagined the hurt in his voice and hurried on, "I've been really busy at the shop." Although that was true, it wasn't, of course, why she hadn't been answering her phone.

"I understand," he said. Though he didn't sound like he understood at all. "I'm sorry to call so late. I hope I didn't wake you."

"No, I'm still up." *Talking to my ghost,* she added to herself. *Asking him to see if he can hook me up with my dead husband.*

"Did you talk to your husband's friend?"

Did his voice sound a little anxious when he asked that? Audrey wondered. *And if so, why?* "Yeah. He's going to look into Edward Dryden and Nicholas Pearson both and see what he finds. He seems to think Edward's a perfectly legitimate businessman, though."

"I hate to say I told you so."

"Then tell me something else," she said, doing her best not to sound irritated, annoyed, and snarky.

"I talked to my guy, too," he told her. "And he found out some interesting stuff about Pearson."

"That was fast."

"Yeah, well, when you pay someone that much money, they'd better be." Before she could comment on that, he hurried on, "Can we meet somewhere tomorrow?"

Although she told herself it would be a bad idea to see him in person, she couldn't see any way to avoid it. Maybe she could tomorrow, but she couldn't forever. "Sure," she said.

She started to say something about dinner, then decided

that might be asking for trouble, because that was becoming a habit. A *dating* habit, at that. So she started to invite him over to her house, but wasn't sure that was such a good idea, either.

He took the matter out of her hands, however, when he said, "Why don't you come over to my place after you close up shop for the day?"

Oooh, that was the worst idea of all, she thought. So, unable to come up with anything else, she told him, "Actually, I think I'm going to have to work kind of late tomorrow. Why don't you come by here on your way home?" Because of the three choices, that seemed the least dangerous. Audrey could be in control on her own turf, right? Never mind that her control always fled whenever she was around Nathaniel.

He said nothing for a moment, and she feared he would press her on the come-on-a-my-house thing. But all he said was, "I'll bring dinner with me. You like Chinese?"

"I love Chinese. Bring me anything lo mein."

"Will do. See you around seven?"

"That will be fine," Audrey said. She just wished a little lo mein was all it took to make things fine.

· Twelve ·

CECILIA WAS DREAMING. SHE KNEW SHE WAS dreaming, even before she looked down at the strange outfit she was wearing—a dark red satin dress trimmed in gold whose overly frilly straps fell from both shoulders. It was, she was almost positive, the same dress she'd seen on one of the dancing girls in the movie *Show Boat* when she was a kid. Likewise from *Show Boat* was the dancehall scenery she'd conjured for the backdrop of her dream—all crystal chandeliers and red brocade wallpaper and polished hardwood floors—not to mention the Dixieland jazz band playing in the corner of the room. Though they played with infinitely less verve and fewer tambourines than they had in *Show Boat*. Thank God.

What she hadn't borrowed from *Show Boat* for her dream was Silas Summerfield, since she distinctly remembered Cap'n Andy Hawks being played by Joe E. Brown, and he'd worn some ridiculous Hollywood getup that had been even more embellished than the dancing girls' dresses. Silas had way more in common with charming gambler Howard Keel, though he didn't look like the type to break into song. His captain's uniform, she was sure, was the actual one he'd worn on his own riverboat, since somehow she knew he was in her dream as himself, and not some Tinseltown-generated idea she'd dredged up from the back of her brain. He was dressed almost completely in black, from the toes of his black boots to the cap tilted jauntily—because what else would a nineteenth-century riverboat captain be but jaunty?—on his head. The only things that weren't black were his crisp white shirt—bound at the collar with a black string tie—the double row of brass buttons on his jacket, and the tidy gold trim of his epaulets.

He stood in the doorway of the dance hall, his gaze fixed on hers, the night behind him as black as his clothes, splashed with stars that twinkled like his buttons. When he entered, he immediately swept his cap from his head and tucked it under one arm, and strode leisurely—but purposefully—toward the table where she sat. Except for the band, the room was empty, but even the musicians seemed to fade to the background as Silas drew nearer. The song they were playing became muted and mellow, the perfect accompaniment for the frosty bottle of champagne that suddenly appeared on the table, chilling in a sweaty silver ice bucket beside two elegant long-stemmed flutes.

Silas said not a word when he joined her, only tilted his head forward in acknowledgement and reached for the champagne, to open it. The cork left the bottle with a wet, crisp *pop*, then he tilted the bottle over each glass until they were both filled with sparkling, pale gold wine. After tucking the bottle back into its nest of ice, he handed one glass to Cecilia, then lifted the other into the air.

"To you, my dear," he said. "The most beautiful woman aboard."

Cecilia sipped the wine, savoring the clean, bracing taste of it, relishing the way it cooled her throat on the way down. Wow. She never got this kind of detail in her dreams. This was really, really . . . cool.

"Well, this is different," she said as she lowered the glass to the table again. "Usually I only have anxiety dreams. I can't find my car in the parking garage or can't find my room in a hotel. Or I have fifteen minutes to bake a hundred wedding cakes. That kind of thing. I can safely say I've never dreamed I was a dancehall girl."

He smiled at that. "You're not a dancehall girl in this dream, either," he told her.

"I'm not?"

He shook his head, still smiling.

"Then what am I?"

He inhaled a deep breath and released it slowly. "Well, to put it in the crassest of terms, Cecilia, you're my . . . woman."

A thrill of something hot and not altogether unpleasant rolled through her midsection at hearing him say what he had, the way he had said it—so knowingly, so confidently, so possessively. Hearing any other man say something like that in the same way would have terrified Cecilia. Hearing it from Silas, though, wasn't scary at all. In fact, hearing Silas say it somehow made her feel oddly safe. Safe in a way she'd never felt before. As if she didn't have to look over her shoulder all the time anymore. As if she didn't have to worry about Vincent anymore. Because if Vincent dared to show his face, Silas, her man—Wow, that felt really good to say that—would protect her completely.

She told herself she should be ashamed of herself, liking the idea of a man's protection. She was a twenty-first-century woman. She'd been taking care of herself since she was a teenager. Yeah, well, okay, except for those years with Vincent. But even then, her sense of self-preservation had kicked in at some point, and she'd gotten herself away. She'd rescued herself from her abuser. She didn't need anyone else's protection.

Except that, for some reason, the idea of someone else protecting her suddenly felt kind of nice. It was hard taking care of yourself all the time when you were by yourself. It was scary. It was lonely. What was so terrible about wanting—maybe even needing—a little extra help?

"There's nothing wrong with that, Cecilia," Silas said. "It doesn't matter what century a man is born in. Any man who doesn't feel a fundamental compulsion to take care of the people he loves isn't fit to call himself a man."

She lifted her chin. "And any woman who doesn't feel compelled to do the same thing isn't fit to call herself a woman."

He grinned again, and nodded. "I dare say I'm beginning to like this stronger, more independent version of American womanhood. Provided you don't grow so strong and independent that we men become unnecessary."

She started to tell him that twenty-first-century society had already made men pretty much unnecessary in a lot of ways, thanks to sex toys, sperm banks, and cloning. Then she decided he probably wasn't ready for that aspect of twenty-first-century life, and it might be better to protect him for as long as she could. Besides, men did still come in handy when there was heavy lifting to be done. And even the most ingenious vibrator left a lot to be desired when it came to unclogging a drain.

"You'll never be unnecessary," she assured him. Because any man as beautiful and decent as Silas was would always, always, be needed.

He pulled out the chair beside hers—not the one opposite, she noted—and folded himself into it, setting his cap carefully on the other side of the table. He looked at her hands, cupped one on top of the other, and, after only a small hesitation, covered them with one of his. She braced herself for the staggering shock wave that had shuddered through her when they'd come into contact with each other before, but all she felt this time was the warmth of his bare fingers curling gently over hers. When their gazes met again, she saw that he was as surprised—and delighted—as she by the discovery. But what was truly surprising, not to mention delightful, was Cecilia's reaction to that touch. Because she had become convinced over the past year that she would never welcome a man's touch again.

It was the reason she'd had trouble keeping a job until the

one at Finery. Thanks to what she had suffered during her time with Vincent, she couldn't bear the touch of masculine flesh against her own. She didn't fare much better just being in the same room with a man. Finn and Stephen had been the only exceptions, and only then because of their orientation. No matter how nice the man, or how gentle his disposition, or how unthreatening his demeanor, he made Cecilia feel, at best, uncomfortable, and, at worst, petrified.

Until now. Until Silas.

Of course, it was only because this was a dream, she thought, and everything around her, including Silas, was lacking in substance. He couldn't threaten her, because he didn't exist. Not the way other men did. He was a ghost. A fantasy. A dream.

He twined his fingers with hers, and a thrill of something warm and liquid rushed through her. Funny, but her dreams had never been tactile before.

"This is just a dream, right?" she asked him, just to be sure.

He nodded, his expression saddening some. "Alas, yes. But I had some success conversing with Audrey by entering one of her dreams that first night. I thought perhaps, since you haven't been able to see me before, it might work with you, too."

"How do you do it?" she said.

"I don't," he told her. "You do. By thinking of me during the day, it opens a door in your subconscious I'm able to enter once you're asleep. Which means, Cecilia . . ." He lifted her hand to his mouth and brushed his lips lightly over the backs of her fingers, his warm breath caressing her flesh and making her heart rate triple. ". . . that you were thinking about me today."

She started to deny it, then smiled. What would be the point? "Well, it's kind of hard not to think about you when I feel you brooding behind me all day."

He had started to kiss her hand again, but let it drop a little. She tried not to feel too bereft. "I do not brood," he stated.

She lifted her hand to his mouth again, silently inviting another kiss. Which was extraordinary, because even if Cecilia might have thought she could eventually touch a man without flinching, she'd *never* thought she would want one to kiss her again. Even more amazing, she found herself wanting to kiss him, too. "Well, you're certainly not brooding now," she said a little breathlessly.

He turned her hand over so that her palm was facing up, then bent his head to place a chaste kiss in its center. "I am not," he agreed. "At the moment, I am trying to convince my lovely Cecilia to dance with me."

She had begun to feel dreamily mellow—and not a little aroused—by the warm brush of his mouth over her flesh, but his announcement that he wanted to dance with her doused every wonderful sensation she'd experienced up to that point. Holding hands with a man, even allowing him to kiss her hand, was one thing. Dancing, especially the way they danced in Silas's time, all up close and personal, was something else entirely. Sitting down, he was much less threatening—never mind that this was a dream and all that stuff was relative anyway. Standing up, and virtually surrounding her, as he would be in a dance, was unthinkable.

"Come, Cecilia, you know me better than that," he said softly, once again reading her mind.

Which he of course was going to be able to do, since he was currently wandering around in her brain, being privy to all kinds of things. A lot of which, she couldn't help musing further, she probably didn't want him to be privy to.

"You know I would never hurt you," he added softly.

Her mouth dropped open at that, and the warmth that had seeped into her began to quickly recede, replaced with the sort of chill that swept in on the most brutal winter days. Because Vincent had uttered those very words to her more than once, and in the same cajoling way. *C'mon, Georgia*, he'd say to her old self whenever she told him to stop doing whatever he was doing because it hurt her—be it yelling at her or telling her she looked like a whore in that dress or sleeping with the new hostess at the restaurant. *You know I'd never hurt you.*

And then he had. Every single day. Even before he'd raised a fist to her, he'd hurt her with his words. His actions. His incessant need to dominate. He'd hurt her for years. Deliberately. Almost gleefully. And Cecilia had promised herself she would never let anyone hurt her like that again.

And now Silas was telling her he would never hurt her. How could she be expected to trust him?

"You can trust me, my dear," he said softly, "because I'm not whoever it was who made you feel this way."

She arrowed her brows downward, wondering just how much access Silas had to her thoughts. She didn't think she could bear it if he knew what kind of person she'd been with Vincent. How weak and uncertain, how timid and frightened. "How much do you know about him?" she asked softly.

His dark gaze held hers, so intent that he seemed to be trying to peer right into her soul. Finally, he said, "You have buried him very deeply, Cecilia. I know nothing of him in particular. I know only what you feel for him. Anger. Resentment. Fear."

She said nothing in response to that, but she didn't look away. He turned her hand in his again and wove their fingers together, returning both to the table.

"I only hope," he said softly, "that, in time, you will tell me about him. About you. About that part of your life."

"I don't talk about that," she replied swiftly. "Ever. I just want to forget it happened."

He nodded slowly. "I understand. Unfortunately, though, our memories have a bad habit of not leaving us. Particularly the ones we most wish would go."

There wasn't a whole lot to say in response to that, and indeed Silas didn't seem to expect a reply. Because, still holding her hand, he stood, giving her arm a gentle tug. "Dance with me," he said.

As if cued by his words, the band in the corner of the room segued into a slow, moody number, one Cecilia couldn't recall ever hearing before. And in spite of her earlier feelings about not wanting to dance with him, she reminded herself that this was a dream, not real, so everything was going to be just be fine.

She followed him to the center of the floor, and before she even came to a stop, he was sweeping her into his arms and spinning her around and around. Her steps never faltered, even though she had no idea how to dance this way. Silas held her hand in his and roped his arm around her waist, and she settled her other hand on his broad shoulder. The wool of his jacket was rough beneath her fingertips, and his palm against hers was calloused and strong. His body was hard in all the places hers was soft, angled where hers was curved, yet somehow, they fit together perfectly. The mellow music filled her ears, Silas's masculine scent filled her nose, and utter happiness filled her heart.

She really must be dreaming, she thought, because nothing in life had ever felt this good. But—

"Just whose dream is this, anyway?" she asked him. "I've been thinking all this time it's mine, but I don't know how to dance like this. And I've never heard this song before."

He had started to smile as soon as she asked that first question, in a way that told her he'd had this discussion before, with someone else. "I told you earlier how I'd discovered this was an effective means of communication with Audrey that first day," he said. "But what I discovered after the fact was that, when she dreamed of me, and I entered her subconscious, I brought my subconscious with me. So that her dream became mine, and my dream became hers, so there were elements of both of our experiences to be enjoyed."

"I'm not sure I follow you," Cecilia said. "Do ghosts sleep? Do they dream?"

"No, I don't sleep," he said in a way that told her he and Audrey had already talked about that, too. "But I still carry with me the dreams I had in life, and they mingle with the dreams of those with whom I . . . connect," he finally concluded. "Now that you have dreamed of me once,

Cecilia, you may again. And whenever you do, a part of me will become a part of you. And a part of you will become part of me."

She still wasn't sure she understood. But she decided that, ultimately, it didn't matter. What mattered was that they could touch in her dreams without sparking that strange shock. More important, in her dreams, she welcomed his touch. It had been a long time since she'd touched a man intimately. A long time since she'd wanted to touch a man that way. Now, as she pressed her body to Silas's, she remembered what it was like to enjoy this sensation with someone who truly cared about her. She had forgotten how nice it could be between two people, but as he opened his hand over the small of her back and pushed her closer still, she began to remember. When she tilted her head back to smile at him, he bent and brushed his lips lightly over hers before nuzzling her temple and kissing her there, too. The fire inside her leapt higher, moving into her chest and between her legs, making her feel things—and want things—she hadn't felt or wanted in a very long time.

"Good thing this is only a dream," she said softly. "Otherwise, I might be tempted to do something tonight I'd regret in the morning."

She heard him chuckle softly, the sound rumbling in his chest and making her laugh, too.

"What could possibly be regrettable about anything that might happen tonight?" he asked.

"Oh, please," she replied. "Sex complicates everything between a man and a woman."

"My darling Cecilia, sex is the only thing between a man and a woman that isn't complicated. Don't be such a Victorian."

She did laugh at that, feeling whatever tension was left inside her evaporate. For a long time, the two of them only danced, to a long slow number that seemed to last forever. Which would have been fine with her. The way she felt in her dream, she never wanted to wake up again. In fact, the way she felt in her dream, she wanted to stay with Silas for—

With a gasp and a start, Cecilia awoke, rearing backward in a chair, feeling utterly disoriented, and trying to remember where she was and what she had been doing. Dancing, she recalled. With Silas. No, wait. That had been in the dream. Before that, she she'd been . . .

She opened her eyes and saw that she was sitting in Audrey's office, and her memory came flooding back. She'd been tallying the day's receipts for Finery, sitting at Audrey's desk in Audrey's office, filling out the final paperwork before going home. She'd been so exhausted, she'd laid her head down for just a moment, but she must have nodded off to sleep. Nodded off and dreamed of Silas.

Wow, and it had been one of those weird, realistic dreams, too. The kind you woke up from and it took a few minutes to get acclimated to actual reality. It truly had felt like she was back in time, on a paddle wheeler somewhere on the Ohio, and Silas was there kissing her. No, not a kiss. Not quite. Just a soft brush of his mouth over her lips and temple. Only a breathy, searing hint of what might have come if she'd slept a little longer. The dream had ended before he'd gotten around to *really* kissing her.

Dammit.

And then she remembered something else about the dream. She remembered she'd been able to experience sensually everything going on around her. She'd tasted the champagne. She'd heard the music. She'd felt the scratchy fabric of his jacket. She'd . . . touched Silas. Really touched him. As if he were flesh and blood. He'd felt like flesh and blood. She'd felt the warmth of his bare hand over her own, heard the beating of his heart beneath her ear when they danced, and she'd gotten goose bumps when he brushed his lips so tenderly over hers. It had felt so real. *He* had felt so real. And she had genuinely enjoyed touching him.

But now he was gone. She was alone again. Only this time, somehow, she felt even more alone than she had before. And where before, solitude had brought her comfort, now, suddenly, solitude felt so . . . solitary.

She made herself forget about the dream—for now, at

least, since it wasn't the kind of dream that was easily forgotten—and finished tallying the receipts and filling out the bank deposit slip. Then she put everything in the safe so Audrey could take care of it in the morning. She called up to the third floor to her employer and neighbor—and, she couldn't help thinking, friend—that she was finished for the day and would be going home. Audrey called back her thanks and said she would see Cecilia tomorrow.

After gathering her purse and jacket, Cecilia headed down to the first floor, pausing, as she always did, at Silas's portrait to whisper a soft good-bye to him, as well. This time, though, she also lifted her hand to stroke his oil-on-canvas fingers. "Good night, Silas," she said. And then, still warm from the aftereffects of her dream, she kissed her fingertips and lifted her hand to press it against his heart.

"Good night, Cecilia," she heard him say from behind her. But when she spun around to reply to him, her breath caught in her throat. Because standing in the hallway, as if he'd followed her right out of her dream, was Silas. He was dressed more casually than he'd been in her dream—gone was the jacket and string tie—but was otherwise exactly as he had been when she danced with him, right down to the mischievous, affectionate twinkle in his eyes.

"Silas," she said, smiling, something warm and happy effervescing inside her. "I can see you."

·Thirteen·

NATHANIEL HESITATED BEFORE LIFTING HIS HAND TO the big brass door knocker on Audrey's front door, telling himself there was no reason to feel like a sixteen-year-old kid on his first car date. Unfortunately, he couldn't convince himself. He still felt edgy and anxious about seeing her again after the way they'd parted ways the other night. He reminded himself that he and Audrey weren't kids, and they could face the aftermath of a simple kiss like two adults. He was, after all, a man of forty-one, and she was a woman of . . . thirtysomething.

Strange, but he wasn't sure exactly how old she was. He knew what year she'd graduated from high school, but had she been seventeen or eighteen when she donned cap and gown? Really, now that he thought about it, he realized he knew very little of her, save the facts he had gleaned about her online: where and when she'd gone to school; what she did for a living; that she'd been happily married before becoming a widow. But he knew none of the small things that went into making her Audrey Magill. What had her childhood been like? What was her favorite color? What kind of music did she listen to? What types of books did she like to read? What were her hobbies? What kind of food did she like, other than Chinese and Chow Wagon?

That brought his attention back to the brown paper bag in his hand, inside which was the quickly cooling dinner he'd promised to bring tonight, for this not-a-date-just-getting-caught-up . . . event. To prove that he knew it was not-a-date, he truly had come straight from work—after a stop for their not-a-date dinner—and still wore what he'd had on all day, a dark gray suit with slate blue dress shirt. Though he'd tugged loose his splashy Jerry Garcia necktie and unbuttoned the top two buttons of his shirt in a not-a-date fashion that was the result of wanting to be comfortable and nothing more. Because, in case he hadn't mentioned it, this was not-a-date.

Biting back an irritated sound, he lifted his hand to the big brass knocker and rapped a few times, then waited for sounds of life on the other side. He didn't have to wait long. In fact, the door opened so quickly, he halfway wondered if Audrey had been standing on the other side looking through the peephole while he mustered the nerve to knock. She, too, seemed to be making clear her knowledge that this was not-a-date, because she was still dressed in what she'd probably been wearing all day, too, a straight black skirt and lightweight sweater the color of good cabernet, her hair pulled back from her face, as it always was. But where before she'd always worn a ponytail or braid, this time the style was more severe, a prim bun perched at the back of her head, as if she *really* wanted to make clear that this was not-a-date.

"Hi," she said when she saw him, the single word coming out breathless and nervous.

He held up the brown sack as if it were a spiritual offering. "I bring sustenance for what promises to be a long night." When Audrey's eyes went wide, he realized how what he had said could be misconstrued by anyone who was *not* out on not-a-date. "Oh, man, that came out all wrong." He pretended not to notice that she still looked anxious and uncomfortable. "I just meant we have a lot to talk about, that's all."

She nodded silently and stepped aside, something he hoped meant he should come in. Warily, he took a step forward, and when it looked like she wasn't going to throw anything at him, braved a few more. Eventually he crossed the threshold and then—yes!—he was inside the house without any more missteps. At her nervous invitation, he followed her through the living room that she'd turned into her hat shop, through another room that had doubtless originally been intended as the dining room, but which she'd filled with more hat displays, into a kitchen whose door probably remained closed during the day to give the impression of this building being a business, not a home.

The kitchen was plenty homey, though, its terra-cotta tiles, granite counters, and sage green cabinets giving it an old world *cucina* feel. Copper pots dangled from an overhead grid, and plants sprang up from painted pots in a greenhouse window over the sink, some of which Nathaniel recognized as herbs, some of which were obviously just ornamental. He set the bag of food on a scarred wooden table, noting that Audrey had already set two places on it. On the up side, she'd included wineglasses, which could be interpreted as oh-yes-it-is-too-a-date. On the down side, the places were set on opposite sides of the table instead of side by side.

"So, what other food do you like besides Chinese and Chow Wagon?" he asked as he began withdrawing white paper cartons from the bag.

She looked puzzled by the question. "Why do you ask?"

He shrugged, hoping the gesture looked casual. "Just curious."

"I like just about everything," she told him.

"Any favorites?"

She smiled. "Indian."

He started to say that next time, he'd hit Shalimar or Royal India or India Palace on his way—not that any of those was on his way—then figured they probably weren't supposed to talk about a next time. Even if there would be a next time of some kind. Just probably not the kind he was thinking he'd like it to be.

"So . . . what's your favorite color?" he asked as he began opening the cartons he'd removed from the bag.

She expelled a single, anxious chuckle. "What difference does it make?"

He smiled, hoping the gesture looked casual. "Just making conversation."

She narrowed her eyes at him a little, then said, "Green."

"What's the best book you ever read?"

This time there were two chuckles, but they still sounded anxious. "Nathaniel . . ."

"I've run out of things to read," he said, hoping the statement sounded casual. "I'm always open to recommendations."

She expelled an impatient little sound, but managed a small smile. "I don't know. I guess something by Agatha Christie or Anya Seton. I read for entertainment. Nothing too heavy. Something to take me out of my world and into another one. After years of crunching numbers all day, I like to set my brain free when I read."

He nodded. "Good to know." Then, because he figured luck wasn't much use if you couldn't press it from time to time, he added, "Music? What performers do you like?"

She did laugh at that, and finally, finally, seemed to relax a little. "Nathaniel, why are you asking me this stuff?"

He'd finished opening everything by now, so moved to the counter where a single bottle of wine and a corkscrew sat. Pointing at them in silent question, she nodded, so he went about opening the wine. He was grateful to have the task, because it gave him a good reason for avoiding her gaze.

"I just want to know more about you, Audrey," he said honestly. "It occurred to me today that even though you're in the position of saving my soul, and I'm in the position of relying on you to do that, we know almost nothing about each other, other than the basic essentials of name, occupation, education, and . . ." He hesitated only a moment before concluding, "Marital status."

She dropped her gaze at that, and pink bloomed on each cheek. Okay, so they knew what it was like to kiss each other, too, he amended to himself. Which was extremely good knowledge to have. It still wasn't enough knowledge. He wanted more. And not just knowledge of her raindrops-on-roses favorite things. He wanted to know everything there was to know about Audrey Magill. He wanted to know all the deepest, darkest secrets she carried inside. And he wanted to know every last naked inch of her outside.

But he was getting way ahead of himself. Not surprising, considering the fact that this was territory he'd never explored before. He wasn't used to pursuing women. Mostly because he'd never met one he particularly wanted to pursue. Anything resembling a pursuit that he may have undertaken in the past had been largely perfunctory, since, invariably, the women in question wanted very much to be caught.

Audrey, he knew, wasn't the type to come around on her own. Even though she wanted him at least on some level— there was no denying she'd enjoyed that kiss the other night as much as he had—she was too devoted to the memory of her husband to take the first step. Or even the second step. Or the third, fourth, or fifth. And Nathaniel didn't want to move too quickly or push too hard, lest he scare her off completely. So how did a man go about pursuing—seducing?—a woman who was still in love with another man? Especially when it was likely she would always love that other man? How could he compete with a cherished memory, unless it was to win some affection—or something—from Audrey himself? And how could he win some affection—or something—from her if she didn't even know him?

"My favorite writer is William Faulkner," he said. "And my favorite color is blue. I like Indian food, too, but I like Latin cuisine even more. My favorite performer is Wynton Marsalis, followed closely by his brother Branford. For what it's worth, I don't really have any hobbies these days, but I still have a stamp collection I started as a kid, and I confess that, from time to time, whenever some interesting stamp crosses my desk, I tuck the envelope into a drawer for later extraction." He paused for only a moment before adding, "And my childhood sucked. But I guess it could have been worse. I don't suppose I have any more issues than anyone else in the world does."

He'd watched Audrey carefully as he spoke, and took heart in the fact that she didn't look like she wanted to reach for the phone and call some mental health hotline. Even better, once he was finished, she nodded slowly and said, "My hobby used to be making hats. Now that it's my career, I don't have a lot of time for anything else. I like all kinds of music, but my favorite is probably jazz, too. My childhood was pretty idyllic, actually. My parents doted on me, being the dream-fulfilling only child. On Christmas morning, you could barely see the floor for all the presents. We camped at Red River Gorge every fall and went to King's Island every summer." She shrugged. "But I have issues, too. Mostly I wonder why all the people I love leave me when I need them most."

He wanted to tell her he wasn't going anywhere, wanted to make clear he had every intention of staying in her life as long as she would have him. But he couldn't say that yet, not honestly. At this point, he had no way of knowing how long he would be anywhere. What happened if they didn't get his soul back? How long could a person exist without one? And what kind of existence would it be if he was, in the literal sense, soulless?

He knew there were people who thought he'd lost his soul a long time ago. He'd been called soulless more than once in his adult life. It hadn't been that long ago that he'd told Audrey himself that if he lost his soul, it would be one less thing he'd have to worry about. And hell, at the time, he'd meant it. But that was before he'd gotten to know Audrey. Back when he was, you know . . . soulless. He didn't want to be that way anymore.

So in response to her remark about the people she loved leaving her when she needed them most, Nathaniel only nodded slowly his understanding. Because even if he hadn't understood that before, having never loved anyone, he was beginning to understand it now.

All he said, though, was, "I got chicken, beef, *and* vegetable lo mein. Which do you prefer?"

IT WAS NEARLY DARK, THE LEFTOVERS HAD BEEN divided equally, and the wine bottle was empty when Nathaniel and Audrey finally got around to the reason they'd agreed to meet for not-dinner. In between, she had to admit, they passed a fairly nice hour talking about things other than lost souls, problematic land development, and haunted houses. For instance, Audrey learned that Nathaniel's pick in this year's Derby was the same as hers: Silk Purse, the upstart filly who was a late entry, and whose trainer was taking the world—or, at the very least, Louisville—by storm.

She also learned that Nathaniel had been given two coveted tickets on the *Belle of Louisville* for the Great Steamboat Race on Wednesday that he hadn't planned on using unless he could find someone to tag along. He'd thrown her a meaningful look when he said it, but he hadn't asked if she wanted to tag along. And where Audrey would have thought she would be grateful not to be invited—even if it *would* be a lot of fun to be on the *Belle* during the race— she instead found herself feeling a little disappointed that he hadn't asked.

Which was all the more reason she should be grateful, she told herself. Even if thinking that way made no sense at all.

They were still seated at her kitchen table, but where there had been plenty of light pouring in through the window when they first sat down, now the kitchen was bathed only in the amber light of a small boudoir lamp atop the refrigerator, something that gave the room a warmer,

cozier feel. Nathaniel had removed his suit jacket before
they ate, and now his tie hung unfettered from his collar,
and he'd rolled back the cuffs of his shirt to nearly his
elbow, revealing the strong forearms beneath. He leaned
back in his chair, but his hand rested near the base of his
glass, fingering the stem idly as he studied the ruby red
spirit within.

The scene was much too mellow and pleasant for Audrey's
comfort, so she asked without preamble, "What did your guy
find out about Nicholas Pearson?"

Nathaniel glanced up at that, his gaze unfocused, as if
he'd forgotten where he was or why he was here. Then he
shook off his preoccupation almost literally and said, "A
lot, actually. None of it good."

Audrey leaned forward, bracing her elbows on the table,
and tried not to notice how much closer it brought her to
Nathaniel, and how his scent—a mixture of something soapy,
something spicy, and something utterly, overwhelmingly
male—surrounded her. Of course, she could have leaned
back in her chair again to retreat from his manliness, but she
didn't want to be hasty.

"Like what?" she asked.

He traced the base of his glass with an idle finger,
drawing her eye. Back and forth his middle finger arced on
the half of the circle that faced him before sliding up the
slender stem. Then his thumb began to draw leisurely lines
on the bowl of the glass, up and down . . . up and down . . .
up . . . and . . . down . . . He skimmed his fingertips and
the pad of his thumb over the curves of the glass in a way
that was almost erotic, the same way she imagined he
would guide them over a woman's breast.

Her eyes fluttered closed as images of that very thing
unfolded in her brain. Those hard, blunt fingers sliding
along her collarbone and between her breasts, sifting along
the lower curve of one before moving to circle the nipple of
the other. Then they were tripping down over her ribs and
torso, that long index finger dipping into her navel and out
again, then lower still, into the nest of curls between her

legs, then the damp flesh of her sex, opening her, furrowing through the warm, sensitive folds of skin to penetrate her with long, languid strokes, over and over and—

She snapped her eyes open, only to find Nathaniel gazing at her as if she'd lost her mind . . . or something. Darting her gaze over his shoulder, she lifted her wine to her mouth for a long quaff, never mind that quaffing wine was something she hadn't done since college.

"For one thing," he said in reply to her question, his voice edged with something akin to . . .

Well. Akin to the very thing Audrey had just been feeling herself. She quaffed her wine again.

"For one thing," he tried again, his voice leveling off some this time, "The name Nicholas Pearson has definite ties to organized crime in New Jersey."

Well, that certainly caught her attention enough to make her almost forget about erotic finger action on a wineglass. Almost. "Like to the Teflon Don?" she asked.

"Not that branch of the mob," he told her. "And not that high up. Nicholas Pearson was more of a fringe guy. But he was a wannabe above-the-fringe guy who had aspirations of breaking into that higher echelon. No one took him very seriously, though. They let him in on petty stuff, but mostly used him to take care of problems."

Audrey didn't like the sound of that. "What kind of problems?"

"Problems like people who didn't make timely payments or do things they were supposed to do. Nicholas Pearson was the one who broke fingers and knee caps and beat the hell out of people."

That was petty stuff? Audrey wondered. Then she realized Nathaniel was talking about the guy in the past tense. "You talk like he doesn't work for the mob anymore."

"He doesn't. At least not up in New Jersey. He disappeared about five years ago after being tied to a triple murder."

Yikes. "So how does he fit in with Edward Dryden?"

"I have an idea," Nathaniel said, "but I want to hear

about what you learned at your end first, from . . . your husband's . . . ex-partner."

It didn't escape her notice that he'd stumbled over Sean's name to the point where he couldn't say it. Not that she didn't sympathize. She often had trouble saying Sean's name, too. But that was because she loved and missed him so much. Why would Nathaniel have trouble saying Sean's name?

"So did you hear from . . . Leo is it?"

She nodded. "Actually, he got back to me a lot faster than I thought he would. I didn't expect to hear from him 'till tomorrow."

"What did Leo find out?"

"Nothing like your guy did," she said. "He's still looking, but called today to tell me there weren't any outstanding warrants for the guy. So there must not have been charges pressed in that triple murder."

"No," Nathaniel agreed. "There weren't. And a lot of what my guy found out was doubtless rumor and innuendo. But it would be well-founded rumor and innuendo for him to pass it along," he added before she had a chance to object. "What did Leo find out about Edward?"

"He said Edward Dryden is as squeaky clean as they come," she told him. "That there isn't a whiff of scandal about the guy. In fact," she continued, "Leo told me today he's beginning to think Edward is a little *too* clean. A little *too* scandal-free."

"Meaning?"

"Meaning that everybody has *something* in their background that should show up on a thorough check. Parking violation. Workplace complaint. Something. Especially a guy who works as a developer. Even the best ones who are totally legit have complaints lodged against them about something, even if they're by some perfectionist malcontent client who has nothing better to do with his time than lodge charges against people. But Edward has none."

"Interesting," Nathaniel said. "But what I find even more interesting is that Edward set up his development business in Louisville about four and a half years ago. Before that . . ." His voice trailed off, but he smiled a secretive little smile.

"What?" Audrey asked.

He mimicked her position, bracing his elbows on the table and leaning forward, something that brought his face to within inches of her own. Wow, had she thought his scent surrounded her before? Now she was fairly swimming in it. Not that she was complaining. It was a very nice scent.

"Before that," he said, "this man who now makes his living as a *very* successful developer was working as a middle school English teacher in Vermont."

Audrey found the, ah, development, curious. "That's some career change to make, virtually overnight."

Nathaniel shrugged. "I really didn't give it much thought when I did Edward's initial background check. People, especially of a certain age, sometimes make drastic career changes. For all I knew, the guy paid his way through his English degree working construction and wanted to go back to his roots." He eyed her intently. "Now, though, looking at Edward in a different light . . ."

He left the statement unfinished. So Audrey finished it for him. "Looking at Edward in a different light, it looks like maybe Edward Dryden started off as something . . . and maybe even someone . . . else."

Nathaniel nodded slowly.

"So six months after Nicholas Pearson drops off the face of the earth," Audrey said, "Edward Dryden shows up in Louisville with an entirely new career."

"And then a ghost who's haunting your house," Nathaniel added, "and who has access to things you and I can only imagine, connects the two names in a way that, although hazy, is still connected."

"So how do we prove Nicholas and Edward are the same guy?" she asked. "Other than the fact that they've never been photographed together, I mean. For that matter, how do we even know they *are* the same guy? We're making a lot of assumptions here and jumping to a lot of conclusions."

"Maybe," he concurred. "Which is why . . ." He reached behind himself for the jacket he'd slung over the back of the chair, reached into the inside breast pocket, and withdrew a key. Then he finished the statement, ". . . we're going to need to do a little sleuthing on our own."

"What's that?" Audrey asked.

"A key to the offices of Dryden Properties."

Her mouth fell open at that. "And just how did you find yourself in possession of said key?"

"It's a copy," he told her. He smiled and lifted a finger to his lips in an I've-got-a-secret way. "But I can't reveal my sources."

"You don't have to," she said. "You paid your detective to get that."

His response to that was an almost imperceptible lift to one corner of his mouth that made something in Audrey's midsection do a funny little flip-flop. "I'm not saying."

"Why aren't you paying him to use it?" she asked further. "You can't possibly be thinking you're going to break into his offices yourself."

"Technically, it's not breaking in," he said. "Since we have a key, we won't have to break anything."

"Whoa, whoa, whoa," she said. "What do you mean 'we'?"

But he ignored her question, continuing, "Technically, it will just be illegal entry."

"*Just* illegal entry?" she echoed. "So that means what? The judge will only give us five to ten instead of seven to twelve?"

He shook his head. "It means we can get in and out without Edward ever knowing we were there."

"And just what would *we* be looking for?" Audrey asked, hoping he noted that her emphasis on the *we* was sarcastic and not meant to indicate that she had any intention of joining him in something like this.

"Anything out of the ordinary," he told her.

She shook her head. "Again, I ask you. Why not pay your shady PI to do this?"

"Because my shady PI won't know what's out of the ordinary. He doesn't have enough knowledge of my or Edward's business to know what to look for. I do."

"And why should I go along with this?" Audrey wanted to know.

Nathaniel smiled again. "Because it will be a great adventure?"

"It won't be that great."

"All right. How about so that you can report back to Silas Summerfield after the fact?"

She narrowed her eyes at him. "What do you mean?"

"I mean you can be his eyes and ears. You told me that night at Buck's that he's able to get into your thoughts, right?"

She nodded. She had told him that. Just before she'd gone to the women's room and he'd snaked the check out from under her and paid it. "Yeah . . ." she said.

"So if you go with me and scope the place out, then when you come back here, you can give Silas . . . I don't know, a virtual tour or something. And maybe he'll 'see' something, for lack of a better word, that triggers something for him."

"It might be worth attempting, Audrey."

Those last words came not from Nathaniel, but Silas. When she turned toward the direction from which they'd come, she saw him leaning against the counter, his arms crossed over his midsection, studying her and Nathaniel with much interest.

"Silas is here," she told Nathaniel, still looking at the ghost. "He thinks it might be a good idea for me to do exactly what you're suggesting."

"Great minds and all that," Nathaniel said. "Must run in the Summerfield blood."

"Do you really think it's a good idea?" she asked Silas.

"Well, I'm not sure I'd say it's *good*," he told her. "But it isn't terrible, either." He pushed away from the counter and covered the short distance that lay between them. "The thing is, Audrey, I don't have any ideas that are better. And time is running out," he added.

Something in her chest knotted hard at that. "What do you mean?"

"I mean there's been no progress whatever in winning back Nathaniel's soul. It's been gradually drifting away for two weeks now. It won't stay anchored where it is much longer."

"But you said before that as long as there was still time to undo the deal, Nathaniel's soul was safe. That his soul wouldn't be lost until the buildings were up."

"Yes, well, either I was wrong about that, or something has happened to make the development more permanent. Because the boy's soul is losing ground."

Now something heavy and cold settled in the pit of Audrey's stomach. "How can that be?"

"I don't know. I only know that we . . . you," he corrected himself, "don't have as much time as we once thought. We . . . you . . . need to find a way for Nathaniel to sever his ties to Edward Dryden and scuttle that development as soon as you possibly can. If that means breaking into the man's office . . ."

"It won't be breaking in," she said. "It will be illegal entry."

"Then you need to illegally enter and find whatever you can to help Nathaniel. And you need to do it now."

She turned to look at Nathaniel, and judging by the expression on his face, even though he'd only heard one side of her conversation, he'd gotten the gist—and then some— of what was going on.

"When do we do this?" she asked.

"Are you busy Saturday night?"

· Fourteen ·

FOR ALL THE DOWNTOWN DEVELOPMENT PROJECTS Dryden Properties had under way, the offices for the company were actually located in the 'burbs. In eastern Jefferson County, to be exact, in an area noted for being untainted by things like widespread break-ins and petty theft.

Or even illegal entry.

Audrey and Nathaniel would have had a much easier time masking their activities—or, at least, having them explained away as random—had Edward located his place of business in one of the areas where he actually did business. Not that he was developing any seedy, dangerous neighborhoods—more was the pity—but had his office been located in a more urban environment, it would have been closer to pockets of restless youth who were prone to things like . . .

Well, illegal entry, for example.

But since there were no restless youth to be had this evening, Nathaniel and Audrey would just have to rely on their restless selves. He'd promised her, after all, that they could be in and out without Edward ever knowing they had been there. Provided they went in and out as quickly as possible and did it at a time of night when no one in their right minds would be at the office, even a workaholic like Edward Dryden who spent more time at work than at home. That last was something Nathaniel had assured Audrey he knew a thing or two about—not that he'd had to do much to assure her of that—and he was positive, absolutely, completely, utterly positive, that no one would be around at three A.M on a Sunday morning.

Which was how the two of them came to be sitting in his car—his *other* car, not the more conspicuous Porsche, though as far as Audrey was concerned, a Jaguar sedan was still plenty conspicuous—in the parking lot of the building where Edward kept his offices. Fortunately, the parking lot was in the back of the building instead of the front, which abutted a shopping center that would have been wildly busy any other time. In fact, the first time they had driven through to case the joint—and, really, she had to stop watching film noir if she was starting to use phrases like "case the joint" in her everyday jargon—there had still been a few cars in the parking lot belonging to employees of a couple of nearby restaurants. As of their last pass, however, the shopping center had been nearly vacant. This was as close to deserted as the area was ever going to be.

"It's after three," Nathaniel said from the driver's seat beside her.

He was dressed completely in black, from his trousers to his turtleneck to his leather driving gloves. Audrey was similarly attired, in black jeans and sweater, her own gloves a leopard print velvet, since she only owned mittens otherwise, and she'd never seen anyone with mittens breaking and entering—oh, pardon her, she meant *entering illegally*, of course—on TV.

"It's now or never," he said.

She inhaled a deep, slow breath at the announcement and released it slowly, hoping to steady the rapid-fire beating of her heart. Audrey Fine Magill had never committed a crime in her life. She hadn't earned so much as a parking ticket, ever. Certainly she realized why they had to do what they were doing, and she told herself they did have a key that Nathaniel had acquired, albeit without the owner's knowledge. If they were caught here, in the middle of the night, on a weekend, dressed completely in black, it was going to look a tad suspicious. If a security guard stumbled upon them, they'd have some 'splainin' to do. And if Dryden or one of his stooges—really needed to lay off the film noir—caught them . . .

Well. If Edward was who or what Audrey and Nathaniel suspected him of being, that didn't bear thinking about.

But they weren't going to get caught, she promised herself. It was three A.M. on a Sunday morning, the parking lot was deserted, and they were wearing black. It was everything a private dick and his swell girl Friday needed for success.

Gee, maybe they could stop at the all night rental place and pick up *The Big Sleep* on the way home . . .

Then Nathaniel was opening the driver's side door, and both the overhead light and open-door chime came on, looking and sounding like Big Ben in the dark, silent surroundings.

Some private dick and swell girl Friday they were turning out to be.

Hurriedly, they both exited the black Jag and closed the doors as quietly as possible. With one expressive glance over the hood at each other, Nathaniel nodded once, and they made their way to the building. It was new, brick, made to look like something tourists saw in Williamsburg, and, since the neighborhood was partly residential, partly white collar, and all upscale, not overly secured against pesky plebeian things like crime.

She hoped.

The soft scrape of their feet on the asphalt sounded like a hopped up crowd at a Linkin Park concert to Audrey's ears, and the scratch of the key in the exterior door sounded like a stampede of wildebeests. Her heart rate quadrupled as she waited for Nathaniel to get the door open, and just as the knob turned, a car with a major muffler problem drove past on the other side of the building, quickening her pulse even more. The door, of course, had a squeaky spring that sounded like giant fingernails on a massive blackboard, and when the door finally pushed open, it was with a *whoosh* that sounded like a tsunami.

Not that she was being hyperbolic or anything.

Then Nathaniel was pulling her in behind him and closing the door again. "Phase one complete," he whispered. "You still with me?"

She nodded, not sure she trusted her voice at the moment. The way sound had been magnifying for her, she'd probably sound like the call to the gate at Churchill Downs. Nathaniel must have sensed her anxiety, because he cupped a hand on her shoulder and gave it a gentle squeeze. Funny, though, how that only made her heart hammer faster still.

He flicked on a small penlight and aimed it at the stairs. "Dryden Properties is the door on the right at the top. You want to go first, or should I?"

Silently, she pointed a finger at him. He nodded once, then started up. She followed immediately behind him, unable to keep from curling her fingers into the fabric of his shirt in her irrational fear of losing him. She reminded herself that it was only a stairwell and that there weren't a whole lot of ways to go. But even a swell girl Friday had her off days.

Nathaniel dispatched the door to Dryden Properties with considerably less cacophony than the door downstairs, and then they were inside. He leaned back against the door to inhale a few deep breaths before proceeding, and Audrey realized he was no less anxious about doing this than she was. Instead of worrying her, that made her feel better for some reason. His discomfort over doing something he knew he shouldn't made her think maybe Silas was wrong about his soul moving farther away from rescue. Surely if it had gone too far, Nathaniel would have no qualms about doing this.

Heartened some, she braved speaking aloud. Okay, so it was in a whisper, so the "loud" part of "aloud" was relative. "Tell me again exactly what we're looking for."

There was enough light afforded from the streetlamps in the parking lot beyond for her to see him turn and look at her. "How about a big red arrow that says, 'Clues here'?" he whispered back.

"Very funny."

"Look for anything that might be associated with me or Summerfield Associates," he told her. "Or anything that has words like *whack* or references to taking someone for a ride. And also any weapons of mass destruction."

Yeah, right. *If this were a film noir*, she thought, *they'd start rifling through the filing cabinets, and, at some point, turn up a bottle of whiskey and a Maltese falcon.* This being the twenty-first century, however—

"The computer," Audrey said. "But what if it's password protected?"

"Let's hope it's not."

"Are the computers at your office password protected?" she asked.

"Mine is," he told her. "Irene's is. But the ones for the secretaries and paralegals aren't."

"So we start with the ones out here and work our way inward."

"I'll do that," he said. "You try the filing cabinet."

He pointed toward the opposite wall, and, sure enough, there sat a trio of filing cabinets. Nice to know some things didn't change. When she made her way over to them, she saw that one was locked, which, of course, meant that was where she should start. She strode back to the desk closest to the entrance, figuring it belonged to the receptionist or secretary, the one most likely to keep track of the key.

Nathaniel was at that desk, too, booting up the computer, and she tried to reach around him for the drawer in the center. When he saw what she was doing, he took a step to the left to make room for her. But Audrey didn't anticipate the move, so ended up colliding with him. When he reached out to steady her, he brushed his arm over her breasts, but it was dark enough that she didn't think he realized what he'd done. She realized it, though, her breath hitching in her chest and heat filling her belly at the intimate touch.

"Sorry," she said a little breathlessly. She took a giant step backward and crossed her arms over her chest. "I was going to see if there was a key to the filing cabinet in there."

For a moment, Nathaniel only looked at her, and she thought maybe he knew what he'd done after all. Then, sounding a little breathless himself, he said, "Right. Uh, go ahead. I'll stand here." And then he, too, took a giant step backward.

Audrey moved quickly, finally finding the key in the bottom drawer, and went back to her task. She found nothing about Nathaniel's company in the locked cabinet— or any WMDs, either—so she hastily checked the others. Nothing.

She located a door opposite the one through which they'd entered and deduced it was Dryden's office. After returning the filing cabinet key to its drawer, she made her way to the other door. It wasn't locked, but the office was darker, due to the blinds being closed on the solitary window. Audrey flicked on the penlight Nathaniel had given her and shot a small circle of light around the room, until she saw a solitary filing cabinet in the corner. She passed Dryden's desk as she went and, just for the hell of it, sat down and started pulling at drawers.

Much to her surprise, none was locked. So what could she do but start rifling through them? Carefully, but thoroughly.

At the very back of the second drawer she checked, she found a file containing some photographs. Nothing out of the ordinary, just a lot of shots of one man in various states of vacation and recreation with family and friends. It was safe to assume that the man who was a common denominator in all of them was Edward Dryden, and when Audrey tried to remember the grainy photo of the man she'd seen in the paper that morning two weeks ago after dreaming about Silas that first time, she was fairly certain it was him. In one photo, he was standing on the deck of a sport fishing boat with two other men. Another looked like a picnic in a park somewhere. Another showed him with a group of people at Churchill Downs.

Nothing incriminating, she thought again. But maybe worth having. She located a copier in the corner of the room and quickly made copies of each of the photographs before returning them to their rightful place. Then she went to the filing cabinet to see if she could find anything there. It didn't take long for her to discover a file whose tab read *Summerfield Associates*, which she pulled from the drawer at the same time Nathaniel opened the door to the outer office and entered.

"Any luck?" he whispered.

"Maybe," she told him.

She explained about the photographs and showed him the file she'd found. He glanced hurriedly through it, but didn't seem to be surprised by anything he found.

"It's duplicates of everything I have in my files," he said, his voice tinged with disappointment. "There's nothing helpful here."

"Did you find anything on the computer?"

He shook his head. "Nothing. Not even any encrypted files that might look fishy. It's just a typical office computer with typical office files. I'll check the one in here, too, but it probably won't be any more helpful."

It didn't take long to confirm precisely that, leaving them both where they had started when they entered—with knowledge of nothing new. Certainly they could hand the photos over to Leo and Nathaniel's investigator, but chances were slim that there would be anything useful among them, either. It wasn't like Dryden had ever shied away from cameras.

Nathaniel looked at his watch. "It's going on six. I don't think we're going to discover anything else." He emitted a single anxious chuckle at that. "Not that we really discovered anything to being with."

Without thinking, Audrey lifted a hand to his shoulder and gave it a gentle squeeze. Even through the fabric of his sweater, she felt the coldness of his skin beneath. Was it her imagination or did it seem even colder than it had before? *Surely not*, she immediately told herself. It had to be her imagination. His skin had been like ice for two weeks. You couldn't get any colder than ice. Could you?

"Don't worry," she told him as they crossed the outer office toward the main entrance, hoping she sounded more reassuring than she felt. "Something will come up that will make everything okay."

He looked at the hand on his shoulder, then lifted his own to cover hers. He was about to say something when the creak of the building's exterior door below erupted, sounding even louder than it had when she and Nathaniel had entered. Some kind of watchman, she thought. Nathaniel was right— nobody came to work this early in the morning on a weekend. She hoped. Panicked, she turned to look at him and saw that he'd heard the same thing.

Thinking fast, Audrey pulled him toward a sofa situated to hide the copier and make the office look less officelike. There was just enough room behind it for the two of them to crouch unseen. But Nathaniel stumbled in the dark, pitching forward against Audrey. She was able to turn around and steady him before he fell—some—and together, they managed, fortunately, to make it to the floor behind the sofa without causing a ruckus.

Unfortunately, however, they didn't land in the most comfortable position, with Audrey on her back and Nathaniel atop her. He was able to catch himself on his elbows before he would have crushed her, but he didn't have time to do anything more, because the outer office door opened, and they heard someone whistling.

Whistling the "William Tell Overture" of all things. Though, Audrey had to admit, it was the perfect accompaniment for her rapidly beating heart. The staccato hammering of her pulse, however, wasn't due entirely to the fact that there was someone on the other side of that

door who could walk in any minute and find her and
Nathaniel in flagrante delecto. It was also due to the fact
that it wasn't just the "delecto" that was "flagrante" at the
moment. It was also the Audrey. In fact, at the moment, the
Audrey was more "flagrante" than she'd ever been in her
life. And it had far less to do with the security guard out
there than it did the illegal enterer on top of her.

She felt Nathaniel's weight pushing down on her from her
chest to her thighs, his warm breath stirring the hair at her
temple and dampening her skin. His body was cold at first,
but within seconds of coming into contact with hers grew
hotter, something that only heightened her own body heat.
She did her best to keep her breathing shallow, but every
time she inhaled, her chest rose to press harder against his,
and even that small contact made her senses come alive. It
must have had the same effect on him, because she felt him
grow hard where her thigh was wedged between his legs,
and the knowledge that he was becoming so aroused only
doubled her awareness of him.

The whistling outside grew louder, drew closer, and
Audrey gulped in a breath to hold it. But that only trapped
the scent of Nathaniel inside her, intoxicating her. She saw
the beam of a flashlight arc over the wall above her and
closed her eyes, as if that might make her disappear. But all
it did was make her more aware of the man lying atop her.
Of his hard body pressing into hers, of his mouth, so close
that she felt his lips graze her cheek, of his cock pushing
against her leg as if demanding release. Then the whistling
was moving away again, and the door to Edward's office
was closing, and then the outer door was closing, and then,
suddenly, Nathaniel was kissing her and kissing her and
kissing her, and she was wrapping her arms around him
and kissing him back.

His mouth was hungry on hers, insistent, demanding. She
felt his hand seize her rib cage, the curve of his thumb and
forefinger cradling the lower swell of her breast, and she
lifted her arm to rope it around his neck, giving him better
access. He immediately covered her breast with sure fingers,

palming her generously before skimming lower again, down to her hip. It was as if he wasn't sure where to touch her, so he touched her everywhere, lingering nowhere, setting fires all over her body. She drove her fingers into his silky hair and splayed them open over his back, then cupped his nape and shoulders, then started all over again.

For long minutes, they clung to each other, warring for possession of the kiss, neither willing to concede. It was Nathaniel who finally came to his senses long enough to point out the precariousness of their situation, then offer a solution to the problem.

"Come home with me," he whispered breathlessly into her ear before nibbling the lobe. "I want to make love to you, Audrey. No security guards, no ghosts. Just you and me and my bed. All day."

A shudder of heat shot down her spine at his roughly uttered words, bundling in her belly like a pile of hot embers. Embers that had been smoldering for years, ready to burst into flame at the first breath of air that stirred them, only to be gusted to explosion by a single embrace. It had been so long since she had felt like this. So long since a man's touch had set her body on fire. So long since that coil of heat in her midsection had snugged tight with the promise of delicious release to come. So long . . .

So long . . .

Audrey had always loved sex. She'd become active in college and had been with a half dozen men before Sean entered her life. With her, sex had always been spontaneous, vigorous, and adventurous. She'd been an uninhibited and playful lover, both demanding and generous in her exploits. And although Sean had been more conventional in his lovemaking than she and had drawn the line at some of the things Audrey enjoyed most, sex with him had been, for the most part, enjoyable, and, for the most part, satisfying.

Since his death, she'd almost forgotten what it could be like between two people. Had almost forgotten the tempestuous sensations a single touch could arouse. As if cued by the thought, Nathaniel dipped his head to the sensitive curve where her shoulder joined her neck and brushed his lips over the tender flesh. At the same time, he nudged the hand on her rib cage higher to cradle her lower breast before covering it completely. She sucked in her breath at the shiver that coursed through her, tangling her fingers convulsively in his hair again.

"Come home with me, Audrey," he repeated roughly.

And then, without even realizing she had made a decision, she pressed her lips to his forehead and told him, "Yes."

THEY SPOKE NOT A WORD ON THE DRIVE TO Nathaniel's house. They held hands, clutched shoulders, rubbed thighs, stroked hair. Thanks to the early hour, there was virtually no traffic to hinder their journey, and Audrey felt as rushed and impatient as the sleek black car as it cut through the dusky morning. After what seemed an interminable amount of time, Nathaniel turned into his parking garage, then they were in the elevator ascending to his home.

No sooner had the metal doors folded closed, however, than they turned to each other in a scorching embrace. Nathaniel hauled her up against him, turning their bodies so that Audrey was pressed against the elevator wall and he was crowding himself against her. He snatched the elastic band from her hair so that it tumbled free down around her shoulders, burying one hand in the silky mass before splaying his fingers open over the crown of her head, tipping it back so that he could plunder her mouth at will. He tasted her deeply, their tongues tangled in a quickstep dance, then he dropped his other hand to her hip. Lower and lower he pressed his fingers, until he cradled the lower curve of her fanny in his palm and pushed her forward, into the hard ridge of his erection.

Audrey uttered a wild little sound that erupted from deep inside her, then lifted her leg to wrap it around both of his. She writhed against him, reveling in the way he

swelled even larger, cupping her own hand over his taut
buttocks to propel him harder into herself. For a moment,
they mimicked through their clothes the union they would
be enjoying later, until a soft chime announced their arrival
on Nathaniel's floor and they tumbled into the hallway
beyond. Within moments, they were inside his condo, and
he was pushing the door closed behind them and throwing
his hand over a switch plate to turn on a light. As pale gold
from a nearby lamp bathed them in amber, he pulled
Audrey into his arms again.

They wasted no time ridding each other of their clothes.
Audrey tugged his turtleneck free of his trousers at the same
time he gripped the hem of her sweater and began to yank it
higher. She released the buckle of his belt long enough for
him to pull her sweater over her head, then he hesitated long
enough for her to jerk his shirt over his own. She took a
moment to soak in the glorious sight of him half-naked, all
broad shoulders and sinewy strength and rock hard male.
His chest was a masterpiece of muscle and dark hair, hair
that arrowed down over a flat torso, disappearing into the
unbuttoned waistband of his pants.

But it was his arms that were her undoing. Where most
women considered other parts of a man more compelling,
Audrey's mouth had always gone dry over a nice set of
biceps or a particularly salient triceps. And the camber of
muscle on Nathaniel's arms was . . .

Oh, my.

She inhaled a slow breath as she traced the pad of her
finger over an exceptionally well formed shoulder, releasing
it in a quaver of longing as she followed an elegant line of
sinew down to his very nicely achieved forearm. His skin
was like silken steel beneath her touch, smooth, hot, and
responsive. When she finally returned her gaze to his face, it
was to see the longing in her own heart reflecting back at her
tenfold.

Reaching behind herself, she flicked open the catch of
her bra and let the garment tumble forward over her arms
and to the ground, freeing her generous breasts. His eyes

darkened when she did, and he took a single step forward, bringing his body nearly flush with her own. But instead of pulling her into his arms, his hand moved to the heavy ring that swung between her breasts. Sean's ring. The ring she had worn since her husband's death. The ring she hadn't removed once, for any reason. Now Nathaniel caught that ring in the palm of his hand and looked at her with a silent question.

Audrey swallowed hard, looking down at the ring, at Nathaniel's hand, at her naked breasts. She waited for the feeling of guilt she thought she should feel at what was to come. Waited for the awkwardness that should make it feel as if it were Sean, not his ring, coming between them. But in that moment, she only had feelings for Nathaniel. Desire for Nathaniel. Need for Nathaniel. And something else, too. She was afraid to say just what. But it was for Nathaniel, too.

She moved her hands behind her neck and reached for the clasp of the chain. She even went so far as to push the tiny catch that would release it. But she couldn't make herself go through with it. Couldn't take that last step that would once and for all remove her from her husband. Instead, she reached for the ring in Nathaniel's hand and, with a quick, deft move, pushed it behind herself, so that it hung down her back.

"I'm sorry, Nathaniel, but it's the best I can do," she said softly.

She waited to see if he would stop, if he would pick up her bra and sweater and hand them back to her, telling her he'd take her home. Instead, after only a small hesitation, he reached for her again, pulling her into his arms, covering her mouth with his. The feel of his naked chest against hers was almost more than Audrey could bear. He warmed quickly against her, opening his hands over her shoulder blades, splaying his fingers wide across her bare back. Then she felt his fingers skimming downward, toward the waistband of her trousers, over the contours of her fanny, her hips, and back to the dip of her waist.

As if of one mind, they parted enough to undress each

other the rest of the way, moving slowly as they did toward the center of the living room. The furnishings were utterly male, darkly paneled walls and floor, rich, jewel-toned Orientals, oxblood leather chairs and lushly upholstered forest green sofa. An oil-on-canvas hunt scene hung over the fireplace, and the mantel boasted more masculine trophies—wooden ships, a heavy clock, an abstract marble sculpture. The view beyond the veritable wall of windows across the room was of nothing but fragile morning sky made barely pink by the first creeping rays of sunlight.

By the time they reached the sofa, they had shed the remainder of their clothes. Without ceremony, Nathaniel sat, pulling Audrey into his lap to face him. After kissing her again, he hefted her breast in one hand, rubbing his thumb leisurely over the stiff peak of her nipple. She gasped when he did, and he plunged his tongue deeper into her mouth, then moved his other hand behind her, slipping into the crevice of her ass. At that, she moaned, rearing her head backward, so he pulled her breast to his mouth instead. He sucked her deep inside, laving her nipple now with the flat of his tongue, then teasing it with the tip, all the while tracing his finger leisurely along the elegant line of her derriere.

Audrey gripped his shoulder with one hand and dropped the other between her legs, petting herself to increase her pleasure. When Nathaniel realized what she was doing, he slid his hand around to her front, joining her fingers in the damp folds of her flesh until she thought she would come apart in his hand.

And then she was on her back on the couch, and his head was between her legs, and he was tasting her there as deeply and as hungrily as he had been devouring her mouth. Again and again he lapped at her, pushing her legs wider to give himself better access, then darted the tip of his tongue against that most sensitive little part of her. She cried out as she felt her orgasm building in her belly, gasping for breath, groping for something to hold onto. She tangled the fingers of both hands in his hair, holding him insistently where he was. Loving her orally was something Sean had refused to do, thinking it unseemly. It was something she had missed *so much*. More and more greedily Nathaniel consumed her, and more quickly her climax built, until she was crying out his name, again and again and again, and her body was trembling with her release.

And then Nathaniel was beside her, holding her, whispering words that both soothed and aroused, touching her in ways that both pacified and excited her. She moved her own hand between their bodies and palmed the damp head of his cock, then lowered her hand and closed it snugly around him. He was so big, so hard, so ready for her, and her breath hitched in her chest at the thought of what was to come. She tilted back her head and kissed him, then leaned forward, urging him onto his back this time. Then she assumed the position he had held for her, taking him into her mouth and savoring him.

This, too, was something she had enjoyed giving to her lovers in the past, and it was something with which Sean had never been comfortable. Audrey had forgotten how powerful she felt when pleasuring a man this way, how much she enjoyed knowing he was at her mercy, and how incredibly intimate such acts could be when shared. As she pulled him more deeply inside, Nathaniel sifted his fingers through her hair, curved his hands over her shoulders, sucked in one deep breath after another. She relished him for long, erotic moments, until he tightened his fingers in her hair and murmured that he was close to coming.

Reluctantly, she withdrew, covering him with her hand again, stroking him softly as she rose and extended a hand toward him, helping him back to sitting. She started to straddle him, but he excused himself for a moment, whispering that there was one not-so-minor detail to see to. For a moment, she couldn't imagine what he was talking about. But when he returned with a condom, she smiled.

"Oh, yeah," she said softly as he took care of that not-so-minor detail. "It's been so long, I forgot about—"

"You didn't forget much," he replied with a grin. He reached for her, helping her back into his lap, until she was sitting astride him, her hands on his shoulders, her legs parted wide.

She actually blushed at his comment. "Actually, any memories of . . . that . . . are even more distant. Sean would never . . ." She let her voice trail off, hoping her meaning was clear, dropping her gaze to his chest, where she traced a slow circle around his heart.

He lifted both hands to her breasts, holding them gently, palming them lightly. "Sean would never what?" he asked quietly.

She was surprised to realize she was naked with another man discussing her husband. Even more surprising, the situation didn't feel at all strange. Nevertheless, she hesitated a moment before continuing. "Sean was pretty . . . traditional . . . when it came to sex. Woman on top was about as exotic as he would ever go. So we never . . ." She sighed. "Oral sex was out of the question."

She looked at his face again, but his expression revealed nothing. "You and your husband never had oral sex?"

She shook her head.

"Never?"

"No."

"So this is something you never shared with him?"

She shook her head again. "There's a lot I didn't share with him sexually," she said.

Nathaniel said nothing in response to that, only lowered his gaze to her breasts before bringing one to his mouth and sucking it deeply. He moved his other hand between her legs and stroked her, gently tapping the tender bud of her clitoris. Audrey closed her eyes and threw her head back, clutching his shoulders, squeezing her thighs against his to lift herself higher. When she lowered herself again, Nathaniel guided himself inside her, and she filled herself with him, shuddering at the depth of his entry. Never had she felt so full in her life, so replete, so whole, so ready to explode. And then he urged her upward, moving himself inside her, and she realized there was still so much more to come.

She lowered herself on him again, and he seemed to plunge even deeper this time, so she rose and fell again. With every new plummet, he seemed to fill her more than before, until she wasn't sure where her body ended and his began, or if her body ended at all. They seemed to fuse into one sensuously moving, sexually responsive being, all heat and damp and utterly arousing sensation. Nathaniel gripped her hips harder as he increased his thrusting, and Audrey slid her arms from his sweaty shoulders to circle the ample biceps she'd admired before. Just as the hot coil inside her began to curl tighter, he turned their bodies so that she was on her back with her legs circling his waist, and he was on his knees, pummeling into her again and again and again.

And then they were coming together, crying out as one their completion, their bodies colliding one final time before he was collapsing beside her, pulling her close and kissing her again. This time, though, the kisses lacked the ferocity and hunger of those first ones. This time, the kisses were gentle and sated and long.

"We never made it to your bed," she finally said softly against his mouth.

He chuckled low. "Oh, we will, Audrey. We will. We have all day."

WHEN HE'D TOLD AUDREY THEY WOULD HAVE ALL DAY, Nathaniel had meant it. Even after darkness fell Sunday night, he and Audrey still lay in his bed, their naked bodies twined together, basking in the aftermath of a third coupling. Of course, for this last, the coupling had come in the form of oral satisfaction, but it had still been precisely that: satisfying. He couldn't believe her husband had denied her something she took such unmitigated, uninhibited pleasure in doing. But he'd be lying if he didn't admit he enjoyed the fact that he and Audrey shared something she hadn't with Sean. Maybe that was selfish, but there it was

all the same. There was something he could give her that
her husband had not. Something more than his love.

Because he was beginning to suspect that his feelings
for Audrey went that deep. He wasn't sure when it had
happened or how or why. Maybe it was because she was
the first woman he'd had to rely on, or the first woman he'd
spent time getting to know, or the first woman with whom
he'd shared something other than a physical attraction. For
all he knew, his feelings for her had taken root the moment
she stepped into his office and stood up to him. Then, when
he'd learned more about her, discovered what kind of
person she was, she'd started to creep into places inside
him that had been cold and empty for a long, long time.
Many of them had always been empty, but Audrey walked
right in and started unpacking and made those places cozy
and warm.

Warm, he thought. That was indeed how she made him
feel. But she'd rescued him from more than just the
physical cold that had plagued him for the past two weeks.
She'd rescued him from the emotional chill that had been
part of him for longer than he could remember.

He looked down at her face, pressed to his naked chest,
her eyes closed in shallow slumber. Faint circles darkened
the pale skin beneath her eyes, but she looked content
otherwise. They hadn't spent the entire day in bed, of
course. He'd fixed her breakfast after that first time, and
they'd passed the morning together sharing coffee and the
Sunday paper. He'd loaned her a pair of sweatpants and a
Louisville Cardinals T-shirt that had swallowed her, and
had experienced a thrill of something raw and masculine at
seeing her dressed in his clothes. Around noon, they'd
found *The Thin Man* on On-Demand, and then Nathaniel
had pulled his own copy of *After the Thin Man* from his
DVD collection to make it a proper double feature. For
dinner, they'd ordered a pizza from Bearno's, and he'd
opened a bottle of Chateau Letour he'd been saving for a
special occasion to go with.

It had been the sort of day any couple might share on a lazy weekend, and it had been as comfortable as if it were the sort of thing the two of them did all the time. It was almost as if they'd agreed by mutual consent to pretend just that. After that first exchange about Sean, Audrey hadn't mentioned her husband, and Nathaniel had been content to leave it that way. Eventually, though, this day was going to end, and they would have to return to the problems facing them. They would have to find the key to freeing Nathaniel from his ties to Edward. They would have to topple Edward's plans to develop the block of Main Street he wanted to develop.

And they would have to figure out where this thing between them was going.

Her left hand lay open on his chest not far from her face, her gold wedding band snug on her third finger, where it had always been. Her hair hid the still turned backward chain with her husband's ring, but she still wore that, too. He'd halfway thought—and wholly hoped—that there would come a point during their lovemaking where she would finally remove both, but she hadn't. What would happen, he wondered, if, when she opened her eyes, the ring her husband had given her once upon a time was the first thing she saw?

He circled a strand of black hair around his finger, coiling it again and again, until his finger disappeared. The small motion must have woken her, because she stirred in her sleep and opened her eyes. Instead of looking at the ring on her finger, however, she immediately looked up at Nathaniel. For a moment, she seemed a little disoriented, as if she didn't know where she was. Then her eyes focused and, after only a small hesitation and only a small furrow of her brow, she smiled.

"What time is it?" she asked sleepily.

He looked at the clock on the nightstand. "It's just past nine."

She expelled an incredulous sound at that and pushed herself up to sitting. "I have to get going."

He hesitated only a moment before offering, "You could stay the night."

She couldn't possibly know how significant an offer that was. Nathaniel had never invited a woman to spend the night at his place before. Normally, he didn't want women here in the morning when he awoke. Hell, normally he didn't want women here at all. He didn't want to share any part of his private life with anyone that way. But especially in the morning. What if she woke up before he did and saw him lying there at his most vulnerable?

The thought of that happening with Audrey didn't bother him as much as it did with other women. Not that he wanted her to wake up and look over and see him drooling . . . But even if she did, she was the kind of woman who would probably smile, then wipe his mouth with the edge of the sheet and snuggle in close again. At least, that was what she would do if she felt the same way about him that he felt about her. Just how did she feel about him anyway?

"I have to go," she said again. Still softly, but more insistently this time. Which, he supposed, was an answer to his own mental question.

"I'll drive you," he said.

"No, that's okay," she told him. "I can call a cab."

Strike two, he couldn't help thinking. Nevertheless, he insisted, "I'm not going to let you spend the day here with me like this, then take a cab home. That's just too . . ."

"Tawdry?" she finished for him.

"Impolite," he corrected her.

She lifted a hand to his face, pressing her palm lightly to his cheek. She looked, somehow, like she was going to say something very, very important. But all that came out was, "It's okay, Nathaniel. I'd rather take a cab. I need to take a cab. Okay?"

He tried to understand. She needed some space. Needed to think. Needed to do whatever women did after they had unexpected sex with an unexpected man in an unexpected place. He just wished he knew what to say to make her realize it had been anything but that to him.

Holding the sheet to herself, she reached for the oversized
T-shirt she'd worn earlier and pulled it over her head, clearly
no longer comfortable with her nudity. That was made more
obvious when she stood and tugged it down over her thighs,
even though it covered all of her that needed covering.

"My clothes?" she asked.

He'd picked up all of their clothing earlier, while she was
sleeping and nodded toward the chair where he'd tossed
them. She picked through the pile of black to separate her
things from his, then turned and threw him a sheepish look.

"I'll, um . . . I'll change in the bathroom," she said
uncomfortably. "Could you . . . call a cab for me?"

He nodded, but she'd already turned away, so he wasn't
sure she saw it. Then he pushed his side of the covers away
and slung his feet over the bed. After a quarter of a century of
being sexually active, it had finally happened to Nathaniel.
The awkward morning after. And it wasn't even morning.

· Fifteen ·

CECILIA TALLIED THE LAST OF MONDAY'S RECEIPTS for Finery, entered the appropriate figures into their proper places on the computer spreadsheet, filled out the bank deposit slip, and put everything in the safe in Audrey's office. Then she glanced down at her watch. Six twenty-seven. She had three minutes to freshen up before her gentleman caller arrived.

She grabbed her purse and hurried down the second-floor hallway to the tiny bathroom at the end that was, for all intents and purposes, the company washroom. There, she dusted her face with a little powder and poofed her hair as best she could, then swiped a touch of gloss over her lips. She'd never been big on makeup, but a little color never hurt, right? And she did so want to look her best. She swept a hand down over the pale green column dress to smooth out the worst of the wrinkles, then opened the door. She glanced quickly down the hallway and, seeing no one, made her way to the stairs. Audrey had left right after Finery's closing to attend a Derby fashion event, so Cecilia had promised to lock up. And if she hadn't quite said exactly *when* she would be locking up . . .

But Audrey wouldn't mind. Thanks to Nathaniel Summerfield, the mysterious—but very hunky—guy who kept calling and showing up lately, Cecilia was confident her employer-neighbor-friend was sympathetic to matters of the heart.

Her own heart turned over as she made her way down the stairs and found Silas waiting for her in the showroom. He was dressed as he always was, in his black trousers and white shirt, so she'd come to the conclusion that wardrobe selections on the other side weren't what they were here in the real world. But that was okay, since Silas looked eminently yummy in his nineteenth-century togs.

The real world, she echoed to herself. Hah. This world hadn't felt real since that dream she'd had of dancing with Silas. Ever since waking from that, she'd felt as if *this* life was the shadow of reality, not her dream life. And since that dream, there had been others. Cecilia had found that there was nothing to make a lunch hour pass more pleasantly than taking a little nap. She'd had lunch with Silas almost every day, in her dreams. And in every one of them, they'd been able to touch and hold hands and dance and . . .

Well, they hadn't done *that* yet. He hadn't even kissed her again. But they'd danced on his riverboat again, and they'd walked along the Ohio, both in his time and in hers. And they'd shared a picnic in Central Park. Her dreams, which had once been filled with dark shapes, menacing shadows, and faceless ogres all representing Vincent had become idyllic scenes of romance with Silas. Two weeks ago, Cecilia had dreaded falling asleep. Now, at least for those times when she could catch a few winks at work, she looked forward to drifting off.

And even in her apartment, where Silas couldn't follow, because his portrait was here, she still dreamed of him at night. Regular dreams that were insubstantial and sometimes brief, but her head still filled with images of Silas instead of the man who used to terrify her.

And even without being able to touch him in her dreams, she could still enjoy his company whenever she was here. And she did, every chance she had. Cecilia enjoyed working late these days. Because working late meant uninterrupted time with Audrey Magill's ghost.

No, not Audrey's ghost, she thought as she stepped down from the last stair and into the living room. Maybe Silas was haunting her friend's house, but he didn't belong to her. Not the way he belonged to Cecilia.

"Good evening, Cecilia," he greeted her as he crossed the room to stand before her.

"Hi, Silas," she returned, almost shyly.

She still wasn't sure what had happened to make him visible to her now. Silas seemed to think that by dreaming about him, she'd opened a portal into her soul that allowed him to pass through the barriers she'd erected around her heart in the wake of her experiences with Vincent. Cecilia wondered if maybe it was just that she'd grown to trust him enough to let him in. Honestly, at this point, she didn't care what had caused it. She only knew that being able to see Silas like this, and being able to touch him in her dreams, was almost like having him around for real.

She just wished she knew how long he would be able to stay.

"How was your day?" he asked.

She smiled. "It was good. But I missed you. You know, I wouldn't mind if you popped in every now and then, just to wave or something."

He shook his head. "You need time to be with other people, Cecilia. You don't need me skulking around watching you all the time."

She eyed him curiously. It was an odd thing for him to say, unless he knew something about her past. And since she'd told him almost nothing about that . . .

"Why do you say that?" she asked.

He arched a dark brow in speculation. "Perhaps because it's true?"

"Yeah, but . . ." She shifted her weight to one foot,

crossing her arms over her midsection. "How much do you
know about me?"

He lifted a hand toward her face, then seemed to
remember he couldn't touch her now the way he could in her
dreams. With a small frown of disappointment, he dropped
his hand back to his side. "I know only what you've told me.
And what I saw during that brief glimpse inside. That you
were hurt badly. The rest is conjecture on my part. But," he
added, "I'm very good at conjecturing."

So he was, she thought. Still, this wasn't something she
wanted to talk about.

"I can't stay long," she told him. "I'm only scheduled to
work 'til seven, and I don't want to take advantage of
Audrey."

"I understand."

"But we have a little time. What would you like to do?"

She hadn't meant the question to be anything but a
conversation starter, but a look came over Silas's face in
response that was wholly unexpected. Part bleakness, part
sadness, part desperation . . . and all heartbreaking.

"What?" she asked. "What did I say?"

He shook his head. "Nothing. Everything. Oh, Cecilia,
there's so much I would like to do. Yet I have no way of
knowing how long I have left here, and I'm bound by that
damnable painting. It is lovely to escape with you in dreams.
But I would like, just once, to do something in the here and
now that would give me a taste of this time."

"Well, pick one thing," she said impulsively. "One thing
that it would be possible to do. Right now. Maybe we can
figure out a way to do it."

He strode slowly to the window and looked out at
the street. "I should like to see the river," he said. "I miss
the river. She's a splendid mistress, the Ohio. And the
Mississippi is an even more magnificent creature. To be here
now, like this, so close to the water and yet not be able to see it
and smell it and experience it, is a poignant loss indeed."

Wow. Cecilia had never heard him talk like that before.
He sounded almost poetic. She liked this pensive side of

him. "Sometimes I miss the ocean," she said, tracing his footsteps to join him at the window. "I grew up in the Bay area . . . San Francisco," she clarified, "and although I like the river, too, it's not the same as the Pacific. The ocean is so much more breathtaking and has so many more moods."

He spun around to look at her, his dark brows arrowed downward. "Ah, but that isn't true at all. The Ohio is as intemperate a body of water as any. In the summer, she can be warm and playful, her surface rippling like the lace of a petticoat. And in winter, she sometimes freezes, and it takes a gentle, but steadfast man to find her most yielding facets and ease them open. In the spring and fall, she's completely unpredictable, fiery and temperamental one minute, generous and obliging the next. But through it all, she is a tough, feisty, steadfast individual."

Cecilia smiled. He really did make the river sound like a woman. And the way he'd looked at her when he'd talked about her winter moods, she'd somehow known he was talking about more than the Ohio. She warmed a little inside at the thought of Silas gently but steadfastly finding *her* most yielding facets. Then she marveled that such a thought could make her feel warm. Usually, the thought of any man getting close to her facets or any other part of her made her freeze up harder and colder than the river would.

"You know, a woman could get jealous, listening to you talk about your mistress the way you do."

Now his dark brows arched higher. "Are you jealous, Cecilia?"

Her face grew warm at the question. Try as she would to form a complete thought, nothing would quite gel in her brain. Nor would the words come out of her mouth right when she tried to say what she meant. "I didn't . . . I don't . . . It's not that . . ."

He grinned at her inability to finish a statement. "You needn't feel jealous, you know. Compared to you, my dear, the river is a pallid, lackluster thing. I would far rather spend time with you than with she."

Now heat blossomed in Cecilia's belly, too. But all she said was, "You still miss her."

He expelled a quiet sound of resignation. "Yes. I do."

A thought occurred to her. "So if you're bound to that damnable painting, and I took that damnable painting for a little ride, then you'd be forced to come along, right?"

He narrowed his eyes at her. "A ride?"

She nodded, grinning.

"In your motorcar, you mean?"

"That's what I mean."

He gave the idea some thought, then he smiled, too. "I only rode in a motorcar when I was alive once. It was an exhilarating experience."

She laughed at that. "Oh, you ain't seen nothin' yet. Cars have come a long way since your time. How fast did you go that one time you rode in a car?"

"It was ridiculously fast," he told her. "Almost twenty-five miles an hour."

"Hah," Cecilia said. "The speed limit on Third Street is thirty-five now. On the expressways, it's fifty-five."

"Fifty-five miles in one hour?" he asked incredulously. "Do you mean to tell me you could drive from here to Frankfort in an hour?"

"Less," she said. "Because once you get outside the county, the speed limit goes up to seventy."

His mouth dropped open at that. "Impossible," he said. "Nothing can go that fast."

Cecilia stood and made her way to the stairwell, then took the stairs two at a time. When she stood in the second-floor landing, she gripped his portrait in confident hands and released it from its hook on the wall. Then she carefully pulled it down until she was gazing eye to eye with Silas Summerfield's oil-on-canvas image.

"Better fasten your seat belt, Silas," she told him. "Because, compared to what you're used to, it's going to be a bumpy ride."

* * *

ACTUALLY, SILAS THOUGHT A HALF HOUR LATER, THE
ride had been quite pleasant. Certainly smoother than any
carriage he'd ever ridden in. Or even the trolley. Of course,
that could be because of the fact that, in his current state,
he was made of ether and couldn't feel even the most
heinous jolt of her motorcar. His portrait, which was
strapped to the seating behind his in much the way Cecilia
was strapped to the driver's chair, might beg to differ. Still,
he had but to look at the road down which her little car
traveled to see that it was infinitely smoother than the
streets of his day. And the pneumatic tires of motorcars
bore the weight of their vehicles with considerably more
care than had the metal-covered wooden wheels of the
carriages to which he had grown accustomed in his day.
And as for the scenes passing by . . .

Despite the disrepair into which of some of the houses in
his neighborhood had fallen, in many ways, the area had
changed little since his time. His section of the Southern
Extension—or, as Audrey and, evidently, its other current
occupants referred to it, Old Louisville—had originally
been populated by only a handful of quite grand mansions
on St. James Square. But by the time Silas died, smaller,
though by no means small, houses had sprung up all around
those, lining Second, Third, Fourth, and Fifth Streets,
shoulder to shoulder, for blocks on end. These homes had
filled with families in his time who weren't quite so well off
as their more flamboyant neighbors, but who were people of
means, nonetheless.

Silas had bought his house on Third Street when he
retired and took occupancy of it immediately after its
completion in 1881. He'd wanted room to spread out after
having virtually lived his entire adult life in the confines of
his boat, and the houses of the Southern Extension had
definitely offered that.

The trees lining the streets now were considerably larger
than the ones that had grown there in his day. Their roots had
spread far enough and grown fat enough now to buckle the
walkways, and their branches stretched wide across the

avenues to create shady byways where before the sunlight
had flowed down unobstructed. The signs on many of the
storefronts, if not identical to the ones in his day, were
certainly still in keeping with the style of their original shops
and businesses, but many others were lit with electricity and
neon gas. Many of the houses, too, Silas noted, were no
longer private homes, but places of commerce and society.
Others, he was surprised to see, had been converted to
apartments.

The car bounced over two metal rungs in the street, with
Cecilia neither slowing, nor looking left or right, before
hitting them.

"Does the trolley no longer run?" he asked.

"Not the one you're used to," she said. "There's the
Frankfort Avenue Trolley, which is especially fun on FAT
Friday when it goes up and down Frankfort Avenue for free,
stopping at restaurants and shops and art galleries. And
there's another on Main Street that's similar. But neither is
really a trolley. They're both buses altered to look like
trolleys."

"The mood of my time with the convenience of yours,"
he said.

She nodded. "Except I imagine you didn't have to worry
about exhaust fumes when you rode the trolley."

"No," he said. "And I don't imagine you're able to enjoy
the grind and clank of the gears whenever the trolley man
changes course or speed."

"No, but I was able to enjoy that in San Francisco," she
said with a smile. "The trolleys there haven't changed much
since your time. I loved riding them. They're enchanting."

"Enchanting," he echoed, swiveling his head first one
way and then the other. Another car passed them on his
side, its exterior rusted and dented, belching black smoke
in its wake. "I wish I could say the same thing about your
time."

"Hey, it's not like you lived in the Golden Age, pal," she
reminded him without taking her eyes from the road.
"Anyone who wasn't white and male—and rich—in your

time had to endure all manner of social and professional inequity. Children were put to work in sweatshops. Women couldn't vote. Justice, or a lack thereof, was based on the color of a person's skin. The sky was sooty with coal ash and the water was poisonous in some places. People died of illnesses that are immensely curable now." She glanced over at him with a wry expression. "Should I go on?"

"That won't be necessary," he assured her. He had, after all, already heard this from Audrey.

In spite of that, Cecilia did continue. "You lived a privileged life, Silas. The kind of life most people didn't have back then."

"And I worked hard to earn it," he retorted.

"I'm not saying you didn't. I'm just saying there was good and bad then, just like there is now."

"True enough," he conceded. And, too, he thought further with another glance at Cecilia, this time did have one or two things to recommend it that his hadn't, not the least of which was women like the one he was with at the moment. He'd always supposed the reason he had never remarried after losing his wife was because he found the lure of the river life too strong. Having spent some—quite enjoyable—time now with both Audrey and Cecilia, however, he was beginning to think perhaps it was because the women of his time, most of them, at any rate, simply did not suit him. Certainly, there had been women in Louisville a century or two ago he had admired. But they had all either moved in social circles other than his own, or they had been married, or they, like he, were wed to their professions or causes.

He wished he knew his fate with regard to this world, whether he would be able to stay here once he and Audrey had completed their mission of saving Nathaniel's soul. There was a part of him that almost hoped they weren't successful, so that he might be condemned to haunt her house forever. Because, lately, it didn't seem like such a condemnation to be relegated back to earth. Lately, it had begun to feel much more like a blessing.

Cecilia drove down Fourth Street—his own street, she had told him, was now a one-way avenue that headed away from the river—and as they drew nearer to Broadway, many of the buildings became more modern and less to his liking. At some point after his death, architects seemed to have lost their creativity and sense of style and had begun to manufacture boxes of dubious originality and little flair. He complained to Cecilia about their lack of splendor and pointed out how that was made more obvious when they were plunked down beside the Beaux Art and Italianate beauty of the Brown or Seelbach Hotels, which he was delighted to see still remained, and which he remembered well from his day. Other structures went by in a blur as she took him on a quick tour, barely noticeable, until Cecilia braked for a stoplight at the intersection of Fourth and Main, whereupon Silas looked to his right and saw something of a quite intriguing nature.

"What's that place?" he asked, gesturing toward a collection of geometric shapes heaped upon each other, fashioned from what appeared to be glass in varying shades.

"That's the Kentucky Center," Cecilia told him. "Also known as the Center for the Arts. It's cool, isn't it?"

"Cool?" he echoed.

She smiled. "Splendid," she clarified, echoing one of the words he'd used earlier, but which her tone suggested wasn't used much today.

He considered the structure for another moment, then nodded. "Yes," he said, surprised by his reaction. "It is rather splendid. I should like to see the inside sometime."

She looked over her shoulder at his portrait, then back at Silas. "Stephen and Finn have season tickets to the Broadway Series, but I'm not sure how people would feel about sitting next to a portrait. Maybe we could swing it, though. The inside is as cool-slash-splendid as the outside. There's this wall sculpture made of demolished cars you'd probably find interesting, in light of your newfound passion for motorcars."

Before he could reply to that, the traffic signal turned

green, and Cecilia turned the steering wheel to the right. "Before you get too smug about old architectural styles versus new, take a look to your right at the Humana Building."

She slowed the car as Silas complied with her instructions, and he found himself not just looking right, but looking up, as well. Up, up, up, at a massive edifice fashioned from what looked like pink granite, with a ground floor façade of black and gold, over which flowed a . . .

"Is that a waterfall?" he asked, shocked.

"Yeah," she replied. "Pretty damned splendid, huh?"

He nodded. "Very cool." He considered the building for another moment before adding, "It reminds me, though, of a giant cash register."

She laughed at that. "You wouldn't be the first to think so."

She sped up then, and suddenly nothing looked familiar to Silas, especially after they turned left and headed under the entrance to a massive bridge and an elevated highway that blocked both the sunlight and any chance for a beautiful view. Then suddenly, out of nowhere, he saw it—the Ohio River, wide and muddy and serene. It disappeared again when Cecilia took another turn, but after a few more twists and turns, it appeared once more . . . until it disappeared again behind restaurants and parks and hills.

"That's all?" Silas asked. "Has the city grown so much that it's hidden the river completely from view?"

"Be patient," she told him. "There's a park a few miles up River Road where we can stop and enjoy the view for as long as we want."

True to her word, it wasn't long before she was turning her car into what a sign proclaimed was CARRIE GAULBERT COX PARK. There was an expansive blacktop parking lot, but it was surrounded by even more expansive green space that was dotted here and there by pavilions for picnicking, and bisected by boat ramps where one might load small craft. By now, the sun had fallen in the sky to where it barely hovered over the trees on the opposite bank, where the shallow foothills of southern Indiana rose and fell. In Silas's time, those hills had been great green bumps, vacant of any buildings. Now, though, he could see both private homes and shipyards. The river rippled calm and brown beneath both, the soft waves catching the late afternoon sun and dancing with it before passing it off to another current.

"This is lovely," he said. "The river looks quite beautiful this evening." He turned to look at her, offering her a grateful smile. "Thank you, Cecilia."

She smiled back. "You're welcome."

They both turned to look at the river, neither saying anything for a stretch of time. Then he heard her sigh with something akin to serenity.

"I actually come to Cox Park a lot," she said. "When I lived in San Francisco, whenever I needed to get away from—" She halted abruptly, and the tranquil little smile that had curved her lips suddenly fled. Quickly, she hurried on, "Whenever I needed to get away for a while and be by myself, I used to go to the beach and watch the ocean. It always made me feel better after—"

She halted again, and for one brief moment, Silas felt a pinch of fear and anguish yank at his midsection, and he knew it was Cecilia's own anxiety spilling out of her and into him. But she reined it in quickly enough that he didn't have time to explore it. Nor was he able to determine its origin. He only knew what he had suspected before, that something had happened to her before she moved to Louisville that continued to cause her anguish. It was something she kept buried deep inside her. Something she was unwilling to share with anyone.

Something Silas very much wished she would share with him.

But he knew he must tread cautiously if he hoped to learn anything about whatever it was. So he made his tone solicitous—a wildly uncommon demeanor for him—when he asked, "And did you often find it necessary to get away for a while and be by yourself when you were living in San Francisco, Cecilia?"

She said nothing at first, only continued to gaze at the river as if she hadn't heard him. So Silas returned his attention to the river, too. Maybe if she thought his curiosity was only idle, she would be more inclined to answer. And perhaps, if he was very lucky, some part of her reply might even include the truth.

For a long time, she only sat silently, pensively, and Silas didn't pester her to say anything more. The passage of time was something with which he was supremely comfortable, since time had become his truest companion in the afterlife. And even before he died, he had been a patient man when it came to waiting for what he truly wanted. Patience was a trait of anyone who was accustomed to river life. Travel on such waterways was leisurely, even indolent. There was no point in hurrying on a river, because the river would carry you at whatever speed it happened to be churning in that day. Even with a paddle wheeler, the captain's needs and requirements could only go so far. It was the river who made most of the decisions, and she generally took her time in making them.

Like the river, Cecilia could take all the time she needed, as far as Silas was concerned. He had no desire to rush the passage of time with her. But just as he was becoming accustomed to the silence—she relented.

"Yes," she said softly. "I often needed time to myself in San Francisco."

Not wanting to press his luck, but needing to know, Silas echoed, again, very cautiously, "To get away, you said."

She hesitated, then nodded. "Yes," she repeated. "To get away."

He started to ask her from what she needed to get away, then, because he knew it was the more correct question, he amended, "From whom?"

She had continued to watch the river as she talked to him, but now she turned to meet his gaze. Instead of answering, however, she asked, "If I say something to a ghost, is that like talking to myself? I mean, you couldn't go around blabbing to everyone, could you?" Her expression grew troubled. "Although, since Audrey can hear you, I guess you could tell her . . ."

Silas began to guide his hand toward her face to touch her, then remembered that he could not, so lowered it to his lap again. "Cecilia, even if I were alive, I would never violate any trust you placed in me."

She nodded slowly. But she confided nothing, something that told him she wasn't quite convinced.

He lifted his hand to rest it on the back of her seat—strange that he was able to affect that pose, and many others, when he couldn't feel what he was doing—then pushed his fingers as close to her shoulder as he dared without actually making contact. But even without touching her, he could feel . . . something . . . surrounding her that reminded him of the fear and pain she kept inside. Some aura of distress that was humming just beneath her surface and was gradually leaking out. Whatever she was holding on to, she wouldn't be able to do it forever. Eventually, whatever it was was going to break free and spill out of her.

"That first day we met," he ventured carefully, "when you and I . . . collided," he said, thinking that word was as good as any for what happened, "in that scant second when the two of us were one, I could sense your thoughts and feelings. Or, at least, some aspect of them." He smiled what he hoped was a reassuring smile. "You're quite good at guarding your emotions, Cecilia, but they're very, very strong. I wonder, though," he added, "if you understand how strong you are yourself. You're stronger, I think, than your emotions. Stronger than even you realize."

She inhaled a deep breath and released it slowly, as if she were trying to do the very thing he was talking about, keeping her feelings tightly braced and staying stronger than they were. But her dark eyes grew damp as she completed the gesture, suddenly looking even larger and more expressive than they had before. She blinked, once, and a fat tear tumbled from each eye. Immediately, she swiped at one of them, but the other kept traveling down her cheek, pausing at the bow of her jawline where it was poised to drop. In that moment, Silas knew a keen torment, because he wanted so desperately to lift a finger to that tear and brush it away.

Unable to stop himself—or perhaps he simply didn't want to stop himself—that was precisely what he did. Except that, of course, he wasn't able to move the tear. And when the pad of his thumb raked softly over her skin, instead of feeling the warmth and smoothness of her flesh, he only succeeded in sparking another jolt of discovery that shook him to his very core.

It wasn't quite like before, however. There was no overwhelming rush of sorrow or dread the way there had been when she'd plunged her hand through his chest. Since the contact was lighter this time, so was Silas's awareness of her feelings. But, too, since Cecilia had let some of her guard down, Silas was able to understand more of what generated her response this time than he had been before.

It was indeed a who, not a what, she had needed to escape in San Francisco. A man. A man she had once trusted, and who had betrayed that trust most heinously.

"You loved him," Silas said when he realized that, too. But he felt no stab of disappointment in recognizing that, no twinge of envy. He felt what Cecilia did—shades of melancholy, traces of lingering fear.

She nodded slowly. Then, with clear reluctance, she shifted her body so that his fingers were no longer in contact with her flesh. She still wasn't willing to share her feelings with him. Not that intimately. Not yet, at any rate.

She did, however, tell him what he had hungered to know. "His name was Vincent Strayer. *Is* Vincent Strayer," she corrected herself. "I mean, it's not like he's dead."

"Unlike some people," Silas pointed out unnecessarily.

She braved a smile at that. "You're more alive than Vincent could ever hope to be. Certainly you're more human."

He dipped his head in both acknowledgment and gratitude.

Her smile fell when she returned to the subject of this

Vincent. "I met him six years ago. He owned the restaurant where I worked. He was very handsome. Very charming. And quite a bit older than me."

"I'm quite a bit older than you, too," Silas reminded her.

He was treated to another quick smile, but there was still a fleeting sadness in the gesture. "But you and I aren't . . . We're not . . ." She shook her head, as if giving up on trying to put voice to whatever she was thinking, then settled on, "You're not like him."

"And what was he like?"

She inhaled another one of those deep, thoughtful breaths, but this time, when she exhaled, there was a raggedness to her respiration that hadn't been there before. "At first, he was wonderful," she said. "I thought he was attentive and loving and fascinated by me. But looking back, I can see now that he was a classic emotional abuser." She met Silas's gaze again. "I guess they didn't call them that in your time, did they? That's a twentieth-century thing."

"No, that wasn't what we called men who mistreated women in my time," Silas concurred. "Those of us who were decent had other, infinitely less polite, designations for them. But that is by no means a 'twentieth-century thing,' as you called it. And I am saddened to find it still occurs. Though I suppose, the nature of men being what it is, I am not entirely surprised, unfortunately."

She nodded, but said nothing.

When it looked as if her silence would remain a chronic condition, Silas asked pointedly, "Tell me about this Vincent who was wonderful at first."

She looked back at the river and sighed again, but this time there was an impatient quality to the sound. "I was with him for five years," she said. "The first couple were, I thought at the time, great. I thought Vincent was so in love with me. He wanted to be with me all the time. He lavished me with gifts and praise. Took me on romantic weekends. Every time I turned around, he was there. At work, at home, socializing . . . We did everything together."

Silas said nothing, for he feared he knew where this was

going. He had known more than one man like Vincent when he was alive. They didn't collect women because they loved them. They collected women because they wanted to own them.

"And on those rare occasions when he and I were apart," Cecilia continued, still watching the slowly rippling waters of the muddy Ohio, "he called constantly, wanting to know how my day was. What I'd done, who I'd seen, where I'd gone. I thought it was because he cared about my experiences. I thought it was because he loved me. Maybe even more than I loved him."

Ah, Silas thought, *there was a telling statement.* The fact that Cecilia knew, even early on, that whatever behavior Vincent was displaying, it veered from the sort of feelings she had for him. She loved him. But what he felt for her was something else.

"I'm not sure I can pinpoint when I realized something was wrong," she said. "It just gradually started occurring to me that my friends weren't calling me anymore, and I wasn't calling them. Not that I had a lot of friends," she conceded, "or family, for that matter. But I had a few friends. Until Vincent subtly separated me from them."

She looked at Silas again. "I can see now how it happened. Whenever I was invited out somewhere, to anything, Vincent always pouted and said he'd made special plans he wanted to surprise me with and now I was ruining the surprise. Or, even worse, he'd say I didn't love him as much as he loved me, because I wanted to spend time with other people instead of him. He always turned it around on me and made me feel guilty, and then I'd have to work doubly hard to prove my love to him. Prove my love," she repeated derisively. "As if love is something you have to prove to someone. That just shows how far gone I was."

"Or how lonely you were," Silas said softly.

Her brows arrowed downward. "Maybe. I suppose I was emotionally vulnerable when I met him. And alone. And lonely. I was such an easy mark. Which is exactly what guys like Vincent look for in a woman."

The observation didn't invite comment, so Silas said nothing.

"I still can't believe I let it go on as long as I did," she continued. "Every day, he got a little more possessive, a little more demanding, a little more domineering. Every time he came into a room, I felt this panic sort of creeping in. And then, one day, the panic wasn't creeping anymore, it was exploding. I could never do anything right, nothing was ever to his liking. He'd find fault in every little thing. The way I wore my hair, the color shirt I had on, the music I had playing on the radio. At work, even when the restaurant was getting rave reviews and the critics were praising my desserts as the best part of their dining experience, Vincent would tell me it wasn't good enough. For years, he just kept chipping away at my confidence until I felt like a failure. Until I felt like I was nothing without him. He made me feel like I should be grateful he would deign to be with me, since no one else would ever want a loser like me."

"Which was precisely the way he wanted you to feel."

She nodded again.

"And yet," Silas said, "some part of you must have realized that wasn't true, otherwise you would still be with him."

Again she turned to stare at the river, evidently finding it easier to talk to him when she wasn't looking at him. "About a year and a half ago," she said, her voice so soft, Silas had to strain to hear it, "we were supposed to go to a party given by another restaurateur, a man who was supposedly Vincent's friend, but who Vincent viewed as more of a rival. And I was just . . ." Another sigh, this one weary-sounding. "Exhausted," she finished. "Physically, emotionally, in every way a person can be exhausted. We'd had a wedding reception at the restaurant the night before, and it had gone on well into the morning. I'd gotten maybe two hours of sleep before I had to get up and to go back to work. When I came home that evening—Vincent stayed home and slept in, by the way—I knew there was no way

I'd be able to make it through a night of partying. I was that close to collapse. I told Vincent to make my apologies and go without me, to tell them I was sick, which, quite frankly, was exactly what I was."

When she hesitated before continuing, Silas asked, "And what did Vincent say to that?"

"Nothing," Cecilia told him. "He didn't say a word. He just grabbed me by the arm and dragged me into the bedroom, then shoved me to the floor and went to the closet. He jerked something out for me to wear, threw it at me, and then, for good measure, he . . ." She closed her eyes. "He kicked me. In the stomach. Hard."

Something red hot and menacing boiled up inside Silas at hearing that, but he let her finish.

"He probably would have done more, but he didn't want me to look like someone had just beaten me up when we went out. And we did go out," she said. "I was terrified of what he would do if I refused. But I knew that was the end of it. Instead of putting me in my place, which was what Vincent intended for that kick to do, it was my wake-up call that I needed to get away from him. But it was months before I could do that. He watched me like a hawk."

"And I don't imagine he made it pleasant."

She closed her eyes. "No."

Telling himself not to ask, but needing to know, Silas ventured, "Cecilia, did he—"

But she hurried on before he could finish. "Finally, there was a night when Vincent had to stay late at the restaurant, and I left and came home and started packing. And only the barest essentials. I left behind every article of clothing and every piece of jewelry he ever gave me, only took the things I'd bought for myself. And I almost made it out with an hour-long lead on him. What I didn't realize was that Vincent's assistant, Dolan, who was really more like a bodyguard, was home, and that he'd received instructions from Vincent a long time ago to keep an eye on me when Vincent wasn't around."

She lifted a hand to cover her eyes and started to shiver. Again, Silas wished he could reach out to touch her. But he only sat helplessly and let her finish.

"I was almost to the front door when Dolan caught me," she said. "He saw the suitcase, saw how frantic I was, and knew right off what I was doing. I bolted for the front door, but he got there first. He picked me up and carried me back to the bedroom, locked me in, and called Vincent." Her eyes still closed, her hand trembling now as much as her body, Cecilia said, "He beat the hell out of me that night, Silas. And he . . . he . . ." Now her breathing was shaky, too. "And he . . . did other things . . . things I'd just as soon not talk about. Or think about." She dropped her hand, opened her eyes, and continued to look at the river. "Not that I can help that last. But I'm doing better."

The red hot rage inside Silas very nearly exploded then. That any man would lift a hand to Cecilia, that he would mistreat her in the most demeaning way made him want to commit murder. But only after mistreating the fiend in a way that was comparable—and then some—to the pain he had inflicted himself. Were Silas made of flesh and blood, he would hie himself to San Francisco on the next train and beat the man bloody.

Barely able to keep his voice level, he said, "Surely someone notified the police. A neighbor. A coworker. Surely, this man paid for what he did to you."

"Yeah, I reported the incident," she said. "From my hospital bed. The cops questioned Vincent for forty-five minutes and let him go. No charges were filed."

"*What?*" Silas asked incredulously.

"It was his word against mine," she said wearily. "He said I'd been beaten up by a man I was seeing on the sly and who I was trying to protect, pinning it on Vincent. And Dolan backed him up."

"But that's outrageous," Silas objected. "Vincent—"

"Vincent is a very prominent citizen," she interrupted him. "He's friends with lawyers and judges and politicians. He donates money to social causes and sponsors all kinds of community events. He is loved by the San Francisco community. The cops didn't believe me—no one believed me. They all believed him. I was nobody. I was nothing."

"You were never nothing, Cecilia," Silas said vehemently. "Vincent may have tried to make you feel that way, but it isn't true. You're a remarkable woman, to have survived what you did at the hands of that animal and come out of it being the gracious, vivacious, decent, wonderful woman you are."

She nodded again, a little slower this time. "Yeah, that's me. Gracious, vivacious, decent."

"And wonderful," he added, hoping his smile looked reassuring when he was still seething inside. "Don't forget wonderful."

She said nothing for a moment, then, very quietly, told him, "As soon as I was able to walk, I left the hospital. I didn't even check myself out. I'd kept one bank account Vincent didn't know about, one that had a couple thousand bucks in it. I cashed out and left San Francisco and never looked back. Spent the next few months staying with friends and acquaintances around the country until I looked up Stephen here. And here I've stayed." She turned to him again. "There are times when I wake up in the middle of the night, afraid he's looking for me and that he'll find me. But really, he's probably forgotten all about me by now. I've put that part of my life behind me as well as I can and am finally beginning to heal." Her expression softened some as she added, "That's due in large part to you, you know." She looked out at the river a final time, then back at him. "I should get you home. If Audrey gets back and sees your portrait gone, she'll worry. Can't have that."

No, he supposed not. But then, he wasn't the one anyone should be worrying about. Of all of them, it was Cecilia who commanded concern at the moment.

She'd claimed she was beginning to heal, he echoed to himself. But it didn't sound like healing to him. It sounded like bandaging without antiseptic and hoping infection didn't set in later. The only way to heal the sort of wound Cecilia had was to excise the infection that was making it fester. There was still pain and fear in her, thanks to this Vincent character. As long as she didn't feel safe from him, she would never be able to put that part of her life completely behind her. And the only way she would feel safe from him was to know unequivocally that he could never, ever, hurt her again.

But Silas wouldn't press her on this. Not now. Maybe not ever. One thing, however, was certain, Silas knew. Vincent Strayer should not be allowed to walk the earth a free, untormented man, having done what he did to Cecilia. Having done what he may have done to other women. Having done what he might very well do again. Justice must be served. Somehow. At some point. By someone.

Fortunately, Silas had a very good idea where to start.

· Sixteen ·

LATE MONDAY EVENING FOUND AUDREY SITTING AT her kitchen table in pale blue, cloud-spattered pajama pants and a white tank top, an open bottle of wine and half-empty glass of pinot noir sitting in front of her. The only light in the room spilled through the window from a streetlight in the alley out back, falling in an almost perfect rectangle of lavender illumination on the table. In the center of that almost perfect rectangle of lavender lay Audrey's left hand, palm down. As she lifted her wine for another sip with her right hand, she gazed down at her left. At the third finger of her left hand, precisely. Where the lavender lamplight glinted off the gold of her wedding band, turning it almost silver.

   She enjoyed a long, leisurely drink of the wine, savoring the full, heady flavor in her mouth for a moment before swallowing. It was the same label Nathaniel had ordered for them at Buck's that first night they went out. She'd had no idea how expensive it was until she'd gone to look for it. She'd paid seventy-five dollars retail. It must have cost twice that in the restaurant. No wonder he hadn't let her pay the bill that night.

Impulsively, she put down the glass and reached for the chain that had remained around her neck the last three years, tugging free Sean's ring from beneath her shirt and cupping it in her right palm. She hadn't removed the ring or chain once since putting them on. Not once. Not for Nathaniel. Not for anything. There had been nights when she'd rolled over on the big ring and woken herself from the discomfort of having it lodged between her chest and the mattress, but she still hadn't taken it off. Times when she'd attended formal events where a plain gold chain disappearing into a neckline had looked out of place, but she'd worn it anyway. And once, when an airport metal detector had gone off and the security guard had said she would have to remove all her jewelry before being allowed through, she'd cashed in her ticket and opted to drive the six hours to Atlanta instead.

The guard had thought her ridiculous. And maybe she had been. At the time, there had been no question that she would opt to keep the necklace on. Because at the time, she'd thought removing it would mean breaking some tie to Sean. The same way removing her wedding ring would cease to make her married to Sean.

But she wasn't married to Sean, she reminded herself. Not legally. Not technically. Not physically. And after the day she'd spent with Nathaniel yesterday, not—

Well. Not something else, either. She hadn't stopped loving her husband, so it wasn't that she'd ceased to be emotionally tied to him. And he still occupied a place inside her, so she'd hadn't stopped being spiritually tied to him, either. But if she were still married to Sean in the ways that counted, she would feel guilty for having made love with Nathaniel yesterday, and she didn't feel guilty at all. She felt confused, uncertain, and not a little fearful. But she didn't feel guilty.

She had thought she would have to duck his calls today, but her private line hadn't rung once. Nor had he tried to reach her at Finery. She would have thought that would make her panicky. Would have thought that would convince her he was only after one thing from her, and having gotten it, had lost interest. In another place and time, with another man, she might have come to that very conclusion. But she didn't feel that way with Nathaniel. She knew him well enough by now to know he cared for her. No man could have made love to her with the care and intimacy he had without having some kind of affection for her. He was giving her time and space, that was all. Time and space he thought she needed, to come to terms with what was happening between them.

Strangely, it had ended up being time and space that allowed Audrey to realize she didn't need any time or space after all.

She reached behind her neck and unfastened the clasp of the chain, holding it in place for a moment with both hands, her heart hammering hard in her chest, as if she were about to undertake some monumental, life-threatening risk. Then, very, very slowly, she removed the necklace and ring and set them on the table. The ring lay in the wan lavender light, its black stone looking surprisingly dull and cold. Audrey sat motionless, breathless, waiting for something to happen. Something portentous and ominous, something creepy and uncanny, something mystical and ethereal.

Something.

But nothing happened. The wind didn't pick up outside. The floorboards didn't creak. Nothing flew from the cabinet to shatter on the floor. No misty shape appeared in the doorway to lift a ghostly finger of accusation.

Nothing changed inside Audrey, either. She still felt exactly the same way she felt five minutes ago. Confused. Uncertain. Not a little fearful. And it was still Nathaniel, not Sean, who circled in her thoughts.

Her gaze fell to the ring on her left hand. It was in a shadow now, no longer glistening. With her right hand, she lifted the glass and emptied it, then immediately filled it with more wine. She lifted that glass, too, and drank generously before replacing it on the table, then moved her right hand to her left. The ring came free with one tug, moving easily over her knuckle to the end of her fingertip. After only one small hesitation, she withdrew her wedding band completely, then set it beside Sean's ring, in the rectangle of violet light. The small, undecorated band looked utterly incongruous next to its heavy, artfully inscribed neighbor. A small indentation remained on her finger, the only remnant now of her tie to a man who had left her years ago.

Again, she awaited any change in the Earth's orbit or a shift in the current dimension or a crack in the fabric of time. But there was nothing. Nothing but she and a half-empty bottle, and a half-empty glass, and two completely empty rings.

But not, she couldn't help noticing, an empty heart.

In fact, her heart suddenly felt fuller than it had ever felt before. Because instead of feelings for one man, she had feelings for two. She still loved Sean. She would always love Sean. But there was something else there, too. Something for someone besides Sean. There was . . . affection . . . for Nathaniel, as well.

Funny, how that could be possible. How new love could be generated without borrowing from the old. How the heart could hold an infinite supply of the stuff. How the brain could make new rooms for new experiences, new memories, new people, without closing the doors of any of the others in its vast warren of thoughts.

"Audrey."

Before she even had a chance to get a grip on those revelations, Silas's voice cut through the darkness, tugging her out of her thoughts of both the past and the future and into the present instead. He stepped out of a shadow at the far corner of her kitchen and crossed the room to join her at the table, taking the seat opposite hers, where Nathaniel had sat not so long ago.

"Hey, Silas," she said softly. She was about to ask him where he'd been for the past couple of days, then she remembered that for at least one of those days, she hadn't been home herself.

Before she could say anything at all, however, he told her, "Audrey, I've found him."

She knew immediately who he was referring to, and the air left her lungs in a soft whoosh. He'd located her dead husband in the afterlife. And his timing couldn't have been more—

Well. Maybe there had been a shift in the current dimension or a crack in the fabric of time after all.

"You found Sean?" she asked in spite of her certainty.

He nodded. "And I spoke to him."

Something caught in her throat at the announcement. "But you said you couldn't do that."

"Yes, well, I seem to have finally discovered that portal between this life and that one. And I've discovered I can come and go as freely as I want. Anyone who wants to can, actually. And a surprising number already have."

So many thoughts began to tumble through Audrey's mind then that she could barely get a grip on any of them. She wanted, of course, to know about Sean. Instead, she heard herself ask, "My parents? Have you seen them?"

He said nothing for a moment, as if that wasn't the question he had expected to answer first. "I have, actually," he told her. "They asked me all about you and were happy to hear you followed your dream of making hats. Your mother, especially, expressed her delight that you listened to her all those times she told you to follow your heart."

Audrey smiled at that. It was something her mother had told her often, from the time she had been able to understand what it meant to follow her heart. She'd done her best to follow her mother's advice. But it hadn't just been with quitting her accounting job to start her millinery business. It had been when she married Sean, too. And now . . .

Now her heart was telling her to follow a new path.

"Sean?" she finally asked Silas. "Has he ever come through that . . . portal?"

"Yes," Silas told her, his voice softening. "Years ago. Shortly after his death. He came several times. To make sure you were getting along all right. And because he missed you."

Which explained all those episodes in that first year after his death, Audrey thought. It didn't explain, though, why there hadn't been others.

"Did you talk to Sean, as well?" she asked Silas.

"I did."

"And you told him I'd asked about him?"

"Yes."

"You told him I wanted to talk to him, too, the way I talk to you?"

"I told him that, as well, yes."

But Sean wasn't here, she told herself unnecessarily. If he had come through before, then he knew the way. And if she could talk to Silas the way she did, then she should be able to talk to Sean, too. She'd been thinking all this time that the reason he hadn't returned to her the way Silas had was because he hadn't known how, or perhaps because he hadn't realized how much Audrey missed him. But if he'd come before, he must have seen for himself how much she was grieving for him. Why hadn't he shown himself the way Silas had?

Silas must have sensed her turmoil, because he told her, "He loved you very much in life, Audrey. And he continues to love you now. It's just that he . . . Well, he . . . He . . ."

"He doesn't love me enough," she finished quietly, surprised at how easily she was able to speak the thought aloud. "Not enough to come back and stay."

After only a small hesitation, Silas nodded. "I'm afraid there is no other way to put it," he told her. Then he hurried on, "You have to understand, Audrey, that many people, after they die, find themselves in a place that is extremely pleasant. It is entirely free of fear and sadness and want. There is no fatigue, no worry, no pain. It is a state of absolute peace and utter contentment. For many, it is the state they had always hoped to have in life but could never manage.

And once they finally experience it . . ." He lifted a shoulder, then let it drop. "They simply don't want to leave. Not for anything."

"But you left," Audrey pointed out.

"I did," he agreed. "Because I had something to do here that superseded everything else in importance for me. I needed to ensure that my family name remained unsullied, and I had to save my descendant from going to a place that is quite the opposite of the one I left, one filled with fear, sadness, want, fatigue, worry, and pain. A state of absolute torment and utter despair. Saving Nathaniel from that, to me, was far more important than absolute peace and utter contentment. Had I allowed him to continue down the path he was headed, peace and contentment for me would have been impossible.

"Had you found yourself in the same sort of position Nathaniel is in," he continued, "Sean, I am confident, would have come to your aid. But he knows that won't happen to you, Audrey. He knows you can make it on your own. He knows you will move on after his death. He knows you don't need him." He smiled gently. "Not the way Nathaniel needs you."

"But I do need Sean," Audrey said softly. Then she realized that wasn't true, really. Not anymore.

Silas eyed her with much interest. "Since his death, you've donated his things to people who can use them, have sold the house the two of you once shared, have started your own business that is promising to be quite successful. You've woken up every morning and you've done whatever needed to be done. You did that from the day after his death 'til now."

"But—"

"You are a very strong woman, Audrey Magill. You can take care of yourself and the others around you. You've been doing that all your life, even in the wake of your husband's death. Sean knows that. He knows you are fine on your own. He saw that for himself when he returned that first year after he was gone. And he wants you to move on with your life."

"But what about—"

"He doesn't feel a need to come back, Audrey. He hasn't for some time now. For you or . . . or for him."

"So what you're saying"—she finally made herself accept—"is that Sean is perfectly content. Without me."

"It's not that he doesn't still love you, Audrey," Silas assured her. "But he has found happiness where he is."

Audrey said nothing, giving herself a moment to figure out how she felt. On one hand, it gave her comfort to know that Sean was in a place where he was happy and at peace. On the other hand, the realization that he had found that without her being around made her feel—

Huh. That was strange. What she felt was a twinge of melancholy mixed with . . . relief? With hopefulness? With . . .

Happiness?

Out of nowhere, Nathaniel's face rose up to replace Sean's, and Audrey realized that, like Sean, she had moved on, too. Without him. She'd feared making love with Nathaniel would feel like a betrayal of Sean. Would almost be adulterous, because she still considered herself a married woman. But it hadn't felt that way at all. That day she'd spent with Nathaniel at his condo had been the most wonderful day she'd enjoyed in years. Being with him had made her feel whole for the first time since Sean's death. He'd filled all the places that had felt empty since she'd lost Sean. But he filled them in ways that were different from her husband.

Her feelings for Nathaniel, too, were different from the ones she'd had for her husband. Her love for Sean had been gentle and comfortable and pleasant, just as Sean had been himself. And he had made her *feel* gentle, comfortable, and pleasant. With Nathaniel, her feelings were intense, energetic, and passionate. Just as Nathaniel was himself. Just as *he* made her feel.

Two very different men. Two very different loves. Neither better or worse than the other. But both important. Both vital. Both essential to her happiness.

"Silas," she said, "I have to go."

He smiled at her. "My dear, do I need to point out that it's after midnight?"

She shook her head. "No, that's perfect, actually. Midnight is when ghosts come out and all manner of supernatural phenomena occur."

"I beg your pardon, madam. I come and go whenever I wish."

She smiled. "So you do. Is that going to continue? Or will you be leaving once we clear up that pesky lost soul business with your great-great-whatever grandson?"

He arched a dark eyebrow. "I shall be here for a while longer."

"Because of Nathaniel's soul?"

"That, too," he said. "But there is another—"

"Cecilia," Audrey said before he could finish.

"Yes."

"I thought there was something going on between the two of you."

Maybe it was just a trick of the light, but Audrey could have sworn he actually blushed at that. All he said, however, was, "She is a lovely woman."

"She is that."

"And there is a matter of some unfinished business that I need to see to for her." Audrey started to ask what that might be, but he hurried on, "Once that is cleared up, however, if it is within my power to do so, yes, I intend to remain."

Audrey's rising spirits sobered at that. "If it's within your power," she repeated. "So you still don't know what's going to happen when all is said and done?"

"I do not."

She nodded slowly, then said the only thing she knew to say. "Don't wait up for me, Silas. I may be a while."

IT WAS NEARLY MIDNIGHT WHEN NATHANIEL HEARD the knock on his front door, but he was nowhere close to going to bed, in spite of having donned a pair of silk pajama pants in midnight blue and knotted a robe of the same fabric around his waist. In fact, he was standing on his balcony again, gazing at the apartment house on Everett, thinking how much he wouldn't mind being again the kid who had lived there. That kid had had so many opportunities he couldn't see, so much potential he didn't realize, so many chances to live a good life and be happy. He wished he could go back for ten minutes to point out to that kid how great he had it, how much he could bring to the world, how different—how much better—his life could be from the one he envisioned.

He also wished he could tell that kid that, someday, he'd find complete happiness with another human being. Unfortunately, Nathaniel feared that would be a big, fat lie.

He hadn't tried to call Audrey today, even though he'd received news from his PI that sounded very promising. After the way they'd parted last night, with her wanting to take a cab instead of letting him drive her home, he'd thought maybe she was having second thoughts about what had happened. About what might still happen. She hadn't removed her husband's ring or her wedding band, even when she'd been giving herself to Nathaniel. Because she still loved Sean, he knew. More than she . . . cared for . . . Nathaniel. More than she might ever . . . care for . . . Nathaniel.

The knock at the door stirred him from his thoughts about Audrey . . . until he crossed the room and looked through the peephole and saw her standing on the other side of the door.

"Audrey," he said by way of a greeting after tugging open the door. "What are you doing here?" Immediately, he added, "I mean, not that I'm not happy to see you, but . . ."

She smiled at that, a little uncertainly. "Are you?" she asked.

How could she doubt it? "Of course. Why wouldn't I be?"

She lifted one shoulder and let it drop, but there was nothing casual in the shrug. "Maybe because I was too blind yesterday to realize what was going on between us? Or, at least, what I hope is going on between us."

Something inside him that had been clenched tight started to ease up at her words. "And what do you hope is going on between us?" he asked.

Instead of answering his question, she asked one of her own. "Can I come in?"

He chuckled nervously and stepped aside, sweeping his hand to the interior of the room in silent invitation. "Of course. I'm sorry. I'm just surprised to see you here so late."

She had started to walk past him the moment he moved aside, but spun around quickly at his last words. Very softly, her gaze fixed with his, she said, "I hope I'm not too late."

He wasn't sure if she was talking about the hour or something else. Either way, however, the answer was, "No. It's never too late for me, Audrey."

She smiled again, a little more confidently this time. "Good. I was hoping you'd say that."

He closed the door and leaned back against it, not sure what to say or do. He figured if Audrey was here at this time of night, she had her reasons for coming. So he waited for her to continue. He'd wait for her no matter what. No matter how long.

For the first time, he noticed how she was dressed—she'd pulled a hooded sweatshirt on over what looked like pajama pants and an undershirt of some kind. He grinned at the realization. Not only had she come here for a reason, but whatever it was must have been some nighttime epiphany that was so important, she hadn't bothered to get dressed first. She hadn't even worn proper shoes, having slipped her feet into bedroom flip-flops. But she had an overnight bag slung over one shoulder, so she'd at least taken the time to ensure she was ready for an overnight stay. At least he hoped that was what the bag meant.

When she saw where his gaze lay, she pulled the bag from her shoulder and let it drop to the floor. "I decided to close the shop tomorrow and give Cecilia and me a day off," she said. "And I was hoping maybe you could give yourself a day off, too."

"Not a problem," he told her. "Especially if you're here." And then, because he still didn't quite trust what he hoped was happening, he added, "You are going to be here, aren't you? I mean, that bag doesn't mean you're leaving town or something."

She shook her head. "Why would I leave when I finally know where I belong?"

His heart beat faster in his chest, and that strange warmth seeped into his belly again. It began to spread farther and grow warmer when she unzipped her sweatshirt and shed it, dropping it, too, to the floor. Because his gaze went immediately to where the gold chain with her husband's ring should have been, and he saw that it was gone. Inevitably, his gaze flew to her left hand next, and when he saw that she'd also removed her wedding band, that knot that had been easing inside him broke completely free.

"Your ring," he said, returning his gaze to her face. "Sean's ring . . ."

"I put them both in a safe place," she said. "I put them . . . away."

She covered the scant space that still lay between them and cupped her left hand over Nathaniel's jaw. His body warmed immediately under her touch, and he lifted his hand, too, to curl his fingers around her nape.

"Sean is my past now," she said. "I'll always love him, and I'll always carry a piece of him in my heart. But you, Nathaniel, are my present. And, I hope, my future, too."

He dipped his head forward, pressing his forehead to hers. "I can think of nothing I'd rather be than your future," he told her. "Unless it's your present. I don't want to be without you, ever. Anywhere. Even if something goes wrong, and I end up on the other side, separated from you, I'd find you, Audrey. I'd come back from wherever they send me, and I'd find you. I'd be with you. My soul belongs with yours. And I'll do whatever I have to do to make sure our souls are together forever. No matter—"

He wasn't able to finish, because she pushed herself up on tiptoe and crushed her mouth to his. He hauled her against himself, and she roped her arms around him, and for long moments, they only kissed and touched and reminded each other of how good it had been between them. How good it would be again. How good it could be forever. Then he swept her up into his arms and carried her to his bed.

Where yesterday, there had been urgency and passion in their coupling, now there was the addition of serenity and tenderness. *And love,* Nathaniel thought. Of course, that had been there yesterday, too, at least for him. But now Audrey acknowledged that, too. He knew she loved him, because she showed him, in every caress of her fingers on his skin and every word she murmured into his ear. So what could he do but show her how much he loved her, too?

He turned their bodies so that they lay on the bed crossways, Audrey on her back and he at her side. He draped one of his legs over both of hers and stretched an arm across her breasts, then kissed her jaw, her cheek, her temple, her forehead. Then he moved down to brush his lips over her throat, her collarbone, and her breast. He flattened his tongue over her nipple before drawing her breast deeply into his mouth to lave it again. He palmed her other breast with his free hand, hooking the nipple between the V of his index and middle fingers, kneading her gently and bringing a small, needy sound from deep inside her.

When she opened her legs and rubbed herself against his thigh, Nathaniel understood what she needed and, after running the tip of his tongue along the lower curve of her breast, he moved downward, tasting her navel and dragging open-mouthed kisses along the tender skin beneath. Then he was moving lower still, pushing Audrey's legs wider to duck his head between them and run his tongue over the damp, heated folds of her flesh. He lapped slowly with the flat of his tongue, then drew circles with the tip. Scooting his hands beneath her fanny he pushed her closer to his mouth, parting her with his thumbs so that he could dart his tongue more insistently against her. Then he penetrated her with one finger, going slow and deep.

He felt her body begin to quiver then, and sensing how close she was to climax, Nathaniel moved to kneel before her. Circling her ankles with sure fingers, he pulled her forward, burying himself inside her—deep, *deep* inside her. Then he draped her legs over his shoulders and lowered his body to hers, braced his elbows on the mattress on each side of her and thrust himself deeper still. Over and over, he bucked against her, opening Audrey wider to receive him. She curled her fingers over his shoulders as he thrust, until they both cried out with their completion. For a long moment, they clung to each other, his body shuddering in the last of its release. Then Nathaniel was relaxing, falling to the bed beside Audrey, one hand curved over her waist, the other arcing over her head.

Audrey snuggled close and sighed against him, her left hand flat on his chest. He covered that hand with his own, stroking the indentation left by her ring.

She needs a new one to put there, he thought. *Someday. Soon.*

He stroked a hand lightly over her hair and said softly, "I have some good news."

She looked up at him, her expression hopeful. Her voice was, too, when she said, "What is it? Is it about Edward?"

He nodded, threading his fingers through the dark silk of her hair. "My PI has found proof that Edward Dryden and Nicholas Pearson are in fact the same man. At least they are now. That wasn't always the case. There's evidence to suggest that in an effort to disappear after that triple murder he was rumored to have committed—and it appears that was much more than a rumor—Pearson also killed a man named Edward Dryden, assumed his identity, and proceeded to start anew here, in a city where no one knew him or the original Dryden and where he could take advantage of both business-friendly policies and downtown-revitalization efforts to start his own company."

"He was trying to go legit?" Audrey asked doubtfully.

"Who knows?" Nathaniel replied. "Maybe. Or maybe he was just biding his time, waiting for an opportunity to start his own crime syndicate or something."

"But that's why he seemed so squeaky clean when he came to town," she said. "Because he'd stolen another man's life."

Nathaniel nodded soberly. "In more ways than one. Mick, my investigator, turned over everything he discovered to your friend Leo, and Leo's brought in the FBI, since much of the evidence, in addition to the murder charge, involves interstate and organized crime."

Audrey pushed herself up from his chest, bringing her face level with his. "And it's solid evidence?" she asked.

Still afraid to hope, but feeling that way anyhow, Nathaniel told her, "It seems to be. Mick said they were going to bring Edward . . . I mean, Nicholas . . . in for questioning. Today."

"That's fantastic," Audrey said. "When will you know something for sure?"

"Any time now, I hope. If it's true that Edward isn't who he says he is, then any contract I signed with him—any contract anyone signed with him—is null and void."

"You won't be associated with a criminal anymore."

"Nope. And neither will anyone else linked to Edward's development. The whole project will be scuttled."

"You'll get your soul back."

"Yep," he agreed. "And to make sure I keep it in good standing, I'm going to do whatever I have to do to make sure the land Edward wanted to develop is turned into the very thing the city wanted to put there: affordable housing for single-parent families, complete with facilities to make their lives easier."

"That would, without question, ensure your soul stays put for the rest of your life."

"And that it goes someplace warm and happy afterward,"

he added. He threaded his fingers through her hair again, tucking it behind one ear. "Just like yours."

She opened her hand over his heart, and he felt the warmth of her touch to his very . . . soul. His real soul. As in, one that had been returned to him. Because the place in his heart that had felt so empty after signing the contract with Edward suddenly felt full again.

"Audrey," he said. "Don't touch me."

She arrowed her brows downward, looking stricken. "What?"

In spite of her distress, he chuckled. Warmly, at that. "No, I didn't mean it like that. I meant, move your hand. Move to the other side of the bed. Don't have any physical contact with me."

"Nathaniel, what . . . ?"

"I think my soul is back."

Now her eyes went wide. She snatched her hand back and moved to the opposite side of the mattress, as far as she could go without falling off. He waited for the chill to return, as it always did whenever she wasn't touching him. Waited for that bone deep, desolate, hopeless cold to settle into his every pore. But it didn't come. Although he didn't feel as warm as he had with Audrey snuggled beside him, neither did he feel in any way cold. He was about to tell her that when the phone rang beside his bed. He looked at the caller ID and laughed out loud when he saw who it was, then snatched it up and pressed it to his ear.

Before he even uttered a greeting, a familiar voice on the other side said, "Sorry to call so late, but you told me you wanted to know the minute it happened, no matter the time. They just arrested Edward Dryden, AKA Nicholas Pearson, and charged him with half a dozen crimes. Including identity theft, fraud, and a little thing called murder. Any business you—or anyone else—had with the guy is now concluded."

"Thanks for the report, Mick," Nathaniel told his PI. "I appreciate all the work you did on this thing."

"I'll write up my report and courier it to your office

tomorrow. And the feds are going to want to talk to you about this."

"Send the report to me here at home, and tell anyone who needs to find me that I'll be here." He looked over at Audrey, who smiled and began to make her way back across the big bed. "All day," he added before dropping the phone back into its cradle without even saying good-bye. Mick would understand. In spite of being a shady PI, the guy had a good soul.

Audrey stopped before touching him again, but she pointed to his chest and smiled. "How's the weather in there?"

"Balmy and warm," he told her. He dropped his gaze to her naked breasts and grinned. "And getting warmer all the time."

"You got your soul back," she said.

"I got my soul back," he confirmed.

"So that was good news you received just now?"

"Excellent news," he assured her. "Best news I've had since . . ." He grinned again. "Well. Since a woman named Mrs. Magill entered my office and told me my soul was in danger."

"That wasn't good news," she reminded him.

"Maybe not. But the messenger brought a lot more with her than dire predictions. She brought salvation, too."

Audrey covered his heart again, then leaned forward to kiss his cheek. "And you, Mr. Summerfield, have returned the favor tenfold."

It wasn't the only favor he did her that night. And salvation wasn't the only thing she brought him. It may have taken a lost soul for Audrey and Nathaniel to find what was missing from both their lives. But once found, neither was going to let love go too far.

Epilogue

CECILIA HAVENS WAS PAINTING THE LIVING ROOM OF her new apartment overlooking the Ohio River when Stephen and Finn arrived with a basket full of treats from the restaurant and some interesting news. The three of them settled into the living room, the one room Cecilia had finished decorating with furnishings more suited to a rambling Victorian house in Old Louisville than a one-bedroom condo in a recently completed highrise. The fireplace was one of those portable gas ones that turned on with the flip of a switch, and above it, she'd hung a housewarming gift from Audrey—the portrait of Silas Summerfield.

Finn and Stephen made themselves comfortable as she poured tea, the three of them chatting about the recent wedding of Audrey and Nathaniel and the new development going up downtown, and about how the newlyweds had drafted all three of them to volunteer in the charity they'd begun to fund scholarships for the kids who would be living in that development. But as Cecilia sliced the cheesecake she'd prepared for the visit, Stephen dropped an interesting tidbit into the conversation.

"You might be interested to know, Cecilia, that Vincent Strayer has been hospitalized."

Her hand stilled in her task, and her fingers twitched involuntarily on the knife. "What?"

Stephen helped himself to one of the slices she'd completed and blithely repeated, "Vincent has been hospitalized. A mental hospital."

Now Cecilia looked up, her mouth open, her eyes narrowed. "What are you talking about?"

Stephen leaned back on the sofa and smiled. "Evidently, he went a teensy bit crazy. We heard all about it from the manager of one of his restaurants."

When Cecilia said nothing, only continued to gaze at him blankly, he continued, "He thought he was being haunted. By, oh . . . like fifty ghosts. All women who had been mistreated by their husbands or lovers when they were alive. Or so he said."

Cecilia turned to look at the portrait over the fireplace, telling herself she only imagined the way Silas's smug little grin grew more smug.

"Yeah," Stephen continued, "every time the guy turned around, there was another woman there terrorizing him. So he said. At work, at home, at play . . . No matter where Vincent went—so he said—there was another ghost scaring him stiff." He winked at Finn. "But not in a good way. It finally got to the point where he just . . . went nuts. Completely bonkers. God knows when he'll get out. Since, even in the hospital, he says he's still being tormented by dead women."

"My goodness, that must be hell," Finn said, reaching for his own cheesecake. "So what kind is this, Cecilia, honey? Is it that orange one again? I love that one."

"Uh, yeah," she told him. "It is the orange one. Only I tried something a little different with the Cointreau this time. Tell me if you taste a difference."

The two men visited the entire afternoon, and no sooner had they left than Silas materialized in the doorway between the living room and dining room.

"Silas, what did you do?" Cecilia asked with a smile.

"I thought Vincent might be lonely after you left him," he said. "I thought he'd like to have other women like you to keep him company."

"That was . . . very thoughtful of you," she replied.

"Yes, I thought so, too."

"So . . . what do you want to do tonight?" she asked. "We could watch *The Ghost and Mrs. Muir* again if you want."

He shook his head. "No, I think I should like to sit out on the balcony with you and watch the river. And then . . ." He threw her a look she could only compare to soulful. "Then, you should go to sleep. Because I have plans for us in your dreams tonight."

She arched an eyebrow at him. "Oh?"

He nodded. "Wear that red thing I like so much to see you in."

She laughed. "Okay. But only if you wear what I like to see you in."

He smiled his slyest smile. "Nothing?"

"That would be it, yes."

He chuckled in a way that sent hot shivers down her spine. "Oh, Cecilia. You have been so good for my soul."

"And you," she said, "make my life absolute heaven."

Dear Reader,

I hope you've enjoyed reading about Louisville during Derby time, which is my favorite time of year in my hometown. Once again, however, I've taken some literary license for the sake of keeping reality fictional. For instance, addresses on Third Street in Old Louisville actually include four numbers, not three, as Audrey's does in the book. And 1400 Willow, where Nathaniel lives, actually only has twenty-one floors, so Nathaniel would be living on the roof, were he actually living on the twenty-second. And please forgive me, my fellow Louisvillians, for playing fast and loose with a few streets and locations downtown for the sake of Cecilia's tour with Silas.

Some aspects of the story are, however, true. Old Louisville really is considered one of the most haunted neighborhoods in the country, and there have indeed been whole books written about it. If you'd like to learn more, I'd recommend local author David Dominé's *Ghosts of Old Louisville*. Or visit the website at www.ghostsofoldlouisville .com. If you ever visit Louisville, you can even take a tour of haunted Old Louisville. Maybe, if you're very lucky, you may run into a riverboat captain or two . . .

Happy reading!
Elizabeth

NATALIE BECKETT SURVEYED THE ARCHITECTURAL wonder that was the ballroom of Emmet and Clementine Hotchkiss's palatial estate and decided that only a complete loser could mess up a party thrown against a backdrop like this. It was as if she'd just walked into the court of Louis XIV, from the cloud-and-cherub-spattered ceiling to the gilded moldings to the beveled Palladian windows that virtually formed the far wall. The late afternoon sun spilled through those windows now, imbuing the room with a luscious golden light, but at night, all those crystal chandeliers hanging overhead would toss diamonds onto the inlaid hardwood floor. Yep, it would take an abject, absolute loser not to be able to throw an amazing, full-to-the-gills party in this place.

Which made Natalie an abject, absolute loser.

Clementine Hotchkiss was the ideal client, one who had spoken those words every professional event planner longed to hear: "Money is no object." Even better, she'd meant it. Clementine had been Natalie's aunt's best friend since college, and she and Mr. Hotchkiss were soiled to their undergarments by their filthy lucre. Clementine had told Natalie to do whatever she wanted with regard to the party—theme, decorations, catering, you name it—that she was turning the party over into Natalie's trusted, talented hands, and please, just let Clementine know to whom she should make out the checks and for how much. There was no way anyone could mess up a golden professional opportunity like the one Clementine had offered. No one except an utter, unmitigated loser.

An utter, unmitigated loser like . . . oh, say . . . Natalie.

She'd had plenty of time to plan the party, too, since Clementine had hired her eight months ago, the very week Natalie had hung out her shingle for Party Favors, her event-planning business. And Clementine was hosting the bash on the quintessential evening to have a party in Louisville—the night before the most famous horse race in the world, the Kentucky Derby. *Everybody* in Louisville was in a party mood on Derby Eve. The two weeks leading up to the race were the city's equivalent of Mardi Gras. Derby parties were easier to plan than birthday parties, because there were no conflicting events. It was Derby. Period. Everyone kept that weekend open for celebrating. Only a party planner who was a pure and profound loser would crash and burn planning a Derby party.

Which made Natalie Beckett a pure and profound loser.

Because even though everything had worked in Natalie's favor from the beginning for Clementine Hotchkiss's Derby Eve party two weeks from today, almost no one was planning to come to it. Even though the invitations had gone out six weeks ago—and save-the-date cards had gone out six months ago—Clementine had received few RSVPs in the affirmative. The majority of the two hundred guests she'd invited hadn't bothered to return the cards at all.

Which, okay, one could interpret to mean those guests might still be planning to come. But Natalie wasn't going to bank on it, since unreturned RSVPs almost always were negative RSVPs. At this point, even Clementine probably wasn't expecting much. But she was polite enough—or perhaps deluded enough—to pretend Natalie could still turn this thing around.

That delusion . . . ah, she meant optimism, of course . . . was made evident when Clementine asked, "So what do you think, Natalie? Shall we put the buffet on the left or the right?"

Buffet? Natalie repeated to herself. Oh, she didn't think they were going to need a buffet. A tube of saltines and a box of Velveeta ought to take care of the catering very nicely. They probably wouldn't even have to break out the Chinet.

She turned to her client, who was the epitome of a society grande dame relaxing at home with her sleek silver pageboy and black velvet headband, and her black velour running suit, which, it went without saying, had never, *ever*, been worn to run. Clementine had rings decorating nearly every finger—she didn't abide that silly rule about never wearing precious gems before cocktail hour—and clutched a teeny little Westie named Rolondo to her chest. Rolondo evidently didn't buy into that precious gems thing, either, because Natalie would bet those were genuine rubies studding the little guy's collar.

But then, Natalie was no slouch·in the fashion department, at least when she was working. As she pondered her answer to her client's potentially loaded question, she lifted a perfectly manicured hand to the sweep of perfectly styled silver-blond hair that fell to her shoulders—perfect because she'd just had both done before coming to visit Clementine. Of course, by evening, when Natalie arrived home, the nails would be chipped and nibbled, and the hair would be in a stubby ponytail that pulled a little too much to the left. But for now, she used the same perfectly manicured hand to straighten the flawless collar of her flawless champagne-colored suit—which, by evening, would revert to jeans and a *Pinky and the Brain* T-shirt. Then she conjured her most dazzling smile for her client, the one she'd learned in cotillion class as a child and perfected long before she made her debut thirteen years ago.

Her parents had spared no expense when it came to bringing up their only daughter right, after all. And by *right*, Ernest and Dody Beckett meant for her to be the pampered wife of a commodities broker or a commercial banker or, barring that, a corporate vice-president on his way to the top. They'd thought she was crazy, pursuing something as frivolous as a college degree—in, of all pointless majors, business—when she knew she would have access to her trust fund upon turning eighteen and could land herself a perfectly good husband like that nice Dean Waterman, who had been mooning over her for years, and where had they gone wrong, having a daughter who wanted to go to college and start her own business? Merciful heavens.

"Clementine," Natalie said in the soothe-the-client voice she'd also perfected years ago—right around the time her first business venture went under—"I think we should put a buffet on the left *and* the right."

Clementine's eyes went as round as silver dollars. "Oh, my. Do you think that's wise? I mean, considering how few RSVPs have come back in the affirmative . . ."

Okay, so clearly Clementine wasn't as delusional as Natalie had suspected. That just meant Natalie would have to be delusional enough for the two of them.

Piece o' cake.

She lifted a hand and waved it in airy nonchalance. "Pay it no mind, Clementine. People often wait 'til the last minute to RSVP. Especially for something like a Derby Eve party, when they have so many prospects to choose from."

Which, of course, was one of the reasons Natalie was such an abject, unmitigated loser when it came to planning this party. Clementine's Derby Eve party was vying with a dozen, better established, Derby Eve parties when it came to attracting guests. Since those other parties had been around so much longer—decades longer, some of them—they were able to pull in the cream of local society, not to mention the bulk of visiting A-list celebrities. The guests to the Barnstable-Brown party alone—easily the most venerable of

Derby Eve parties—could light up Tinseltown, Broadway, *and* the Grand Ole Opry. But the Grand Gala and Mint Jubilee were closing in for sheer star power.

So far, the brightest star power Natalie had been able to harness was a first-round reject of the now-defunct—for obvious reasons—reality series *Pimp My Toddler*. And as it was, little Tiffany was going to have to be home by eight if she wanted to make her bedtime. It would all be downhill after that.

Oh, Natalie was *such* a loser.

"Then you think we should move forward as if the majority of the guest list is coming?" Clementine asked.

"Oh, you bet," Natalie assured her. She was, after all, even better at harnessing delusions than she was celebrities. "Just you wait, Clementine. A week from today, those RSVPs are going to be pouring in with the little 'Of course we can come' boxes checked." She smiled a coy smile that was even more convincing than her debutante one. "I have a little secret weapon I'm saving for the right time."

Clementine's overly painted eyebrows shot up at that. "What secret weapon?"

Natalie lifted her finger to her lips and mimicked a shushing motion. Then she whispered conspiratorially, "It's a secret."

Clementine's expression turned concerned. "Yes, dear, but don't you think you could share it with me? The hostess?" she clarified. Then, as if that weren't clarification enough, elaborated, "The hostess who's signing all those checks?"

Natalie took Clementine's hand in hers and uttered those immortal words of self-employed people everywhere: "Trust me." Then, before her client could object further, added, "I've been planning parties like yours for eight months now, Clementine. I assure you, I know what I'm doing."

Which was true, since Natalie knew that what she was doing was failing miserably. Although she had indeed been planning parties for eight months, Clementine's was by far the most ambitious, way outpacing the handful of birthday parties, two bat mitvahs, one retirement gathering, and a series of bunco nights, at least one of which was best forgotten, since Natalie had misunderstood the hostess of that one and, thinking it was a bachelorette party, had sent a male stripper dressed like a gladiator into a roomful of octogenarians. Not that the party hadn't received rave reviews afterward, mind you, but Mrs. Parrish's Bible-reading group really hadn't come prepared for it. Beyond those events, Natalie had put together an eighth grade graduation, a kindergarten reunion, and one debut, which had mostly served to remind her how awkward and uncomfortable she'd been at her own debut.

Not exactly a success story, she thought, not for the first time.

"Then the new business is faring well, dear?" Clementine asked.

"Oh, very well," Natalie said. Figuratively speaking, at least. Provided *very well* figuratively meant *absolute unmitigated failure*.

Under any other circumstances—like, say, if Clementine Hotchkiss had never met Natalie's aunt—the question would have been perfectly harmless and in no way noteworthy. But there was every chance that Clementine was asking it on behalf of Natalie's aunt—who would report back to Natalie's mother—which meant she was fishing for information about the status of Party Favors. And there was no way Natalie was going to give her client information that might find its way right back to her mother. Especially since she'd been sidestepping her mother's similar inquiries so long and so often that Natalie had invented a whole new dance—the subterfuge samba. If her mother inhaled even the slightest whiff of the stench that Party Favors had become, she'd be circling the steaming pile of Natalie's latest business failure like flies on horse doody.

But then, Party Favors was only one of many steaming piles Natalie had left in her wake over the past seven years—if one could pardon the crass, extremely socially unacceptable metaphor. Ever since earning her business degree, Natalie Beckett had been trying to launch a business of some kind, always with disappointing results. Okay, okay, always with disastrous results.

What was ironic, though, was that Natalie didn't have to rely on a business to make her way in the world. The Becketts were one of Louisville's premier families—Natalie's parents lived right up the road from Clementine, in the third mansion on the right—and she'd had access to a very generous trust fund from the time she turned eighteen. Natalie didn't want to rely on a trust fund. She wanted even less to rely on a wealthy husband. Natalie wanted a career. She wanted to be something more than Dody and Ernest Beckett's daughter and Lynette and Forrest Beckett's sister. She wanted to do more with her life than volunteer for medical research, social awareness, artistic expansion, educational development, or all of the above. And she wanted to be more than a pampered wife and pampering mother, too. She wanted to be . . .

Successful. On her own terms. Make her own way in the world. Unfortunately, the only path she'd been able to hew through the jungle of life so far had led to failure, with a brief stopover at disaster.

As if she'd just spoken that last thought aloud, Clementine said, "I'm so glad things are working out this time. I confess I had to wonder about the last business venture you undertook. I just couldn't imagine there being a big demand for doggie massage."

"Well, there was a little more to it than that," Natalie began to object. She'd offered poochie pedicure as part of the service, too. Not to mention canine coiffure.

"And what was the one before the doggie massage?" Clementine asked. "Something about the hanging gardens of Babylon."

"Hanging Gardens of Baby Bibb," Natalie corrected. At the time, the name had seemed so terribly clever. Now it just seemed to make absolutely no sense. "Organic hydroponics," she clarified for her client. Not that that would probably clear anything up for Clementine, since the only hydro she probably knew anything about was the alpha hydroxy she bought at the Lancôme counter.

"That was it," Clementine said. She cocked her head thoughtfully to one side. "You know, Mr. Hotchkiss actually considered investing in that hanging gardens venture."

This was news to Natalie. Maybe if he had followed through, she could have done a little better with the enterprise, and it would have lasted longer than nine days. "Really?" she asked. "What made him change his mind?"

Clementine smiled, then patted her shoulder. "He sobered up, dear."

Ah.

"It's just as well those businesses didn't flourish," Clementine said now. With remarkable tact. "Party Favors is something you seem much more suited to. Having been the darling of so many parties yourself over the years, it would make sense that planning them would be something you're good at."

Yeah, well, that had been the theory, Natalie thought. Unfortunately, it had worked about as well as the theory of Communism.

"You always were the center of attention at any celebration," Clementine recalled further.

Of course, that was mostly because Natalie had also been the center of catastrophe at any celebration. Which, now that she thought about it, was something she should have considered before launching a party planning business.

Gee, hindsight really was twenty-twenty.

Her client sighed with much feeling. "I must confess, Natalie, that I still have a few misgivings about the party."

Only a few? Natalie thought. Wow, she had way more than that. But she told Clementine in her soothing voice again, "That's only natural. But don't worry. Everything is moving along exactly as it's supposed to." And although that wasn't completely true, there were some things that were, and it wouldn't hurt to remind Clementine of those truths. "The caterers *I* hired for you *eight months ago*," she said, "are now running a restaurant that's become one of the hottest tickets in town. Everyone wanted them for their Derby Eve parties, but you already had them, Clementine. And I just found out this week that the jazz band *I* hired *five months ago* are going to be featured in the *Scene* tomorrow as the city's latest locally grown success who are *this close* to signing with a national record label. Everyone will want them for their parties, Clementine, but you'll already have them."

And that, truly, was where Natalie's talents lay. She could spot talent and predict trends months before anyone else caught on—well, doggie massage parlors and organic hydroponics aside. She knew talent when she saw it, and she'd been hoping that would be enough to move her event planning business ahead of all the others. She truly was suited to this. She really had planned an excellent party for Clementine. They just didn't have enough clout in the Derby Eve milieu to command big crowds, that was all.

Not yet, anyway.

Because Natalie was determined that she would not fail in this venture. She *was* good at this. She *could* make a go of it. She *would* ensure that Party Favors was a rousing success.

Just as soon as she figured out how to bring people to Clementine Hotchkiss's party.

"Don't worry, Clementine," she said again. "I *promise* your Derby Eve bash will be the one people are talking about come Derby Day."

It had to be, Natalie told herself. Because if it wasn't, the next event she'd be planning would be a wedding. Her own. To a man she'd rather bury than marry.

BY THE TIME NATALIE ARRIVED BACK AT HER OLD Louisville office, she'd managed to shove thoughts of Dean Waterman back to the farthest, darkest recesses of her brain, which was where they belonged. No, actually, the farthest, darkest recesses of her brain were still too nice a place for Dean. She didn't care how much her parents liked him or how convinced they were that he was the man she should be tied to for the rest of her life. And she didn't care that Dean had been saying since childhood that someday he would make Natalie his Mrs., and that, to this day, he continued to make no secret of the fact that he was convinced she would be the perfect wife for him.

Dean Waterman was the very definition of smarmy. And cloying. And supercilious. And icky. And he'd been that way since she met him at the age of ten, in cotillion class. Between the sweaty palms and the prepubescent complexion and the hair goo his mother had made him use all the time, Natalie had always been on the edge of her seat, waiting to see if Dean would slide out of his.

These days, he bore no resemblance to the rat-faced little kid he'd been. Braces had fixed his overbite, Lasik had corrected his myopia, and puberty had filled him out. Natalie might have even considered him handsome, if it hadn't been for the cloying smarminess. He was still plenty oily, metaphorically speaking. And he was still definitely icky. But in a moment of weakness, on an evening when her parents had been hammering her even harder than usual about making a go of Party Favors, she'd made a bargain with them. If Clementine Hotchkiss's Derby Eve party didn't come off as a *huge* success, then Natalie would close up shop and refrain from plunging into another business venture . . . and date Dean Waterman—exclusively—for six months.

Not that the *exclusively* part was any big deal since Natalie hadn't dated anyone more than once or twice for more than a year. It was the *date Dean Waterman* part that made her stomach clench. God, what had she been thinking to agree to such a thing? She'd just been so tired of her parents harping on her, and so certain she would make Party Favors a success. She honestly hadn't thought it would come down to actually having to go out with Dean. For six months. Exclusively.

Not to mention the fact that Clementine's party, like all the big Derby Eve parties, was a fund-raiser, and her choice of recipients was a local group dedicated to keeping at-risk kids off the streets. The large check Clementine had hoped to turn over to Kids, Inc., after charging a hundred and fifty dollars to each of her wealthy guests was looking to be more like a buck and a half. And a buck and a half wasn't going to go far in building a facility that would teach those kids about running a business or scholarships to help them someday do just that.

The word *loser* began to circle through Natalie's brain again, so she shoved it back into the shadows alongside thoughts of Dean. Yeah. They went nicely together. Then she turned to her computer and pulled up the web page for the *Courier-Journal* to see who the latest celebrities were coming to town for Derby. The local paper began their Derby celeb watch in January, and Natalie had been keeping close tabs on who was coming and when they were arriving. Scoring major players in the sports, entertainment, and business communities was a big part of ensuring the success of a Derby party, but most of the famous people coming to town had committed to parties before she even opened Party Favors. Every time she saw a new celebrity listed, Natalie contacted that person's representative to extend a personal invite to Clementine's party.

At best, she received a polite thanks, but no thanks. At worst, her invitation went completely ignored. At second to worst, it was accepted, by some celebreality type who was so far down the list, they actually referred to themselves as "celebrealities." In addition to the cast-off from *Pimp My Toddler* for Clementine's yes list, Natalie had scored an auditioner for *American Idol* who hadn't made it to Hollywood, but who had risen to fame—fifteen minutes of it, anyway—because Simon had dubbed him with one of those sound bites that got airtime again and again. This one involved a cattle prod to a part of the young man's anatomy that one normally didn't want a cattle prod anywhere near.

She'd also added an actor who had once played a politically incorrect Native American on *F-Troop*. And a college basketball player it was rumored might possibly, perhaps, maybe, if the stars were aligned, go in the twenty-sixth round of the NBA draft.

Today's celebrity pickings, she saw were pretty slim, even though the race—and parties—were just two weeks away. A cable channel talk show host, a decorator from an HGTV series, and a marginally successful podcaster.

Ah, what the hell, Natalie thought. It wasn't like she had a lot of choice.

She was about to head off to Google to see who repped whom when her gaze lit on the sidebar of today's headlines, and a name popped out at her. A name which, although written in the same tiny font as the rest of the news and with the same dispassionate reporting, might as well have been etched in gold on her computer monitor in letters eight feet high. And they might as well have been accompanied by a crack of thunder and a bolt of lightning, and the skies splitting open, and a chorus of angels belting out "Hallelujah."

Russell Mullholland, the headlines said, had come to town.

Clicking on the headline, Natalie discovered that the man who defined the term "reclusive billionaire" had just shown up in Louisville at some point earlier in the week, without announcement or fanfare, because he owned a horse that would be running in the Kentucky Derby. Meaning, she concluded, that he would be here for the two weeks leading up to the race, including Derby Eve. And since no one had known he was coming, there was a chance, however small, that he hadn't committed to any parties yet. In fact, due to the whole reclusive billionaire thing, even if he had been invited to other parties, there was a good chance he hadn't accepted any of them.

Yet.

Hungrily, Natalie read the rest of the article. Evidently

Mr. Mullholland and his adolescent son had been spotted crossing the lobby of the Brown Hotel yesterday, surrounded by a cadre of bodyguards, which was the first anyone knew that he had planned to be in Louisville. There was a photograph accompanying the article, but it was virtually impossible to see what Mullholland looked like, because, even if his head hadn't been bent the way it was, he was wearing a hat and sunglasses, and what was left of his face was obscured by a very large man with a very determined look on his face.

Strangely, it was that man, and not the buried billionaire, who really captured Natalie's attention. He stood a full head above everyone around him and somehow seemed to be looking everywhere at once. His hair was dark, quite possibly black, and he didn't appear to have shaved for some time. His clothing was fairly nondescript, what looked like khaki trousers and a dark-colored polo, and shouldn't have called attention to him. But his rugged good looks coupled with that wary expression simply commanded her gaze.

Security detail, she thought. The guy had to be one of Mullholland's bodyguards. No self-respecting reclusive billionaire would be without security. Her gaze went back to the indistinct billionaire, since that was where her attention needed to be, even though what she really wanted to do was inspect the bodyguard further. Russell Mullholland had catapulted onto the celebrity scene about a year and a half ago after designing what would become *the* game system of gamers everywhere. The Mullholland GameViper had been talked about for months before it was made available, the gossip and hype turning it into the Holy Grail of game systems. When it finally was launched—strategically, six weeks before Christmas—there had been a frenzy to see who could get their hands on one.

Natalie wasn't much into gaming herself, but she knew plenty of guys and a couple of girls who had camped outside Best Buys and GameStops for days in the hopes of scoring a GameViper for themselves. Even at that, few had succeeded. In the year-and-a-half since its introduction, there had been a half-dozen additional pushes for a limited number of systems, and between the sale of those and the games designed specifically for the GameViper, which went for close to sixty bucks a pop—not to mention the way the company's stock had gone straight through the roof—Russell Mullholland had become a billionaire virtually overnight.

He'd become a recluse nearly as quickly.

Natalie had seen photos of Mullholland where he *wasn't* ducking the paparazzi and knew there was a reason why he'd been voted one of *People* magazine's Most Beautiful Men. Blond and blue-eyed, with one of those smiles that made a woman want to melt into a puddle of ruined womanhood at his feet. Even without the billions, he was too yummy for words. Add to that the fact that he was a single dad who'd been struggling to raise a son after losing his wife to cancer when the boy was a toddler, and it made him irresistible to even the most cold-hearted woman.

Evidently one of the things he'd invested his millions in was Thoroughbreds, all named after his games, one of whom was close to being a favorite in the race. Mullholland had come to town with his son, Dylan, the article said, but it also cautioned not to expect to catch too many glimpses of him, since he had routinely declined all invitations to make appearances at a variety of Derby-related events.

Oh, he had, had he? Natalie thought. Well, she'd just see about that. He hadn't received his invitation to Clementine's Derby Eve bash yet.

Her gaze strayed to the big bodyguard shielding the billionaire with his body. She wasn't about to let a little thing like a security detail get between her and *the* Russell Mullholland. The billionaire would be the perfect party favor for Clementine's gala. *Everyone* wanted to get a glimpse of Russell Mullholland. If Natalie could convince him to attend the party, *everyone* else would come, too. Clementine's fete would be *the* place to be on Derby Eve, and it would be all people talked about the next day. Natalie would be lauded as the party maven of all party mavens, and Party Favors would be a huge success. Clementine could hand an even bigger check over to Kids, Inc., and Natalie would have work out the wazoo.

And Dean Waterman, the slimy little jerk, would be nothing but an oil slick in the narrows of her mind.

ALSO BY
USA TODAY BESTSELLING AUTHOR

ELIZABETH BEVARLY

FAST & LOOSE

"Lots of fun, lots of style, lots of heart."
—*New York Times* bestselling author Christina Dodd

Hotshot Thoroughbred trainer Cole Early needs
a place to stay during the Kentucky Derby. His
only option is a snug little bungalow being rented out by local glass artist Lulu Flannery. And
though her house is filled with indulgences to
please Cole's five senses, he'll have to tame his
rowdy ways to coax some passion out of Lulu.

**"Elizabeth Bevarly's novels glow
with charm and sexy fun."**
—*New York Times* bestselling author Lisa Kleypas

penguin.com

M307T0608